HOLLYWOOD LEGENDS
BOOK ONE

Dreaming
with a
Broken Heart

MARY J. WILLIAMS

Copyright © 2016 by Mary J. Williams.

All Rights Reserved. No part of this publication may be copied, reproduced in any format, by any means, electronic or otherwise, without prior consent from the copyright owner and publisher of this book.

First Printing, 2016

About the Author

Want to know how to motivate yourself to write a book? Have your favorite football team lose the Super Bowl. On the last play. With an interception. The next day I was so depressed I tuned out all media. No TV, no internet, no newspapers — nothing. And I started to write. I'm still writing. As you can see, a little motivation can do wonders. Football will play a big part in my next series of books due out next year. And since I'm writing the ending? No interceptions. Guaranteed. Happy reading everyone.

Mary J. Williams

How to Get in Touch

Please visit me at these sites, sign up for my newsletter or leave a message.

http://www.maryjwilliams.net/home.html

https://www.facebook.com/Mary-J-Williams-1561851657385417

https://twitter.com/maryjwilliams05

https://www.pinterest.com/maryj0675/

https://www.instagram.com/2015romance/

https://www.goodreads.com/author/show/5648619.Mary_J_Williams

More Books by Mary J. Williams

Harper Falls Series

If I Loved You
If Tomorrow Never Comes
If You Only Knew
If I Had You (Christmas in Harper Falls)

Contents

Prologue 1
Chapter One 4
Chapter Two 12
Chapter Three 25
Chapter Four 44
Chapter Five 53
Chapter Six 71
Chapter Seven 93
Chapter Eight 114
Chapter Nine 135
Chapter Ten 154
Chapter Eleven 163
Chapter Twelve 198
Chapter Thirteen 214
Chapter Fourteen 228
Chapter Fifteen 247
Chapter Sixteen 259
Chapter Seventeen 269
Epilogue 290
How to Get in Touch 293

For All The Dreamers

Prologue

THE ROOM WAS dark. Too dark for Garrett's liking. A little stuffy, a slight antiseptic smell with an overlay of sex. That's what you got from a cheap motel and furtive lovemaking. Odors and memories you'd just as soon forget.

The sounds from behind the closed bathroom door indicated his partner was trying to remove all traces of their recent activities. It shouldn't hurt. This wasn't the first time, and damn his weak resolve, it wouldn't be the last.

If he smoked, he would have something to do with his hands. Watching his father struggle with lung cancer put the fear of God in him and his brothers at an early age. All four of them had their vices; smoking wasn't one of them.

Get up. Get dressed. For once, be the first to leave. Even if he could find the balls to walk out on her, he couldn't leave her alone at this time of night. In this part of town.

God, it was like a furnace in here. Despite having the AC wall unit on high, Garrett knew it must be hotter in here than outside. The sheet riding low on his hips was too much. Damn modesty. The room was too dark to see anything; if she didn't like seeing his naked body, she could turn away. Garrett whipped off the coarse cotton material at the same moment the bathroom door opened.

"You don't have to go," Garrett said to the shadowed figure.

"Yes, I do."

She always made sure the light was off. Her silhouette showed a tall woman, thin. Too thin. Even by L.A. standards. She was gaining weight — slowly. Garrett could attest to that. He knew it was a struggle. One she fought every day.

Garrett felt the anger drain from his body — his heart melt. Her demands were not capricious whims. They weren't her attempt to gain the upper hand. Her goal was not to manipulate. She had her reasons. They were real. Legitimate.

"It's still early."

Garrett kept his voice low and even. Shouting didn't help. She never fought back. Retreat. That was her coping mechanism. The last time he blew up it was two weeks before she would take his calls.

"I…" she cleared her voice. "His flight gets in at midnight."

"Don't be there."

"You know how he gets."

Garrett knew all right. She was devoted to a man who treated her like crap, forgot her existence ninety percent of the time, yet expected her to be there when he decided to come home. His fists clenched the mattress. It was the only thing preventing him from grabbing her, begging her to stay. *For once, pick me.*

"I don't know when I can see you again."

I don't know if I ever want to see you again. Garrett thought the words. He would never verbalize them. She was his drug of choice. Weeks passed. The need for her grew. Outwardly, his life looked smooth as glass. Inside, the itch grew.

Garrett became an expert at compartmentalizing. His work never suffered. His family never suspected. No one had the slightest clue about what was raging inside of him. *She* knew. Because she shared his unbreakable habit. Enablers. That's what they were. It was sick. Sometimes, like tonight, he hated himself. He wished he could hate her. Then, maybe, he could walk away.

"I'll be out of town for the next month."

Garrett wished he could see her face. Was she sorry he'd be gone? Relieved? Would she miss him half as much as he was going to miss her?

"Take care."

Garrett waited a second, letting the motel room door close behind her. Jumping up, rushing to the window, he pulled back the thin, dingy curtain. He never walked her to the taxi. Even the minutest chance of them being seen was too much.

The ritual of watching until she was safely inside the vehicle, seat belt on, doors locked, was something he never ignored. Nothing bad would happen to her when he was around. It was when he wasn't there that trouble found her. One more frustration. It wasn't his place to protect her. Knowing that drove him crazy.

Garrett grabbed his jeans from a nearby chair, pulling them on. Unlike her, he wouldn't clean up before he left. He would carry the smell of her with him — let it fill the interior of his car. Tomorrow he would pretend it was still there.

Damn it. Enough. He deserved more than this. They both did. One month. When he got back, one way or another, things were going to change.

Chapter One

HOLLYWOOD. DREAMS FULFILLED. Dreams crushed. It happened every day. Wide-eyed kids still came hoping to be a star. More often than not, they went back home — a nobody. Iowa, Nebraska, Texas, Georgia. Insert state here. Small town, big city. It didn't matter. The movie industry seemed vast from the outside. In truth, it was the most insular of worlds. Making it took determination, perseverance, and a whole lot of luck. Talent was so far down the list it wasn't funny.

Connections. That was what got you through the door. If you had a recognizable name, the door swung wide, the smiles welcoming. If you couldn't pull your weight once you were inside, no one hesitated to kick you out. That famous name only got you so far. The rest was on your shoulders.

Sink or swim. No life preservers were thrown your way. If anything, you were fitted with cement shoes. The only thing this town loved more than a winner was the child of a Hollywood legend falling flat on his face.

Garrett Landis felt the weight of those expectations every time he stepped on a movie set. His father set the bar so high none of his sons was expected to reach his lofty heights. The fact that all four seemed well on their way to not only matching Caleb Landis' achievements, but surpassing them, caused quite a stir.

Resentment simmered under the surface of hearty backslapping and insincere ass kissing. Their father taught his boys many things. In this business, never turn your back on friend or foe. Treat everyone with respect, from the lowliest crew member to the head of the studio. The most important thing? In this business, trust no one — except brothers. Eight years after making his first low-budget independent film, Garrett followed those rules without question. The Gospel according to Caleb Landis. His father's words were his bible. His brothers were his rock.

Wyatt, the oldest, followed directly in their father's footsteps. He was a hard-ass, bottom-line producer. Nathaniel, Garrett's fraternal twin, was the daredevil of the bunch. He was the most in-demand stuntman in Hollywood. Baby brother Colton was blessed with movie star looks. His charisma leaped off the screen, pulling in even the most cynical audience member. Or so one critic wrote after seeing Colt's first movie. Individually, each Landis brother was formidable. Together, they dominated almost every branch of the industry.

"How can we be behind schedule when we haven't shot a single frame?"

"Welcome to the glamorous world of moviemaking."

Garrett grinned when he answered his assistant director, Hamish Floyd. This was their fourth collaboration. The first two made a nice profit. Number three broke box office records. Expectations for *Exile* went through the roof the second Garrett's name became attached. With Wyatt behind the scenes, the movie's success was practically guaranteed.

Garrett didn't believe in sure things. He worked hard on every project, no matter the size. Bigger budget, more potential headaches. That included a prima donna leading lady who couldn't get her ass on set at the designated hour. Garrett refused to start leaking money on day one.

"You want me to coax America's sweetheart of the week out of her trailer?"

"You'd never get past her PA," Garrett told Hamish. "Lynne Cornish thinks one hit movie and a few magazine covers give her the right to make her own rules. She's going to find out on this movie set, there is only one set of rules — mine."

"She has a contract."

"Wyatt's standard contract. She signed it. Her mistake if her lawyers didn't read the fine print."

Contracts were fluid. *Before* they were finalized. Each actor, depending on their box office leverage, could get their people to make demands, tweak the perks. The basics were non-negotiable. Under no circumstance, barring personal injury, a death in the family, or a genuine nervous breakdown, was an actor allowed to delay production. Once, you were warned. Twice, bye-bye. As far as Garrett's big brother was concerned, potential loss of a lead actor was the reason they paid huge insurance premiums. It hadn't happened to Garrett. Not yet. There was always a first time.

Tim Bodine, Lynne Cornish's PA, waylaid Garrett before he was halfway to her trailer.

"Lynne isn't feeling well."

"She was fine an hour ago."

When she was flirting with every man on the set. Apparently, Ms. Cornish could drag herself to any early breakfast if adoring men were present. She found out quickly that Garrett wasn't among them. Whether her sudden *illness* was a result of a hurt ego or plain laziness, he didn't give a damn. Starting right now, Lynne Cornish needed to know who was boss.

"Does she need a doctor?"

"Nooo." Tim drew out the word.

The PA's lack of concern only ratcheted up Garrett's annoyance.

"Five minutes."

"What?" Tim yelled at Garrett's retreating figure. When there was no response, the man hurried to catch up. "She can't make it in five minutes. Lynne doesn't think today will work for her. At all."

Garrett rounded on the smaller man. He topped him by at least eight inches. Tim was slight, Garrett muscular. Yet that wasn't what had the PA stepping back several feet. It was the look in Garrett's steely eyes.

This man exuded confidence. Strength, both physical and psychological, radiated from his core. You didn't mess with Garrett Landis. Not if you had half a brain.

"She was looking a little better when I left her trailer," Tim said, clearing his throat. "She wanted to speak with you. *Privately.*"

Well, shit. Garrett didn't see that coming. Lynne made it clear, early on — she was interested. He made it equally clear he wasn't. End of story. They would have a friendly, professional relationship. Finding out his beautiful leading lady was angling for more didn't hold the thrill it once had. It made Garrett... tired. His personal life was full of enough turmoil — he didn't need the added drama of an on-set romance.

"I don't have the time, or inclination, Tim."

To Garrett's surprise, the PA blushed. In Hollywood, that ability was knocked out of a person fast.

"I can't guarantee anything."

"Then Lynne will be out of a job. How long do you think you'll last after that?"

Tim Bodine looked like a smart man. One capable of cajoling his uncooperative employer. Garrett didn't care what it took to get his star in front of the camera as long as it happened. Immediately.

"Five minutes?" Tim asked, a little panicked.

"I'll give you ten."

Garrett wondered if it was too late to get out of feature films. Animation. That sounded good. No location shoots. Voice-over actors happy to skip wardrobe fittings and hours in the makeup chair. A little direction on his part. Mostly setting the scene. One or two takes. Right now, it sounded like heaven.

"What's the word?" Hamish asked him.

"Bitch?"

"Any chance she'll be joining us in the near future?"

"Your guess is as good as mine."

Garrett looked around. They were ready to go. Cameras primed, leading man looking as impatient as Garrett felt. At least he'd lucked out with Paul McNally. He was a professional through and through. No power plays. No outlandish demands. There was no propositioning the director. Paul's first job was a small part in a Caleb Landis production. He was a great actor. More importantly, he was a friend. Garrett felt lucky to work with him.

"Once again, you've lived up to your reputation," Hamish said with admiration. "You really are a miracle worker."

Garrett looked over his shoulder. Lynne Cornish. In full costume and makeup. A little pouty. He could work with that. It complimented the scene.

"Tell them five."

"We're shooting in five minutes, people," Hamish called out Garrett's directions. "Pee now or forever hold it."

Garrett moved over to camera A, checking the shot. Perfect. This was his world. He knew what he was doing. No one questioned his authority or failed to jump at his command. Unlike his personal life, his professional life stayed on a clear path.

Unwanted, a quick image filled his mind. A woman. In the shadows. Frustrated by the intrusion, Garrett shook it off. He called for the actors to take their marks. He wouldn't let her get in his head today. He had hundreds of people depending on him to stay focused. Rolling his shoulders a couple of times, he looked around to make sure everyone was ready.

The clapperboard was struck. Garrett felt the familiar energy begin to build. With a sigh of satisfaction, he opened his mouth.

"Action!"

THE ROOM WAS perfect.

Even so, Jade Marlow made one final inspection. The ballroom sparkled. The floors were polished, the tables set with an eye towards casual elegance. People would be amazed how much work it took to achieve *casual*. Jade knew. This was what she did. This was her world. It was the only place she had total and complete control.

"Ms. Marlow. The shrimp arrived."

"Thank you, Teresa. Crisis averted."

"We had a backup plan," the caterer laughed. "Shellfish can be iffy, even when delivered on time. I brought twice as many of the stuffed mushroom caps. Who would care if we had four hors d'oeuvres instead of five?"

My father. Jade kept her hands from clenching; her teeth were another matter. *Relax your jaw, Jade. The last thing you need, with a soon to be house full of guests, is a headache.* Jade took a deep breath, then another. Not so long ago, breathing in and out wouldn't have been enough. Certain triggers, like the thought of her father's disapproval, required a pill. Those little pink ones. The ones she flushed down the toilet a month ago. She kept that bit of information to herself. As far as her father was concerned, a medicated Jade was a superior Jade.

Those days were over. Jade was getting stronger. Inch by inch. Second by second. That meant she filled the prescription on a regular basis. Then disposed of them. She continued the weekly visits with her parental-approved therapist. Then went to see her own the next day.

Slowly but surely, she was regaining control of her life. Without her father's knowledge. She wasn't strong enough to fight his objections. Not yet. Soon. When she was, she would tell him to mind his own business. She would pack her bags and leave his home. A little apartment sounded nice. For the first time in her life, she would have a place all her own.

Unbidden, she wondered what Garrett would think of her plans. Not that it mattered, she assured herself. She would never again live her life for someone else's approval. When she made her move, it would be for herself. Period.

"Jade. Darling."

"Melinda."

Jade put on her best hostess face. Melinda Hurst was not a friend or acquaintance. More like a viper. Seeking out weakness then striking. Her greatest pleasure was the pain of others. For some time, Jade had been her favorite target.

I can do this, Jade thought. *Nothing she says matters. They are only words.*

"That dress," Melinda gave the garment a long, thorough look. "Last year's Donna Karan?"

Is that your best first shot? You're slipping, Melinda.

"This year's Jonas Westgate."

"Oh, God," Melinda cackled. "Not one of your *projects*. Jade, darling; it's one thing to give a bit of seed money to an up-and-coming designer. Take my advice. Think again before you wear one of his creations. The cut, the color. He obviously didn't have any clue how to drape your… How shall I put this? Your unfortunate figure."

A few months ago, those words would have hit their mark. The slightest criticism would crush Jade's almost non-existent self-esteem. Now? Part of her wanted to run. Or cry. Hide. Pull off the dress and burn it. That wasn't going to happen. Jade was stronger now. Maybe stronger than she'd ever been. The dress was fabulous. She knew it. The soft green complimented her pale skin, brought out the emerald in her hazel eyes. Her *unfortunate figure* looked slim and elegant. The flowing material accented rather than detracted. She had few curves. Though her painfully thin form was gradually filling out again, Jade knew she looked her best. Melinda wasn't going to take that away from her.

"I thought about wearing a sack, Melinda." Jade paused, looking the other woman up and down. "Where did you get your dress?"

Jade moved away, leaving Melinda to decide if mousy Jade Marlow had just cut her down a few notches. *Damn right, I did.* Jade did a mental fist pump. It might be time to stop measuring her progress in baby steps. She was up on her feet. Her legs were steady. Soon she would be back to her old self. Then she could work on improving *that* model. So much work to do. Jade pulled her shoulders back. She was getting there. She *would* get there.

"Why are you standing here instead of greeting guests?"

Jade felt her confidence slip. There was one person who could pull her down. It was going to take a lot longer to get past a lifetime of thoughtless jabs, barbs, and outright cruelty. You couldn't overcome twenty-eight years in a few months.

Her shoulders a little less straight, but no less determined, Jade turned. The false smile in place. Not that he would know the difference. Genuine, fake. He never noticed. As long as she was there when he needed her, like tonight, he didn't care.

That knowledge once crushed her. Now, Jade saw it as an advantage. She was gradually slipping away from his control. Before he could regain his hold on the invisible ropes that bound her to his side, she would be gone. For good.

"Don't worry, Father. You know I wouldn't neglect my duties."

"See that you don't. And for Christ's sake, fix your hair. It looks like an abandoned bird's nest."

Jade's footsteps faltered. Maybe her legs weren't as steady as she thought. Back to baby steps. She wouldn't let it get her down. She was moving forward, no matter the size of the strides. That was what mattered.

Chapter Two

"WELCOME HOME, GARRETT."

"Thanks, Sally. Remind me. No more location shoots in the desert. You know what? Let's cut out location shoots altogether."

Garrett's office manager didn't bother to answer. He said the same thing every time. In a week, he would forget every problem inherent with taking his movie on the road. His enthusiasm for his job and all its pitfalls never waned for long.

"You have a nice tan."

"Great. Now I have to worry about skin cancer," Garrett grumbled. When he saw the stack of mail on his desk, he veered right, flopping down on the leather couch.

"Did you use the sunscreen I sent you?"

"You mean the stuff that attracted every bug in a twenty-mile radius?"

Sally shook her head. "I don't understand it. Everyone I know uses that cream. You're the only one with a bug problem."

"Must be my naturally sweet disposition that attracts them."

"Right," Sally scoffed. She picked up the mail, depositing it on the table in front of him. "This won't magically disappear."

"Isn't taking care of that crap what I pay you to do?"

"Shoveling crap is not in my job description. I *do* take care of ninety percent of your correspondence. I leave you with the bare minimum. Personal things."

"My life is an open book, Sal," Garrett laughed. "In Hollywood, there are no *personal things*."

Except Jade. What he had with her went beyond personal. It was elemental. Essential.

"Buck up, Garrett. Open an envelope. You might enjoy the experience."

"I never have," he muttered. "Tell me some good news."

"You're stalling."

"True," he conceded. "I still want something happy to start my day."

"Trina is pregnant."

"That is great news." Garrett grinned. "I refuse to believe you're going to be a grandmother."

Sally Penski was forty-eight years old. She looked fifteen years younger. Efficient, friendly, and organized. She kept him running. Schedules. Meetings. Essential things Garrett had no desire to deal with. She texted him most of the time. Emailed occasionally. In an emergency, she called.

Garrett was not entirely certain how she came to work for him. Nine years ago, he had barely moved into his office when she was there — arranging things. Had his father sent her? Both denied it. She claimed she answered an advertisement in the paper. Since he hadn't placed any ads, how was that possible? Sally had the office up and running quickly and with little drama.

It was three months before it occurred to Garrett that he had never officially hired her. By then, it didn't matter. To this day, it was a mystery unlikely to be solved. Sally certainly wasn't telling.

"Your brother called."

"So?" Garrett reluctantly began sorting through the mail. "The surprise would be if one of them *hadn't* called."

"Wyatt."

"Ah."

"He wants to meet with you at eleven."

"Did he say why?"

"Money."

"What else." Wyatt's favorite subject.

Sally left the way she did everything — quietly.

Garrett threw the envelope back on the table, promising himself he would get back to it later. He grabbed a bottle of water from the fridge, then propped his feet up. He was running on three hours of fitful sleep. Lying down for a nap was a tempting thought. A brief thirty minutes sounded like heaven. Unfortunately, he had a busy day ahead. Squeezing Wyatt in would be a challenge. Then there were script revisions, meetings with the head of costumes. He needed to go over the storyboards for tomorrow's shoot.

It would be easier now that they were back in L.A. He would be in his own bed, for starters. No matter how he tried, he didn't sleep when on location. On long shoots, there were nights when he wondered why he bothered. He would eventually give up. His time was better spent working.

It wasn't the healthiest of lifestyles. Yet he wouldn't change jobs for anything. He could live with temporary insomnia if that was the price he paid to make his movies. It was in his blood. His father claimed the business was in their DNA. Garrett couldn't argue.

His parents were the definition of legends. When town's most powerful producer married its hottest screen siren, they became Hollywood royalty. Their four sons princes. He and his brothers grew up on film sets. They cut their teeth in editing rooms, learned to walk around camera cables and sound equipment.

Garrett remembered the moment he knew directing was his calling. His mother, Callie Flynn, was filming what many considered her greatest movie, *The Sun Goes Down*. Garrett was seven, running around, getting into everything. He had a nanny, not that it mattered. He was impossible to keep track of. The crew indulged him. If he asked a question, they answered without hesitation. The director, who was missing his own son, took Garrett under his wing.

By the end of the shoot, Garrett was hooked. From then on, he used his envious position to learn everything possible. He went to film school, always anxious to learn more. By his sophomore year, he knew it was a waste of his time. They taught things he already knew from experience. He quit school, made a low-budget horror flick, and never looked back.

Garrett gave up trying to rest. His mind was too busy. Standing, he stretched his long body, scrubbing a hand over his face. It was his mother's face — so to speak. A very male version. She was tall by Hollywood standards. He inherited her height, her cheekbones, and dark brown, red-tinged hair. To be honest, Colt shared the same traits. The difference was the eyes. His brothers' eyes were blue, like their father. Garrett was the only one who had his mother's changeable pale silver.

The camera loved those eyes. Directors became obsessed with close-ups. The shade deepened depending on her mood. Stormy. Misty. Intense. They shaded from hot gunmetal to chilly slate. Her eyes told the story. The emotions played out in colors. Callie was a master at using this anomaly to draw the audience in. Anger? No problem. Happiness? Piece of cake.

The only one she couldn't fake — the color no audience ever saw. The deep purple of love. Caleb Landis knew that shade; he saw it every day for the last thirty-six years.

Garrett wondered if his eyes turned that color when he was with Jade? Did he love her? Or was it only a gnawing obsession that would burn itself out? He knew the answer. For the first time, he was glad they had never had sex in the light. Like his mother, if his eyes gave him away, he didn't want Jade to know. Not now. Not unless there was a drastic change in their twisted relationship. His words would never give him away. He didn't want his eyes to.

With a sigh, Garrett glanced at his watch. Ten-thirty. He hit the intercom.

"Yes, Mr. Landis?" Dominic, Wyatt's assistant, answered a second after the first buzz. He always did. Not even Sally was that good. Super capable or slightly creepy? Garrett could never decide.

"Can we move the meeting up a few minutes?"

Garrett could imagine the calculations running through the man's head. In Wyatt's world, half an hour *was not* a few minutes. He had his time micromanaged down to the second. It should have made him an annoying son of a bitch. It didn't. His brother was one of Garrett's favorite people. It had nothing to do with being related. They were *siblings* and friends.

"He's on the phone with Dubai."

"How is old Dubai? I haven't spoken to him in years."

Silence. Hell, Garrett swore he could hear crickets. Dominic had no discernible sense of humor. Luckily, Wyatt was fine with that. His assistant wasn't there to entertain or be entertained. His job was to keep things running smoothly. Most important, keep the boss man free from unnecessary interruptions. Garrett was never sure if Dominic considered him a necessity or an annoyance.

"He wrapped up a bit early. You may see him now."

"You *know* I'm his brother."

Garrett heard Dominic huff.

"Not during office hours."

GARRETT GREW UP in Beverly Hills. The huge estate his parents purchased in the early eighties was a never-ending playground for four growing boys. Tennis courts, two swimming pools, an endless lawn for games of every kind. Every year since the last of the children moved out, his parents talked about downsizing. Why did they need so much space? Grandchildren? None of their sons seemed in any hurry to provide them with the renewed patter of little feet.

Wyatt received the brunt of that complaint. Garrett and Nate were catching up. Colt was only two years behind, yet he seemed exempt.

Why? Movies stars were different. He had years to play the field. Or play with his leading ladies.

For all their less than subtle hints, Caleb Landis and Callie Flynn never tried to change their children. Their decisions, from their professions to their love lives, were their own. They were loving, generous parents. Not all Beverly Hills kids could make the same claim.

Spoiled, pampered, their egos as big as the industry they dominated. Somehow, with all the privileges they were afforded, the Landis boys avoided the clichéd pitfalls associated with too much money and too much fame. Their father would never have permitted it. He ruled with an iron fist in a velvet glove, not afraid to hug his sons when needed or kick some ass when warranted.

Garrett pulled his Lamborghini to a stop next to Wyatt's Bentley. The wide driveway also contained a classic Porsche and a decked-out Ford F450. It looked like Colt and Nate beat him here too. The way production on *Exile* was going, it was a surprise he made it at all. A night with good food and family was exactly what he needed.

"Garrett!"

"Nate," Garrett laughed as his twin lifted him off his feet. "Let me down, you idiot."

"Getting soft?" Nate sat Garrett on the ground, giving him a quick punch in the stomach.

Well-versed in his brother's methods, Garrett stepped back. Between his quick reflexes and Nate pulling his punch, he barely felt it. If he'd wanted to, Nate could send a man to the hospital with one fist to the midsection.

Garrett counted himself lucky they were family. Around puberty, Nate's growth spurt shot him past his twin by almost three inches. As a stuntman, he was nothing but solid, lean muscle. Garrett exercised. Took care of himself. Nate's body was his business.

"When did you get back from Costa Rica?"

"This afternoon." Nate draped an arm over Garrett's shoulder. "Never again. I can't sleep in those lousy trailers. I need my own bed. After dinner, I'm sacking out for ten hours straight. What's so funny?"

"Us," Garrett said. "I think we developed our sleeping quirks in the womb. I can't sleep on location, neither can you."

"Blame Mom?" Nate seemed horrified at the thought.

"Never." Garrett shook his head. "We hit the parental jackpot."

"And that is one of the many reasons I love my boys."

Callie Flynn opened her arms. When she had Garrett and Nate in a warm embrace, she sighed. There was nothing better than having all her chicks back in the nest. The fact that they returned on a regular basis — willingly — filled her heart to near bursting. The love and respect she and Caleb received had her counting her blessings. Every day.

"Who is this gorgeous woman?" Keeping an arm around his mother's trim waist, Garrett stood far enough away to look her up and down. "You get younger every time I see you, Mom."

"Why thank you, Garrett." Callie beamed. "A woman can never hear that enough."

"It would make it easier if you stopped looking like a teenager and started looking like the mother of four grown men," Nate grinned down at the woman he adored. "I've lost track of the times some jerk has told me how hot you are. Put on fifty pounds. Get some wrinkles. It will save me from having to threaten guys with an ass-kicking."

"Don't be ridiculous. As your mother, I'm flattered," Callie smiled. "As an actress who has spent the majority of her life being judged by her looks? I'm thrilled. As a fifty-six-year-old woman? I'm freaking ecstatic."

"Why is that, my love?"

Caleb Landis came into the room at the end of the conversation. He didn't care why. He approved of anything that made his darling wife happy.

"Nate seems to think I'm *too* beautiful." She winked at Garrett. "Can you imagine?"

"Sacrilege." The big voice boomed out of a man who in every way was bigger than life. Well over six feet tall, with a shock of thick white hair, his body was strong and straight. At sixty-two, he had the energy of a man half his age. He came to Hollywood hungry for success.

Everything he had, the money, the fame, the awards, came from his hard work and the ability to spot a winner. His track record as a movie producer was legendary. A trait he'd passed down to his sons.

The sound of their father's voice brought Wyatt and Colt from the kitchen.

"You are the most beautiful, desirable, intelligent woman ever put on this Earth. It's our job, as the men in your life, to worship the ground you walk on. Understood?"

The last was directed at Nate, not his wife.

"Is this asshole… Sorry, Mom." Colt winced. "Is Nate being a jerk?"

Callie hid her smile. Her boys didn't curse in front of their mother. Not because she was a wilting flower whose ears would melt. She was pragmatic enough to understand that she was living with four men — they were going to use salty language. She didn't want sons who spewed f-bombs at the drop of a hat. Curtailing their use of four letter words around her made them think twice when out in the world. Or so she told herself.

"Hey," Nate protested. "How did this get turned around on me? I casually mention that having a legendary beauty for a mother can sometimes be problematic and all of a sudden I'm a bad guy?"

"I've had to beat other men off with a stick for decades. It's the very happy price you have to pay when you love a woman so beautiful inside *and* out."

Garrett was used to the open, sometimes over-the-top, affection his parents displayed. Everything they did was big. The way they loved, the way they fought. The way they made up. One time after an epic argument, he and his brothers didn't see them for three days. At thirteen, Garrett had been old enough to know what they were doing behind the closed bedroom doors.

At the time, it was embarrassing. A few years later, when it happened again, he admired their stamina. Now, for the first time, Garrett envied not only loving someone that much; he longed to have it for himself. He found it was easy to give away his heart. The hard part was getting one in return.

"You seem pensive tonight." Colt handed Garrett an ice-cold longneck beer. "Problems with the new movie?"

"Other than a leading lady who thinks she's God's gift?" Garrett took a long draw from the bottle. "Actors."

"Hey, don't lump all actors together. Some of us are easy peasy to work with." Colt laughed, his blues eyes sparkling.

Those eyes, and the handsome face that went with them, graced hundreds of magazine covers over the past few years. Colt was blessed with a face the camera loved. On top of that, he could act. Not just another pretty face, one critic declared after Colt's last film. Garrett was proud. In public, he let the world know just how proud. In private, this was the baby of the family. Putting him in his place was a mandatory older brother obligation.

"Easy peasy? More like easy. Period. You need to pace yourself, Colt. At the rate you're going, you'll run out of starlets to sleep with." Garrett shook his head in mock despair. "What then?"

Colt chuckled good-naturedly. He was the easygoing Landis. You could poke, prod, and goad him for hours. He was famously tolerant of invasive paparazzi and overly enthusiastic fans. Colt never complained about long delays on the set or lost his temper when the script was changed at the last minute. Oh, he had a temper. The boiling point was high. Which meant when he finally *did* reach it, watch out.

"You've been stuck behind that camera too long, Garrett. Hollywood has an endless supply of beautiful women. Wave after wave. Day after day. They come by car, train, bus." Colt sighed happily at the thought.

"Don't you get tired of the same, vapid conversation?" Garrett snapped his fingers, bringing Colt's attention back to him. "Oh, that's right, you barely know their names. Being able to discuss current affairs is not a requirement."

"Stop giving Colt a hard time. With his track record, he gets points for making it this long without an STD." Wyatt joined them, a glass of iced tea in his hand. He didn't drink. Not anymore.

"No glove, no love," Colt said.

"Charming."

"Don't scoff, Garrett." Callie slipped an arm around his waist, squeezing affectionately. His mother was a toucher. Hugs were mandatory in the Landis family. "I hope you're as careful as your brother."

Garrett kissed the top of his mother's head.

"I don't have as many reasons to be. But yes," he quickly added. "I'm always careful."

"Good. Now." She looped her arm through his. "Let's eat. Lorena's spaghetti and meatballs await."

There wasn't anything the long-time Landis family cook made that four hungry boys hadn't devoured. Spaghetti and meatballs were Garrett's favorite. The family settled around the dining room table, each automatically taking their usual spots. The conversation was easy, the topics eclectic. Work, politics, climate change. Garrett tucked into the pasta and spicy sauce. He hadn't realized how hungry he was until the generous plate of food was in front of him.

"We went to an auction at Anson Marlow's house night before last."

Garrett's hand paused, the fork full of food halfway to his mouth. Swallowing, hoping to clear the sudden lump in his throat, Garrett ate the spaghetti. He chewed and chewed, listening intently to what his mother was saying.

"I didn't think you socialized with him," Wyatt said as he reached for a piece of hot garlic bread.

"We don't," Caleb stated emphatically. "The auction was to help survivors of that earthquake up north. I wanted to send a check. Your mother insisted we make an appearance. I swear if we end up with one more useless piece of *charity* artwork, we'll need to build on another room to store the crap."

"Careful, Caleb," his wife warned. "You're turning into a grumpy old man. Next you'll be schlepping around in baggy pants with the waistband pulled up under your armpits and yelling at kids to stay off the lawn."

"I didn't hear you complaining about this *old man* this morning. I believe you grabbed my ass and called me God."

"Honestly." Nate shook his head in amazement. "Do you two ever stop?"

"Hopefully, not until they're putting me in the ground."

"In another forty or fifty years," Callie added, her deep purple eyes locked with the blue of her husband's. "Where was I?"

Colt smiled indulgently. When Caleb and Callie looked at each other in that way, they often became distracted.

"You went to a benefit?"

"That's right," Callie nodded, smiling at her youngest. "Anson Marlow might not be my favorite person, but when he does something, it's first class all the way. Not that he does anything except sign the checks. Jade plans every aspect, from the flowers to the gift bags. The details were impeccably thought out."

"You saw Jade?"

Garrett held his breath waiting for the answer to Colt's question. The question he had so desperately wanted to ask.

Callie's eyes turned a misty gray, concern written on her face. "I think it's the first time she's been out in public for over a year. I'm afraid many of the people there came because they heard she was going to make an appearance."

"Christ," Wyatt said in disgust. "Why can't they leave the woman in peace? After what happened, who could blame her if she bought a cabin in the woods and became a hermit."

"It would be tempting," Callie agreed.

"How did she look?"

"Thin," she told Nate. "Stronger than I expected. Jade always had an air of fragility about her. Years of being emotionally bulldozed into submission will do that, I suppose. Of course, none of us knew what was going on behind closed doors."

"Her father knew."

Callie didn't blink at the ferocity in Garrett's words. She saw it as normal, what anyone would feel. Basic human compassion. What his mother didn't know, there was nothing basic about Garrett's feelings. They ran deeper than the surface — bone deep.

"That's only a rumor, Garrett. One that was hushed up quickly."

Garrett turned his gaze, meeting eyes exactly like his own.

"Do you think anything goes on in that house without Anson Marlow knowing about it?"

"There isn't any doubt Marlow knew." Caleb's words dripped with contempt. "He let his own daughter suffer untold abuse, rather than taint his family with scandal."

"Do you really think that's why he didn't intervene?" Callie was shocked at the thought.

"You can count on it. The man is pond scum." Caleb pushed his empty plate away. No seconds tonight. The conversation effectively killed his appetite. "Oh, he's smart. Brilliant in his own way. He pulled himself up from nothing. Worked hard, married well. Extremely well. He's a cold son of a bitch. You can't blame his wife for leaving him."

"I can blame her for not taking Jade when she did," Callie said heatedly. "You don't abandon a small child. Not to a cold, cruel bastard."

"Why is she still there?" Colt asked after a few moments of silence. "Why stay in that house, with that man?"

"Sometimes there's comfort in familiarity." Callie looked around the table, grateful for her blessings. Not everyone had not one, but five unwavering pillars for support. "From what I understand, Jade has no one."

Bullshit, Garrett wanted to shout. *She has me*. But did she know it? Had he ever told her?

"She still young," Caleb reasoned. "It isn't too late for her to find her own way."

"She needs a friend."

"And that friend is you?" Caleb asked his wife.

"I've been thinking about it. Why not?" Callie asked her husband defiantly. Unlike Jade, Callie knew how to stand up for herself and what she thought was right. Then she backtracked. "I don't want to come off as a crusading do-gooder. Do you think it's a bad idea?"

"Nope," Caleb said, smiling when he saw the surprise in her eyes. "Do me a favor, though?"

"What?"

"Let this new relationship bloom away from Marlow's house. It will be best for Jade and you if her father isn't in the vicinity."

"Agreed." Callie felt a jolt of energy. "I've always suspected that underneath Jade's smooth, cool exterior lay some heat. Maybe if she has a friend who will listen, or just be there, she might find a way to push some of that buried passion to the surface."

Passion. Garrett knew Jade possessed plenty of that. When they were alone. In bed. In the dark. Like his mother suspected, it was something she'd always had. A spark that drew him the first time they met. The one that kept him going back, hoping for more than she was willing to give.

Later that evening, Garrett was still thinking about that spark. The drive to his Laurel Canyon home gave him plenty of time to let his mind wander back to the first time he spoke to Jade for any length of time.

For years, they wandered in and out of the same parties, concerts, and charity events. Los Angeles. Beverly Hills. Hollywood. They were strangely insular communities. If you had money. Add the movie business, the social circles became even smaller.

Garrett knew Jade Marlow by sight. Her porcelain skin and red hair set her apart. The cool, aloof air she projected kept most men away. She was beautiful. No denying that. He'd heard her described as icy. Too cold to bother when there were so many warm-blooded, willing women to be had with much less effort.

It was a hot August night that Garrett found out how wrong everyone was about Jade Marlow.

Chapter Three

THREE YEARS EARLIER

"WHY DID I let you talk me into attending this party? Every year it's the same thing. Boring food, boring people." Nate took a swig of whiskey, grimacing. "Are they watering down the Jack?"

"Did you ever think that you might be the problem?" Garrett asked. He sampled his own drink. No doubt. It wasn't straight whiskey. And it wasn't Jack Daniels. "Other than the booze, you should look at yourself and ask why you're so restless. This room is filled with beautiful women. Find one. Take her home. Screw your brains out."

Nate yawned.

Garrett laughed. "If that idea bores you, there really is something wrong."

"Ha, ha." Nate rotated his neck, trying to work out some of the kinks, and perhaps loosen the tie he wore because it was the thing to do. He knew how to dress for formal occasions. Owned several custom-made tuxedos. His mother insisted. That didn't mean he had to like putting one on. He liked worn jeans, a soft t-shirt, and broken-in work boots. Tonight all he wanted was his bed — alone.

"Tough shoot?" Garrett asked.

Nate was a stuntman. A damn good one. He worked his way up until, for the first time, he was running the show. It was what he wanted — dreamed of. It also meant a lot more work and responsibility. Now, instead of just himself, he had the safety of his crew to think about.

By the looks of his brother, Garrett wondered if he was losing a few nights' sleep worrying.

"Yeah," Nate acknowledged. "Made tougher by an asshole director who won't let the experts do their jobs. This guy is a micro-manager, Garrett. And before you jump to his defense, let me tell you why it's a problem."

Garrett nodded. Nate called it. He was automatically going to defend a fellow director. He understood the need to keep all aspects of the movie under control. He also knew if Nate was complaining, he had a good reason.

"This morning's stunt was fairly routine. A fight. Two men. A plate glass window."

"Nothing is routine during a stunt. You are too good at your job to ever think that."

"Too right," Nate agreed. If anyone understood, it was his brother — his twin. "Try telling that to Arnie Schmidt. He seems to think if it looks easy, it is easy. After all, it isn't real glass."

Garrett winced. The breakaway glass used in stunts was safe. It wasn't foolproof. That's why they were professionals. Because they were good at their jobs, making sure everything ran smoothly, there was a perception what they did wasn't complicated. Thinking that way was the first step to a potential tragedy.

"I hope you set him straight."

"It didn't come to blows, if that's what you're asking." Nate grinned. "It was a close thing. Luckily, the jerk backed down. The stunt is in the can. I'm hoping he's learned his lesson."

"You don't sound convinced," Garrett said. All his sympathy was with his brother.

"I'm not. There's enough strain on the job without having to pull this guy's fingers out of my pie."

"We are still talking about stunt work? Is Arnie getting touchy with your personal pie?"

"Shut the fuck up," Nate laughed. Count on Garrett to make a joke. *That's* why he was glad he had someone to bounce his problems off. Feeling some of the tension lifting, Nate looked around the room. This time he really looked.

"You know, you're right. There are some damn sexy women here tonight."

Garrett smiled, watching his brother scope out the room. The low wolf whistle shifted his attention to the woman across the room who managed to grab Nate's attention.

"Jade Marlow," Nate said with obvious appreciation. "I always wondered if she was as cool as she seemed. In bed, does she turn into the wildcat all that red hair suggests?"

"Do you want to find out?"

For some reason, Garrett dreaded Nate's answer. Not that *he* was interested. She wasn't his type. Too aloof. Not enough curves. If Nate wanted to find out if the layer of ice around Jade Marlow was a thin veneer or glacier thick, why should he care?

"Tempting." Nate gave Jade another considering look, then shrugged. "Tonight, I'm too tired. I don't want a challenge. I want a sure thing. Ah, Nina Polk. Just what the doctor ordered."

He didn't track Nate's progress. If he left with Nina, good for him. Garrett's attention was on a tall redhead in a pale yellow dress. Were her eyes green? In all the years they bumped around the same circles, Garrett couldn't remember getting close enough to notice. His breath hissed through his teeth when Jade chose that moment to lift her gaze. For a second, their eyes met and held. Not green. Not brown. Hazel? He needed to move closer, wanting to be sure.

Instead of moving in a straight line, Garrett made a serpentine pattern through the crowd. He greeted friends, exchanged pleasantries. The whole time keeping track of Jade.

Luck was with him. She stepped away from her group. Telling himself there was nothing creepy or stalkerish about following her, Garrett kept pace. When she exited the room, out the tall French doors, and onto the balcony, Garrett smiled, saying a silent *thank you* when he found the area deserted except for the two of them.

"Hello."

Jade's happy greeting was unexpected. Garrett imagined having to coax her to start a conversation. Much to his delight, she made the first move.

"Hello."

From a distance, Jade Marlow was a beautiful woman. Up close, she was exquisite. Her flawless skin glowed like rich cream in the moonlight. Garrett decided right there that he wanted to taste every inch.

"I'm Jade."

"I'm Garrett."

"I know who you are," she smiled tentatively. "Everyone knows the Landis family."

Garrett thought she seemed a little shy. Funny. The world saw a cool, ice queen. He saw a woman who was a little unsure. Maybe a little shy. It was all about perspective.

"Everyone knows Jade Marlow," Garrett told her. She looked pleased and a little surprised by his words.

"Really? Everyone?"

"Absolutely." Garrett moved closer. "Which makes me wonder. If everyone knows *us*, why have *we* never met?"

Jade shrugged, turning away.

"I'm sorry. Did you want to be alone?"

He hoped not, but if she asked, he would leave.

"No!" Jade gave a low, husky laugh.

Garrett racked his brain for a way to make her do it again. The sound made him happy. And horny. Quite a combination.

"That was a desperate sounding no, wasn't it?" Jade asked. "I don't want you to go. Unless *you* want to."

Her eyes. Garrett felt a catch in his breathing. Lord, what eyes. Not green. Not brown. Hazel. There were little flecks of a hundred colors swirling like a beautiful kaleidoscope. *Did he want to go?* Hell, no.

"I like it out here."

Garrett moved to stand beside her. The view of the Hollywood Hills, all lit up, was one of his favorites. Everything looked shiny and bright — the way Hollywood should look.

"I like standing with you," Garrett turned his head and smiled. "You smell amazing, by the way."

Oh, there it was. A little blush. A true redhead's blush. It told him so much. Cold women's cheeks didn't turn that lovely shade of pink over such an innocent compliment.

"You're a fake, Jade Marlow. You have everyone thinking you're made of ice. I see plenty of heat."

"Do you know me well enough to decide that?" Jade asked. Her voice was low, her eyes snapping with displeasure.

Shy, but with backbone. Garrett felt his interest ratchet up several notches. Beautiful women were a dime a dozen in Hollywood. Interesting ones were harder to come by. The combination was almost irresistible.

"I don't know you at all, Jade. But I'd like to."

"I...," Jade took a deep breath. She looked at Garrett for a moment. "I have a big decision to make. Will you help me?"

"Tell me about it."

"No. Not now."

A mystery? He could live with that. Some more time with Jade was what he wanted.

"What do you need me to do?"

"Take me for a drive. I don't care where." Jade looked back through the French doors. "Away from here."

Garrett didn't hesitate. "I'll get my car and meet you out front. Say ten minutes?"

"Is five too soon?"

Garrett grinned. "Five, it is."

Getting his car from the valet was an adventure. It cost him two hundred bucks and the promise of an extra job in his next film to be ready and waiting when Jade arrived. Five minutes on the nose. Garrett helped her into the passenger side, once again taking in the scent of spicy oranges. As she settled into her seat, the long length of her shapely legs drew his eyes. They went on forever.

"We should go," Jade told him, her eyes darting toward the house.

"Are you being followed?"

"Not yet."

Deciding questions could wait, Garrett closed the door, skirted the front of the car, before climbing in behind the wheel. Jade said she didn't care where they went so he headed up Mulholland Drive.

Garrett drove with an easy skill. The winding road could be dangerous. Especially at night. They were in no hurry, so he went at a leisurely pace, barely hitting the speed limit.

He hated blasting the air conditioner at night, preferring the feel of the air from an open window on his face.

"Will the breeze bother you?" Garrett knew from experience that some women did not appreciate having their hair messed up.

"Hmm?" Jade frowned, her mind obviously a million miles away.

"The windows. Do you mind if I open them?"

"Oh," she smiled. "No. Not at all. I prefer it to air conditioning."

Garrett returned her smile. She was a gem. Or rather, rare Jade. He chuckled at his whimsical thoughts. Lordy, he needed to get a hold of himself. *Rare Jade?* Where the hell had that come from?

"Tell me what's so funny. I could use a laugh."

"Smile like that again and I will tell you anything."

"I've heard the Landis brothers cornered the market on charm." Jade's smile widened. "This is the first time I've seen it in action. For once, there was no false advertising."

"Charm is a subjective thing, Jade." Since they were on a straight stretch of road, Garrett spared her a brief glance. Damn, she was beautiful in the moonlight. "Other women might not enjoy my brand."

"I doubt you have any problem talking women around — whatever it is you want."

Garrett didn't deny her words. He liked getting his way. He was good at making sure he got it. Right now, all he wanted was to give her what she needed.

"You said you had a decision to make. How can I help?"

"Drive. Talk."

"About?"

Jade leaned her head back, her eyes closed, and sighed. "Anything. Nothing. Just talk."

So that's what Garrett did. He told Jade about the last movie he made. Searching his brain, he relayed the craziest moments that at the time made him want to tear his hair out. Now, they made her smile — laugh. Every frustration became worth it when he heard that husky sound. She didn't respond in any other way, letting him go on and on. She relaxed, though, slipping her feet from her stiletto pumps. Her hands that were once clenched fists were now open, palms up on her lap. His words, and the miles they traveled, seemingly taking her farther and farther away from her troubles.

Garrett finished his story. He didn't feel the need to fill the silence; instead, kept driving, enjoying the company. The summer air became sweeter the higher they traveled into the hills. He realized he didn't do this enough. There wasn't time. Busy schedule — busy life. There was something to be said for driving with no destination. They had no place to be. They had no reason to hurry.

"I never do this," Jade said quietly.

"Go for meandering drives through the Hollywood Hills? Me neither."

"Well, yes." She smiled again, not opening her eyes. "I meant I don't take off with men I've just met. I don't take off with men. Or women."

"What do you do?" Garrett was genuinely curious. What made getting out of bed each morning worthwhile for Jade?

"I... exist." She scoffed at her own words. "Wow. How overly dramatic does that sound? Poor little rich girl Jade Marlow. She lives in a mansion with servants to carry out her every whim. Designer clothes, expensive cars. Yearly trips to Europe. What woman wouldn't trade places with me in a heartbeat?"

"Sounds incredible." Incredibly boring. Garrett glanced at Jade's hands. Fists. Clenched. Great. An hour of relaxation gone in a few minutes. "Who would you change places with, if you had the choice?"

"That's a loaded question." Jade turned her head toward him, her eyes still closed. "What we see of other people's lives is usually what they want us to see. Scripted, so to speak. I could pick a seemingly perfect family. Happy Mom and Dad. Rosy-cheeked children. What happens when that door closes every night? I don't want to know."

"Untold horrors?" Garrett asked. He pulled the car onto a secluded side road. Turning off the engine, he looked at Jade. "Why would your mind go there?"

"Because I don't live with any of that." Jade's eyes opened and he saw a tired resignation Garrett didn't understand. "I've thought about leaving my father's house. But why? I'm not abused. All he asks is that I'm there when he's in town. He wants a companion. The rest of the time, I can come and go as I please."

"Are you happy?"

"I think so." Jade frowned. "I'm not unhappy. And as my father reminds me whenever I get restless, there's nothing wrong with consistency."

"Jesus, Jade. Really?" Garrett took her hand, smoothing out the fist. He massaged the back of her fingers with the pad of his thumb. "Consistency is one thing. Not living your own life is another. What do you do for excitement?"

"Take off for late night rides with strange men?" Jade lifted her gaze from their joined hand. "Is it pathetic that you're the most excitement I've ever had?"

"We won't call it pathetic." Garrett lightly kissed the back of her hand. "We'll call it a start."

"More like a one-off."

"It doesn't have to be," Garrett assured her. He didn't want this to be the beginning *and* the end. Why should it be?

"Garrett? I have another favor to ask." Jade's smile was tentative — a little shy. "Have I exceeded my limit?"

"With one car trip? Hardly. Ask away."

"Will you kiss me?"

"Oh, Jade. Honey." Garrett pulled her into his arms, the console between them a minor barrier. "You'd be doing *me* the favor. I've wanted to taste you all evening."

Garrett couldn't remember the last time he thought about how he would kiss a woman. Maybe as an untried teenager on his first date? Then he worried about how to turn his head or if he should use his tongue. With Jade, his thoughts weren't about technique. He wanted this to be a kiss she never forgot. If he knocked out the memory of every other man in the process, that would be a nice added bonus.

At the first touch of her lips against his, he stopped thinking at all.

Jade's mouth was soft under his. Her sweet breath came out as a sigh. Garrett's fingers slid into her hair, the silky strands caressing his skin. All of her was satin smooth, the skin of her cheek, the curve of her lips. His sighs mingled with hers. This wasn't a kiss. It was a feast and he was a starving man who couldn't get enough. Her taste was instantly addictive. A lifetime wouldn't satisfy his craving.

Garrett pulled Jade closer until they were chest to chest. For such a slender woman, her breasts were wonderfully full and soft. The thin material of her dress was little protection from his roving hand. He cupped the firm mound, running his thumb over her peaked nipple.

"What are you doing?" Jade breathed the words into his ear.

"You don't like me touching you?"

"I like it too much."

Garrett smiled, his teeth nipping at her bottom lip. "No such thing as *too* much."

"I wasn't supposed to like it at all."

Garrett let her pull away, a frown on his face.

"You asked me to kiss you hoping… What?"

"I wanted it to be nice. Pleasant."

"I don't know what to say. Sorry?"

Jade laughed. It wasn't a happy sound.

"It's my fault," she said. "That wasn't my first kiss."

"I wouldn't think so."

"It was the first time a kiss has, I don't know. Worked me up?" Jade shrugged. "Kissing is nice. Affectionate."

"Kissing, when done properly, is hot as hell, Jade. Nice and affectionate is reserved for family members and friends. Lovers are a different matter."

"We aren't lovers."

"Fine." Garrett nodded. His eyes met hers, the color a deep, intense gray. "Soon to be lovers."

"No."

"I hear the regret in your voice. Why? We're both unattached." Garrett paused. "Are you married?"

"Not yet."

"Engaged?"

"That's the decision I need to make," Jade turned away. "My father thinks I should marry. It's time."

"Time? What does that mean?"

"I'm getting older and he wants grandchildren."

"What are you? Twenty-two? Twenty-three?"

"Twenty-five next week."

"Ancient." Garrett took her hand again. He liked touching her. "My parents want grandchildren, Jade. That doesn't mean they push my brothers and me to get married."

"My father doesn't push," Jade assured Garrett. "He bulldozes. In this case, though, I think he's right. I want to get married. Someday."

"Someday is good."

"I'm not seeing anyone special." Jade sighed. "I never see anyone special. About a week ago, my father pointed that out quite forcefully. Since I wasn't capable of finding a suitable husband, he would find one for me. Or rather, he's *found* a suitable husband."

"Then let your father marry this guy. You don't have to tie yourself to a stranger."

The whole idea was appalling. He couldn't understand how Jade could be so calm.

"He isn't a stranger. Stephen works for my father. I went on a few dates with him last year."

"Were his kisses pleasant?"

"His kiss," Jade emphasized the singular, "was fine."

"Fine being a step down from pleasant?"

"He's handsome, well-spoken. Stephen fits in socially." Jade smiled. It didn't reach her eyes. "I like the idea of having my own home, Garrett."

"You want to get away from your father. I understand that. You don't have to get married to do that, Jade."

Seeing her hesitation, Garrett took a big leap.

"Come away with me."

"Garrett…"

"Hear me out. I'm going to Vancouver tomorrow to scout movie locations. Two weeks in Canada. Have you ever been?"

"No."

"It's beautiful. We'll take our time. Eat at some great restaurants. See the sights." Garrett gave her his most charming smile. "Separate rooms. Or not. That will be up to you. No pressure. I promise."

"There wouldn't be separate rooms," Jade said. "We both know that."

"No. But it will be your choice."

"I can't, Garrett."

"You can."

"I have three charity events in the next week. I'm chairing one; the others are very dear to me."

"Jade…"

"Take me home, Garrett." When he would have protested, she squeezed his hand. Her eyes begging him to understand. "Please."

Garrett started the car without another word. There were plenty of things he wanted to say. Instead, they rode in silence. He knew where she lived. The Marlow estate wasn't far from his parents' place. He and Jade grew up a few houses apart. They went to the same school. Only a few years separated them. Yet this was the first time they had spoken more than a few words. Now, when it was too late.

The hell with that, Garrett thought. Jade wasn't married. She wasn't engaged. She certainly had no strong feelings for *Stephen*. Who said it was too late?

Garrett pulled to a stop outside the gated house.

"Don't."

Jade stopped him when he would have pushed the intercom.

"I'm not letting you walk to the house, Jade."

"It isn't that far."

"Far enough."

Garrett pushed the button then waited for the gates to open. He drove the short distance to the house. Before Jade could make her escape, he put a hand on her arm.

"Tell me you were tempted."

"I wanted to say yes the second you asked," Jade told him.

"I want to see you again, Jade." Garrett lifted her chin until her eyes met his. "Two weeks. That isn't long."

"In this case, it might as well be forever."

Before Garrett could answer, the passenger side door opened.

"Jade."

Jade winced. The voice wasn't loud or harsh. It was firm. Commanding. Cold.

"Get in the house. Stephen was worried about you."

"Stephen can kiss my…"

"Garrett." Jade shook her head. "It's fine. Honestly." She looked at her father. "I'll only be a moment."

"Now, Jade."

She sighed. There was more than regret in her hazel eyes. Sadness. And something Garrett couldn't quite define.

"You don't have to go, Jade. I'll take you anywhere you want."

"This is home."

There was no fear. Resignation. That was it. He saw it in her eyes and heard it in her voice. For some reason, that alarmed him more than anything.

"Two weeks." He was giving her a lifeline. All she needed to do was grab on.

"Thank you for driving me home, Garrett."

Jade slipped from the car. Before she could say anything else, her father slammed the door. He escorted her up the steps and into the house. Garrett waited until they were completely out of sight before he pulled away.

He *would* see her again. Nothing would stop him. Not an over-controlling father or a would-be husband. God, it was going to be a long two weeks.

GARRETT KNEW LESS than a week into his trip that he'd found the perfect spot to shoot his movie. A rural setting that could pass for Michigan in the nineteen-twenties. The lake he was particularly interested in was exactly as the screenwriter described. A log cabin sat on the shore of the north side. The inside was too modern; that they could get around. The outside suited his vision.

Which was a good thing. Garrett's budget was tight. There wasn't room to build what he needed. Coming in on time, with money to spare meant solidifying his reputation. He worked fast, cheap, and produced a quality product. None of his movies lost money. He planned on keeping it that way.

Next up was Garrett's first "studio" film. Bigger budget, better locations. He could finally afford to take his time. Every shot would be planned out. No more flying by the seat of his pants because the money was running low. Not that he planned on going overboard. He was too much his father's son to waste money. Letting a film run over budget was not in his DNA.

"What do you think?"

"Hamish," Garrett slapped his AD on the back. "I hope you like trees. Starting next month, this is our home. One month of roughing it. No takeout pizza or egg foo yung at two in the morning. Think you can handle it?"

Hamish shrugged. He grew up dirt poor in Scotland. If his father lost his job or someone got sick, food became a premium they couldn't afford. Since coming to the States, he'd gotten used to eating regularly.

As long as that didn't change, he could handle the boondocks.

"Down the road about a mile, there's a bonny widow and her sister. They've invited us to dinner." Hamish wiggled his bushy, black eyebrows. "I got the impression *dessert* was part of the package."

Garrett looked at his friend. They were close to the same age. They had similar appetites. During their last shoot, it was the co-eds — college roommates who weren't shy about having sex in the same room. After six, long celibate weeks and a few too many beers, neither was Garrett. The next morning he swore never again. If they couldn't find separate rooms, he would go back to his old standby. Masturbation was a lonely form of gratification. Still, it beat the hell out of getting a glimpse of Hamish's ass in mid-thrust.

"I'll pass."

"Come on. They have their own bedrooms. No sharing." Hamish had to hurry when Garrett started walking around the lake. He was eight inches shorter. With shorter legs, it took three steps to keep up with Garrett's one. "Besides, the older one's front teeth are missing."

"I know I'll be sorry I asked," Garrett said. "Why is that a good thing?"

"All gums on the blowjob."

Hamish covered his teeth with his lips, providing Garrett with a visual he wouldn't soon forget.

"Tempting."

"Are we on?"

Garrett shook his head. "They're all yours."

"Why?"

Their plan was to stay in the cabin tonight, and then head out early. They were done a week early. The only thing left was fine-tuning the details. Garrett was happy to leave the haggling to Wyatt. It was his job as the producer of the film. Besides, he was good at it. It was taken care of on conference calls that bored the tears out of Garrett.

He wanted nothing more than a good night's sleep. They were scheduled on the eleven-thirty flight to Los Angeles. If he were lucky, the plane would be on time. By seven tonight, he hoped to be having dinner with Jade.

Thoughts of her crept into his mind at the damnedest times. It wasn't constant. He had a job to do. He was focused and professional. That didn't stop him from thinking about Jade's smile. Or her laugh. When he was alone at night, visions of her long, silky legs wrapped around him teased his sleep.

"I'm not up to it, Hamish," Garrett told his friend. It wasn't a lie. "Can we leave it at that?"

"Sure." Hamish gave Garrett a speculative look before letting it go. "Maybe the sisters will be willing to share. Hamish Floyd can handle two at once."

The next morning, Hamish looked worse than what the cat dragged in. Garrett didn't ask how the evening went and for once, Hamish didn't volunteer the information. It was a story that would eventually get told. Probably on a long, cold shoot when there was nothing else to talk about.

The flight back to L.A. was blessedly uneventful. Hamish slept while Garrett poured over his notes, jotting down thoughts while they were fresh in his mind. Vancouver was going to be the last thing on his mind tonight. He planned on devoting all his attention on Jade.

"Do you want to share a cab?"

Hamish was awake. Barely. His bleary eyes focused on Garrett long enough to acknowledge the question.

"Make sure the driver takes the quiet way home," Hamish mumbled. He settled into the back of the cab, asleep before Garrett joined him. What quiet way? This was L.A. This time of day there was no such thing. Garrett shook his head. He doubted Hamish knew what he was saying.

Garrett gave the driver the address. He was about to call Jade when his phone rang.

"Wyatt. Your timing, as usual, is impeccable."

"Good flight?"

"Smooth," he said. "What's up?"

"I wanted you to know I finalized the Vancouver deal. You're all set."

"That was fast." Even for Wyatt, this was record time.

"They were amenable to our terms. There was no reason to delay." Garrett heard Wyatt shuffling papers. "I know you must be dead tired, but Mom is having the family over for dinner tonight. I told her I'd mention it."

"The entire family?"

There was a pause. "Colt is in Europe promoting *Freelance*. Nate should be there."

"And Stephanie?"

There was another, longer pause. Wyatt's wife was a no-show more often than not these days. A wise man wouldn't ask. Garrett's concern for his brother superseded wisdom.

"Unlikely."

"Wyatt —"

"What should I tell Mom?"

"I can't make it. I'll call Mom and explain."

"Good. I'll see you tomorrow?"

"Tomorrow."

Garrett felt a wave of concern. He didn't like the defeated tone of Wyatt's voice. A rocky marriage combined with an alcoholic wife was beginning to take their toll. Something had to give. Soon.

After the cab had dropped Hamish off, Garrett decided to stop by to see his mother. He used the ride to get in touch with Jade. The twinge of guilt he should feel for using his connections to acquire her phone number didn't come. All's fair, after all.

The call went straight to voicemail. Damn. He was hoping to talk in case she hesitated over having dinner. It was hard to charm a lady in a text. Though not impossible. He left a message and a text. *Tonight at seven? Tomorrow anytime?* He put the ball in her court. He would wait a few days in case he had to jump the net to retrieve it.

Garrett paid the cab driver. Normally he wouldn't take the time to peruse the outside of his childhood home. He spent eighteen years here; he knew what it looked like. Today, he noticed something different. The color. In the span of one short week, the color had changed from robin's egg blue to yellow. He imagined his mother had a fancy name for the bright, cheery color. He imagined his father rolling his eyes. Something about the huge mansion was always being updated, added on, or decorated. Dad didn't really mind. He loved the woman too much. If it made her happy, it made him happy.

"Garrett."

Garrett grinned at his mother's enthusiastic greeting. One week or one hour, she welcomed her family with the same vigor. He caught her in his arm, swinging her around. Closing his eyes, his inhaled. Vanilla. She was a screen goddess to the rest of the world. To him, she was Mom.

"How is the most beautiful woman in the world?"

"Thrilled to have one of her traveling brood back in the nest." Taking his hand, she led him into the house. "This is a lovely bonus. I wasn't expecting you until later."

"Unfortunately, I can't make it for dinner."

Garrett followed her through the large foyer. Sunlight everywhere. It was what sold her on the house. They continued, passing through the library and out to the patio. The pool sparkled, the flowers bloomed in an array of bright colors, and the lawn was a deep, healthy green. Perfect. His mother wouldn't have settled for less.

"A date?" Callie asked. She poured him a glass of lemonade. "You know that's the only thing I consider an acceptable excuse."

"Of course. I know the house rules."

Garrett took a cookie from the plate. He couldn't remember a time when drinks and cookies weren't out in case company stopped by.

"Is she wonderful? The potential love of your life?"

"Mom." Garrett shook his head. "Only you can get away with questions like that."

"Why?" Callie asked the question tongue in cheek. She already knew the answer.

"Because I love you."

"Hearing that never gets old." Callie gently kissed Garrett's forehead before joining him at the table. "Spill, young man. Who is she?"

"It's early days, Mom. I'm interested, not in love." He took a sip of the tart, sweet liquid. "If things progress, I'll let you know."

"Hmm." Callie's gray eyes met his own. "Fair enough. I expect updates. Understood?"

"Scout's honor."

"Ha," she scoffed. "None of my sons was a boy scout. Boy *terrors*, yes."

"They were healthy, inquisitive, energetic boys. In other words, perfectly normal," his father said as he walked onto the patio.

Caleb Landis pulled his son up, giving him a hug. Garrett knew this game. Squeeze hard, harder than the other guy. Even pushing sixty, his father held his own. As usual, the contest ended in a draw.

"We gave you and Mom a run for your money," Garrett said. He kissed his father's cheek before retaking his seat.

"You've kept me young. You can't afford to get old with four sons nipping at your heels." Caleb thanked his wife when she handed him a glass of iced tea. "Tell me about Vancouver."

The family business occupied the next hour. Movies. If someone wasn't filming a movie, he, or she, was in pre- or post-production. Now, between them, they had six projects in various stages. Caleb and Callie were about to start their seventh movie together.

"Enough business," Garrett finally declared. "What's new on the home front? Besides the color of the house."

"Isn't it lovely?" Callie exclaimed. "Daffodil Delight. It makes me smile."

"What does it make you do?" he asked his father.

"If it makes Callie happy, it makes me happy."

Garrett grinned. Exactly the answer he expected.

"There was a surprise in the neighborhood."

"Another skunk infestation?"

"Bite your tongue." Callie shuddered. "No, something much more pleasant. A wedding."

"That isn't news," Garrett said, reaching for another cookie. Chocolate chip was his favorite. "Tell me someone in Beverly Hills *didn't* get married last week. *That* would be a surprise."

"Well, this had the gossips on high alert. Jade Marlow eloped."

Garrett couldn't have heard right. Jade? Married? How could it happen so fast?

"Who?" he asked, hoping for a different name.

"Jade Marlow," his mother confirmed. "I don't suppose you or your brothers know her very well. She's a lovely young woman. Some people call her icy. I think she's shy."

"When did this happen?"

"Day before yesterday. Her father is a big name, so of course it's news. The reports say the couple ran off to Hawaii." Callie sighed. "It's very romantic. According to the neighborhood know-it-alls, no one knew Jade had a serious boyfriend. Stephen something or other. I hear he works for her father."

Garrett only half-listened, catching bits and pieces of secondhand information. All the while, he had one thought. *She didn't wait for me.* It was stupid. Why would she wait? One extended conversation and a hot kiss. She didn't know him. They connected. That was true. It was *not* love at first sight, by either of them. He wanted her. That night, if she had said the word. Now, she was off limits.

"Garrett."

"Yes?"

"Where were you, baby?" Callie asked with a frown. "You drifted a million miles away."

No. Not a million miles. Only a few blocks down the street. He felt a twinge of regret. Okay. Maybe more than a twinge. He'd spent a week anticipating Jade in his arms. He couldn't miss what he never had. Or something like that. He hoped Jade found what she was looking for. Garrett sincerely wished her happiness in her new home — with her new husband.

"I was thinking. I can go out on a date anytime. I'd rather have dinner with my family." He winked at his mother. "If the invitation is still open."

"Don't be silly." Callie frowned. "What about the young woman? Won't she be offended if you cancel at the last minute?"

"She won't give it a second thought."

Chapter Four

PRESENT DAY

JADE STEPPED FROM the shower. She liked it hot. The steam filled the room, obscuring the mirror over the sink. The only one she owned. She always kept her back to it until she was fully dressed. The steam was a safety net — a buffer just in case she slipped up and caught a glimpse of something she refused to look at.

She went through her usual routine. Drying her body. Lotion, top to bottom. With her hair still wrapped in a towel, she covered herself with an outfit that suited that day's well-planned activities. Then, and only then, she moved to the mirror.

Jade methodically dried her hair, pulling it back into a simple style. Her makeup was minimal. A bit of concealer to hide the dark circles under her eyes. A touch of mascara. Blush was essential. Not too much. She didn't want to look like a sad clown. Then a light coat of lip-gloss.

Jade Marlow was ready to face the world.

"Good morning, Miss Marlow."

"Good morning, Angie."

Jade held her head up high, her back ramrod straight. Through everything. The pain, the humiliation. Jade never let the world see her cower. She had done enough of that in private.

"Mr. Marlow would like a word with you in his office."

Seven in the morning. Her father knew she left her room every day at the same time. If he wanted something, he informed one of the servants to tell Jade. The only time this varied was during her two-year marriage. Then the servant waited until she came down from the west wing. It wouldn't be seemly to interrupt a married couple in their rooms. God forbid anyone saw her after a night of Stephen's *attention*.

If possible, Jade's back became straighter with every step. Taking a deep breath, she knocked on the solid oak door.

"Come in."

"You wished to see me, Father?"

Always Father. Never Dad. Certainly not Daddy. The difference spoke volumes to anyone who cared to listen. Anson Marlow's money had a way of making people deaf.

"Sit down." The gruff command came without a glance up from the papers on his desk."

"Very well."

Jade waited patiently, ankles crossed, hands folded neatly in her lap. This was nothing new. Her father always kept her waiting. She was never certain if it was one more way of showing her who was in charge, or if he didn't think of her at all. If she dallied, not answering his summons immediately, the rafters would ring with his displeasure.

There was a time she would sit — her mind racing. *Had she done something wrong? Was he displeased? What could it be?* She never guessed. The possibilities were endless. Now, she didn't care. Her mind was as calm as her expression. She counted the books on the shelves instead of the myriad of faults her father found in her.

"Why was there a delivery van parked in front of the house at six o'clock?"

"Flowers."

"Obviously, Jade." Anson sighed. *You idiot* was implied. Loudly. "It had Maxine's Florist emblazoned in bright pink on the side. Why do we need more flowers? At six A.M.?"

"I'm hosting the *Ladies Who Lunch* this afternoon. The floral arrangements needed to be in place before the table settings."

Jade didn't mention that the get-together was her father's idea. He knew it. The look she gave him was placid. Unblinking. *Was that a crack she saw in his disapproving frown?* Again, she didn't care.

"What is wrong with you lately?"

"I'm not sure what you mean."

Jade was a statue. She didn't flinch when her father growled. She didn't sweat or fidget. That's what was different. If he couldn't tell, it was his problem. She did not intend to share her newfound ability to ignore his insults. Instead of nervous heat, her body felt wonderfully cool. What was it? Oh, yes. Jade was in her *Zen state.*

"You're smiling." His tone was accusatory.

"Am I?" That didn't happen very often. Especially around her father. "I'm anticipating this afternoon's luncheon. You know how much I enjoy the company of the Beverly Hills elite."

Lies. All lies. One after the other. Another layer to the new Jade. She used to be a lousy liar. She found the more she prevaricated, the easier it became. Nothing major. White lies. It was practice for when she was ready to tell the biggest lie of her life. Jade felt her pulse jump. *Soon.*

"Was there anything else, Father? I need to check with Cook about some last minute menu changes. It seems Mrs. Granger is now gluten-free. Isn't that wonderful?"

"Good God. No wonder Stephen cheated. You have the personality of a limp rag."

Is that why he beat me? Jade wanted to ask. *Oh, no. He beat her because she was annoying and talked too much. Or maybe she didn't talk enough.* The reasons were endless. Every slap justified. Every punch her fault.

Jade breathed in and out. Find your center. Stephen's fists can't hurt you anymore. Neither can your father's words.

"Will you be in for lunch?"

Anson gave Jade another long, speculative look before he finally answered.

"And take the chance of running into those biddies? Their husbands' money is what I care about. I'm counting on some heavy investments in the next few months. Don't screw this up, Jade."

"Of course not, Father."

Jade rose to her feet, nodded in her father's general direction, and then left the room. Once outside the closed door, she held out her hand. Not exactly steady as a rock, but damn close. A tiny tremor, which she quickly controlled. She hoped that Jittery Jade was no more.

Jade looked at her watch. Eight o'clock. Instead of heading straight for the kitchen, she took a detour into the art gallery. No one came in here except to dust or to show off. Her father's vanity room, filled with paintings and sculptures Anson Marlow neither appreciated nor understood. He presented the items to guests as though he'd created them. Jade stood by in case anyone asked a question he couldn't answer. She made it short and sweet before blending back into the woodwork. This was his place to shine, not hers.

The room was the perfect place to make a phone call she didn't want anyone to hear. Or to text her secret lover. The thought made Jade shiver. Not with fear or dread. Sexual anticipation was something new. She felt it briefly three years ago in the car of a stranger. Now, she only needed to think Garrett's name and her body came alive.

She knew he was back in Los Angeles. Garrett Landis was a high-profile director from a high-profile family. Where he went, cameras invariably followed. It made him easy to keep track of. It also made having a clandestine affair tricky. To say the least. Add her name to the mix — the notorious Jade Marlow — and they were playing with fire.

The smart thing would be to end it before their cover was blown. Jade toyed with her phone. Garrett wasn't happy with their arrangement. How difficult would it be to convince him? She felt a twinge in her gut. Not difficult at all. She was more trouble than she was worth.

Shaking off what she recognized as the beginning of a pity party,

Jade quickly typed out the message, sending it before she could change her mind.

Meet me. Ten p.m.?

Jade slipped her phone into her pocket. There was no need to name a meeting place. Garrett knew. She would be on pins and needles until she received an answer.

Schooling her features, Jade walked from the room, heading for the kitchen. She didn't glance around. If one of the staff observed her exit, it didn't matter. She knew they reported everything to her father. The trick was never looking guilty. Cool, calm, and collected.

She was viewed one of two ways. An ice queen or a pathetic victim. One person recognized the passion she kept in check.

What would the *Ladies Who Lunch* say if she stood up and announced *Garrett Landis is my lover?* Jade imagined they would be too shocked to say anything. Shocked, disbelieving. Envious. They would go home to their boring, pudgy husbands knowing Jade Marlow had a man *they* could only fantasize about.

Tempting. But not worth the fallout. No. Garrett must remain her secret. For both their sakes.

THE DAILIES WERE good. Better than that. They were fantastic. For all her pain in the ass antics, Lynne Cornish could act. The camera loved her big blue eyes. Her chemistry with Paul McNally was off the charts. They steamed up every scene.

Once the camera stopped rolling, she reverted to a five-year-old who pouted if denied her slightest whims. For his sanity, Garrett avoided her whenever humanly possible.

"She's something else, isn't she?"

Garrett started to share with Hamish *exactly* what he thought of Lynne Cornish when he saw the look on his friend's face.

"You have got to be shitting me," Garrett groaned.

"What?"

Hamish appeared clueless.

"When did you start screwing our star?"

Garrett wondered if Hamish would deny it. He could see the indecision on the other man's face. Fortunately, he never held out long when Garrett stared him down.

"I'm not."

"Hamish..."

"Screwing connotes two animals giving in to their baser instincts," Hamish said. "What Lynne and I feel is far deeper, Garrett."

Garrett waited, holding his breath. If Hamish declared he and that harpy were soulmates, he might lose his lunch.

"We're soulmates."

Garrett's lunch stayed put. His temper, on the other hand, rose to just short of boiling.

"Fuck that." He signaled Hamish to follow him. He knew his top was about to blow — he didn't want to do it in front of witnesses.

The walk to his office did nothing to cool him down. Each step sent his blood pressure surging. He waited until they were safely behind closed doors before letting loose.

"Have you lost your *wee Scottish mind*?"

"I—"

"Of all the stupid, irresponsible—" Garrett threw his hands up. "Why? That's what I want to know. I know the rule stating no consorting with the cast is unwritten, Hamish. That doesn't make it any less important."

"I know, Garrett. I didn't set out to fall in love."

"Oh, come on."

"I don't expect you to understand. I'm not sure *I* do." Hamish gave Garrett a helpless shrug. "Things started innocently enough."

"Don't they always?"

"I guess I deserve the sarcasm. How often have we derided the idiots who start on set affairs?"

Assuming the question was rhetorical, Garrett kept his mouth shut.

"I know that look."

Garrett simply raised his eyebrows.

"You think I'm an idiot."

"I believe the words stupid and irresponsible have already been used," Garrett said. His anger was fading. Instead, he was baffled. "Let's put aside the reasons why this is a bad idea. When the hell did you have the time?"

"When we were on location."

Hamish flopped down on the leather couch. He tapped his left foot to an uncertain rhythm. *Nerves*, Garrett thought. That little telltale tick that only someone who knew the man well would recognize.

"Without anyone noticing?" Garrett was impressed. There was nothing as insular as a movie set — especially one miles away from civilization. You couldn't pick your nose without it becoming news.

"We only talked," Hamish said. "A few kisses. Last night was the first time we…"

"Fucked?"

"Made love," Hamish corrected.

Garrett wanted to pound his head against the wall. Hell, he wanted to pound Hamish's head. *Anywhere*. This was not good. Right now, everything was sunshine and cotton candy. The chances of it staying that way until they finished shooting were next to nil. Lynne might believe she was in love. Hamish certainly did. When she became bored and turned her attention to a hunky extra or an adoring crew member, then what? Shit? Meet fan.

Unfortunately, Garrett was in a no-win situation. Telling Hamish his love affair would end in disaster was the fastest way to lose a friend and alienate his Assistant Director. Keeping his mouth shut meant dealing with the inevitable fallout. There was no choice. He would keep his fingers crossed love in bloom didn't wither until after he called a wrap on *Exile*.

"Keep it low profile," Garrett said.

"Thanks, man." Hamish jumped up, a bundle of anticipatory energy. "Are we done for the day?"

"Go."

When he was alone, Garrett sighed. There was work to do. Nothing stood still on a movie shoot. The script was solid. Barring any unforeseen disasters, they would finish ahead of schedule. Unfortunately, there were always problems. It was part of his job to limit the frequency and severity. The big bonus was, there were no location shoots left. Blue screen. Special effects. A few intimate moments between his stars. Post-production would take over a year. *Exile* would be a tent-pole release summer after next. A blockbuster — fingers crossed.

As problems went, Hamish and Lynne were an annoying headache, not a migraine. Publicity could handle the mess — if necessary.

Garrett turned on his phone, checking missed calls and texts. *Carved in stone rule*: No phone calls during dailies. He didn't want the distraction. Also, in a life where his phone was a vital tool he was never without, it was nice to have an excuse to tune it out for a few hours.

Most of the messages he ignored. Reminders from his PA about meetings — time and place. Wyatt needed five minutes. *When didn't he?* Dad's birthday was coming up soon. That was a can't-miss event. Garrett bought the present months ago when he was in Costa Rica. Caleb Landis loved wildly colorful shirts. It was a quirk his sons indulged. At one time, they had contests to see who could find the most outrageous print. Now, his closets stuffed, the Landis boys only purchased an addition to the collection when they stumbled across something unique. Garrett couldn't wait to see his father's face when he opened the package. Hula-hooping pink crocodiles. He'd snatched it up the minute he saw it.

Garrett's smile morphed into a thoughtful frown when he came to a text sent that morning. *Jade.* His heart rate kicked up. Even the thought of her made his mouth go dry and his dick harden. He had a lot of nerve questioning Hamish's judgment when his own was so messed up. He wanted Jade. Any way he could have her.

With a sigh, Garrett typed a response. *Yes.* His thumb hesitated a second then hit send.

Garrett leaned back in his chair. He closed his eyes, rotating his head from side to side. So much for changing the status quo. He was stuck because there was no choice. There hadn't been from that day six months ago when he saw her again. He didn't regret his decisions. That would mean removing Jade from his life. Forgetting her taste. The way she felt in his arms. The sounds she made when he brought her to an orgasm. Life with Jade was frustrating. Life without her? Unthinkable.

Chapter Five

SIX MONTHS EARLIER

GARRETT HEARD THE whispers.
Do you think what they say is true? I heard she almost bled to death. She almost didn't make it. I wonder what she did to make her husband want to kill her.

The ignorance in that last sentence made Garrett sick. It made him want to shake the speaker until the stupidity became dislodged. Unfortunately, he didn't know how to *siphon in* the ounce of intelligence it took to understand no one asked to have her husband beat her senseless then carve her up with a knife.

The irony wasn't lost on Garrett. Violence against Jade. Violence raging through him. He wanted to believe there was a difference. He knew he would never raise a hand against a woman, no matter the provocation. Walk away. Yell. Break something. Punch a bag, not your wife. There were always alternatives. Just as there always was a group who believed the victim was at fault.

Garrett left his untouched sandwich on the table. He needed to get out of the restaurant. The moment he was clear of the building, he took several deep breaths. Los Angeles air wasn't the cleanest. Still, anything was better than the stagnant atmosphere he just left.

He should have stayed in his office and ordered in. The problem with that? Wyatt. Big brother was becoming concerned with Garrett's suddenly solitary habits. Home. The office. Home. That was his routine. Work was his excuse. Post-production on his last movie needed all his attention. It was difficult to roll that one out when the movie industry was the family business. When his brother was his producer.

Ever since the news of Jade's hospitalization, Garrett's concentration came and went. Knowing what she suffered at the hands of a man who should have cherished her tore at his guts. He thought of her occasionally over the past two and a half years. He pictured her as she looked when they drove through the Hollywood Hills. Beautiful and a little sad.

She married. It was a little disappointing but not earth shattering. He wanted her to be happy. He believed she was. Finding out how wrong that belief was made him wish he had never stopped driving that night. Would it have changed anything? Probably not. Unfortunately, he would never know.

The first news reports claimed Stephen Marsh, son-in-law of famed industrialist Anson Marlow, was under arrest for attacking his wife. There was no mention of Jade's name, as though she was the least important person in the story. Garrett knew, though.

For days, he scoured the internet, called contacts. He searched for information. There was little to be had. Somehow, Anson Marlow managed to keep the gruesome details under wraps. That lasted a week. Slowly, drop by appalling drop, the world learned of the horrors Jade endured. Not just that last night, but also over the entire marriage.

Garrett paced. A drink sounded like a good idea. Why didn't he keep whiskey in his office? He sighed. Crap. Wyatt's wife. They had stopped leaving alcohol around about four years ago. Stephanie could sniff it out like a bloodhound. Ultimately, nothing the family did helped. After her death, it never occurred to Garrett to restock his office. The only reason he kept it in the first place was for business meetings. This was the first time he could remember actively craving a drink. All things considered, it was probably for the best that the office, hell, the building, was alcohol-free. The way he was feeling, stopping with one shot would be a challenge.

Garrett picked up his phone. The temptation to call Jade became more and more difficult to ignore. He still had her listed. Last week, he checked with the same friend who got him the number to make sure it hadn't changed. Now he fought with himself over the advisability of using it.

Jade didn't go out in public. That he knew. Her release from the hospital occurred late one night, two weeks after she first arrived. Anson Marlow cleverly circulated a false story saying she would be going home later that afternoon then sneaked her out in a laundry truck. No one saw her then or since.

Did she have anyone, Garrett wondered. A friend to talk to? Or to just sit with? Rumors swirled. They ranged from Jade being hideously disfigured to her mental fragility. Her poor father didn't want to have her institutionalized. Instead, he kept her sedated. She was locked way so she couldn't hurt herself or anyone else.

That last part cost Garrett the most sleep. The thought of that lovely, laughing woman being treated like Rochester's wife in *Jane Eyre* made him toss and turn with worry. Not that he believed the speculation. Like everything else in this town, the truth was often bent and twisted so often it became unrecognizable from the lie.

Still, Garrett knew Anson Marlow's reputation. It suited his purposes; he was capable of making sure Jade stayed a virtual prisoner. He wanted to make sure her withdrawal from the world was her own choice.

Garrett wanted Jade to know she had a friend. If she needed him — for anything — he was only a phone call away.

Running a distracted hand through his hair, Garrett again picked up the phone. Before he could talk himself out of it, his finger tapped Jade's name. Then he waited.

"Hello?" a woman answered.

Not Jade. Because she couldn't answer? Was she incapable of talking on the phone, or did she not want to be bothered? If that was the case, why not let it go to voice mail? Garrett shook off the questions. The only way to find out was to ask.

"May I speak with Jade?"

"Ms. Marlow is unavailable."

"Unavailable or drugged out of her mind?"

Way to play it cool, Garrett. A simple phone call; that was all this was supposed to be. Instead, he practically accused some unknown person of keeping Jade whacked-out on tranquilizers.

"Who is this?"

"A friend."

There was a pause.

"A friend who happens to be a reporter?"

Fair question, Garrett acknowledged. If this woman was there not as Jade's jailer, but to protect her privacy, questioning a caller's motives made sense.

"Definitely a friend." Then, after a little consideration, Garrett added, "Or rather an old acquaintance who would like to be Jade's friend. Will you tell her Garrett called? I'm available at any time."

"Wait." The woman paused before continuing. "I'll ask if she wants to talk to you. Give me a minute?"

"Take your time."

Not drugged. Unless the woman was throwing him a red herring. Or maybe he was becoming a victim of his profession. The world was not a movie script full of impossible intrigue. Conspiracies happened all the time on the silver screen — less frequently in real life.

"Hello?"

Again, not Jade.

"Yes, I'm still here."

"Ms. Marlow wonders if you could call back tomorrow. Around ten a.m.?"

"Absolutely." Garrett felt a lightening of the weight he carried around. Not complete relief. It was a start. "Tell Ms. Marlow she'll be hearing from me."

"Mr. ah..."

"Landis."

"Mr. Landis. Please, don't forget to call." The woman's voice was earnest, almost desperate. "She needs a friend. I think, maybe, more than anything. And one more thing," she whispered.

"Yes?" Garrett leaned forward as if she was in the room.

"Don't tell anyone."

Garrett sat unmoving for several minutes after he hung up. So much for imagined danger. Something strange was going on. Whoever the woman was, she was looking out for Jade. Did she work for Anson Marlow? That was a silly question. Jade's father had to be paying the woman's salary. Was part of her job description to keep friends away?

Suddenly full of energy, Garrett jumped from his chair. None of his questions would be answered today. Grabbing his keys, he headed out. A long swim in his parents' pool followed dinner. Then a long visit. He would still toss and turn. He knew there would be little sleep tonight. Until then, he had his family to help ease the next few hours.

And Jade? What did she have? *Who* did she have? One caring, yet ineffectual woman. A woman paid by Anson Marlow.

That was about to change, Garrett promised himself. Soon, Jade would have him. He hoped that she would let him in.

The next morning at ten o'clock on the dot, Garrett made the call.

"Hello? Garrett?"

Jade. He knew her voice immediately. A little tentative. A bit unsure. He wanted to reach through the phone, gather her into his arms, and promise to keep her safe.

"Jade."

After running this conversation through his head a thousand times, now the moment had arrived, he didn't know what to say.

"I..." Garrett heard her take a deep breath. "I'm sorry I couldn't speak with you yesterday. I was meeting with my, well, I guess there isn't a pretty way of putting it. I was meeting with my psychiatrist."

"Is she helping you?"

"*He*. And no, I don't think he is. But as he and my father keep reminding me, it's early days."

"Would you be more comfortable with a different shrink?"

Jade didn't answer. *Crap. Maybe shrink was an indelicate word. No, not indelicate. Thoughtless.*

"Thank you, Garrett, for not pussyfooting around the elephant in the room. I don't speak with many people these days. The ones I do seem very uncomfortable with any mention of therapy. Of course, most people think I'm crazy."

"Are you?"

Again, a pause. He should never joke over the phone. Any nuance was lost.

"I know you're kidding."

"I was," Garrett assured her. "How could you tell?"

"You have a very expressive voice. I suppose growing up with a gifted actress as a mother, some of it was bound to rub off."

The opening he was looking for. Family was a safe subject. An entertaining one. Garrett launched into a series of stories. Light. Funny. There was no need for Jade to answer. For the next hour, he segued from one anecdote to another, not waiting for Jade to respond. He wanted her to relax. Or rather, he wanted her to find the sound of his voice relaxing. When she needed to let go for a little while, she would think of him and call.

"Your brother did not fill a room at the London Savoy with ping pong balls."

"He did," Garrett said. He grinned. There was more life in her voice. He could almost picture her smiling.

"An entire room?"

"I swear. It was a closet—"

"Ah." Jade jumped on that little detail.

"Colt was only ten. Admittedly, he had some help. A few bucks to the maid's brother and he had a co-conspirator. Still. The mastermind was a ten-year-old boy. You aren't impressed?"

"Maybe," Jade conceded. "Were your parents angry?"

"No, but the hotel manager who opened the closet door was. The man had no sense of humor."

"Why have I never heard this story before? Colton Landis is the biggest movie star in the world. People would eat that up."

"The hotel managed to keep it under wraps. They didn't want it to get around how easily it was to pull off a stunt like that." Garrett laughed when he remembered the pride on his father's face. *Ten years old.* "My parents were happy to avoid any publicity. Now it's a family story we roll out from time to time."

"Still—"

"Jade! Where the hell are you? Dr. Phillips is waiting."

"I need to go."

Garrett hated the fear he heard in Jade's voice. Fear and resignation.

"Jade? Can I call you again tomorrow?"

"Do you want to?"

"Very much."

"*Jade!*"

Anson Marlow's voice was closer that time.

"Yes. Please," Jade whispered. The phone went dead.

Garrett's first instinct was to rush over to the Marlow house. He wouldn't let her father get away with bullying Jade. She needed gentleness. Kindness. Two things Anson Marlow didn't appear capable of giving her.

He sat back in his chair. He wasn't going anywhere. Unless he thought someone was physically abusing her again, he would bide his time. Jade needed a slow build. Phone calls to start. Soon he would ask to meet. Not for long. Wherever she was comfortable. She would set the pace and the rules.

His assistant stuck her head through the office door, reminding him he had a production meeting in ten minutes. His life went on. It was a busy life. Jam-packed with work, family, and the occasional short-term relationship. Garrett liked it that way. He wasn't happy when he had extra time on his hands.

He didn't have time for Jade. Not really. What he started today was not a casual thing. Garrett was committing himself to helping a woman without knowing how deep he needed to go. *Pull away now*, a voice told him. *She isn't lover material. Not now. She is fragile. Damaged. Even if you weren't so busy, what makes you think you're qualified?*

None of that mattered. He was determined to help Jade Marlow even though he wasn't certain why. For now, all that mattered was Jade. The rest he would figure out as he went along.

They spoke every day. Garrett called at the same time. Jade answered after the first ring. He wanted to believe she was anxious to hear his voice. That might be part of it. When she asked if she could start calling him, he knew she was worried about being discovered. She didn't want to be overheard. A ring, or even a vibration, might be intercepted. Garrett was her secret and it seemed she wanted to keep it that way.

"I missed breakfast," Wyatt strolled into his office mid-week. It was five minutes to ten. Five minutes until Jade.

"Sorry to hear it. Why don't you take an early lunch?"

In other words, get out of my office. Garrett kept a calm face. He didn't say anything else. Inside, he was willing his brother to leave.

"Want to join me?"

"Nope," Garrett said, his eyes darting towards the clock. "I'm stuffed. Pancakes at Mom and Dad's."

"You've been spending a lot of time in Beverly Hills lately." Wyatt gave him a speculative look. "Any reason?"

"Other than liking my parents' company?" Garrett shook his head. "Nope."

"You're a good son," Wyatt said. "One that is full of shit."

"Hey—"

"There has to be another reason you're hanging out in Beverly Hills." Wyatt slowly smiled. "Who is she?"

Garrett felt his throat tighten. He didn't need to keep Jade a secret from his family. No one would object to him helping her. For some reason, he wasn't ready to share Jade.

"She?" Answer a question with a question. A great avoidance tactic. One Wyatt knew very well.

"Now I'm *certain* there's a woman. You are a straight shooter, brother. Colt charms, Nate bulldozes, and I can wheedle a deal with the best of them."

"What am I?"

"You tell the truth. You never lied. Not really." Wyatt laughed. "Not that you didn't try a few times. Usually when you were covering for Nate. Even for your twin brother, you couldn't lie your way out of a paper bag."

"I can lie." Wyatt's look told Garrett he wasn't convinced. "When it's important. Helping Nate put one over on Mom and Dad hit low on the importance scale."

"Fine. Keep your secrets." Wyatt moved towards the door. He stopped, looking back at his brother. "Is she married?"

"Of course not."

Fuck. He knew the second the words were out of his mouth he was sunk. The grin on Wyatt's mouth confirmed it.

"Enjoy your lady, Garrett. If you want to talk, you know where to find me."

What he wanted to do was kick Wyatt in the ass. He had fallen for that particular trick since they were boys. It seemed he never learned. He didn't have long to worry about it. His phone rang. Jade. Right on time.

"Hi."

"Can we meet?"

Not what he was expecting. Garrett didn't ask questions. He didn't hesitate.

"Name the place and time. I'll be there."

Jade's choice of meeting place was a surprise. To put it mildly.

Garrett didn't have time to argue. Jade whispered the location, told him she would text the rest of the details, then immediately hung up. He tried calling her back. He wanted to suggest half a dozen alternatives that were out of the way in neighborhoods where you could walk alone.

Night *and* day. Unfortunately, Jade turned her phone off. He left a message.

Jade didn't get back to him. As a result, Garrett found himself driving to a seedy motel in Gramercy Park. Wisely, he borrowed Hamish's nondescript car. Brown, dust, dented. He often wondered why a man who could afford any model he wanted would drive a rundown piece of crap. Tonight he was grateful for his friend's questionable taste. It wouldn't draw undue attention amidst similar makes and models.

In the text, Jade asked him to check in, and then text her the room number. He was happy to get there first. If the place were a vermin-infested hole, he would insist they leave. Surprisingly, the room, though shabby, appeared clean.

Garrett set the key on the scarred table. So far, he was following her instructions to a T. What she wanted him to do next had him hesitating.

"Turn off all the lights. Make sure the curtains are tightly drawn. Leave the door ajar. Sit as far away from the door as possible. Don't look at me. Please. Not even a glance."

He wondered if the gossip was right. Had Jade's scumbag husband cut up her face? Was her body scarred as well as her soul? Why ask to meet? Perhaps this was a test. For both of them.

Not liking it, yet trying to understand, Garrett made the room as light tight as possible. He was fixing the curtains when he heard the approaching tap of heels. Quickly, he walked across the room. He sat with his back to the door. He didn't plan on looking at her. He would honor Jade's wishes. He hoped seeing him turned away would give her an added layer of security.

The door slowly creaked open.

"Garrett?"

"I'm over here."

He waited while she followed the sound of his voice. Apparently satisfied, she shut the door.

"Thank you."

"I want to help you, Jade. If this is what you need, I'm fine with it."

Not fine. More like resigned. Jade didn't need to know that.

"It must sound very cloak and dagger."

Garrett listened to what sounded like a coat being removed. That made sense. It had to be ninety degrees in the room. He turned on the air conditioner as soon as he arrived. The wall unit was noisy — and ineffective.

"Did you have trouble finding the place?"

"No." Garrett heard the rustle of silk. His body reacted. Christ. Pavlov's dogs. Even a hint of something sexy and his dick started to harden. Down, boy. For all he knew, she might be wearing very expensive bloomers. Bloomers weren't a turn on, right? It seemed nobody sent his dick that memo.

Since he couldn't ask her what she was wearing without coming across as a pervert, Garrett settled on a more innocuous subject.

"What kind of car did you drive?"

"I took the bus."

"Are you kidding? You walked all the way from the bus stop? In this neighborhood?"

"It was fine," Jade assured him in a low, quiet voice. "No one bothered me."

"Then you were damn lucky." Under any other circumstances, Garrett would have given her hell. Such stupidity deserved a reaming out. Instead, he breathed deeply. She was safe. That's all that mattered.

"When we leave, I'll call you a cab."

"Fine."

Garrett waited. This was Jade's play. Wasn't it up to her to make the first move? Or first speech? Shit. Whatever. It was up to her.

"I wanted to thank you."

"For?"

"Calling." There was another pause. "Not that other people haven't been in touch. Reporters. Neighbors. Women I went to school with who I haven't spoken with in years."

"Rubberneckers." Garrett knew the type.

"Yes," Jade sighed. It sounded achingly sad. "You were the first who mentioned friendship. I've been so isolated. So alone. God, I sound pathetic."

"No," Garrett assured her. "You sound like a woman who has been through hell and is trying to come out the other side. Needing a friend isn't weak, Jade. *Needing* isn't weak."

"Tell that to my father."

"I'd be happy to."

The sound Jade made wasn't a laugh. Not quite. It was too harsh. A raspy bark as though it was too long since she had any reason to let happiness travel through her throat. *All it takes is practice*, Garrett thought. One laugh a day, to start. He could help with that.

"My father isn't easily convinced. When he's right, the world and their opinions be damned."

"What does your therapist say?"

"Psychiatrist," Jade said. "According to Dr. Phillips there is a *huge* distinction."

"Pompous ass," Garrett muttered.

"Yes!" Jade exclaimed. "That's what I told my father after my first session."

"I take it your father didn't agree."

"I see Dr. Phillips every other day. Does that answer your question?"

"Jesus, Jade! Every other day?" Garrett couldn't imagine. "Don't you run out of things to say?"

"That hasn't been a problem with you." Jade's heartfelt words were softly spoken. Garrett heard every single one.

"Jade—"

"Dr. Phillips likes repetition," she hurried on. "I tell him the same thing over and over. He nods. Eventually, Jade is all better. No, not better. I'm erasing the past. Soon, it will be like it never happened."

Garrett heard the bitterness. Who could blame her? Her father, with that idiot doctor's help, was trying to rewrite history. Anson Marlow pushed his daughter into the marriage. The abuse she suffered took place in Marlow's home. What better way to sweep it all under the rug than to act like it never happened. There was so much wrong with that. Garrett didn't know where to start.

"You need someone else, Jade. Throw that Phillips character out on his ass."

"My father is insistent. And," she sighed. "He's paying the bills."

Why hadn't he thought of that? Money. Jade's job was to act as hostess for her father. She ran his home. While Anson Marlow received years of free labor, Jade received what? A roof over her head? A husband who almost killed her? Hardly a fair trade.

"Let me help." Garrett tried to word his proposition so it wasn't offensive. "I'll pay for a new therapist. It's what any friend would do, Jade."

"I have money, Garrett."

"You do?"

"Not a lot. My mother left me some in trust. It came to me when I turned twenty-one."

"Your mother? I thought—"

"I don't want to talk about her."

Her words had heat. More heat than any subject they had touched on. The woman who abandoned Jade to be raised by Anson Marlow was obviously a sore subject. Garrett let it drop.

"I can help you find a doctor. I know plenty of people in therapy. This is Los Angeles."

"I'm already seeing someone. A woman. Promise not to tell anyone? My father can never know."

"What you tell me stays between us, Jade. Always." Garrett frowned. "Have you dropped Phillips?"

"No. I still see him. My father is determined."

"Demented."

"Excuse me?"

Why pull his punches now? He could tell Jade was stronger than anyone gave her credit for. Bent — not broken. Healing more every day.

"I said your father is demented. You should be his priority."

"It's hard to change a lifetime's habits, Garrett. I'm more of an annoyance. An obligation. As far as my father is concerned, my marriage is one more thing I managed to screw up."

"He blames you?" Again with that crap. What the hell?

"Not in so many words." Jade sighed. "Then again, my father could write a book on passive aggressive behavior. Dr. Phillips would have a field day."

"Will you tell me about your therapist? Not what you talk about," Garrett rushed to qualify. "Do you like her? Trust her?"

"I do like her," Jade said. "Trust is harder. That takes time. But I'm getting there."

"Good. I'm glad."

"Garrett?"

"Yes?"

"I want to ask you something. A favor."

"I won't say you can ask me anything," Garrett teased. "I stop at murder. Pretty much anything else. Shoot."

"Feel free to say no."

"Okay."

"It's a biggie."

"Jade," Garrett chastised softly.

"Right." He could hear her take a deep breath. "Will you have sex with me?"

"Yes."

"Wait. What?" Jade paused. "Just like that?"

"You know I want you, Jade." Garrett chose his words carefully, tiptoeing through this particular minefield. "I wanted you that night over two years ago. That hasn't changed."

"I have."

"So have I," Garrett told her. "Not that I'm comparing us. I'm simply saying, time moves along and we move with it. I know more than I did. At least I hope I do. The one thing that hasn't changed is my desire for you."

"I...," Jade hesitated. "I don't want to raise your expectations,

Garrett. I wasn't a virgin when I got married. I like sex. Not that I had a lot of experience. It was nice. After... With Stephen...," she seemed to choke on the name. "Let's just say he wasn't worried about my enjoyment. Or participation."

"Shit." Garrett gripped the arms of the chair so hard he was surprised they didn't snap.

"I want to like it again."

"Of course you do."

"Now do you understand why I want you to think about what I'm asking? I don't know how I'll react when you touch me. Most of the time, with... Stephen," again, she hesitated over the name. "I felt frozen inside. A coping mechanism, according to my therapist."

"That sounds logical."

"I suppose. My point is I don't know if I can thaw. I want to. I want to be me again. I'd like you to help."

"Do you want to start tonight?" Garrett didn't know if he was crazy. He certainly had no qualifications to help a woman get past sexual abuse. He only knew he had to try.

"No!" Jade exclaimed. "I mean it never occurred to me you would say yes. Not without thinking about it."

"Your pace, Jade," Garrett assured her. "When you're ready, I'm your man."

"Thank you. I should be going."

"I'll call that cab."

Garrett pulled up the number. The driver knew Garrett. He knew his tip would be sizable. Even so, he hesitated when he was told the neighborhood. An extra hundred dispelled the man's reluctance.

"Half an hour," Garrett told Jade.

"You don't have to wait."

He didn't answer. What could he say to such a ridiculous statement? The smell of Pine-Sol and stale smoke swirled through the room, pushed by the antiquated air conditioner. Garrett sat, his back still to Jade. There was no talk for several minutes before he asked *her* a favor.

"May I see your face?"

"You know what I look like."

Panic. That's what he heard. Jade's breathing deepened — he could hear it from across the room. His request wasn't made from morbid curiosity. He wanted her to know she could show him anything. Her scars inside and out. He wouldn't turn away from her either.

"It's okay," Garrett said reassuringly. "I understand. Too soon."

"He didn't cut my face."

The words were rushed, like jumping into a cold lake or pulling off a Band-Aid. Quick. To reduce the shock and pain.

"Oh, honey…" How could a man respond to that? Good? *Her husband cut her.* It was horrifying for Garrett to think about it. Jade lived through it.

"I've lost so much weight," Jade explained. "Even before the… even before. I couldn't bring myself to eat. Not because I wanted to starve — honestly. Or maybe I did. I don't know anymore, Garrett."

"Are you eating now?" *Please say yes.*

"I'm eating more." Jade sighed. "Everything tastes like dust. Or chalk. Except chocolate pudding. Unfortunately, my doctor tells me I can't live on that alone."

"Calcium. It has to be good for your bones."

"That's what I said." There was surprise and a bit of humor in her voice.

"If I keep the lights out, will you sit on my lap? Nothing will happen. Let me hold you until the cab gets here."

"I'm a rack of bones."

"You are Jade," Garrett told her firmly. "That's all I care about."

Garrett didn't know how much time passed. One minute? Two? When he heard Jade's first step, he let out the breath he had been holding. When she stood in front of him, he could see her outline.

"It's been a long time since anyone held me."

Garrett took her hand. Delicate. Almost fragile. Yet it gripped his with surprising strength. Like Jade herself. Deceptively strong.

"I'm here, Jade."

Garrett guided her onto his lap. She weighed nothing. Less than a child. Jade wore a thick sweater that should have stifled her in the evening heat. With the natural layer of insulation gone from her body, she needed protection. From the elements — from the world.

At first, Jade held herself away from him. Stiff and upright. Garrett didn't speak. Instead, he rubbed a hand up and down her back in what he hoped was a soothing motion. Slowly, she began to relax until she was curled close, her head resting on his shoulder.

"I'm sorry."

"For what?" Garrett asked.

"It must be like holding a sack of bones."

There were tears in her voice. *Good*, Garrett thought. *Let it out.* Didn't his mother say there was nothing as therapeutic as a good cry? He wondered how often Jade let herself go? Not often enough.

"I'm a little embarrassed," Garrett told her.

"You are? Why?"

"I promised you nothing would happen. And it won't," he said. "I can't seem to control my body when I'm around you."

"What...?" Jade shifted slightly. "Oh."

"Oh, indeed. Instead of providing platonic comfort, I have a hard-on. I'd yell, *down, boy*, but what would be the use? That part of me has always had a mind of its own."

Jade didn't seem put off. If anything, she relaxed even more.

"It's a relief," Jade sighed. "I was afraid I might repulse you."

"Hardly." This time he was the one who moved. Ever so slightly. "No pun intended."

Garrett was rewarded by the best sound in the world. Jade's laughter. It was a brief chuckle, but it counted.

"Jade, honey. You smell like heaven. Vanilla? Lemons?"

"Yes," Jade whispered. Her arms snuck around his waist.

"I remember spicy oranges the last time we were this close."

"We never got this close," she reminded him.

"Mmm." Garrett breathed deeply. "It was worth the wait."

They sat, content to hold each other. Words weren't necessary. Not right now. When Garrett's phone buzzed, signaling the cab was waiting, there was a bond between them. New. Tentative. Yet unmistakable.

"When can we meet again?"

Jade slipped from his lap.

"Thursday?"

Two days. Garrett ran through his schedule. No night shoots. In fact, the next month would be routine. He was free whenever she was.

"Why don't you let me pick the place?"

"No," Jade said. She picked up her purse before putting her hand on the doorknob. "This is fine."

"Will you tell me why? Why here?"

Jade opened the door, looking at him over her shoulder. The lights from the parking lot were harsh, making Garrett squint. Her face was completely shadowed.

"According to the gardener, it's where everybody rendezvous."

Before Garrett could respond to her outrageous statement, Jade firmly closed the door. He rushed to the window, making sure she was safely in the cab and on her way.

The gardener? Really? Garrett shook his head. There had to be more to *that* story.

There was.

Chapter Six

THURSDAY NIGHT COULDN'T come soon enough. He kept looking at his watch, fidgeting. He willed the long-winded backers meeting to end. No one seemed to notice his restlessness — except Wyatt. He was grateful his brother kept his observation to himself.

In the same borrowed car, Garrett drove through the streets of L.A. He purposefully left home early. He didn't want to risk Jade arriving before he did. They spoke that morning. And the morning before.

With the arrangements for their second rendezvous in place, Garrett hadn't known if she would continue their daily calls. He was very pleased when, exactly at ten, his phone rang.

As conversations went, it was generic. Strictly vanilla. If anyone tapped the line, he would have been bored to tears. Garrett wasn't anyone. He was the man Jade Marlow propositioned. She wanted his help. She wanted to be guided back to the sexually living. Was he nervous? Sure. A little. He didn't take it lightly. Was he confident he could give her what she needed? Damn straight.

What Jade didn't know was how much further he planned on taking her. She would never describe his lovemaking as *nice*. *Pleasant?* Why bother? When he was finished, neither of them would be able to think straight. Then, he planned on starting all over again.

That was for later. Right now, he was taking it slow. For the next few weeks, Garrett Landis was a fucking snail.

The motel had not undergone a miraculous transformation in forty-eight hours. It was still dingy and run-down. In the corner, by the broken ice machine, a drunk urinated on the door of unit seven. Unlucky for some.

Garrett, as he had the other night, collected the key wearing dark Wayfarers and a Dodgers cap pulled low. The night manager, if that's what he was, seemed uninterested in the celebrity status of his customer. TMZ would pay a tidy sum to find out who Jade Marlow was meeting. And where. Toss in the name Landis, the man could name his price. Luckily, he was more interested in Family Feud and his bag of Cheetos.

Garrett signed in. *John Smith*. He couldn't resist. Cash was accepted — preferred. He gingerly took the key from his orange-stained hands, and then made his way to the unit at the far end of the parking lot.

Once inside, Garrett set the backpack he brought with him on the table. Not a speck of dust. Someone took pride in her work. There was no way to turn this sow's ear into a silk purse, but the cleaning person made an effort. Knowing he and Jade were unlikely to contract typhus was the only thing that kept him from insisting they move to a different location.

Taking off his sunglasses and cap, Garrett went through the same routine as the last time. Air conditioner on. Lights out. Curtains pulled tight. This time, though, when he sat to wait, he faced the door.

Garrett settled back. To pass the time, he ran through the script changes he wanted to make before starting his next movie. The screenplay was solid. The best to come his way. However, solid did not mean perfect. The writer seemed amicable to work with him. The tweaks he wanted to make were minor, yet intrinsically vital to the flow of the story. It could be the difference between a good movie and a great one.

The speech the female lead made halfway through the film was running through Garrett's head when he heard the sound of a car pulling to a stop outside the door. Standing, he put one finger on the edge of the curtain giving him a sliver to look through. He was just in time to see Jade slide from the cab.

As though sensing his gaze, Jade managed to keep her face averted while she paid the driver. Not that it would have mattered. She wore a large, floppy hat with her hair tucked inside. The brim drooped over her profile. When he was certain she was safely delivered, Garrett retook his seat.

"Have I kept you waiting?"

"No."

She didn't voice an objection when she saw him facing her. Was that progress? Or did she realize the room was too dark for it to matter?

"I was delayed."

She removed her hat, shaking her head. Long tresses tumbled down around her shoulders. Garrett inhaled sharply. Jesus, that was sexy. All done in silhouette, he felt as if he was watching a crazy kind of peep show. It teased glorious images, just out of reach, and then never delivered.

One day soon, he promised himself, *Jade will trust you enough to turn on that light*. Until then, he would remain a shadowed voyeur. Not the perfect arrangement. For now, he could live with it.

"Anything serious?"

"Hmm?"

Jade ran her hand through her hair, arching her back. The image, along with her deep, husky sigh, shot straight to Garrett's dick. Crazy libido.

"Jade. Honey."

"Yes?"

"You are so damn sexy."

Jade froze. Slowly, her head turned toward him.

"Are you making fun of me?"

"What?" Garrett asked. Was she crazy?

"Then you're being kind," Jade whispered. "I'm about as sexy as a limp rag."

"Then I have a limp rag fetish of which I wasn't aware," Garrett said. "Right now, I'm hard as a rock. Not the first time, if you recall."

"You should see your doctor about that, Garrett. Getting excited over a walking bag of bones is not normal."

"Fuck that," Garrett shouted. He regretted the outburst immediately when Jade flinched. What was wrong with him? She needed delicacy. Jade wasn't there five minutes. He was shouting and mentioning about erections. Smooth.

"*Don't shout at me, Garrett,*" she yelled back.

Jade gasped, her hand going to her mouth. Garrett jumped from his seat. He took one step, ready to comfort her, when he heard something that froze him in his tracks. Her laughter. Not brief or subdued. The sound was... joyous.

"That sounds good."

"It feels good," she told him. "I can't remember the last time I laughed like that."

"When was the last time you yelled at someone?"

"Years." Jade laughed again. This time with a bit of sadness. "My therapist assured me my backbone would return. Eventually."

"I like her." Garrett wanted to send the woman a roomful of roses. Whatever she was doing, it was helping Jade find herself.

"I needed to trust the person." Jade cocked her head to the side. Even though he couldn't see her eyes, he could feel her gaze. "I knew you wouldn't hurt me."

"Not all men hit, Jade."

"No," she nodded. "My father uses words instead of fists. It's a different kind of pain."

Garrett didn't know how to respond to that. He wasn't going to throw platitudes at her. Or threaten her father with bodily harm, tempting as the thought was. When she wanted to talk, he would listen. Right now, he had something else in mind.

"Let's eat."

"I beg your pardon?"

"Food. I had an early lunch. I've been so busy. I didn't have time for anything since. I'm starving."

Garrett unzipped the backpack, pulling out the containers stored inside. On the way here, he stopped at his favorite takeout place for hamburgers and French fries. It seemed like a safe choice. Plenty of ketchup and mustard. A couple of Cokes. The last covered bowl was for later. A surprise.

"I'm not hungry, Garrett."

"Then keep me company," he said as he removed the lids.

The smell of greasy goodness quickly filled the room, making his mouth water. He told Jade the truth. It was long past his usual mealtime. What he didn't tell her was he deliberately skipped dinner. He wanted to eat with her.

"Sit."

There were two chairs in the room. The one he used while waiting for Jade, and the one he held out for her now.

"I'll wait over here."

She tried moving toward the bed. Garrett stopped her. Taking her hand, he gently tugged until the chair was behind her. Then he pushed.

"There," Garrett said, satisfied.

His eyes were used to the dark room, enabling him to see well enough to eat. And see Jade's shadowed face. If she would look up.

"Sure you won't join me?" he asked, waggling a French fry at her.

Jade slowly raised her chin. Her eyes didn't meet his; they were fixed on the fry.

"Are they hot?"

"And salty." Garrett let it hover over the pool of red sauce on his plate. "Ketchup?"

"Please."

Garrett made a quick swoop, and then held his hand out. When Jade tried to take the French fry, he pulled back.

"Open up."

"Bossy," Jade said, smiling slightly. She opened her mouth.

"What do you think?" Garrett asked, watching her eyes close as she savored the mouthful.

"That is the best French fry ever."

"Everything tastes better when you eat with a friend. Want another?"

Jade shook her head. "I want a plate full."

Grinning, Garrett loaded a paper plate with fries and ketchup.

"Burger?" He waved the still wrapped sandwich under Jade's nose.

"Is it plain?"

Garrett drew back in horror.

"Don't insult me or Alf. He makes a bacon cheeseburger so fantastic, cows bow in reverence."

He could tell Jade was tempted. After a moment, she said, "Maybe a bite?"

"Wait."

Garrett rummaged around in the backpack. He pulled out a single candle, setting it on the table between them.

"Garrett..." The worry in her voice made him hesitate. Was he doing the right thing? Was he pushing too hard? Too fast? He would leave it up to Jade to decide. If she protested, he would pull back.

"Trust me," Garrett said as he struck a match. "Everything is better by candlelight."

Jade blinked, her eyes wide — vulnerable. *A man could drown in those eyes.*

"No," Garrett whispered. "Don't turn away, Jade."

Tentatively, Garrett lifted his hand, then hesitated when Jade's eyes widened. To his relief, she didn't flinch. Instead, she jutted her chin out almost daring him. His touch was gentle — almost a caress — turning her face toward him and the flickering light.

"Your skin is like fine silk," Garrett said. He ran his thumb over her cheek.

He now knew why she was reluctant to show him her face. Gaunt, he supposed was the word. Alarmingly so. Yet what Garrett saw didn't make him want to turn away. He wanted to gather her close so he could protect her from a world that put the sadness in her large, expressive eyes.

"Our fries are getting cold," Jade sighed. Her face turned toward his hand, giving the palm a soft kiss before she pulled back.

"So they are." Garrett swallowed. That kiss. That small gesture moved him more than he could say. Almost as much as the *thank you*, he saw in her eyes.

They made small talk for the rest of the meal. Garrett was happy when Jade ate a third of her hamburger and most of her French fries. Conversation helped. She didn't have time to think about what she was putting in her mouth when Garrett entertained her. Location shoots were a breeding ground for hilarious anecdotes.

"You did not fall into a portable toilet."

"Not in, as much as through," Garrett chuckled ruefully. It was funny now. Then? Not so much. "When you work with actors known for pulling practical jokes, sometimes you become collateral damage."

"That must have been…"

"Disgusting," Garrett finished for her. "Crap, urine, and blue… dye, I guess. Whatever that chemical is they use in those things. After that, I made sure we rented the environmentally friendlier toilets. Once you've walked around for a week looking like a mottled Smurf, you never want that to happen again."

Jade smiled. Really smiled. Garrett decided his discomfort had been worth it.

"Did you ever discover the toilet saboteur?"

"Sure," Garrett nodded. "Benjamin Larson."

"Oh, come on," Jade gasped. "Now I know you're kidding me. Benjamin Larson? He's a Shakespearean legend. I saw his Hamlet last year when I was in New York. He was brilliant."

"He *was*," Garrett agreed. "On stage, he is as serious as a heart attack. Off, when he is passing the time on a movie set, he acts like a crazed three-year-old hopped up on too much sugar. And speaking of sugar."

Garrett cleared away their plates, putting them and the leftovers in a plastic bag. Then, giving Jade a spoon, he opened the last container.

"Pudding." Jade's eyes grew wide, the hazel turning almost green. "Chocolate. My parents' cook makes the best — bar none."

"You remembered."

"Surprised?" Garrett took her spoon, scooping up a bit of the creamy dessert.

"You're a busy man," Jade said with a shrug.

"In other words, the men in your life have not paid attention to your likes and dislikes."

Again, Jade shrugged.

"Want to know what I think?" Garrett held the spoon out.

"What do you think?"

"Take a bite, then I'll tell you."

Jade stared for a moment, long enough for Garrett to wonder if she was going to refuse. Finally, she opened her mouth. He held her gaze while her lips closed over the spoon

"Mmm," Jade sighed. "That is much better than the instant stuff."

"Instant? Sacrilege."

"Well?" Jade asked.

"Oh right. I think you need to hang out with a better class of man."

Before she could comment, Garrett offered another bite. Then another.

"Aren't you having some?"

"Thank you for offering."

Before she could pull away, Garrett covered Jade's mouth with his. The kiss was brief. But memorable.

"Sorry." Garrett's smile wasn't the least bit remorseful. "I couldn't resist."

"How was it?" she asked with a touch of unmasked anxiety in her eyes.

"The pudding? Delicious."

"Oh," Jade whispered.

When she tried to turn away, Garrett kissed her again. His tongue outlined the shape of her lips, teasing — asking for entrance. Gradually, Jade opened her mouth. Satisfied, he ended the kiss.

"However, the kiss?" Garrett whispered back. "Addictive."

Against his better judgment, Garrett took Jade in his arms. This time the kiss was no tease. *Take it slow* became *take it all*. Not that he forgot what Jade had been through. One indication his actions caused the slightest distress, he was ready to end the embrace. Before he formed the thought, Jade kissed him back with a passion to equal his own.

Oh, boy, Garrett thought. *Stopping now was going to be murder. He would stop*. He sank deeper into the kiss. *Soon*.

"Tell me to stop." Garrett said the words against her lips.

"No."

Garrett groaned when Jade wrapped her arms around his neck, practically crawling onto his lap. Being good would be so much easier if Jade didn't taste like chocolate-coated sin. He was at his breaking point. Well, maybe just a little longer.

"Jade," Garrett sighed. "Honey, we need to stop. Now."

Summoning the last thread of his willpower, Garrett gently disentangled Jade's arms, setting her back on her chair. Her moist, parted lips looked so inviting he almost pulled her back. The vulnerability in her eyes steeled his resolve. Too much, too soon was not a good idea. He wasn't an out of control teenager with raging hormones. He wasn't controlled by his erection. However, at this moment, it was an extremely close call.

"You want me to help you? Trust me to know how far to go. How *fast* to go." Garrett didn't want there to be any misunderstandings. If they were going to do this, he was in charge.

"I feel ready. Achy."

"Me too." He smiled. Jade seemed surprised by his admission. "Men get achy too."

"I know," she said. "I didn't know they stopped. Especially when the woman is willing."

"I'm not a caveman, Jade. I won't jump on you, grunt a few times, and then pass out while still on top."

"It hasn't always been that bad." Jade played with the edge of a crumpled paper napkin. "I've had lovers who made some effort."

"Spare me the details." Garrett wasn't in a sharing mood. Even if it happened before he knew Jade. "I will say, *some effort*, is the definition of damning with faint praise. Lord, save me from any women describing my love-making in such a manner."

"Take me to bed. Now. I promise I will you praise to the sky."

"Damn straight you will," Garrett told her. "But not tonight."

"Next time?"

Jade asked the question with such earnestness Garrett had to laugh. He couldn't fault her eagerness. He planned on feeding it with patience. Building anticipation. For them both. She needed a gentle hand. He needed... Jade.

"We'll see how it goes," Garrett told her. "Better a little at a time. Now, when can we meet again?"

THE NEXT TWO weeks followed a similar pattern. Work during the day, Jade at night. Not *every* night. Sunday, Monday, Friday. Missing three days was his fault. Something that couldn't be avoided. He had a job where people depended on him to show up on time and be productive. Movies didn't make themselves. It was Garrett's baby. Neither his crew nor his backers cared about what was going on in his love life.

The paparazzi were another matter.

You didn't grow up in Hollywood, the child of superstar parents, without a healthy disdain for the tabloid press and the vultures who fed off of it. Still, Garrett was low on anyone's radar. Or he always had been. A few pictures here and there. Never any scandal attached to him. He was boring. If word got out about his clandestine meetings with Jade Marlow, that would change in a heartbeat.

So, for the first time in his life, Garrett became a skulker. Finding out he was good at it came as a bit of a surprise. Making excuses when friends invited him out for drinks. Leaving his Lamborghini parked at the studio while he drove off in a newly purchased turn-of-the-century Toyota. He couldn't afford to keep borrowing Hamish's car. Not unless he wanted to start answering the inevitable questions.

Putting off his friends and colleagues was a piece of cake. His family? That was another matter altogether.

"Let's go out and get stinking drunk."

Nate walked into his office the way he usually did. No warning and mid-thought. His twin flopped onto the couch, his big body crushing cushions.

"Because?" Garrett was certain he knew the answer.

"My next gig starts the day after tomorrow. They estimate a ten-week shoot. Which means..."

"Closer to fourteen." Garrett finished. Stan Packer was directing the film. The man was notorious for his run overs.

"Exactly," Nate huffed. "I don't drink when I'm on the job. I can live without the stuff; you know that. But on location? In Bumfuck, Tennessee? There is nothing to do but count each other's mosquito bites."

"That can be entertaining."

"No women in the movie or on the crew, little brother."

"Well, damn." Garrett sympathized. He was sexually frustrated and he *had* a woman. Sort of. Nate was staring down more than three months without even a chance of sex. Brutal.

"You shouldn't be getting drunk; you should be getting laid."

"Been there, done that," Nate said with an exaggerated sigh.

"God," Garrett chuckled. "Save me from the day I make sex sound like it was a chore."

"Not a chore," Nate conceded. "A bore. Or rather, so by the numbers I can barely remember it happened. Two hours ago, Garrett. The sex was the equivalent of junk food. It seems great while it's happening. After, you feel empty and unsatisfied."

"When did you start waxing philosophical?"

"Philosophical, hell," Nate scoffed. "I'm saying I need a more imaginative bed partner."

"I think it was you who once pointed out this town has an endless array of choices. Women at every turn."

"Hmm. There are more women than one man can hope to get to. The problem is I haven't been making very good choices lately."

Nate leaned his head back, his eyes closed. He wore his usual. Jeans and a t-shirt. Both were well worn, though fastidiously clean. Black, steel-toed work boots. Around his right wrist, he wore a red and gold braided friendship bracelet — a gift from a young cancer victim Nate met through the Make a Wish Foundation. The boy wanted to grow up to be a stuntman. Through superior medical care and what the doctors called a miracle, that dream, and the boy was still alive. Nate would cut off his hand before he parted with those woven pieces of cloth.

"Dare I ask who your latest disappointment was?"

"Tawny Bright."

"Oh, come on."

Nate lifted one eyelid. Seeing the disbelief on his brother's face, he grinned.

"I swear on my vintage Harley."

"Stripper?"

"Hippies," Nate corrected. "Her parents carried on the family tradition of living off the earth and naming their children ridiculously over-the-top names. I figure you have two choices. Legally change it or embrace the crazy."

"I take it Tawny chose the latter." Garrett loved when his brother stopped by. He had the best stories. Most of which were true.

"Top to bottom. She looks like she stepped out of the touring company of *Hair*. Or maybe *Godspell*. I always thought that one was completely out there."

"It cracks me up that my badass brother knows the difference. Guys with bulging muscles and tattoos aren't supposed to be musical theater fans."

"Ya," Nate nodded. "I'm a fucking enigma. And it's *one* tattoo. Singular. Mom had a fit when she found out about it. She would skin me alive if I got another."

"A badass, musical-loving momma's boy." Garrett ducked when Nate whipped a cushion his way. "Missed me by a mile. You're losing your touch."

"I had my eyes closed."

"Excuses, excuses."

"Speaking of excuses. Wyatt tells me you've been making a lot of them lately."

Nate stretched out on the couch. Since all the Landis men were tall, their furniture ran toward oversized. Normally, Nate's feet would be hanging over an armrest. Instead, his boots barely skimmed the end.

"Wyatt needs to get a life so he can stop worrying about mine."

"Come to think of it, you blew me off a couple of times lately." Nate tucked his hands behind his head then wiggled his eyebrows. "Want to tell me about her?"

"No."

"Ah, ha."

"Christ." Did he never learn? "No, because there isn't anyone to talk about."

"Right." Nate simply shook his head. He let his eyes drift shut. "What's the big secret? Is she married?"

Oh, no. He wasn't falling for that one again.

"What is the obsession with married women?" Garrett countered. "Is there something you want to tell *me*?"

"Fine." Nate yawned. "You'll tell me when you're ready. You always do." He turned onto his side, facing away from Garrett. "You don't mind if I catch a few winks, do you?"

Garrett didn't bother to point out that the big bed in Nate's bedroom would be much more comfortable. His brother owned a house not far from his own. Both places were empty more often than not because they traveled so much. The difference was, if given the chance, Garrett gladly closed off the world for days at a time. He liked his solitude. Nate needed people. He hated an empty room. He always slept better when he knew someone was near. Preferably, someone he loved and trusted. For all his man-whore ways, Nate wanted to settle down. He wanted what their parents had. However, until he found the perfect woman for him, he was happy to play the field. The more, the merrier.

When the intercom on Garrett's desk buzzed, he answered quickly.

Nate had the amazing ability to regulate his level of sleep. When he needed it, he was a light sleeper. The slightest noise would wake him instantly. Other times, like now, a brass band wouldn't disturb him. Still, Garrett kept his voice low.

"Problem?"

"Is that the only reason I contact you?" Wyatt asked.

"Let's call it 70-30." Garrett glanced at Nate. Nope, not even a twitch.

"Then I'm upping the odds for a non-business call. You've been blowing me off lately. How about lunch? We can catch up."

Wyatt was right. Between work and Jade, he wasn't spending much time with his brother. Any of them.

"Nate is here. Dead to the world on my couch."

"Take out?" Wyatt understood that Garrett wasn't leaving Nate alone. "Chinese or Mexican?"

"He's bound to wake up when he smells food," Garrett said. "Make it both."

While he waited, Garrett rocked back and forth in his chair, staring at nothing in particular. Jade aside, he, and his brothers, led fast-paced, hectic, busy lives. They wouldn't have it any other way. Making time for each other was important. He had friends. Nate, Wyatt, and Colt were his *best* friends. Making time, even if it was lunch in his office, was important.

Without another thought, Garrett grabbed his phone, did a quick scroll through the names, and dialed. He grinned with satisfaction when Colt picked up.

"Hey, Garrett. What do you need?"

That was the difference. His brothers, every one of them, had his back. No questions asked.

"Are you free for lunch?"

"I could probably get away for an hour or two. They don't need me until this afternoon. Where and when?"

"My office. Now."

"Wyatt?"

"And Nate."

"Well, hot damn," Colt whooped. "I'll be there in ten."

"Hey. Make it twenty," Garrett cautioned. Once a big brother, always a big brother. "We aren't going anywhere."

"I'M READY, GARRETT."

There was a touch of desperation in Jade's voice. Good. But he wanted more than a touch. He wanted her tearing at his clothes. He wanted her to bed. It seemed only fair. He was a hair's breath away from dropping to his knees. He would promise her anything for one taste of heaven on Earth. One sip of Jade.

"We still have our clothes on, honey. Naked is an important step."

"We can do it this way."

The desperation was still there. So was something else. Fear.

They were in the hotel room, on the old bed, lying face to face. As always, darkness surrounded them. Kissing, caressing. They were getting good at both. Jade liked when he touched her breasts. As long as it was over her shirt and bra. She moaned. Garrett loved the sound. She grew bolder every time. Tonight, she bent her leg, lifting it until it curled around his hip. Garrett shifted his knee, sliding it up until he felt the heat of her very core. Not a moan this time. A gasp.

"Move, Jade. Ride my leg."

Garrett's hand gripped her waist, encouraging her to slide up and down.

"Mmm." The sound came out of Jade in a husky sigh.

"Does that feel good?" He knew the answer but wanted the words from her lips.

"Yes. Please, Garrett. I need... I need..."

"I know what you need."

Garrett knew he could give her an orgasm like this. But he didn't want her to get used to always keeping a barrier between them. He tried several times to touch her. Every time his hand began to slide under the material, she froze. Solid. All progress wiped away.

"One day I will back you up against a wall and take you," Garrett promised. He lowered his voice. "Hard. Fast. No preliminaries. You will get to the point where all I have to do is look at you a certain way and you will be so wet, so ready, you'll come with my first thrust. That won't stop me. I'll make you ride it out, never ending. Up, up, up again." With each word, Garrett rubbed against her a little harder. "You won't come again until I let you. Not until I'm ready."

"*I'm* ready," Jade breathed. Her hands gripped his arms, her head thrown back, leaving her neck vulnerable to his mouth. At the first touch of his lips, she cried out his name.

"That's right, Jade. I want you to remember who you're with. This is *my* touch."

Holding his breath, Garrett edged the hem of her shirt up, and then slid his hand underneath. When he felt Jade begin to stiffen, he bit the side of her neck and shifted his knee, hitting just the right spot between her legs. Jade was too far gone to protest when he pushed up her bra and cupped her bare breast for the first time.

"Let me take your top off," Garrett whispered in her ear.

While Garrett waited for her answer, the pad of his thumb teased her nipple. It hardened quickly, making his mouth water in anticipation. He wanted to taste that lovely little bud. Hell, he wanted to taste every inch of her.

"Stop."

The second Jade said the word Garrett felt his stomach drop. With any other woman, he would coax, cajole — find a way to turn that *stop* into a *go*. Jade wasn't any other woman. His hands dropped away. His leg straightened, leaving her hot, wet core. They no longer touched and not even the heat of the room could stop the cold that settled over him.

"Did I frighten you?" Damn it, Garrett wished he could see her face.

"Yes." Jade pulled in a deep breath. "I'm scared, Garrett. Not of you."

"Then what?"

"I'm... I have scars. On my stomach, below my breasts."

Garrett heard the tears in Jade's voice. Following his instincts, he reached for her.

"No," Jade pulled back. "If you hold me, I know I'll fall to pieces. I should have told you everything before we got this far. It was stupid to think we could have sex without any intimacy."

"Not stupid," Garrett said. "Intimacy isn't a prerequisite for sex." Taking a chance, he reached for her hand. Relief surged through him when her fingers curled around his. "It makes it better, though."

For once Garrett was grateful the room was dark. Sometimes it was easier to share difficult things when you couldn't see the other person's reactions. *The anonymity of the confessional,* so to speak.

"Is this something you want to hear?" Jade asked. "You didn't sign up for the heavy stuff, Garrett. I asked you for sex, not a shoulder to cry on."

"I want to be your friend, Jade. With or without sex, I will always be here for you." Garrett squeezed her hand. "*Always.*"

"I want you."

"Thank God. That whole, with or without sex crap? I meant it, honestly. Let's just say I will be much happier *with* than *without.*"

"I know you're joking."

"Maybe," Garrett admitted. "A little. I *do* want you, Jade. That hasn't changed."

"It might. After you hear what I have to say."

Garrett wanted to assure Jade. He knew the basics of her story. The whole world knew. Having the details filled in would not change his desire for her. A part of him wished she would keep it to herself. Not because he feared losing interest. Because he didn't want to have those images in his brain. Taking a deep breath, he chastised himself. *Jade* needed to do this. *He* needed to listen.

"We were married two months the first time Stephen hit me."

Garrett didn't respond. He sensed the less he said, the easier it would be for Jade to continue.

"I don't remember him having a temper before that. Maybe I wasn't paying attention. My father has always been volatile. I suppose I was used to being around a man who expressed his dissatisfaction loudly."

Garrett couldn't help it. He had to ask.

"Did your father ever hit you?"

"No," Jade said emphatically. "He likes to use words to break a person down, not fists. Stephen didn't have the patience for verbal abuse. Physically knocking me down was faster, and for him, much more satisfying."

Garrett's gut clenched. He wished he could go back and stop what happened. It was impossible and unproductive thinking. He was here; he would listen. He hoped that would help her heal.

"At first, Stephen wasn't careless enough to leave marks that couldn't easily be covered up. My face was off limits. My stomach was his favorite target. He would punch me, and then kick me when I was on the ground. I think I had a miscarriage one of those times. I suspected I was pregnant, but I hadn't seen a doctor. The blood, after Stephen hit me, was too heavy. I knew the baby was gone."

Garrett couldn't stand it a moment longer. If she didn't want to be held, too bad. He needed Jade in his arms. Pulling her close, he breathed a sigh of relief when she didn't object. Instead, she held him back, relaxing in his embrace.

"I'm sorry about the baby."

"Me too." Jade turned her face into the crook of his neck. "I would have loved my child, Garrett. But..."

"What?"

"I'm glad I didn't have Stephen's baby." Garrett felt a shudder run through her body. "Am I a horrible person for feeling that way?"

"For not wanting to bring another human being into an unthinkable situation? Hardly."

"I was weak. I know that. The second I thought I was pregnant I should have walked away. *Run* away. Instead, I stayed behind the wall I'd built up."

"There was no one you could talk to?" Garrett asked. *Like your father?* The question burned in his throat. Where the hell was Anson Marlow? *Why did he let his daughter go through hell when he was living in the same house?*

"You mean my father."

"Yes, Jade. I'm sorry, but what the hell? He had to know."

"Yes," Jade admitted. "Nothing happens in that house without my father finding out. The servants report everything. There was no way to hide the blood on the floor. I was in no condition to clean it up and Stephen didn't even try. He left me there. Left the house. I assume he went drinking with his cronies or to one of the women he slept with instead of me. Believe me. I was more than happy to let someone else take care of that."

"What did you father do?"

"Besides have a maid dispose of the ruined rug? Nothing."

"Fuck."

"Does it help? Cursing, I mean." Jade snuggled closer. "I think I'd like to learn."

"Jade, honey, if there is anyone who had the right to let the swear words loose, it's you." *And then some.*

"I spoke with my father the next day. Enough was enough. I lost his grandchild. He always spoke about his legacy, how important it was to leave something behind. He didn't care if Stephen hit me. I knew that. Surely my losing his future heir would tip the scales in my favor."

"I don't think I'm going to like the answer."

"*I* didn't." Jade sighed. She sounded tired. Garrett pulled her closer, willing her to take some of his strength. "He finally acknowledged there was a problem. Correction. A *minor* problem with my marriage. Not with Stephen. My father handpicked my husband. Fundamentally, he was fine. *I,* on the other hand, was a mess before and still. Now, instead of being a constant thorn in his side, that thorn was irritating Stephen."

"Your father blamed you?" Garrett knew Jade told the truth. Still, it seemed unbelievable that a man would side with the monster who was abusing his daughter.

"He regretted the loss of the child. He suggested the next time I found out I was pregnant, I keep my head down and my mouth shut."

"I'm sorry, Jade."

"I wasn't. It was the proverbial straw, Garrett. The camel's back hadn't snapped. It was lying in a million little pieces. For the first time in my life, I looked at my father with clear eyes. He would never change.

The love I always wanted wasn't going to magically wash over him. Without another word, I went to my room and packed my bags."

"Good for you."

"I should have left it all behind," Jade whispered. "I should have called a cab, gone to a hotel. Stopping to pack almost got me killed."

"Stephen caught you?" Garrett steeled himself for what she was about to say.

"I don't know why he came home early. Bad luck on my part, I guess. He was more hungover than drunk. I remember thinking how handsome he used to be. Maybe I was the problem. During the few years we were married he put on weight, stopped working out."

"It isn't your fault he became a fat, lazy bastard."

"No. I told myself that. I didn't have time to tell Stephen. He took one look at the suitcase and he did something he had never done before. He punched me in the face. The next thing I know Sally, one of the maids, was standing over me screaming. I wanted to ask her what was wrong, but I couldn't form the words. I looked down at my body. There was nothing but red. Blood, everywhere. I wasn't scared. I couldn't feel a thing. The next thing I knew, I woke up in the hospital. Three days later."

The only sound in the room was the air conditioner fan clanking its own odd rhythm. Garrett didn't want to push Jade. He held her close, offering his silent support.

"The doctor told me I almost died," Jade said. The words were so matter-of-fact. The words chilled Garrett to the bone. "I don't know why that didn't frighten me. Maybe I was in shock. I certainly wasn't in any pain. Whatever they pumped into my veins gave me this floaty, I don't give a shit, feeling. Suddenly I understood why people became addicts. For the first time in my life, I was carefree. Why wouldn't I want to keep that feeling?"

"Jade…"

"Don't worry," she assured him. "The doctor gave me a prescription when I left the hospital. I threw it away before I gave into the impulse to have it filled. I knew drugs weren't the answer."

"Going back to your father's house must have been difficult."

"You mean, how could I go back?" Jade shook her head. "I was in no shape to strike out on my own, Garrett. Do you want to know what he did to me? There was so much speculation. Most of it wrong."

"Do you want to tell me?" Garrett asked quietly.

"I think I do. My therapist thinks I need to talk about it. With someone other than her. So far, you've been great. Amazing." Jade kissed the side of his neck. It was a lovely, intimate gesture that Garrett found surprisingly moving.

"Have you remembered what happened?"

"No," Jade said. "It's all secondhand. Sometimes it freaks me out, sometimes I feel completely detached. I can't guarantee what version you'll get."

"I'll take my chances."

"Stephen always carried a knife. One of those with a million and one uses. According to the police, after he knocked me out, he took out the longest blade and started carving. More like hacking, really."

Garrett couldn't control his gasp of shock. It wasn't her description that got to him; it was the calm way Jade told it.

"I guess you're getting detached, Jade."

"Whatever works for you." As soon as he said the words, Garrett realized he meant them. There was no right or wrong way to survive something like what Jade went through. All that mattered was her survival.

"Most of the cuts were shallow. A lot of blood — not much damage. It was the last cut that did the damage," Jade took a deep breath. "A fraction of an inch to the left, he would have hit my liver. Turns out it wasn't the cuts, but the loss of blood that almost killed me. No one is entirely sure how long I lay there before Sally found me."

"She found you in time, thank God."

"Yes. Unfortunately, Stephen got away. He's still out there."

"Do the police have any idea what happened?"

"I'm sure they have their theories. None that they've shared with me."

"What do you think?"

Garrett knew the answer before Jade spoke.

"I think my father either had him killed or helped him get away." She tipped her head, peering at Garrett. "Does that shock you?"

"I wish it did, Jade. But no. After what you've told me, neither of those things would surprise me."

"My life is so fucked up."

"Well, done," Garrett chuckled. "Who said you needed to learn to cuss? You, honey, are a natural."

"I have some ugly scars."

"I don't care."

"I do." Jade's voice lowered. "I don't want you to see them, Garrett. I'm too thin and my stomach is covered with red, puckered lines. I don't care if most of them will eventually fade. I don't care."

"Shh," Garrett said in a soothing voice. He smoothed back the hair from Jade's face, stroking repeatedly. "I promise, until you decide it's time, I won't ask to look."

"We can keep the lights out?"

"Until you're ready."

As Garrett lay holding Jade, he wasn't thinking about her scars. The lights being on or off didn't matter. His worries were centered on Jade's husband. He hoped Anson Marlow *did* have the bastard killed. If not, he hoped the bastard slipped up and the police captured him. Soon. If not, Jade was still in danger.

Chapter Seven

GARRETT THOUGHT LONG and hard about Jade's situation. Last night, after he left the motel and was in his own bed, he spent a sleepless night running everything through his head. Over and over again. He couldn't fix her situation at home. As much as he wanted to storm in, punch her father's lights out, then insist she come with him immediately, that wasn't going to happen — for so many reasons.

First, what would he do with her? Put her up in a hotel? Move her in with him? Neither of them was ready for that; Garrett didn't know if they ever would be. Their relationship was undefined. Lovers? Not yet. Friends? They were making progress in that direction. Getting to know each other bit by bit. It was new. Like Jade. Fragile, yet getting stronger every day.

Garrett *did* know he cared. He couldn't wait around wondering if Jade's husband would someday show up and hurt her again. The next time she might not be lucky enough to get away with a scarred body. Next time, she might die.

"Hey, are you coming down with something?"

Garrett tried to shake off his morbid thoughts, and then turned to Hamish.

"I'm fine. Why do you ask?"

"It's ninety-five in the shade and you just shivered. That can't be normal."

No, Garrett thought. There was nothing normal about imagining a woman dead. If he could do anything to keep Jade safe, he would.

"I'm fine," Garrett assured his friend. "My mind wandered. Let's get back to the task at hand. We have most of our film crew assembled. Who's missing?"

Garrett could tell Hamish wasn't completely convinced something wasn't wrong, but he didn't push the matter.

"The main parts are in place. It's a good group. We've worked with most of them before. Bill Wyman has a new assistant."

Garrett frowned. This was news to him.

"What happened to Felicity?"

"She's moved on," Hamish said.

"In Bill speak, that means he screwed around on her. How many times has that happened since we've known him?"

"This is the third." Hamish shrugged. "Felicity was good. She won't have a problem finding another job. She's ready to take the lead on a film."

"Bill can't be faulted as a teacher and mentor. Professionally, he's exactly who you want to work with. Personally, he's a train wreck. A damn charming train wreck, by all accounts."

"Luckily, we aren't his type," Hamish chuckled.

Bill Wyman was one of the best cinematographers in the business. Or so he told Garrett the first time they worked together. It was Garrett's first time flying solo. Bill's second. Neither of them lacked self-confidence. The potential for a clash of egos was strong. For whatever reason, they worked together like a couple of well-oiled cogs. No friction. No temperamental blow-ups.

This was their fourth movie together. Bill was on his third assistant. The personal drama never affected his work. If anything, a new woman energized him. Garrett couldn't imagine living his life that way. However, it wasn't *his* life. It was Bill's. As long as the work didn't suffer, as far as Garrett was concerned, his cameraman's private life was nobody else's business.

Garrett listened while Hamish updated him on the best candidates to round out the crew. The choices were relatively simple. They liked giving newcomers a break. Whenever possible, they hired at least one person with little or no experience. *Giving a hand up*, was how his father put it. It was a Landis tradition. One Garrett believed in perpetuating. Unfortunately, this time his movie was under a tighter than usual schedule. There would be no time for *teaching moments*. He needed every member of his crew to be fast, efficient, and experienced. Bill's new assistant had him a little worried.

"We start shooting in five days," Garrett said. "Two weeks here in L.A., two in Oregon. I refuse to go over budget, Hamish."

"Hey, Wyatt isn't producing this one," Hamish countered.

"Meaning, unlike my brother, this producer will cut us a little slack?"

"Wyatt does hold the purse strings tight."

"Which is why all of his movies make money," Garrett reminded his friend. "Wyatt is the best."

"Hey, I didn't mean to sound critical," Hamish rushed to reassure Garrett. "I was joking — mostly."

"I'm not offended." Garrett gave Hamish a friendly slap on the back. "Hell, Wyatt would take it as a compliment."

"Too right." Hamish grinned.

"It's important I prove myself when I'm away from my family, Hamish. This one is all me. I'm getting it done on time and under budget. I want to prove I'm not a flash in the pan backed by the Landis name."

"You're too sensitive, Garrett." Hamish shook his head. "You've made your own name."

"I'm getting there," Garrett agreed. "In a few months, when we start *Exile*, no one will question my ability to make any kind of movie I want. Drama, comedy, adventure. I won't be pigeonholed, Hamish. What we do today, every day, is one more step in that direction."

"I'm with you, brother. I plan on riding your coattails to the top of the heap."

"Heap?"

Garrett grinned at the image of him and Hamish crawling over other directors, smashing fingers, bloodying mouths, breaking bones. Whatever it took to get to the top. Considering this was Hollywood, it was damn accurate.

"Heaps of adulation. Heaps of money." Hamish closed his eyes as though he were picturing it all. "Let's not forget the women. I trail behind you and your brothers, consoling the ones not lucky enough to catch your fancies."

"You do fine on your own," Garrett said wryly. "More than fine. Women love that brogue. What did your last girlfriend call you? A Scottish leprechaun?"

"She left off the Scottish part." Hamish gave Garrett a disgruntled look. "She didn't know the difference. Can you believe that? I don't care how great her ass was. When she called me Irish, it was over."

"We all have our lines in the sand."

An hour later, alone in his office, Garrett wondered if, where Jade was concerned, there was something that would make him walk away? As with everything else involving Jade, it was too soon to tell.

Garrett knew one thing. Steps had to be taken to find out what happened to Stephen Marsh. Picking up his phone, he searched his contacts. There it was. He hit the name, hoping the call didn't go to voicemail.

"Garrett," the familiar voice answered after only two rings. "What the hell does my least favorite Landis brother want?"

Garrett knew two things about Jack Winston. He was as easygoing as they came, and when push came to shove, he was one tough son of a bitch. He and his best friend owned a billion-dollar cyber-security empire. Before they hit it big, Jack and Drew Harper *were* the security. They spent several years in Hollywood protecting some of the industry's biggest names.

Garrett's mother and father used the duo on occasion, during movie premieres, or personal appearances. Bodyguards to the stars. They were tough, discreet, and looked good in a tux. More James Bond than Hulk Hogan. Suave — but deadly. One of the few times they had to show their muscle was when an overzealous fan lunged at Garrett's mother when she was promoting a movie. Jack moved so fast, most people were never aware anything happened.

Caleb Landis knew. Jack tried to brush off the incident, saying he was doing his job — nothing more. As far as Caleb and the rest of the Landis men were concerned, Jack was a hero. If he needed a favor. Big or small. Night or day. All he needed to do was ask.

That favor had never been claimed. Now, ironically it was Garrett who needed something from Jack.

"Are you still going on about something that happened five years ago?"

"There is no statute of limitations when it comes to a man's wife."

Garrett rolled his eyes.

"Rose wasn't your wife five years ago," he reminded the other man. "In fact, you didn't know her. How can I be in your dog house for flirting with a completely unattached woman?"

"Flirting?" Jack asked. "According to Rose, you invited her to spend a week in Jamaica. In a villa on a private beach. Clothing discouraged."

He didn't give it away with his voice, yet Garrett knew Jack was grinning. He could easily picture the big man, in his office, feet up on his desk, enjoying every second of the grief he was handing out. Jack didn't give a damn how many men propositioned his wife. As long as it was in the past. Rose O'Brian was a beautiful woman with a personality to match. Garrett met Rose at a party in New York given by a mutual friend. He was attracted, made his pitch. She shot him down with such good humor and charm he ended up with only a minor dent in his ego.

"You know I'm not the only Landis to make a play for Rose."

"The hell you say?" Garrett heard Jack's feet hit the ground. "Which one?" There was an ominous silence. "And when?"

"Relax," Garrett chuckled. "Nate was at the same party where Rose and I met. We're twins, Jack. Sometimes we have the same taste in women. What am I saying? *Rose* appeals to every man's taste."

"That's true," Jack said. "I suppose I can overlook it. Besides, I trust Rose implicitly."

"Of course you do." Garrett couldn't resist one more jab. "By the way, Colt will be on location near Harper Falls next month. Maybe he should stop by."

"How near?"

Well, over four hundred miles, actually. Harper Falls, Washington was located in the upper eastern part of the state on the Columbia River. Colt's movie was filming in Calgary, Alberta. Hardly *dropping in* distance. However, Jack didn't need to know that.

"Just say the word, Jack. Colt is a *very* social person."

"Okay." Jack gave a friendly laugh. "Enough about your pretty boy brother. You called for a reason. What's up?"

Losing the light banter, Garrett gave a brief but detailed outline of the situation. It wasn't necessary to share the most intimate details. Jack got the picture.

"I don't know what to say, Garrett." Jack's voice was filled with compassion. "I'm sorry your friend had to go through that. The bastard husband is gone? Without a trace?"

"I've called a few friends. Done some asking. Not that I've gotten very far. My police connections are more of the fictional variety," Garrett said.

"Alex Fleming runs the physical part of H&W now. He's ex-Army Intelligence. Finding things out is his specialty."

"I appreciate it, Jack. It makes no sense that he could vanish." Garrett paused. "Unless he had help."

"Who do you suspect?"

This was the tricky part. Anson Marlow was a powerful man. His connections ran, not just from coast to coast, but worldwide. Garrett didn't want word of this getting back to Jade's father. That was why he called Jack. The man and his friends were discretion personified.

"Start with Anson Marlow."

"I DON'T THINK this is going to work, Garrett."

The room was as pitch black as possible. The candles from dinner were extinguished, no crack of light slipped through the drawn curtains. Tonight Garrett wanted Jade to feel safe in her cocoon of darkness.

"It is all about touch, Jade."

They stood, side by side, near the bed. Nothing was different from the last few nights they met. Garrett kissed Jade. First with tenderness, his tongue asking for admittance into her mouth, not demanding it. Unlike the first few times, Jade's response was instantaneous. She didn't hesitate to open to him. Her response was no longer shy. She was a full, eager participant.

Jade's arms wound around his neck, pulling him closer. She angled her head, her mouth welcoming. Her confidence grew to the point where she was now the aggressor. She no longer waited for Garrett to initiate every move. Her tongue met his with enthusiasm, not trepidation.

Jade liked to touch — to *be* touched. The pleasure she received from running her hands over his arms, his back, up his legs, was obvious. Garrett loved when her breath quickened from simply exploring the ridges of his stomach muscles.

All this was done fully clothed.

They were making progress. As long as he didn't touch her stomach, Jade let him put his hand under her shirt, cup her breast. That was good, very good — for both of them. Feeling her nipple harden sent a shot of desire through Garrett's body. The catch in her breathing as he teased the hardened tip. The way she whispered his name.

They were making progress. Slow and steady. Tonight he wanted to take it all the way. That meant convincing Jade to remove her clothing.

"I'll take off my jeans and my panties," Jade said, her voice tightening. "Let me leave my shirt on."

"Think about the feel of your bare breasts against my chest," Garrett cajoled gently. "Don't you want to rub against me? Picture it, Jade. Anticipate the sensation of our bare bodies, free of any constraint, touching. The thought makes me so hard."

Garrett felt Jade's hand tracing the skin just above the snap on his jeans. She never touched any lower. She flirted with the area, driving him crazy. However, this time felt different. He held his breath, hoping Jade would take her exploration lower. The breath rushed from Garrett's lungs when, with no preamble, she cupped his erection.

The denim between Jade's hand and Garrett was a minor barrier. The pressure, the light squeeze she gave, felt like a little slice of heaven.

"You *are* hard."

"Does that surprise you?" Garrett asked. "Everything about you is a turn on, Jade."

"Why?"

Jade was the first woman to ask Garrett that question. Why do you find me attractive? What is it about me? In all honesty, it wasn't a question he had ever contemplated. The smell of her hair? The sound of her voice? The way she turned her head when she listened, *really* listened, to what he said?

Sexual attraction was such a subjective thing. Not only that, it was fluid — ever changing. One week you can't live without someone. Her touch, her taste sends you over the moon. The next week she leaves you cold. What changed? Her shampoo? What she ate for breakfast? There was no answer. Not really. Attraction was a mystery better savored than understood.

"I don't know why, Jade." Garrett put his hand over hers, increasing the pressure. "This is yours. I feel it every time I see you. Hell, you don't have to be anywhere near me. The thought of you arouses me."

"I…"

"What?" Garrett urged when her voice faltered.

"I think about you," she said a bit shyly. "When I'm alone at night. In bed."

"Do you touch yourself?"

"Yes."

He sucked in a deep breath. Damn, that was not where he expected this to go. The thought of her masturbating while fantasizing about him? The image almost scorched his brain to ashes.

"One day you are going to give me a detailed account, and I mean *detailed*." Reluctantly, Garrett moved her hand away. "Tonight, we go old school. You." He kissed her. "Me." The kiss was longer. "In bed." His mouth played with hers with long, passionate swipes of his tongue.

"I like the sound of that."

"Naked, Jade. We are going to be naked."

Feeling her pull back, Garrett deepened the kiss. He wouldn't give Jade the chance to lose the heat that was building. He wanted her so out of control she forgot everything. Her pain, her scars. He wanted her to feel beautiful, the way he saw her, inside and out.

Before she could protest, Garrett grabbed the hem of her shirt, pulling it off in one motion. He went to his knees, his arms around her waist, his face pressed against her stomach. Without a word, Garrett pressed his lips to the skin below her ribs. Jade didn't protest. She didn't move. They held their breath as he began to map every inch of her with his kisses.

Garrett felt it — the healed wounds that were daily reminders of something she wanted to forget. When he ran his tongue over a long, jagged ridge, Jade gasped, trying to move away. Her shaking hands pushed at his head.

"Don't, Garrett. It's so ugly. *I'm* ugly."

The tears he heard in Jade's voice ripped at his gut. He would give her anything she asked if it would dry those tears. *Almost* anything. He wouldn't get off his knees. He wouldn't take his lips from her ravaged skin. He had to make her understand. *She wasn't ugly*.

Unbuttoning her jeans, Garrett lowered the zipper, his mouth following slowly behind. When the denim pooled at Jade's feet, he lifted each leg, guiding her until she stood before him in nothing but her underwear.

"Such soft, sweet skin."

Jade stopped trying to push him away. Instead, her hand went to her stomach, splaying across as much of the surface as she could reach. Garrett didn't reassure her with words. He used his mouth, kissing each finger, his teeth lightly nipping.

"That isn't fair, Garrett."

Smiling at the moan Jade couldn't contain, Garrett nuzzled the mound of silk-covered flesh between her legs.

"You didn't ask me to play fair, Jade," he said. "You wanted me to help you feel again. Feel more than you've ever felt before. Do you trust me?"

"Yes."

Jade's response was breathy but giving, without hesitation. Garrett pushed his advantage.

"This is all about you, Jade," Garrett assured her. "What you need. What you want. Do you want to put yourself in my hands? I promise to stop if you want me to."

"No!" Jade cried out. Her hands slid into his hair, holding him in place. "Don't stop. Even if I beg you to."

"Oh, honey." Garrett kissed the inside of Jade's thigh. "You'll be begging, all right." He edged his tongue under the band of elastic. "If you taste half as good as you smell I won't be coming up for a very long time."

"Maybe we could start with something a little less… personal."

Garrett chuckled. That wasn't fear in her voice. Unease, he could deal with. The intrigue he could build on.

"If we do this right, it will be nothing *but* personal. First, let's get rid of these."

Garrett divested Jade of her panties before she could think of a reason to keep them on.

"Are you as pretty down here as I imagine?"

"No one is pretty down there," Jade informed him breathily.

"Now, that is where you're wrong." Garrett kissed the skin of her sloping mound. "A woman's sex is uniquely beautiful. The source of so much pleasure. The bringer of life."

Garrett's tongue teased, and then dipped for his first taste. Mmm. Just as he suspected. Instantly addictive. From the sounds Jade made, she agreed. Giving her a gentle push, Garrett toppled Jade back onto the bed. On his knees, he settled between her legs. He planned on giving her multiple orgasms. And he planned on enjoying every moment.

Jade, it seemed, was through protesting. Garrett could hear her deep breathing. He could feel the tension in her legs.

"Are you thinking of England?"

"What?"

God, he wished he could see more than the shadowy outline of her face. That *what* was tinged with so many emotions. Surprise. Confusion. A big dose of *what the hell are you talking about?* Her expression must be priceless.

"Isn't that the old saying? When a Victorian wife was expected to do her wifely duties, she was told to lie back and think of England. It kept her mind off of her rutting husband," Garrett explained, the whole time running his hands over her legs, satisfied when they started to relax. "I don't think Victorian women were supposed to enjoy sex."

"I counted."

"Counted what?"

On the surface, talking about sex with her husband didn't seem like the best foreplay. Garrett wasn't interested in the surface. Jade's problems were much deeper. If he could help her root some of them out, no subject was off limits.

"I counted how long it took Stephen to finish. I'm happy to say he didn't have much stamina. At least, not with me."

"Wham, bam?"

"And never a thank you, ma'am."

Garrett smiled. *There it was.* Jade had a terrific sense of humor. One of the many things he was discovering about her. If she could laugh, even a little, about her husband's many shortcomings, she would heal much faster.

"Not to brag…," Garrett began, his voice teasing.

"No one starts a sentence like that if they aren't about to brag," Jade pointed out.

Deciding Jade was relaxed and enjoying their banter, Garrett took advantage by sliding his finger between the wet folds. He entered her easily. Lord, she was tight. Thinking about sinking his cock into her was almost his undoing. He had to pull his thoughts away from himself and concentrate on Jade. Her gasp of pleasure helped him refocus.

"As I was saying. Not to brag, but I can go for hours." Garrett punctuated the sentence by taking another taste, his tongue lingering, causing Jade's hips to push forward, silently asking for more.

"Hours?" she sighed. Jade sounded hopeful. *And* disbelieving.

"I understand. You need proof. No problem."

Garrett could tell Jade was close. The movement of her body, the shallow gasps all added up to one thing. He planned on making the first orgasm she received from him a memorable one. Moving his thumb to the side, he replaced it with his mouth.

The flavor of her spicy nectar burst over his taste buds. He lapped them up, savoring every drop. The sounds Jade made were like music, filling the room, drowning out the ancient air conditioner. Garrett heard only Jade. His senses filled with her. When her fingers threaded through his hair, squeezing, pulling him closer, he knew she was just as invested as he was. Then when her legs stiffened. When she cried out in wonder, he knew he was hers. It was too soon to speak the words. There was a long way to go before any declarations could be made. Still, when he thought back, he would remember this as the exact moment he knew Jade Marlow was the only woman for him.

Garrett soothed while Jade floated down. Moving from the floor, he joined her on the bed. He took her in his arms, settling the sheet over their bodies. He didn't speak. Instead, he held on, waiting for her to absorb everything.

"No one has ever done that for me," Jade whispered after a few minutes.

"Given you an orgasm?" Garrett asked.

"That too. But I meant *how* you did it." She sighed, snuggling closer. "Thank you."

"They don't know what they missed." Garrett put his lips close to Jade's ear. "You taste like heaven."

"Garrett…"

"Are you blushing?"

"Probably." Jade hesitated, as though considering her next words. "I want to return the favor."

"Sounds good to me."

Knowing that she meant right now, Garrett held Jade close, stopping her hand when she reached for his erection. He was rock hard. The thought of her mouth around him made his entire body tighten with anticipation. However, tonight that image was not going to become a reality.

"We'll get to it," Garrett assured Jade. And himself. "When I make you feel good, Jade, I don't expect anything in return. Two consenting adults. That's what we are. Sometimes the pleasure is in *giving* pleasure."

"I've never known a man who would turn down a blow job."

"Don't get the idea I'm a self-sacrificing saint," Garrett laughed. "In the future, when you offer again, my answer will be a resounding yes."

"But not tonight."

"Not tonight."

They quietly lay in each other's arms. Garrett toyed with the ends of Jade's long, thick hair, picturing how the red almost glowed in the candlelight while they shared dinner. He tried unsuccessfully to remember Jade in the light of day.

There must have been a time, over the years they lived nearby, that he ran into her. When they were school age, Garrett's parents took him and his brothers on location during summer break. His childhood had been filled with exotic adventures. Egypt, Japan, Argentina. By the time Garrett graduated high school, his passport was full — his education diverse.

"When you were a child, what did you do during summer vacation?"

"That's an odd question," Jade said, her voice slightly muffled. She was nibbling on his chest. As good it felt, it was damn distracting.

"Not odd," he said. "I'm curious about you. Did you travel? Stay home? Have adventures around the neighborhood with friends? Tell me about young Jade."

"There isn't much to tell, Garrett." Jade slid her hand across his stomach, dangerously close to where the sheet covered his lower half.

"Oh, no you don't." Garrett took her hand, kissing the back. He then laced her fingers with his, keeping a firm grasp. "I've shared a lot about my misadventures. You don't have to recite the novel, Jade. Start with the Reader's Digest version."

"Fine," Jade sighed. "My father preferred I socialize with the children of whoever could do him the most good, business-wise. As a result, I hung around with a lot of sullen, over privileged jerks. I can only imagine what they said about me when I wasn't around."

"What makes you think what they said was bad?"

"I was shy and I didn't want to be anywhere near them." Jade's laugh was self-deprecating. "Not the best combination to *win friends and influence people*."

"You forget," Garrett said. "I grew up around those idiots too. With few exceptions, they weren't worth your time or effort."

"Tell that to my father. I tried, honestly. If only to avoid another lecture." Jade shuddered. "God, I hated those lectures. He never raised his voice. That cold, impersonal stare he gave me. *Why can't you make more of an effort to fit in*? My father is big on fitting in. For years, he has tried to whittle away at my annoying edges, desperate to make this square peg fit into a Beverly Hills round hole."

"There's nothing wrong with being unique, Jade."

"Not unique," Jade corrected. "Odd. I'm too tall. Can't do anything about that except relegate me to flat-soled shoes. My eyes are too big, my hair is too red."

"Too red?" Garrett touched the thick, soft-as-silk strands again. "No such thing."

"Mr. Deon didn't agree."

"Why does that name sound familiar?"

"Because about fourteen years ago, he was *the* hairdresser in Beverly Hills," Jade explained. "My father's girlfriend of the moment insisted I go to him. Mr. Deon was *bound* to be able to do something with my Ronald McDonald mop."

"What a bitch," Garrett said. Jade couldn't have been more than what? Thirteen? A vulnerable age. Instead of being a friend, this other woman tore at Jade's insecurities. What was wrong with people?

"Mmm," Jade nodded her head in agreement. "I became a brunette."

"Well, that's not right."

"I'd show you photographic evidence, but I've destroyed every picture from those three years."

"That long?" Garrett asked in amazement.

"She had her claws in tight." Jade shrugged. "When my father moved on, so did the brown hair. Gradually. I was afraid to make a too sudden change. Turns out it didn't matter. One night he was entertaining a business associate. The man's wife commented that I looked much better as a redhead than a brunette. My father, instead of being upset, glanced at me and muttered, *When were you a brunette?*"

"My opinion of your father continues to sink to depths I didn't know existed."

"I was floored."

Garrett rubbed Jade's shoulders, trying to comfort. Anson Marlow displayed a careless cruelty towards Jade that made him sick to his stomach. How could you not care anything about your own daughter? The idea was unfathomable.

"I sound pathetic," Jade said. Before he could protest, she added, "I had a playmate. Manuela, our gardener's daughter. Sometimes she would come with her father and we would play in the backyard. She's the reason I picked this motel."

That surprised Garrett.

"You told her about us?"

"No," Jade shook her head. "She once mentioned that her older sister is a maid here. I knew how much pride the entire family takes in their work, so I thought the chances were good these rooms would be clean. I was right."

"Jade…"

"You have to admit, you could eat off those bathroom floors."

"I'll take your word for it."

Garrett didn't know who was crazier. Jade for picking this place on the off chance the gardener's older daughter was as fastidious as the rest of her family. Or him for continuing to come to this sparkling hellhole. Something needed to change. Soon.

"Garrett?"

"Hmm?"

"Will you...?"

When Jade hesitated, Garrett slid down until they were face to face. Close enough to see her eyes. He felt the frustration again. He wanted to see the changing emotions in those hazel depths. When he gave her pleasure, he wanted to see if the color became more green or gold. Right now, he couldn't tell what she was thinking. He was so sick of existing in the shadows when it came to Jade.

"Will I...?"

"Can we have sex?"

Garrett smiled. Nothing shadowy about that request.

"Let's start by removing that bra."

He reached around, unclasping the back, then slid the piece of silk down Jade's arms.

"Are you excited or cold?"

"Garrett."

"Jade," Garrett chuckled. "I've touched your breasts. Kissed them. I've taken your nipples in my mouth. Your moans have filled this room, so I know you like what I do. Why are you embarrassed?"

"I like it when you do things," she admitted. "I don't know if I can talk about it."

"Does it bother you when *I* talk?" Garrett asked. He traced the slope of her breast until his finger rubbed the tip. "You don't like dirty talk?"

"I *do* like it." Jade whispered the words as though her admission might be heard by someone outside the room. "I like it a lot."

"Good. Because I like talking during sex. I like letting you know what you do to me. How good you feel. Of course, I can't talk when I do this."

Garrett took her nipple in his mouth. The stiff little peak became harder as he sucked, grazing it with his teeth. Like a juicy strawberry — but much sweeter.

"Do you want me to tell you how you feel in my mouth?"

He bit down again, this time a little harder. Jade's moan told him everything he needed to know. She was ready for him to stop holding back quite so much. There were places he could take her that were still off limits — too intense. However, Jade no longer needed pure vanilla. It was time to add a little spice to their play. Words were a great place to start.

"I love it when you make that little sound in the back of your throat."

"What noise?"

When Garrett pinched her nipple between his fingers, biting her neck at the same time, Jade's question turned into a gasp, then a moan, then a tantalizing combination of the two.

"That's the one," Garrett said, smiling. He left a trail of kisses until his lips hovered over hers.

"I didn't know I made a special noise," Jade said.

"Like nothing I've ever heard before." Garrett gave her a light kiss. "Unique. Like the rest of you."

"I'm ordinary, Garrett."

From the tone of her voice, Garrett knew if he could see her eyes, they would be a little sad. He wasn't allowing that. He finally had Jade where he wanted her. Years after that night in his car, they were going to have sex. What the hell. He might as well admit it, if only to himself. He was going to make love to Jade Marlow. A first for him. All was good. Sadness had no place in bed with them.

"Why would I lie to you, Jade?"

"Not lie," she conceded. "Embellish. To make me feel better about myself."

"The first time you asked me to meet you, all you wanted was for me to have sex with you. Am I right?"

"Yes."

"There was nothing in your request about pumping up your ego with kind, insincere compliments." Garrett knew he was pushing the point a little too hard, but he didn't want any doubts left in Jade's mind.

"You're a *kind* man, Garrett."

"I don't think anyone who has worked with me would ever use that word. Slave driver. Asshole. Madman. That I've heard. Kind? Not so much."

Garrett saw her lips curve upward.

"How many of them have you slept with?"

"You have me there," Garrett smiled in return. "I don't do location hook-ups."

"I bet your lovers would agree with me." Jade cupped his face with one hand. "You are exciting, Garrett. You know how to please a woman. Fundamentally, you are the kindest man I have ever known."

Garrett was floored. Who knew that such a simple compliment would bring him as close to tears as he could ever remember? Jade spent her life without one of the most fundamental things he took for granted. Love was complicated. Friendship could come and go. Kindness was so easy. Yet it was what she craved because she spent her life without it.

"I'll accept kind," Garrett teased, hoping to lighten the moment. "*If you admit I'm the sexiest man you've ever met.*"

"That's easy," Jade said, the paused before adding, "I've never met Colton."

"Ha," Garrett scoffed. Thrilled that Jade felt comfortable enough to tease, he was happy to play along. "My brother is all flash, honey. What you see up on the screen and in the magazines? A trick of lights and filters. In person, Colt is a ninety pound weakling with bad skin and thinning hair."

"Wow, Hollywood really can work wonders."

"You have no idea." Garrett rolled on top of Jade, linking his fingers with hers. He held her hands, trapped under his, on each side of her head. "Now, while I worship your delectable skin with my mouth, tell me how sexy *I* am."

"I never knew a man could do the things you do to me," Jade breathed as Garrett licked her ear. "I've read about it in books. God, I hated those books."

"Not sexy enough?" Garrett asked between kisses.

"Too sexy. I was set up for disappointment. I — Oh, God! Garrett, what did you just do?"

Garrett knew exactly what she meant. That little spot right where her neck and shoulder met. When he bit with exactly the right amount of pressure, Jade almost shot out of her skin. However, since they were in a teasing mood, he decided to play dumb. For a little while.

"You mean this?"

Garrett lightly kissed Jade's cheek.

"No."

"This?"

His lips grazed the underside of her jaw.

"That isn't where your mouth was."

"Really?"

Garrett was enjoying himself. There was something to be said for playing in bed. He couldn't remember when he last took the time. Or wanted to. He loved sex. Believed in satisfying himself with willing ladies as often as possible. None of those women made him want to linger the way Jade did.

"Are you going to do it again?" Jade asked with obvious frustration.

"If you do something for me."

"Name it."

"Careful, honey." Garrett loved that he was driving Jade to distraction. "I might ask for something kinky."

"How kinky?"

Garrett could tell Jade was intrigued by the idea. Well, well, well. It appeared Jade wasn't a straight arrow, which was fine with him. He wasn't into anything extreme. Still, he enjoyed a little twist now and then.

"Let's try knocking off those training wheels before you tackle the big hill." Garrett covered Jade's mouth with his. The kiss was hard, intense, and way too brief. They were both breathing harder when he pulled back. "Say something dirty."

"How dirty?"

"Don't panic. Nothing too wild," Garrett reassured her. "Yet. Tell me what you want. One thing you would like."

For a minute, Garrett was afraid she was through playing. He didn't think he was pushing too hard. Still, Jade wasn't experienced. In any way. It might take some time to coax her out of her shell.

"I like when you use your tongue."

There we go. Garrett smiled to himself as he gave Jade what she asked for. Not too wet. He was a man, not a hormone-riddled teenager. He knew the proper balance between what made a woman shudder with passion and what made her shudder with disgust. It was a fine line. One he always stayed on the proper side of.

"Do you like it here?"

Garrett outlined her shape of Jade's ear, biting the lobe.

"And your teeth," Jade gasped. "You always make it feel so good. You bite, always stopping before it hurts. I didn't know I wanted that."

"I plan on opening your world to all the possibilities, Jade. Some of them you'll like." Garrett bit again. "Others, you can decide as we go. Now, about that spot you wanted me to hit again. Right about here."

At the same moment his teeth latched on, he entered her. One smooth motion. Garrett knew Jade was ready for him. The entire evening was leading to this. The meal they shared. The teasing. Even her first orgasm was only a prelude to having him inside her for the first time.

Jade surprised him. Garrett expected a slow build. He was used to her being a little shy at first — unsure. Not this time. The double stimulation of his teeth and his cock turned her into a wild woman. Her legs wrapped around his, urging him on. She pulled her hands free. She grabbed his head, guiding his mouth to hers. This was the first time she took the initiative. She wasn't happy to be led. She knew what she wanted and she was taking it.

"This is going to be fast, Jade," Garrett warned. "You aren't helping slow it down."

"I don't want slow." Jade grabbed his ass, making sure his pace matched the one she wanted. "Hard. Give me everything you have."

The words were music to Garrett's ears. For weeks, he held his desire in check. Giving Jade every consideration, then going home to jerk off in his solitary shower. Being inside her hot, wet, body was better than any dream. She was tight and slick. It only took a minute for him to hit his peak.

"Are you ready to come with me?"

Please say yes.

"I'm coming, Garrett. *Now!*"

Thank God. He tumbled over. His mouth found Jade's, their cries of pleasure mingling in a passionate duet. The slide back to Earth was gradual, his hips still working, trying to wring out every ounce of the moment, wanting it to last.

Garrett collapsed, rolling to the side. He kept Jade in his arms, needing her near. Throwing his head back, he closed his eyes, savoring the feel of her. Nothing could ruin the moment. Not the crappy motel *or* the loud air conditioner.

Garrett wished they were at his house. He would fill the huge tub in his bathroom, pick Jade up, and then make love to her all over again as the warm water lapped around their bodies. He didn't want to think about using the shower here at the motel. Things grew in the corners that he feared would resist even the strongest disinfectant.

At least the sheets were clean. Next time, he would lavish her with the kind of lovemaking experience she deserved. It was time to leave the rattrap motel behind. After weeks of hiding, there was no longer any need. They weren't a one-time thing that had to be kept on the down low.

Now, he needed to convince Jade.

Chapter Eight

PRESENT DAY

JADE WONDERED IF she was making a huge mistake. Having tea with Garrett's mother? Was she out of her mind? Not only was Jade carrying on a secret affair with Callie Flynn's son — she was meeting him that very evening.

The luncheon was a success. At least it seemed that way to Jade. Judging such things was always difficult. You could spend the entire time thinking you put every foot right. Then you find out a week later you had a huge spot on the back of your dress and the *Ladies Who Lunch* club thought you were a mess. At one time, the whole thing would have turned Jade into a shaking mess. Now, she didn't care what those women thought.

Garrett's mother was a different matter altogether. Why hadn't she thought up a plausible excuse? Jade had one right at her fingertips. She could have begged exhaustion. Between the luncheon, which ran until three-thirty, and Jade's recent medical problems, she doubted Callie would have blinked an eye. Only Jade needed to know it was a lie. She was at full strength — mentally and physically.

Now, instead of anticipating her rendezvous with Garrett, Jade searched her closet for the perfect outfit to wear to meet his mother. Should she check with Garrett? Will he be angry? Jade straightened her shoulders. The hell with that. She was through worrying about angering men. Her entire life, she let the fear of her father's cold, cutting words, or her husband's fists, influence her actions. No more. Callie Flynn called *her*. If Garrett had a problem with that, he could take it up with his mother.

Feeling good about her internal pep talk, Jade stopped fussing over what to wear and grabbed a bright yellow sheath off its hanger. Because of the weight she gained in the past few months, Jade wasn't concerned about hiding behind layers of clothing. She would never be curvy; there was no getting around that. Her figure was naturally slender. Another thing she was coming to terms with. Garrett seemed to like her the way she was. More importantly, Jade was beginning to like herself. Inside and out.

Meeting Callie Flynn was one more step toward the woman Jade wanted to be. Confident women didn't cower behind closed doors or agonize over minute details. If one of the film industry's greatest beauties wanted to have tea with Jade Marlow, then tea they would have. As equals. She hoped that the meeting had nothing to do with Garrett.

It was a ridiculous thought. How would Garrett's mother find out something the rest of the world knew nothing about? If even a hint had leaked out, Jade would be all too aware. No, whatever Callie Flynn wanted, it wasn't about her son.

Jade reapplied her makeup while she thought back on the luncheon. *Ladies Who Lunch* was a charitable organization. They did some good, Jade supposed. Fundraisers were always being held. The money distributed to *needy families*. However, when everyone you knew was a multimillionaire, the term *needy* was relative.

The members consisted of some of Beverly Hills' wealthiest wives.

Rather the wives of wealthy men. They were an interesting amalgamation. First wives ruled the roost. Just below them were the second wives — if the first wife died. Next, second wives of divorced husbands. At the bottom? The third, fourth, and fifth trophy wives. If you were twenty or more years younger than your husband, you were allowed to join. Achieving any amount of respect took time and hard work. If you had the staying power, with both the group *and* your marriage, eventually it paid off. You graduated from interloper to the in-crowd.

Jade shuddered at the thought. The last thing she aspired to was acceptance from a group of women she neither liked nor admired. They let her host the luncheon because her home was considered a neutral site and her father had more money than most of their husbands. The main reason they sought Jade out was morbid curiosity.

The gold hoop earrings she chose were simple, understated, and much more Jade's personal style than the flashy gems her father insisted she wear. The world needed to see the Marlow wealth. When they entertained, Jade was given whatever jewelry her father thought appropriate. The moment the guests left, she returned it to him — he locked it in his office safe. Only Anson Marlow had the combination. Or so he thought.

Jade had the numbers memorized. She learned them over time. Catching a number here and there when her father was careless enough to open the safe in her presence. It never occurred to him that she was clever enough to pay attention. He was too arrogant to switch the numbers on a regular basis. For a man who trusted no one when it came to business, Anson Marlow neglected the little things in his home. He believed Jade to be one way. Meek. Boring. Stupid. Easily led.

It was difficult to argue. For most of her life, Jade *was* meek, boring, and easily led. However, she was never stupid. She silently observed. It would shock her father to know how much she knew about his business. The legal transactions. *And* the under the table ones. Some bordered on shady. Others were downright illegal.

She used to fantasize about cleaning out his safe. She would hand over the papers to the proper authorities. The jewels and money she would keep for herself. Jade wouldn't hide what she did. The best part would be the look on her father's face when he realized who the mastermind was behind his downfall. Stupid Jade. Not so stupid after all.

Anson Marlow never looked at his daughter — not really. He didn't when she was a child. He didn't when she was an awkward teenager desperately in need of a parent's guidance. He turned a blind eye to the abuse happening in his own home. Now, he failed to see the woman Jade was becoming. Stronger, more independent. A woman who no longer yearned for his love and approval. A woman capable of bringing his empire crashing down.

Of course, that was not going to happen. Jade did her research. The people her father swindled were not innocent investors losing their hard-earned life savings. They were men and women badder, or worse, than the man they foolishly trusted. It might be satisfying to bring the lot of them down. Unfortunately, it would be messy. Jade had lived with enough mess to last a lifetime. Let them continue to screw each other over. They deserved what they got.

The jewels and the money meant nothing to Jade. Yes, they would ease her way. Having a cushion beyond her dwindling inheritance would be nice. *Nice* was the last thing Jade was looking for. Not anymore. She wanted to see what was beyond the gates she had grown up behind. Jade was ready to break free. Maybe her father would miss her. Most likely, he would not. Happily, Jade would not be around to find out.

For the luncheon, Jade carefully arranged her hair in a French twist. Conservative, neat. Boring. There was that word again. She looked in the mirror. *Really* looked. What she saw surprised her.

Her face was fuller. Her cheekbones no longer hollow. Her eyes still dominated her face, but they didn't stand out like tragic beacons begging for the world to pity her. Trying to be objective, she gave herself a thorough once over.

She was pretty, Jade decided. There was color in her cheeks and a glint in her eyes. To be honest, that was entirely new. Even before her marriage and the subsequent events, Jade rarely sparkled. She was quiet, unobtrusive. Now? There was *more*. Whatever that meant. It was up to her to find out.

Garrett called her beautiful. Thinking of her lover... *Lover*. The mere thought brought a rosy bloom of color that traveled up her neck in a suffusion of heat. She, Jade Marlow, had a lover. A strong, considerate, passionate man who thought of her pleasure before his own.

Jade still wondered how she had the nerve to ask Garrett to meet her. Then she asked him to have sex with her. It had been terrifying. Embarrassing. Sure Garrett would reject her. She kept waiting for the floor to open up, suck her in, and put her out of her misery. Instead, Garrett said yes. Not out of pity or obligation to the poor abuse victim. He agreed because he wanted her. After all these months, the multiple meetings — and orgasms — Jade had no doubt. Garrett wanted *her*. Skinny, uninteresting Jade Marlow.

None of those women she played hostess for today would believe it. Especially if they knew the demands Jade put on Garrett from the beginning. Demands she continued to insist on even though a growing part of her wanted to throw them away. For some time, she found herself wanting to see Garrett when they were together. He had a wonderfully strong, leanly muscled body. Her hands told her that. Her mouth confirmed it. She could see him in the shadows. Now, she wanted to see more.

Fear held her back. What if he couldn't handle her scars? Deep down, Jade knew that wasn't likely. Garrett wasn't the kind of man to walk away because of a series of crisscrossed lines on her stomach. How many times had he traced them with his fingers? Kissed them? Murmured his distress for what she had suffered? Garrett wouldn't turn away in disgust. However, he might pull away. For all her newfound strength and growing confidence, she couldn't quell the fear of losing Garrett. For a few hours, in a dingy, rundown motel, he was hers. The moment the lights came on, all that would change.

One of two things would happen. Either Garrett would fade from her life or he would want to take things public. Jade feared both. The first, because being with him made her feel alive. She felt like a woman. How could she give that up? The second would mean facing cameras, paparazzi, microphones shoved in her face. The combination of her notoriety and Garrett's celebrity status would send the story through the roof.

Jade reached up, pulling out the pins that held her hair rigidly in place. She sighed with relief when the thick tendrils fell onto her shoulders and down her back. That was better. The loose, red strands were symbolic of the new Jade. In the past, she would have picked up a comb. Not today. She liked the slightly wild look, the not-so-perfect style. The new Jade.

With a nod at her reflection, Jade grabbed her purse. Come what may, she was ready to meet the great Callie Flynn head on.

"Miss Marlow?"

Jade sighed. Not three steps out of her bedroom before the maid was dogging her. There was always someone waiting. Where was this person when Stephen was slicing her up like a demented butcher? Why wouldn't her father give her some privacy? What the hell did he think she was going to do?

Straightening her shoulders, a small, pleasant smile plastered on her face, Jade turned.

"Yes?"

"Your father is asking for you."

"Did he say what he wanted?"

That threw the girl. Jade never asked questions. When her father summoned, Jade jumped. *Why* he called for her didn't matter. The fact was he called.

Dressed in her crisp black and white uniform, the young maid's eyes darted around. Clearly in a panic, she searched for someone to help. Jade knew the girl was on her own. There was no need to post guards. One unimportant maid was enough. It was her job to watch, pass on messages, and report. Anson Marlow had no reason to think Jade would question anything. It was obvious the maid had no idea how to answer when a question was asked.

Taking pity on the girl, Jade gave her a friendly smile. The staff was almost entirely new. With only two exceptions, her father had replaced anyone who was here during her marriage to Stephen. Half of them were afraid of her, half pitied her. Most were worried the rumor about her precarious mental health was a fact — not fiction. Judging from the look the maid gave her, the woman fell into the latter camp.

"Please tell my father I'm late for an appointment. I will speak with him when I get back."

"Oh, but..."

Not waiting, Jade proceeded down the stairs, the maid right on her heels. When they reached the landing, Jade kept on going.

"Don't worry," she called, not bothering to turn around. "My father won't fire you."

Jade had no idea if that was true. Reassuring the woman seemed like the easiest way to get out the door without any interruption. If she found out that her father had terminated the maid's employment, Jade would find her another job. One where she didn't have to stand outside a bedroom door, polishing the same table, waiting for the crazy woman to emerge.

Jade paused, letting the sun wash over her. When she had her own place, the one thing she would insist on was some outdoor space. Not too big. A balcony. As long as she could sit with the sun's heat on her face. She had spent too much time in the dark the past few years. A few flowers would be nice. Tended by her, not an army of gardeners whose noses got out of joint when she pulled a weed or picked a rose. God forbid those things be done out of sequence. Whatever that meant.

Soon, Jade thought. *Soon there would be no one to answer to but herself.*

An image of Garrett popped into Jade's mind. She kept him in the dark. Hiding her body. All these months, his patience and caring helped chase away the shadows. Whenever she started to slip back, she would picture him. He kept her sane. Still, she wasn't able to let him turn on the lights when they were together. She felt his growing frustration. Very soon, there would come a time when he would insist.

Would she agree? Would she walk away? Could she do either? Jade didn't know the answer. With a shake of her head, she set those worries aside. Now, her only thought should be about getting through tea with Callie Flynn.

Walking was an option Jade might have considered at another time. Today, the heat and her heels made the decision an easy one. She walked around the side of the house in the opposite direction of the multi-car garage. There was no chance of getting away unnoticed if she tried to drive herself. As with every other aspect of his household, her father insisted on doing things a certain way. He employed a system that he left others to oversee. Rule number one: Jade couldn't take a car without Anson Marlow's permission.

Jade used to tip Julio, her father's driver/mechanic, to let her sneak her car out. He was one of the staff sympathetic to her situation. She hated that they thought of her as that *poor little rich girl*. Still, she wasn't above using it to her advantage. That was before Stephen. Now, Julio was gone. His replacement couldn't be bribed. He was convinced Jade shouldn't be driving. Not with her fragile nerves. It was frustrating — humiliating. So, she stopped trying. If she left the house on her own, she called a cab.

The taxi service was on speed dial. She used them so often and tipped so well, she was guaranteed a ride within an hour — no matter where she was in the city. Here in Beverly Hills, the wait was never more than twenty minutes. Seeing her ride, Jade slipped into the back seat.

"Good afternoon, Miss Marlow."

"How are you, Troy?"

"Great. Business is booming. Where can I take you today?"

"Not far."

She gave him the address. Being so familiar with a cab driver might seem strange to most people. To Jade, it made perfect sense. Over the past six months, Troy had practically become her personal driver.

At first, when he kept turning up, Jade was suspicious. Was he a reporter using the taxi service as a cover? She was a hot story. Magazines, newspapers, television shows. They all wanted interviews.

The more the salacious the details, the better. The answer was no when it happened. It would remain no.

Jade hoped the interest would fade away. So far, no such luck. Reporters tried everything. They weren't permanent fixtures outside the house anymore. Her father put an end to that. He always had someone to call who owed him a favor. Still the offers persisted. As did the pop-up paparazzi.

She figured if Troy were going to write a story, it would have happened by now. Jade decided he was exactly what he seemed. A kind, middle-aged man who took her where she requested, asked no questions, and was satisfied with her very generous tips.

"I'm not sure how long I'll be."

The cab drove through the gates. Jade's name opened them without question. The mansion owned by Callie Flynn and Caleb Landis was legendary. Built in Hollywood's early days by a silent screen goddess, subsequent owners were legends in their own right. Now, the walls housed the town's reigning king and queen.

Jade took a deep breath. She couldn't get the thought out of her head that this meeting was more than a casual get-together. Why now? They lived in the same neighborhood all of Jade's life. Suddenly, Callie Flynn wanted to be friends?

"Give me a call when you're ready," Troy said. He turned, smiling. "I've had a thing for Callie Flynn since I saw her in *Moonglow*."

"You and every man with a pulse." Jade wondered what it was like to have that kind of instant appeal.

"She's even more beautiful now. I love a woman who isn't afraid to age gracefully." Troy gave the kind of sigh a man gave when he knew the object of his desire was way, way out of his league.

"If every woman aged as well as Callie Flynn," Jade laughed, "they wouldn't be afraid either."

Troy sighed again, pulling his gaze away from the door of the Landis home. He smiled at Jade. "Like I said, call me. I'll be around."

Jade watched the taxi drive away. Was she a coward to wish she were in the back seat, her visit over? With a shrug, she turned. *Don't be a baby*, she admonished herself. What was the worst that could happen? *You could blurt out that Garrett is your lover.* Now, isn't that what every mother wants to hear when she's serving afternoon tea?

Before she could ring the doorbell, Jade felt her phone vibrate. She turned off the ringer before leaving home. Unless there was some potential emergency looming, it seemed rude to get a phone call when visiting.

Jade opened her bag to glance at the lighted screen. *Her father.* She could imagine what he wanted. *Where are you?* He would demand. *Why did you leave when you knew I wanted to speak to you?*

She ignored the call. For most of Jade's life, Anson Marlow could have cared less where she was or whom she was with. Since her return from the hospital, he was like a child experiencing separation anxiety. All of it done under the watchful eyes of other people. Was there such a thing as clinginess by proxy?

Either way, Jade knew her father wasn't worried about *her*. His fear was her going rogue. What if she talked to the wrong people? He didn't want all the money he had spent on spin control to be wasted. Since Stephen's disappearance, Anson Marlow controlled what was said and who said it. The little bits of information that were leaked *never* contained a word he hadn't approved. According to the reports, Jade was recovering nicely. Her charitable activities, always important, were once again a priority in her life. Accompanying these little blurbs were flattering photographs. Jade always looked serene. Almost happy.

As far as the world was concerned, Jade Marlow was fully recovered. She was once more Anson Marlow's pampered, privileged daughter. Everything was back to normal. Only a select few knew the truth. In the Marlow home, normal was all kinds of fucked up. It always had been. Only now, thanks to Stephen Marsh, her father's complicity, and Jade's willingness to play the victim, another layer of shit had been added.

What her father didn't see or understand was that Jade was changing. She was getting stronger every day. Inch by inch, she was shoveling her way out. For the first time in her life, she knew what fresh air smelled like and no matter what, she was never going to fall in that putrid hole again.

Jade didn't just ignore the call; she turned the phone off. It might be petty, but she liked the idea of her father's frustration when she didn't pick up. He considered voice mail an insult to his position in life. Jade smiled. A small victory, yet a satisfying one.

The front door opened before Jade could ring the bell. Expecting a butler or maid, she was taken aback to come face to face with none other than Callie Flynn.

"Jade," the woman said as she reached for Jade's hand. "Come in."

Without a word, Jade let herself be pulled into the house. A few details registered. The marble floors, cathedral ceilings. Nothing new there. This *was* Beverly Hills. The color caught Jade's attention. Pops of cheery yellow, vibrant blue and vivid red accented the foyer in a way Jade had never seen before. Her eye was drawn to an abstract painting on one wall, a rug near another. In front of a large mirror, there were flowers in every color in the rainbow.

"I was so happy when you agreed to come over. I know it was last minute."

"I was surprised."

"Of course you were." Callie didn't stop, leading Jade past a long staircase, through what appeared to be a library, and then outside. "Why, we're practically neighbors and this is the first time you've been in my home. If I let myself, I would be ashamed."

The words struck Jade as slightly ridiculous, causing an uncontrollable laugh to escape past her lips. Horrified, Jade quickly apologized.

"I'm sorry," she said. "I wasn't laughing at you."

"I don't know why not," Callie told her with a gentle smile. "I tend to speak my mind. Sometimes that horrifies people; sometimes it amuses them. I much prefer the latter. You have a lovely laugh, Jade. Never be afraid to use it."

Jade was dazzled. Not by the beautiful garden. Or the green lawns that seemed to go on forever. No, Callie Flynn left Jade breathless. A true movie star in an era when that distinction was becoming rarer and rarer There was a glow that seemed to beam from beneath her skin. Callie wore little makeup; her dark hair was pulled into a messy bun. She wore a loose sundress the color of cornflowers and no shoes. She was the most beautiful woman Jade had ever seen.

"Sit."

Jade took the chair opposite Callie, setting her purse on the large, glass-top table.

"Would you like some lemonade?" Callie asked. "I know I invited you to afternoon tea, but it is such a lovely, warm day, I thought something cold would be nice. I also have iced tea, green in deference of my husband's recent health kick."

"Lemonade sounds wonderful."

Callie beamed at Jade's choice. "I never know when my sons might stop by. Lemonade is Garrett's favorite so I keep a pitcher handy."

Jade was grateful she didn't have a mouthful of liquid. The sudden mention of Garrett was such a surprise she was afraid she would have spewed it all over his mother.

"Are you expecting him, or any of them, this afternoon?"

"Don't worry," Callie said, patting Jade's hand. "My boys are sweethearts. No need to be nervous."

Jade sighed. She wasn't nervous, at least not for the reason Callie thought. The possibility of seeing Garrett here at his parents' home hadn't occurred to Jade. It would be awkward if he suddenly appeared. To say the least.

"These are the best lemon cookies ever made. Please, help yourself."

What was it about the Landis family that made them want to feed her? Jade couldn't help smiling at the thought.

"There you go," Callie said with obvious satisfaction when Jade chose not one but two cookies from the plate. "In less than ten minutes, we've shared a laugh, a beverage, and some food. We are well on our way to becoming good friends."

Jade froze for a moment, a cookie halfway to her mouth. Friends? Callie Flynn wanted to be friends? With her?

"Oh, dear," Callie smiled ruefully. "I'm making a hash out of this whole thing." She patted Jade's hand reassuringly. "I forget that you haven't been living in my brain, sharing my thoughts."

"That would be…" Jade searched for the word. One that wouldn't be too insulting. "Unsettling." It seemed like a good choice. *And* accurate.

"Believe me. No one wants to share my brain. Scattered would be putting it mildly."

When Callie's clear, silver gaze met hers, Jade almost gasped. Garrett's eyes. Why hadn't she seen it before? Those eyes were world famous. Even though she hadn't seen *his* in anything but the glow of the moon and the flicker of candlelight, the changeable color was unmistakable.

"Are you all right?" Callie asked with concern.

"I'm sorry," Jade said. "This was a bad idea. I'm not very good one on one. I do much better in crowds where I'm not expected to do anything but make small talk."

Except with Garrett. Jade groaned silently. *Stop thinking about him before you blurt out something highly inappropriate.*

"When you think about it, small talk is an art form. Finding the proper balance. Interested yet not too personal. I never mastered the knack of it."

"Because you have personality." Jade shook her head. "Small talk isn't an art form. It's boring. *I'm* boring."

"Oh, Jade…"

"No," Jade went on quickly. She hated the sympathy she heard in Callie's voice. It wasn't what she wanted. "How pathetic did that sound? I meant I *was* boring. When the most interesting thing to ever happen to you is, well, you know. How sad is that?"

The words hung between them. The most interesting thing to happen to Jade was something you didn't speak about with casual acquaintances. An abusive husband who tried to kill you was *not* afternoon tea conversation.

"It is sad," Callie said firmly. "It's a fact, Jade. Still, it doesn't make *you* sad. *Or* pathetic. It makes you a survivor."

"I am that," Jade agreed with a shrug. "Not that I had anything to do with it. Credit my doctors, not me."

"Yes," Callie nodded. "They saved the physical you. What about your spirit? Your soul? I don't see a quitter, Jade. Though no one would blame you if you had rolled up in a ball for a few months — or years."

"I wanted to," Jade admitted.

Those first few weeks after she was home from the hospital were some of the hardest of Jade's life. She was in pain. The nurse her father hired gave her pills every few hours. They were strong. Too strong. Instead of simply alleviating the pain, they knocked her out. She lost large blocks of time. It frightened her to wake up groggy, only to realize it was no longer Tuesday morning but instead, Wednesday afternoon. Soon, Jade started slipping the pills under her tongue instead of swallowing. When she was alone, she flushed them down the toilet. She could handle the pain if it meant keeping her senses about her.

"Good for you."

Callie's fist pump made Jade laugh. She hadn't planned on sharing any of that. The only other person who knew was Garrett. Another trait mother and son shared. The ability to draw things out of Jade without making her feel embarrassed or self-conscience.

"It was your first step, wasn't it?"

"What do you mean?" Jade asked with a confused frown.

"You decided to take your life back," Callie explained. "One step, Jade. That's all it takes. Since then, how many more have you taken?"

Jade didn't know how it happened. Before she knew it, she was telling Callie things — private things. Most of it Garrett knew. Now, so did his mother.

She started with why she married Stephen. Leaving out her brief encounter with Garrett, Jade explained how it made sense. Her father approved. No, that wasn't it. He pushed — hard — for the marriage. As always, it was easier to go along with what he wanted than put up any resistance.

As for Stephen, though she didn't know him very well. He seemed charming in a cool, detached sort of way. It wasn't until they were married that she found out the mask of civility was as thin and fragile as tissue paper.

Callie asked many of the same questions as Garrett. Did her father know about the abuse? Why didn't he stop it? The answers hadn't changed. How could he not know? As for stopping it? He believed if Jade were a better wife, the abuse would stop.

"Heartless bastard."

"Yes," Jade agreed. Heartless. It described her father perfectly.

Jade didn't linger on the abuse. She did that too often with her therapist. Callie didn't need those images in her head — no one did. That last day was too fuzzy for Jade to share *any* details. Her therapist didn't think she would ever remember it clearly. Thank God for small favors.

When Callie didn't ask why Jade would go back to her father's house after she got out of the hospital, Jade was surprised. She soon found out the other woman understood the situation without explanation.

"Where else would you go?" Callie reasoned. "You were in no condition to look for your own place. Even if you could, what then? No, you were smart to take advantage of your father's resources."

"Take advantage." Jade rolled the concept around in her brain. "I hadn't thought of it like that. I like it. *I'm* taking advantage of *him*."

Callie chuckled. She liked Jade. She was a strong young woman. Stronger than she knew.

"Something tells me that's about to change. When are you moving out?"

"There is no way you could have guessed that." Jade's eyes narrowed. "Are you psychic?"

"No." Callie refilled Jade's glass, a smile on her lips. "I don't believe in ESP, do you?"

"I didn't use to."

"Caleb calls it woman's intuition." Callie rolled her eyes. "I love him enough not to point out that is a dated, chauvinistic term used mostly by men. Like patting us on the head and saying good dog, aren't you clever."

"Ouch."

"I know it sounds extreme," Callie said unapologetically. "I'm not as militant in my women's liberation stance as I used to be. Even Gloria Steinem has mellowed a bit over the years."

"Do you know Gloria Steinem?"

Callie nodded. "We had dinner just last month. Next time she's in town I will be sure to introduce you." Callie hid her smile when Jade's eyes grew wide. "You are exactly the kind of young woman she admires. I agree, by the way."

"I don't know what to say."

How was she supposed to talk when her throat was tightening with emotion? For the first time, Jade knew what it must be like to have a mother to confide in. Damn it, she was *not* going to cry.

"If you need to cry, go right ahead," Callie told her. She gathered Jade into her arms. "In fact, I think I'll join you."

Jade might have held out on her own. However, the second she felt Callie's arms around her, she couldn't hold back the tears.

That was how Caleb Landis found his wife and her guest. Not sobbing. More like gently weeping.

"If I need to kick someone's ass, tell me now. I'll call my four strapping sons for back-up."

"No one's honor needs defending, my love."

Callie sent her husband a reassuring, if somewhat watery smile. She took a napkin, wiping Jade's cheeks before kissing each one. Oh, brother, Jade thought. That simple, sweet gesture almost started the water works going again. The only thing that stopped her was Caleb Landis. It would have been too embarrassing to break down for a second time with him sitting three feet away.

"I thought you were in meetings all day."

"I did. In case you haven't noticed, it's almost seven."

Seven? Jade looked at her watch. Where had the time gone? She was about to thank Callie for a wonderful afternoon when she found herself witness to an intimate moment that she probably should have turned away from, yet couldn't.

Callie didn't greet her husband with a kiss. Instead, she smiled. It was the most expressive smile Jade had ever seen. It radiated over her entire face, lighting it up.

"Your eyes are purple."

Jade was so amazed by the transformation; she didn't realize she had spoken aloud.

"Yes, they are."

Caleb's voice deepened as he said the words. She felt like an intruder. The moment between husband and wife was so intimate. Jade wanted to slide from her chair, leaving them alone.

"There aren't many men lucky enough to know by looking at her if his wife is still in love with him." Caleb lifted Callie's hand to his lips. "I dread the day those expressive eyes stop turning purple for me."

"I've loved you for almost forty years. God willing, we will have another forty or fifty."

"Wow!"

"Are we a little too corny for your taste?" Caleb asked, giving Jade a friendly wink. "Our sons say we should tone it down around guests."

"Jade is not a guest," Callie informed him. "She's a friend. Soon to be a very good one, if I'm not mistaken."

"That is good news. Friends, real ones, are hard to come by."

She would not cry again, Jade promised herself. God, what was wrong with her? At her lowest moments — during her marriage, after she returned from the hospital — she didn't cry as she had today. Finding a sympathetic friend was playing havoc with her normally rigid control.

It wasn't only Callie, Jade realized. It was the Landis family. Even Caleb, who should have intimidated her, instead made her feel welcome. And Garrett... A thought popped into Jade's head. She knew she shouldn't ask. *Don't go there,* some inner voice warned.

Jade didn't know if it was the company, the lemonade, or the cookies. Something made her ignore the warning

"Does Gar... I mean, did any of your sons inherit your eyes?"

"Poor Garrett," Callie laughed. "All through high school, his brothers gave him a hard time when he would date a girl. They would mention her name then gather around to see if his eyes turned purple. It became a game. He was young enough to be self-conscious. It didn't matter that he knew he wasn't in love; he would close his eyes so his brothers couldn't see. They would gang up on him, hold him down — force an eyelid open."

Caleb chuckled. "None of the boys cared one way or the other if Garrett was in love. They liked two things above all others. Giving each other hell and rough housing. Combine the two — they were in heaven."

"Was he..." *Damn it,* Jade chastised herself, *spit it out.* "Was he ever in love?"

"I don't think so," Callie said. "His eyes are very expressive, like mine. It is possible they won't ever turn purple, even when he falls in love."

"It will be interesting to find out." Caleb squeezed Callie's hand.

"The way he *and* his brothers are going, I'm beginning to doubt they possess the love gene. Though they have *liked* a lot of women."

"You might not look like anyone's mother, my love, but on occasion you sound like one."

"I have no idea what you're talking about," Callie huffed.

Jade was getting the idea this was not a new topic.

"The boys like to play the field," Caleb explained to Jade. "Is there anything wrong with that?"

Was he asking her? Hoping he didn't expect an answer, Jade took a sip of lemonade. Discussing the Landis brothers and their sex lives — especially Garrett's — seemed like a topic she should avoid at all costs.

"Now you've embarrassed Jade," Callie admonished her husband.

"No, honestly." Jade smiled at her hosts.

To be honest, embarrassed didn't begin to cover how she was feeling. This was new territory for Jade. Her lovers could be counted on one hand. The number of parents she met *while* that man was her lover? Counting Callie and Caleb? Two. It was fine until the subject veered too close to what she and Garrett did in a seedy motel room several times a week. How could she not think about it?

Time to go. Now. She was hours away from meeting Garrett. The last thing she wanted was thoughts of his parents running through her head at an inopportune moment. Talk about a mood killer.

"Speaking of Garrett," Caleb said.

Jade's hand froze as it reached for her purse. *Now, what?*

"He called just before I left my office. Seems there's been some problem with the second unit. He has to fly up to Vancouver right away. Should be in the air right now."

Jade's heart sank. She wouldn't be seeing Garrett tonight. He probably left a message on her phone. As silly as it was, Jade couldn't wait to hear it. If she couldn't be with him, his voice would have to do.

"I should be going."

"Of course. It is getting late." Callie smiled. "Unless you would like to stay for dinner?"

"Oh, I don't know." Jade almost said yes without thinking. She loved being here. Only a few hours and the Landis house felt more like home than hers ever had. Still, she didn't want to overstay her welcome.

"In case you think Callie is only being polite, don't worry," Caleb said, a twinkle in his eye. "If she didn't want you to stay, she wouldn't ask. Isn't that right, my love?"

"Too true," Callie sighed. "I have no filter when it comes to such things. When I was a struggling actress trying to impress the movie world, I bit my tongue so many times I'm surprised I didn't bite it off. Now that I've become…" she turned to her husband. "What did that article call me?"

"A legendary icon."

Callie rolled her eyes. "God! Can you believe that? It's flattering, but honestly. I'm not *that* old." She sighed. "Never mind. The point is I no longer have to suffer the company of idiots. So, please, stay for dinner. I think Lorena made a pot of corn chowder."

"And her sourdough rolls?" Caleb asked hopefully.

"And cherry pie for dessert."

"This is why I have a personal trainer," Caleb said to Jade. "And a pimped out workout facility in the basement. And two swimming pools.

When a man is married to a *legendary icon*," he patted his flat stomach, "he can't afford to get fat."

"Careful, or I will put my legendary foot up your nicely toned ass." Callie gave him a playful shove. "Go tell Lorena we have one more for dinner."

Jade watched the two with wonder. What was it like to love someone that much for so long?

"If you aren't careful, you won't be able to get rid of me."

As she had when Jade arrived, Callie took her hand, leading her into the house. This time she put an arm around Jade's shoulder.

"From now on, consider our doors open. I will be insulted if you wait for a formal invitation to stop by. Anytime, Jade. Call if you want to talk, stop by for no reason. I'm here for you."

Jade wanted to return the easy affection Callie showed. An arm around the other woman's waist, her head on her shoulder. That kind of thing didn't come casually to Jade. Maybe. In the future. She felt a warm feeling radiate through her body when she thought about that. There would be time to let her guard down with Callie just as she had with Garrett.

Garrett. Wondering if there was a message on her phone would prey on her through dinner if she didn't check.

"May I use the bathroom?"

"Of course." Callie showed her a room just off the foyer. "There is nothing for show, I hate that. Use any of the towels and soap."

One more reason to love Callie. There wasn't a common bathroom in her home that didn't have little soaps or monogrammed hand towels. Why put something out if it couldn't be used?

After shutting the door, Jade quickly made use of the facilities. She carefully washed her hands before eagerly reaching for the phone.

Fifteen messages. Most were from her father. No surprise there. Melinda Hurst. Jade wondered how the awful woman got her phone number. Then instantly answered her own question. Melinda and Anson Marlow were close. Whether he encouraged Melinda or the other woman who wanted another chance to sharpen her claws on Jade, it didn't matter. *Let's do lunch?* Jade deleted the message. *Not in this lifetime.*

Finally, almost at the end of the list was Garrett's name. Not a text. As she hoped, he left a recorded message. Smiling, Jade hit play.

Something has come up in Canada. I won't be able to make it tonight. I don't know when I'll be back in Los Angeles. This could take a day or it could take two weeks. I've gotten hooked on the way you taste, honey. Hey, that's it. You taste like honey." Garrett's voice lowered making Jade's breath catch. "*Spicy Jade honey. I could make a fortune selling it. I'm afraid I'll have withdrawals. Luckily, I've thought of a solution. Phone sex. Midnight. Clothing optional. Text me if you can come. And yes, I meant to make a dirty pun.*"

In her haste, Jade almost dropped her phone. She left him a one-word message. Nothing else was necessary. With a smile, Jade texted *YES!*

Chapter Nine

MIDNIGHT COULDN'T ARRIVE soon enough. Finding ways to pass the time wasn't difficult. She found some of it enjoyable. Some of it not so much.

Jade somehow put thoughts of phone sex with their son out of her head while she shared a delicious meal with Callie and Caleb. As she discovered with Garrett, good company and interesting conversation made it easier for her to eat. She no longer dreaded having food set in front of her. Before, her taste buds seemed dead. Now, she reveled in the flavors of the creamy chowder laced with bacon and onion. The warm sourdough rolls, smeared with butter, melted in her mouth. And the cherry pie? She enjoyed it almost as much as chocolate pudding.

Pleased by how Jade relished the meal, Callie insisted they make it a regular thing. Once a week. They had uncertain schedules so the actual night was left fluid. Jade left with a warm feeling she attributed to good food and better company. She had few real friends. Knowing she could add Callie to the list made her feel like she could have floated home, a full stomach and all.

When the cab dropped her at the usual corner, Jade didn't hurry back to the house. She strolled, taking in the evening air that was laced with honeysuckle and roses. She couldn't remember a time when she felt so relaxed. Unburdened. That was the word. Sharing everything with Callie was another step. A big one.

Jade's therapist listened, was sympathetic. Still, she was paid to do so. Then there was Garrett. Telling him had been hard. Brutally so. He didn't turn away. Now, he was her lover. Her *secret* lover. Hidden from the world and shrouded in the shadows of her making. Until she could be with him in the light, there was a very good chance it would end. Soon.

Jade put that thought aside. She had him for now. Tonight. With a smile, she wrapped her arms around herself. *Phone sex.* That would be something new.

She turned to the entrance of her house, pushing the security pad keys to disengage the lock. The camera followed her movements. When she snuck out to meet Garrett, Jade followed a carefully mapped out path that kept her out of camera range. She was proud of that. Her father was certain his system had no flaws. Maybe someday she would tell him the truth. The look on his face would be worth the inevitable icy dress down.

Tonight, Jade wasn't hiding. Instead of keeping her head down, she looked up, smiled, and then waved. That should confuse whoever had the tedious job of reviewing the footage. Jade glanced at the camera. She never smiled. She never waved. *What the hell was going on?*

Jade wasn't surprised when the front door opened before she reached it. She had left hours ago without explanation. It was after nine. Staying out past dark was another thing Jade never did. Neither the staff nor her father was used to Jade stepping away from a seemingly set in stone routine.

Stepping through the door, Jade gave the nervous-looking maid a serene smile. Let them all wonder what was going on. Before they became used to the *new* her, she planned on being gone.

"Good evening, Miss Marlow. Your father—"

"Let me guess. My father wants to see me." Jade didn't pause. She turned towards the office, her footsteps steady. "He spends so much time worrying where I am, you have to wonder how he manages to run a multi-million dollar empire."

Jade didn't bother to knock. Something else new. Walking in without an invitation was a big no-no. *Too much, too soon?* Jade wondered. Her evening with Callie and Caleb emboldened her. The look her father gave her made her wonder if it was a false bravado that would crumble with his first words of disapproval. She was about to find out.

"Where have you been?"

"I had dinner with friends."

Friends. It felt good to say. It felt even better knowing it was true.

"Lying serves no purpose," he sighed. "I called your acquaintances. Neither of them knew where you were."

Anson Marlow was good. Jade would give him that. In two brief sentences, he called her a liar. And reminded her that she had no real friends. *Acquaintances.* Numbering two. She waited for her heart to start beating faster. The guilt. The shame. The feelings of inadequacy. She waited. And waited. Nothing. Oh, maybe a twinge. You couldn't get rid of a lifetime of triggers overnight. It was happening, though. New Jade.

"Are you amused by this?"

Her father didn't sound angry. He sounded incredulous. Jade was supposed to cower, not smile. By now, she should have confessed all. Her apologies should be pouring out. Apologies he would take as his due but never verbally accept. One more piece of the pattern. It was ugly, passive aggressive shit. Time for a new game. One where only she knew the rules.

"I have no sense of humor, Father."

Jade said it with such matter-of-factness, she could see her father struggling to decide if she were serious or being sarcastic.

"You left this afternoon without leaving word where you could be reached."

"There was nothing planned for this evening. I wasn't needed, so I took some time for myself."

Jade could see her father's frustration mounting. She was evasive without any outright disrespect. How was he supposed to handle that?

"I needed your input on the banquet."

"Which banquet?"

"Parker Shipping."

"The one we're hosting in September?" *Two months from now?*

"Yes."

"I see."

Jade saw all right. Anson Marlow felt his control over his daughter slipping. It was slight. Little things here and there. Nothing he was sure couldn't be fixed. He thought he could pull in the slack by reminding her of her *duties*. Her job was to be his hostess. If he had questions about an event, she was expected to be there to answer them. The fact that the event was months away didn't matter. The banquet was already planned to the last detail. Details they went over together and documented in a folder on his computer.

Jade didn't remind her father of these facts. Instead, she remained silent, waiting for him to speak first. It was one of her father's most effective tools. His icy stare always broke his opponents. Within minutes, he had them babbling confessions, secrets. She knew how it worked. This time, she turned it on him.

Anson waited. And waited. Jade could tell the moment he realized she wasn't going to crack. The shift in their relationship was on an irreversible slide. He no longer held all the power because somewhere along the way, Jade stopped caring. He wanted to control everything and everyone around him. All she wanted was control of her own life — away from here.

Jade turned to leave. She was reaching for the doorknob when Anson broke the silence.

"We can talk about the banquet another time."

"Good night, Father."

Quietly, Jade shut the door behind her. Serenely, she nodded to the maid who must have been hovering in the foyer the entire time. Jade walked to the stairs, calmly climbing. She took one step at a time. The maid saw a composed, young woman, back straight, head held high.

That was on the surface. On the inside, Jade was dancing like a maniac. Happy dance be damned. This was an ecstatic dance.

Her father spoke first. That might not mean much to an outsider, but in a lifetime of one-sided confrontations, it was like beating the National Champions forty-five to nothing. On their home field.

Jade entered her bedroom. She leaned back against the door, a smile on her face, her heart racing. For the first time since she had moved back in here, she took a good look. Pink curtains. Pepto-Bismol pink. Jade winced. White ruffles on the bed skirt, a lacy canopy that until now she barely noticed. Even as a girl the colors hadn't appealed to her. If she were staying, the entire room would have to be done over.

Picking up one of the porcelain dolls that lined the shelf by the window, Jade thought about the years she had wasted in this room. Most of her toys were not for playing with. They were expensive. Look, don't touch. Well, not anymore. In the morning, she would box up the whole lot. She would call Callie. She was bound to know the right charity to donate them. Little girls needed dolls to hold. This lot would do nicely.

Happy, Jade fell back onto her bed. The clock read eleven-fifteen. Deliberately, she set her phone on the end table before heading for the bathroom. She wouldn't be *seeing* Garrett tonight. However, that didn't mean she wasn't going to primp. She needed confidence to be sexy. Or talk dirty. Lord, she had never done that before. Not to any extent.

Grabbing her laptop, Jade googled dirty talk. *Holy crap*! Did people really say those things aloud? To another person? Could she? After filing away twenty-seven words for cock, Jade closed the computer with a snap. She knew how Garrett made her feel. She would follow his lead. He was very good at verbalizing what he was doing, how he was doing it, and what he planned to do.

With a shiver of anticipation, Jade glanced at the clock again. This was going to be the longest thirty minutes of her life.

"WHY DO YOU keep looking at your watch? Is there someplace you need to be?"

Garrett didn't answer Hamish. In twenty minutes, he planned on being in his trailer. Phone to ear, hand to dick. Come hell or high water, he wasn't going to be late.

Since his arrival in Vancouver, he had shuttled from one meeting to another, putting out minor fires a boy scout could have handled. He was tired, annoyed, and bordering on pissed. He was missing hot sex with Jade for this?

"Tell me again why I'm here. These guys are being paid to build us a set. Nothing elaborate. When I was seventeen, I spent one hellish summer in Egypt putting up a fake pyramid — five miles from a real one. They can't manage a simple barn?"

"Tell me how things were in the good old days, Grandpa," Hamish laughed at Garrett.

"Mock if you will. The guy I worked under was a slave-driving son of a bitch, but we got the job done ahead of schedule. Without any workman's comp claims either."

"That Clayton guy banged his thumb with a goddamned hammer," Hamish scoffed. "I've done worse hanging a picture for my mother."

"Things like that become life threatening when you have a big company with plenty of insurance footing the bill. Pay him now before some lawyer convinces him that an owie is actually one step away from gangrene."

"Taken care of. He signed a waiver this afternoon." Hamish said. "And before you ask, yes, I made sure it was the one Wyatt drafted. We destroyed all the others."

"Then I repeat. Why am I here?"

"First, Anders, Clayton's boss, is raising hell about not enough men on the job. Union rules, or some such shit."

"Don't shit on the unions, my friend. They still hold a lot of power."

It was dark on the set. Still, the lights gave him a good idea of how much progress had been made. It wasn't an encouraging sight.

"Anders claims they need ten more men to meet union requirements."

"How many does he have now?"

"Twenty, without Clayton."

"Who hired this fucking asshole?" Garrett demanded. "For this size job, fifteen is standard. He's either too stupid to read the guidelines, or he thinks *we* are. Let me guess he has a cousin who needs a job."

"Three. And a brother. We need to fire the idiot, Garrett."

"Give me a minute." Garrett pulled out his phone. "Wyatt insisted I needed to be here. He might as well share in the fun."

Big brother picked up on the third ring.

"If you aren't dying, I don't want to know."

Garrett gave Hamish a surprised look. Wyatt didn't have a regular sleep pattern. He caught an hour here, a few hours there. He never had problems with after-hours calls.

"Unless you're with a woman, you can kiss my ass."

When his brother didn't immediately respond, Garrett let out a silent whistle. Wyatt and a woman. One he cared enough about not to want to be interrupted.

"Who is she?"

"What's the problem, Garrett?"

Interesting. Wyatt sounded like he was talking through gritted teeth.

"So it's okay for you to ask about my love life, but I can't reciprocate?"

"As I recall, you denied everything. I'm following your lead." Wyatt gave a deep sigh. "It's close to midnight, Garrett. Are you in jail?"

"Nope?"

"The hospital?"

"No blood in sight."

"Then why couldn't this wait until morning?"

"If I had any idea you were occupied, it could have," Garrett assured his brother. "Tell you what. Get back to whomever you're doing. Seven too soon?"

There was another pause.

"Make it eight."

Grinning, Garrett put his phone back in his pocket. Wyatt and a woman. Since Stephanie's death, his brother's love life consisted of one-night stands. Even then, they were few and far between. If Wyatt wasn't at work by seven, it was news.

"Wyatt's seeing someone?"

"That would be my interpretation," Garrett nodded.

"Tight-lipped, irritable. Has to be a woman."

"Hmm," Garrett responded.

Who was he to argue? Half the time Jade kept him in knots, the other half happy as a clam. Hamish, on the other hand, appeared to still be in the honeymoon phase of his fling. No bumps so far. Lynn Cornish was playing the good girl, on *and* off screen. Garrett still predicted a disastrous ending for his friend. To make them all happy, he kept his thoughts to himself and hoped for the best.

"What do we do?" Hamish asked as they walked toward their trailers.

"Woman or not, Wyatt was right. There is nothing to be done until morning. Let's get some sleep."

"Lynn is off tomorrow. I don't plan on sleeping."

"Jesus," Garrett groaned. "Spare me, all right? Go. Enjoy. Just keep it to yourself."

"Will do, boss. With relish."

Garrett chuckled. His friend was getting some. In all likelihood, his brother was similarly occupied. He glanced at his watch. Eleven fifty-eight. In less than two minutes, he planned on heating up the airwaves. When had sex become so complicated?

That was easy. It became complicated when the person he had it with started to matter.

As he crossed the cramped trailer, Garrett kicked off his boots, tore off his t-shirt, and unsnapped his jeans in one continuous motion. He was bare-assed, on the bed, and dialing the phone just as the illuminated clock hit midnight.

"Garrett."

Jade answered after the first ring. She didn't care if she seemed over-eager. For the last ten minutes, she worried he wouldn't call. When she heard the first notes of *Undercover Lover*, relief washed over her. Why wait? She wanted to hear his voice. Even if she knew how, it was not the time to play coy.

"Thank God," Garrett groaned. "You're as anxious as I am, aren't you, honey?"

"I've thought about this since I got your message." She paused, wondering how much she should confess.

"You looked up dirty talk, didn't you?"

"How did you know?"

Garrett relaxed against his pillow. He knew because every day he was getting to know her better. She was a little nervous, so she tried to prepare. He would bet her research didn't last long.

"There's some pretty graphic stuff out there."

"Graphic doesn't begin to describe it. I don't know if I can say some of those things."

"I don't want you to." Garrett turned on the light by his bed. "It wouldn't be you if you used somebody else's words. Jade."

"Yes?"

Garrett took a deep breath. He knew he was about to take a big chance. Still, he felt it was time.

"Do you have Skype on your phone?"

"Garrett…"

"I want to see your face, honey. Turn on your light. Let me see."

Garrett didn't know what to expect. He figured the fact that they were still connected was a good sign.

"I texted you my information. Call me back."

Fingers flying, Garrett made the connection in record time. This time when Jade answered, he saw her beautiful face.

"There you are."

"Are you naked?" Jade asked hoping he would use his phone to let her know. The darkened motel room worked both ways. She longed for memories that weren't draped in shadows.

"Want to see?"

"Yes, please."

With a wink, Garrett slowly started panning down his body. He was a director; he knew the effect of the slow reveal.

"Like it?"

Jade nodded. "You have a beautiful body."

"My ego thanks you," Garrett teased. "Tell me what you like. Give me details."

"I like—" Jade cleared away the crack in her voice. "I like that you have some hair on your chest. Not too much. I remember how it feels against my breasts. My nipples are hard thinking about it."

"Show me," Garrett rasped.

Moving the phone so he could see the screen, Garrett waited silently. His breath quickened when he saw the swell of her breasts over the top of a wispy scrap of lavender lace."

"What are you wearing?"

"A teddy. I bought it for myself when I turned eighteen." Jade moved the lace cup, exposing the hard, dark pink nub. "I've never had the nerve to wear it. Until tonight."

"Thank you," Garrett whispered with a touch of reverence. "Now, touch yourself. If I were there, what would you like me to do?"

This was all new to Jade. Yes, she touched herself. When she was alone. If the lights were out. Even then, she didn't linger. Her hand would slip between her legs, taking care of business. It was nice. A stress reliever. It never occurred to her to start with her breasts. Now Garrett was asking her to do just that — while he watched.

"Jade, honey. I'm waiting."

"I wasn't prepared for this."

All her feelings of inadequacy knocked on the door, trying to crawl back in her head. She knew how destructive they could be so she did her best to keep them at bay. Taking a deep breath, Jade shut out the voices, focusing on one — Garrett.

"This is easy, honey. Everything about you turns me on. I wish I were there. I want to be the one giving you pleasure. Think of my hand touching you. There you go."

Jade pictured Garrett. What color were his eyes? A stormy gray?

Clear silver? His voice urged her on. Knowing he liked what he saw emboldened her. She cupped her breast.

"How does it feel?" Garrett asked.

"Soft. Smooth."

"Mmm, I remember. Run your thumb over your nipple," he urged. "That's right. Do you like that?"

"I like the way your voice makes me feel. I like knowing I excite you."

"Oh, Jade. You have no idea. Look at your phone."

Tilting the screen, Jade gasped. Garrett had his cock in his hand. The long, hard length seemed to reach out for her. Unconsciously, Jade licked her lips, her head moving up and down to the rhythm of Garrett's strokes.

"This is for you, Jade," Garrett informed her. "*You* make me hard. The thought of you. That's all it takes. All day I tried to keep myself from picturing you as you are right now. I can't go around with a permanent hard-on. What would people say?"

"Too much Viagra?" Jade teased even as her mouth watered.

"Not a rumor I want floating out there," Garrett chuckled huskily. "That drug-induced five-hour erection can kill a man's reputation. Hell, they can literally kill a man. You're my drug of choice, Jade. No little blue pills needed."

Realizing she was holding her breath, Jade slowly exhaled. Her breathing was shallow, the flush in her cheeks moving down her body.

"Your face is beautiful. I can see the arousal in your eyes," Garrett told her. "The way your lips are parted. I love how your tongue keeps wetting them. Are they dry?"

Jade nodded.

"Words, honey. Tell what you're feeling."

"My throat is dry. My lips, too."

"And the rest of you?"

Jade closed her eyes. She knew what Garrett was asking. Slowly, her lids opened expecting to see his rock hard cock. Instead, she was looking into eyes the color of burnished steel.

"Are you wet, Jade?"

"Yes," Jade sighed.

"Show me."

Careful to avoid her scars, Jade turned the phone toward the ceiling until she was certain it wouldn't catch a glimpse of her stomach. Just to be sure, she pulled across, leaving her upper and lower body bare.

"I see a pair of gorgeous legs," Garrett said. "Show me what's between them."

Jade swallowed. The embarrassment that had slowly faded tried one last push. *This isn't who you are*, it taunted her. *Pull up the covers; turn off the phone. Go to sleep in your cold, little girl bed. You don't belong with a man like Garrett. He is out of your league.*

"I can do this," Jade firmly informed the voice in her head. "I *want* to do this."

"I know that, honey," Garrett said. "I wouldn't push you if I didn't think it was what you wanted."

"It is." Jade declared firmly.

Slowly, Jade opened her legs. It was slightly awkward. She wanted to angle the phone so that Garrett could see her while she was still able to see him. Suddenly it hit her. She grabbed the spare pillow, arranging it under her knees then propped the phone, hoping to give them both a good angle. She smiled with satisfaction. Garrett's face, clear as a bell.

"Can you see me?"

"I love that the hair is red down here, too."

"Garrett."

"*That* embarrasses you? You should be shouting it from the trees. Redheads are timeless. The fact that you are all natural, honey, makes you the envy of millions. What am I saying? I'm the one who is envied. There isn't a heterosexual man alive that wouldn't bow down in awe if they could trade places with me right now."

"Now you're being silly."

"That is the last thing I am," Garrett assured her. "Silly men do not have raging hard-ons. See?"

"Is it painful?" Jade asked. To her, it was a thing of beauty.

"Mmm, in a good way. I know I'll get my reward."

"Which is?" Jade knew. She wanted to hear him say it.

"I get off while watching you get off. Win-win, honey." Garrett's hand moved firmly up and down his shaft. "Your turn,"

Nervousness turned into anticipation. Jade moved her hand until her fingers hovered between her legs. She remembered how Garrett liked to tease her. He played around the edges before giving her what she wanted. Knowing he was watching, Jade did the same.

"How does it feel?"

"Wet," Jade answered breathlessly. "Hot. Slick. See how easily my fingers slide in? Three at a time, no problem."

"Your fingers are smaller than mine. You're tight, honey. I never use more than two."

"I like the calluses on your fingers," Jade said. "My hands are smoother."

"I know. Like silk running up and down my cock."

"You like the way I touch you?" Jade asked. God, she loved touching him.

"Heaven on Earth."

Without removing her fingers, Jade let her thumb run over her clit. She gasped at how sensitive it was. When she was alone, it felt good. With Garrett, it was out of this world.

"You confessed to thinking of me when you touched yourself," Garrett said, his hand never missing a beat. "How often? What was your fantasy?"

Jade was transfixed. Every time Garrett stroked himself, his erection seemed to get bigger — harder.

"I would get into bed."

"Naked?"

"No," Jade corrected him. "I never worried about what I was wearing. You would remove it as soon as you joined me."

"I like that," Garrett whispered. "Go on."

"I close my eyes. The lights are out yet the moon is so bright the room is illuminated. I know you're near. You circle the bed. I hear your breathing. Inside my head, I'm begging you to pull back the covers. I need your touch. It feels like you're teasing me."

"Anticipation," Garrett murmured. "You like a slow build."

"I want it to last," she admitted.

"It's a safe bet I eventually join you in that bed."

"Oh, yes."

Jade removed her fingers long enough to show Garrett how wet she was. The sound of his swift intake of breath, the way his hand slowed, almost stuttering to a stop on his cock, gave a boost to her ego *and* her confidence.

"We both pretend I'm asleep. You're careful to ease the covers back. I'm peeking, so I see the smile on your face. You're amused at my flannel nightgown."

"Amusing, but not much protection," Garrett warned.

"Depends on what I'm wearing underneath."

"A chastity belt? Though I warn you, I'm excellent at picking locks."

Jade felt a rise in her pulse. A familiar tingle spread through her body. Not yet. She eased back, delaying her orgasm until Garrett was with her.

"You're allowed more than one, honey," Garrett said.

How did he know? What gave her away?

"You see too much," Jade sighed.

"We're lovers. I'm supposed to know your body — anticipate your needs. Let yourself come, Jade. I'll help you get there again."

"We should... you know, together."

Hearing Garrett's chuckle, Jade smiled. He was right. She had a camera pointed at her vagina and she couldn't say the word come?

"Fine," she laughed. "I want to *come* with you."

"Tell me when you're ready," Garrett's voice dropped an octave. "I'm with you."

Jade kept her eyes on Garrett's hand. Faster now, not as measured. Her breath caught in her throat. That was for her. His passion, his arousal. It was about her. The thought sent her flying.

"Now," she cried. "I can't stop it, Garrett."

"Put the camera on your face, Jade," Garrett commanded. His face came on her screen. "Show me what you're feeling."

Jade hoped she aimed the phone in the right direction. When the orgasm hit her full blast, all she could think about was the wave after wave of pleasure radiating through her body. She knew Garrett was there — with her. His shout added another layer of satisfaction as she slowly floated back to Earth.

Jade's breathing slowed. Her heartbeat steadied. Her eyes met Garrett's. No longer steely gray, they were a clear, bright silver. Was that his happy color? The smile on his face said yes.

"I wish I could hold you."

Jade took a deep breath. When he said things like that, she found herself balancing on a slippery slope. Her heart was in the balance. For both their sakes, she couldn't let herself fall.

"Do you know how long you'll be gone?"

Garrett shook his head. "There are some labor problems that need straightening out."

"Ah," Jade said, understanding dawning. "Unions."

"You sound like you've had some experience with them."

"It's difficult." Jade smoothed out the sheet covering her stomach before settling back on her pillow. "In theory, I'm all for unions. They have a history of making life much batter for their members. Still…"

"When you have to deal with them they can be a pain in the ass," Garrett finished for her.

"So says the union member."

"No," Garrett corrected. "Technically, the Director's Guild is not a union. I had to join one when I worked on sets as a jack-of-all-trades. Back then, I belonged to half a dozen of them. Everybody has their own. If I wanted to learn, I had to pay my dues — literally."

"And now?" Jade asked, fascinated. Everything Garrett did while becoming the man he was, seemed thrilling. An adventure. Compared to her formative years, it was.

"I let them all lapse. I wanted to give the orders, not take them."

"You answer to no one but yourself."

Jade said the words, savoring their meaning. To be in control of her life. To make her own decisions. That was her goal. It was so close to being a reality, she could practically taste it.

"When I'm on the set, my word is law." Garrett chuckled ruefully. "The rest of the time, Wyatt thinks he's in charge. I suppose as producer, he is."

"Does that bother you? Answering to your older brother?"

"Better him than someone else."

She watched Garrett slide down the bed, relaxed. Naked. Jade sighed. Modern technology was wonderful. However, it would never replace having a big, solid, gorgeous man within touching distance.

"Do you always work with Wyatt?"

"I've been lucky. Wyatt and my father have produced all but one of my pictures. These days Dad doesn't have much to do with the big budget movies. He prefers what he calls his *vanity projects*. Last year, he co-produced *Wishes* with Sam Laughton."

"I loved that movie." Jade's eyes sparkled with enthusiasm. "The book is one of my all-time favorites. Some *vanity project*. How many Oscars did it win?"

"Seven. Including best picture. That was Dad's third Academy Award."

"Mmm. I have every song from the soundtrack on my phone, iPod, and computer. All I need to hear are first few notes of *Unconditional* to make me a weepy mess."

"I know the composer."

"You know Rose O'Brian? I was thrilled when she won the Oscar for best song. And best score."

"Finally," Garrett laughed. "The lady is impressive. Rose and her husband, Jack Winston are old friends."

It was the perfect opening for Garrett to tell Jade about the investigation he had set in motion. He knew she should know. He *planned* to tell her. Just not tonight. Why put something in her head she couldn't control? When Jack called with some news, *that* would be soon enough for her to know.

"I loved *Grind.*"

Jade listened to the down and dirty song so many times; she sometimes thought the images evoked by the lyrics were tattooed on her brain. Rose O'Brian vividly brought a fantasy world to life with raunchy lyrics set to a pulse-pounding beat. Jade often wondered if anyone really did those things. There was one in particular.

"Tell me your favorite part of the song," Garrett said. His smile held a naughty promise. "Then when I'm back in Los Angeles—"

"Second verse, third line."

Jade groaned silently. She should have taken the time to think about her answer. Instead, she came across as a sex-starved fan girl. She waited for him to tease her. Or worse, laugh at her. She should have known better. He wasn't anyone else. This was Garrett.

Garrett put his free hand behind his head, closing his eyes. "Play it for me."

He didn't speak until the song was over — the final note faded.

"It's been awhile. I'd forgotten how that plea the singer makes to her lover cuts through all the crap. She doesn't want it sweet. The hell with foreplay. All she wants is a hot fuck."

Garrett shifted, rolling his shoulders. When his eyes opened, Jade sucked in a deep breath. The color was the palest smoke. Silvery. Electric. He drew Jade in without a word. The way he looked at her mouth go dry.

"I want a hot fuck."

"I think my corruption of you is almost complete," Garrett declared.

His obvious enjoyment, when she used the unfamiliar word, made Jade feel exactly like a student praised by a respected teacher.

"What else is there?"

"Jade, honey, we haven't scratched the surface." Garrett looked at her, the teasing gone from his voice. "We can go so much deeper. Time is our friend. Soon, there won't be anything that is taboo. All you have to do is ask."

It was a two-way street, Jade realized. She couldn't imagine denying him — no matter what he wanted. That was when it hit her. There was something he wasn't going to ask. Something too personal. Too intimate. She knew in that instant it was what she had to do. For him. For herself.

"Watch."

Steadying her shaking hand, Jade took a deep breath. She knew if Garrett were in the room, she wouldn't have the nerve to do this. No matter how much she trusted him, the fear of rejection kept their lovemaking in the dark. It kept *her* in the dark. The only way to move out of the shadows was to show Garrett everything. Whatever his reaction. It was time to start living in the light.

Leaning over, Jade flipped the switch on the wall. She squinted against the sudden brightness. If she was going to do this, she was going all the way. Pointing the phone toward her stomach, she grabbed the end of the sheet. This wasn't going to be a slow reveal. She wasn't trying to be provocative. She treated it like she would a Band-Aid. She didn't ease the sheet off. No. With one more deep breath, Jade closed her eyes, ripping the cloth from her body.

Jade waited. She didn't look at her scars. There was no need. They were something she lived with every day of her life. An ugly reminder when all she wanted to do was forget.

The larger scars were still puckered, their color an angry red. The crisscross of the others showed the man wielding the knife didn't care what it looked like. His purpose had been to inflict as much pain and damage as possible. In that, he succeeded.

Luck kept her alive. For which Jade was eternally grateful. The scars would fade. The plastic surgeon at the hospital seemed to think he could practically erase them. If she waited a few more months, Garrett would never have to see the marks that marred her once perfect skin. So why not wait? Because she wanted him to understand. If the scars were to disappear tomorrow, she would always carry them around. They ran deep. To some extent, they always would.

"I'm going to hunt that fucker down and skin him alive."

Jade blinked. That was not the response she expected. It surprised her. Almost as much as her response to his words. Skin Stephen alive? Hell, yes! Then, as quickly as she thought it, she knew it wasn't what she wanted.

"What good would that do? He would be dead and you would be in prison. I don't like the sound of that."

"I suppose you're right," Garrett conceded with a sigh. "I'll settle for a slow castration."

"Jesus. Have you always been this bloodthirsty?" Jade asked. She didn't add that the castration part sounded damn good to her. She didn't want to encourage anything that might get him in trouble. Stephen wasn't worth it.

"That bastard seems to bring it out of me."

When the seconds ticked by without another word from Garrett, Jade started to turn the phone away.

"Wait," he said, stopping her. "Do something for me?"

"What?" Jade couldn't imagine what he would ask.

"Hold the phone steady."

"Okay."

"Now, put your free hand in front of the camera."

Puzzled, Jade did what he asked.

"If I were there, I would trace every line with kisses. I would show you how much I want you. All of you. However, I can't do that. Not yet. So I want you to do it for me. Put your finger on one of the scars."

Glad he couldn't see the tears welling up in her eyes, Jade followed Garrett's instructions.

"Do you feel the touch?"

"Yes," Jade whispered.

"Close your eyes. Imagine it's me. Can you do that for me, Jade?"

"Yes."

In her mind, Jade felt Garrett's gentle caress. And the tears fell.

"Soon, Jade. No more crappy motel. No more hiding."

Could it be that easy, Jade wondered. Could they step into the light together? Tonight, she believed anything was possible.

Chapter Ten

JADE SPENT THE morning with a spring in her step. Instead of trying to remember the last time that happened, she let herself enjoy it.

Nothing around her had changed since yesterday. The staff watched her every move. Someone was always dusting, vacuuming, or rearranging in her vicinity. Jade wasn't certain what they were supposed to do if she had a nervous breakdown. Calling for outside help had to be number one on the *Absolutely Not* list. If at all possible, handle it internally.

The image of two men, straightjacket handy, sequestered in a secret room, popped into Jade's mind. What a boring job that would be. And pointless. Jade's sanity was firmly in place. If the men existed, she hoped they were served lunch.

Smiling at her silly thoughts, Jade felt a sudden chill race down her spine. The phantom asylum attendants might not be real. However the threat was. Her father knew people. Getting her committed for *observation* wouldn't be difficult. A few greased palms, a little quid pro quo. Before she knew it, Jade could find herself locked away in a rubber room all her own.

Jade shook off the somber thoughts. The first thing she needed to do was make sure she would be missed. Not that long ago, her disappearance wouldn't have caused a flutter. She could almost hear the conversation

Jade's gone? How long?

A year.

That long? Well, what do you know?

It wouldn't be as easy now. Jade had *people*. Regular friends raised questions when someone they cared about went missing. Important, influential friends insisted on answers. The Landis family carried weight, not only in Los Angeles. They were known all over the world. Jade knew half of them were in her corner. No questions asked. If Garrett's brothers jumped in, there would be an ear-splitting din no one could ignore.

Feeling bouncy again, Jade glided down the front stairs to the foyer as she did every morning. The outside looked the same. Calm. Collected. So different from the woman she showed to Garrett last night. They didn't say goodbye until dawn. They talked about everything and nothing. From the important to the silly. In between, they guided each other through two more orgasms. Phone sex could never replace the real thing. Still, in a pinch, with the right man, Jade would take it.

She wanted breakfast. Pancakes sounded good. Jade laughed. That ought to raise a few eyebrows. She never ate this early. And certainly nothing that heavy. It was bound to get back to her father. Turning toward the kitchen, she shrugged off the thought. Let them scurry around like the rats they were, reporting how Miss Marlow not only had pancakes, she used butter and maple syrup. Shocking! Once she was gone, they could spend their days searching for someone else to gossip about.

"Miss Marlow."

With a sigh, Jade turned. Great. Mandy. One of her father's two assistants. The snarky one. She enjoyed treating Jade as if she was a few clowns short of a circus.

The trick was to let Mandy think she had the upper hand. Jade didn't care if she knew the truth.

"Let me guess. My father wants to see me."

"Immediately," Mandy huffed.

The woman was pretty. Blonde. A little plump. A clone of every other assistant Jade could remember. This one seemed a tad cockier than the rest. Perhaps she was expecting to get up off her knees in the office and move to the bedroom. *After* the honeymoon.

Fool. This peroxide cutie was no closer to that gold ring than any of the others. Anson Marlow would never remarry. Jade was certain of that. There was a good reason he had never divorced her mother. She was the magic get out of relationship free card her father pulled out when one of his woman hinted for him to *put a ring on it*.

Mandy, like all that came before her, had a short shelf life. Six months, maybe a year. If they didn't raise a fuss on their way out, there would be a tidy bonus in their bank account. If he really liked them, he passed them on to one of his business associates. Very last century. Early last century. Think *Mad Men* meets *Best Little Whore House in Texas*.

Normally, Jade tried not to think of other women in derogatory terms. In this case, that was difficult. None of them were forced. They had a choice. Move on to the next boss, or walk away. Most of them picked curtain number one.

Not waiting for Mandy, Jade headed to her father's office. Better to get whatever it was out of the way.

"You are supposed to knock," Mandy called to Jade. The other woman's much shorter legs chugged as fast as they could considering the four-inch pumps on her feet. Another of her father's demands.

Ignoring her, as she always did, Jade turned the doorknob.

"I won't need you this morning, Mandy. There is a list of errands on the table by the front door. Lincoln will drive you."

"Of course, Anson. Call me if you need *anything*."

Anything, Jade wondered. *Dictation? Foot massage? Blowjob?*

"Jade. *Jade!*" Anson barked. "I would ask where your mind is these days, but I already know the answer."

Deciding this was going to be one of those conversations — one sided — Jade took a seat.

"I don't know what you mean, Father. I haven't let my duties slide. Is there a problem I'm unaware of?"

"I was willing to turn a blind eye," her father continued. "Let you get it out of your system." He pulled an envelope from the top drawer of his desk. "After yesterday, I've decided it is time to put an end to it."

"First, yesterday was about me taking some time to myself. What is wrong with that? Second, I have no idea what you are talking about. Put an end to what?"

Anson tapped the envelope with one finger.

"Did you think you could sneak out of the house without anyone noticing?"

Jade stiffened.

"From the expression on your face, I'd say the answer is yes."

Whatever her father knew, it didn't matter. Jade wasn't going to let him bully her. Not this time. Never again.

"It shouldn't be necessary for me to *sneak out*," Jade pointed out. "What does that say about my status in this household? Am I your daughter? Your servant? A virtual prisoner? Tell me, Father. How do you see me?"

"This is exactly what I was talking about." Anson's eyes narrowed. A sure sign he was annoyed. "Why are you questioning me? This is my house. My word is law. When you start forgetting that, it is time to pull in the reins."

"Now I'm a what? A farm animal?"

"Don't be impertinent, Jade." He slid the envelope in front of her. "This is over. Understand? Right now."

Pictures. Before she opened the flap, Jade knew what she would find. Her father had her followed. All these months, thinking she had a beautiful secret all her own. She waited for the feelings of disappointment, embarrassment. Then she waited some more. When it didn't happen, Jade realized it didn't matter that her father knew. Knew the entire time. He didn't say anything until now. At the time, she did have a secret because she believed it to be true. Now, when it no longer mattered, there was no way for him to spoil it. The memories were hers and her father couldn't do anything about it.

With a steady hand, Jade tipped the envelope, letting the pictures slide out. Garrett. Arriving at the motel. Leaving the office. Going into the room. Nothing incriminating.

"These are pictures of a man in glasses and a baseball cap. So?"

"Keep looking."

She was the subject of half a dozen shots. Unlike Garrett, she was easily recognized. Again, nothing to get excited about. She exited a cab then entered a room. The same room as Garrett. That was the last photo. None of them together. She knew the curtains were always tightly drawn. They never turned on a light. These pictures proved nothing.

"When I think about my daughter meeting a man in that part of town. In a seedy motel? What were you thinking?"

Jade returned the pictures to the envelope, and then set them on the desk.

"I have nothing to say, Father."

Jade settled back in her chair. She wasn't pretending not to care what her father thought. She didn't.

"Is that so?" Anson shook his head in amazement. "The furor over the last scandal is finally dying down. Do you want a new one to remind everyone? It won't just be this sordid affair that gets talked about. Everything else will come with it."

"No one knows," Jade countered. When her father simply gave her a steady, unblinking look, she finally understood what this was about. "No one except you."

"I wouldn't want to leak this to the press, Jade. Unless you give me no alternative. Stop seeing this Hamish Floyd. When it's time for you to date again, find someone better than a lowly assistant director. He's an immigrant. A nobody."

Hamish Floyd? Not Garrett? Jade tried to take in what was happening. First, the blatant blackmail. Then finding out her father's PI misidentified the man in the pictures. It was a lot to take in.

"How did you find out who he was?"

"The license plate on that beat up car he drives."

Anson shook his head as though the make of the automobile somehow made all this worse.

"I see," Jade sighed.

Jade *did* see. She hated this. However, her father reminded her of something she let herself forget. Her life was a mess. Between an on-the-run abusive husband and a father who needed to control her, there was no room for a man. Especially a man like Garrett. His family was almost scandal-free. That was saying something in this town. Once his name became linked with hers, he would be forever tainted. She deluded herself if she thought they could go public. Trying for a normal relationship was hard enough. Add to it her baggage and his name? They were doomed before they started.

Her father was going to win. As usual. It was up to her to make sure he never knew the real reason why.

"Very well, Father. I won't see him again." Jade started to get up. Thinking again, she sat back down. "Do you ever get tired of it?"

"I beg your pardon," he asked vaguely. Having dealt with the matter, Anson Marlow had moved on. Jade had resumed her place of low-level importance.

"Aren't you sick of breaking me down every time I show a hint of a backbone?" Jade asked. This was something she had wondered about for a long time. She needed the answer. "Why bother? Why do you care, Father?"

For a moment, she thought he was going to ignore the question. When he finally spoke, Jade wondered why he bothered. One more lie.

"You are a Marlow. There is a standard to uphold." Anson shrugged. "Though it shouldn't be necessary, occasionally you need reminding."

"Bullshit."

"What did you say?"

"Bull. Shit. The stuff that comes out of the back end of a male bovine. You, Father, are full of it."

Jade enjoyed the shock that flitted over her father's face. The red, angry flush that followed she liked even better.

"That kind of language is not permitted in this house, young lady."

"Is that the best you've got? No more threats?" Jade shook her head in amazement. "This isn't about your good name. It's about control. You don't love me. You certainly don't like me. What good am I to you? I'll tell you," she continued before he could respond. "I may be an annoyance, but I'm *your* annoyance. Your flesh and blood. DNA doesn't lie."

"What are you talking about?"

"You had our DNA tested," Jade informed calmly. "Why wouldn't you? Your wife ran off. God forbid she saddle you with another man's child. You had to be sure. Tell me, Father, were you relieved or disappointed when you found out I'm yours?"

"How do you know about that?"

The test results were in the office safe along with his other secrets. Why he kept the results, Jade didn't know or care. When she realized what they were, a big part of her hoped she *wasn't* his daughter. No such luck.

"Does it matter?" Did anything between them matter anymore?

"This is getting us nowhere," Anson said dismissively. "Remember, Jade. Your actions reflect back on me. Drop your playmate. This is my house. You follow my rules."

"Understood." Jade stood to leave. She was at the door when her father left her with one more dictate.

"Clean up the language. I never want to hear you swear again."

"Believe me," Jade said. "It won't be a problem."

Without a backward glance, Jade closed the door. She walked back the way she came. Up the stairs. To her room. When she was alone, she took out her phone. Before her resolve started to crack, she found Garrett's number. Jade wouldn't let herself hesitate. She hit delete. It was a little thing. Symbolic. She had the numbers memorized. However, this way she would have to think before calling him. If she had to do more than push one keypad, she could talk herself out of it.

When she left her room that morning, she thought she had a future with Garrett. Now, she knew it could never be. Was a little taste of happiness better than none at all? What was the saying? You couldn't miss what you never had. Had Garrett been hers? She wanted to think so. She wanted the memories. She would never wish away the time they had together. Remembering would hurt. Still, it was better than not feeling anything.

Once that was taken care of, Jade's next action was one that was long overdue. Taking one suitcase from her closet, she packed the few things she owned that held any value. From her jewelry box, she took her maternal grandmother's pearls. Earrings that belonged to her mother. She left the rest. Tucked underneath the velvet lining, she retrieved her most precious possession. A picture of her mother. As far as she knew, it was the only one that survived. Her father shredded the rest. This one was given to Jade by the lawyer who handled the transfer of the money her mother had left her. It was hers if she wanted it. Those were the only instructions she gave.

At the age of twenty-one, Jade couldn't remember her mother. No one ever spoke of her or described what she looked like. Did she want a picture of the woman who abandoned her? It didn't take her long to decide. Curiosity won out over everything else.

Jade ran her finger over the image. The woman in the photo was smiling. She looked happy. Carefree. She was tall and thin. Her hair was red. If Jade could travel back thirty years, it would be like meeting her twin. *Was this the answer?* Jade wondered as she slipped the picture into her purse. Was her father's contempt directed at the woman in the photo as much as it was to Jade? It would be difficult. How galling to destroy the printed images only to see a living, breathing reminder every day?

Jade packed a few pieces of clothing — the essentials. When she closed the case, it was only half-full. She didn't want or need anything else. The clothes in her closet, half of which had never been worn didn't tempt her. She no longer needed them. She wasn't sure if she had ever wanted them.

Without a backward glance, Jade picked up the suitcase. For the last time, she walked down the staircase and out the front door.

Jade didn't care if the maid scrambled to tell her father. There was nothing he could do. She was twenty-seven years old and leaving home.

Jade Marlow was finally free.

Chapter Eleven

GARRETT FROWNED AT his phone. This was the fourth time his call went to voice mail. He could understand Jade not answering. Why the hell wasn't she getting back to him?

The mess in Vancouver was deeper than he anticipated. The temptation to dump it on someone else grew with every frustrating layer he peeled back. The problem wasn't complicated. It was messy. Unions. They were a touchy bunch. Luckily, they weren't unreasonable. He was making progress. By the end of the week, he expected things to be running smoothly. In the meantime, he was going crazy wondering why he couldn't reach Jade.

Two days had passed. That night. That amazing, beautiful night carried him through the next day. With almost no sleep and too much coffee, Garrett dragged himself from meeting to meeting. He had a job to do, yet all he could think about was Jade.

He considered calling someone to check up on her. Who? His mother was an option. Jade told him about her long visit with his parents. Garrett was thrilled to know his mother had reached out. Jade needed another woman to confide in. From what she said, a nice foundation was in place for their friendship to grow.

What could he say to his mother without giving away his involvement? He wanted his relationship with Jade to become public, but disclosing how it started was another thing. It would be difficult to explain why he was worried without spilling all the details. If he made something up, he would be stuck with the lie for as long as he was with Jade. Since he planned on that being a very long time, starting out with a lie, especially to his mother, wasn't a good idea.

That eliminated his entire family. Garrett felt trapped in a state of limbo. In all likelihood, there was a perfectly reasonable explanation why Jade wasn't answering his calls. He should wait a few more days before raising the alarm. Unfortunately, Jade's situation was unusual. She had an MIA husband who could show up without warning. What if he already had Jade? Her father couldn't be relied upon to call the police. The man could just as easily ignore Jade's disappearance. When questioned, all he had to do was concoct some story about how he thought Jade was visiting friends for a few days. He had no reason to think there was anything amiss. Meanwhile, Stephen Marsh could have snatched Jade off the street and no one was doing anything about it.

Given the choice between overreacting and ignoring a potentially deadly situation, Garrett knew there was no choice. Jade was all that mattered.

Garrett decided the best place to start was the Marlow residence. If he called asking for Jade and she came to the phone, problem solved. If they told him she was out, he would try again later. If he were given the runaround, he would take more drastic measures.

Getting the phone number wasn't a problem. He knew plenty of people who had that information. Charity events, social get-togethers. An unlisted number was easily obtained when you ran in the same social circles.

Taking a calming breath, Garrett dialed the number. He only had to wait through one ring before the phone was answered.

"Hello. Marlow residence."

"May I speak with Miss Marlow?"

The pause that followed did nothing to steady Garrett's nerves.

"Miss *Jade* Marlow?"

"That's right," Garrett said. *Was there more than one Miss Marlow?*

"One moment, please."

With each ticking second, Garrett felt his level of unease rise. After several minutes, he was ready to reach through his phone and strangle the nearest person. What the hell was going on? When someone finally came back, it was not the same woman who answered. Definitely not a good sign.

"Excuse me. To whom am I speaking?"

"To whom am I speaking?" Garrett countered.

"This is Mr. Marlow's associate, Mr. Black. What is your business with Miss Marlow?"

"Personal," Garrett replied. "And none of yours."

"If you are unwilling to state your business, Miss Marlow is unavailable. Call again if you have a specific reason for contacting her. Good day."

That was it. No more hesitating. Garrett wasn't waiting around to find out if Anson Marlow was being a controlling prick, or if Jade was missing and no one was doing anything about it.

Jack Winston would know what to do. Garrett was about to make the call when his phone rang. His mother. He couldn't ignore her call. Hoping a few more minutes wouldn't matter, Garrett answered.

"How is the most beautiful woman in the world?"

Too much, Garrett wondered. His mother was ultra-sensitive to her son's moods. She was sure to see through his attempt to sound upbeat — normal. She was beautiful. It was the tone that might have given him away.

"Is everything all right?"

Shit, Garrett thought, kicking himself for not being a better actor. *Maternal radar.* Even Colt, Oscar nomination and all, had a hard time fooling their mother when something was bothering him. Luckily, Garrett was in a different country. He could fib his way around Callie when they weren't together. If she could see his face, his lies dissolved like tissue paper in a rainstorm.

"Unions."

The one-word answer did the trick. His mother had been in the business long enough to understand. Hell, she belonged to one. On top of that, she was married to a producer. In one way or another, the Landis family dealt with unions every day of their lives.

"Poor baby," Callie cooed sympathetically. "Are they giving you a hard time?"

"No more than would be expected. I should wrap things up in a few days. Getting back to actual movie making will be a relief."

"I'm sure," Callie said. "You'll be here for your father's birthday, won't you?"

"Have I ever missed one?"

Caleb Landis' birthday bashes were legendary. Garrett's earliest memories were of the yearly party her mother threw to celebrate. Each one had a theme. *Turkish Harem. Carnival in Rio.* And one of Garrett's personal favorites, *Under the Sea*. Beautiful waitresses dressed like Ariel from the *Little Mermaid?* Garrett's favorite lobster rolls? His father in a *Sebastian the Crab* costume? Priceless.

"What's this year's theme?"

"It's a surprise." Garrett could hear the excitement in his mother's voice. She loved throwing parties. When it celebrated the birthday of the man she loved, she was in heaven.

"That means a costume will be delivered at the last minute." Garrett groaned. "Please, Mom, I beg you. No skirts."

The Scottish bash she threw two years ago still haunted Garrett. Insisting they dress as accurately as possible, Callie made her husband and sons go commando. Sure, they could have worn underwear. She didn't physically check them at the door. It simply never occurred to any of them to go against Callie's wishes. As a result, Garrett spent a drafty evening hoping his kilt wouldn't fly up.

"All your boy bits will be fully covered," Callie promised with a laugh. "You know, when you were little, I couldn't keep you from dropping your drawers. There was nothing you liked better than running around naked."

"Something I thankfully grew out of." Garrett looked at his watch. Time was getting away from him. "Was that why you called?"

"No. I wanted to know if you sold your old downtown loft. I know you had it on the market."

"No," Garrett frowned, wondering why it mattered. "There have been a few inquiries, but nothing serious."

"That's what I thought. If I vouch for the person, would you consider renting it? At a discount. A big one."

"Mom." Garrett sighed. "Is this one of your rehabilitation projects? I'm not keen on the idea of turning my place over to a crack addict or prostitute. Reformed or not."

"No," Callie reassured him. "Nothing like that. Though you should keep an open mind, sweetheart. Everybody deserves a second chance."

"I agree," Garrett said. "I just don't want them relapsing on my newly refinished hardwood floors."

"Well, that's a discussion for another time. I have a friend who needs a place to stay. Her budget is tight. I had a heck of a time talking her out of a studio on the east side. I shudder when I think of the dirty halls. The place smelled like mildew and I swear I heard something scurrying around in the walls."

"You know I trust your judgment. The money doesn't matter. You decide."

"I knew you'd come through," Callie said with delight. "Jade might put up a fuss. She's on an independent kick that I thoroughly approve of. That's why I didn't suggest she move in here. We have that cute little guest cottage that—"

"Wait," Garrett interrupted. "Jade Marlow? Is she your friend?"

"Oh, that's right. You don't know. Your brothers stopped by for dinner last night so they are up to date."

"Mom." Garrett tried his best to keep the impatience out of his voice. "What about Jade Marlow?"

"She moved out of her father's house. Just like that." He heard

Callie snap her fingers. "It wasn't planned. One morning, she packed a bag and left. Checked into a motel. She won't tell me where. I suspect it's worse than the studio apartment."

"How do you know all this?" *And why didn't he*, Garrett wondered.

"She called me the next day. We met for lunch. I couldn't get very much out of her. Apparently, her father crossed the line one too many times." Callie clucked her tongue sympathetically. "Plus, she was ready. Had been for a while now. Though she didn't say so, I suspect there's a man involved."

"What makes you say that?"

"Intuition," Callie said. "Before you scoff, there is more. When I asked—"

"And of course, you did." Garrett was glad. He wanted to know what Jade said.

"I'm her friend, Garrett." For Callie, that said it all. "She didn't confirm or deny. However, there was sadness in her eyes when I mentioned it. A break-up can shake anyone's world. Between her father and this man, Jade finally found the incentive to take control of her life."

"Break-up?" Garrett practically barked the word. "Is that what she said?"

"I told you, she didn't say very much. I'm going on experience. Before your father, I met quite a few jerks," Callie said with feeling. "None of them broke my heart. I didn't care enough for that. They *did* bruise it. Believe me. It hurts. It also takes a while to get over. My guess is if Jade's heart isn't broken, it certainly is cracked. Deeply. Idiot men."

Garrett didn't know what to say. Jade's heart was broken. How was that possible? None of this jived with the image he carried with him from the other night. He could still see her. Sleepy. Satisfied. Excited about their future. Damn it. How could that have changed in a few days?

More than ever, Garrett felt the frustration of his situation. They were at a delicate stage. The union was coming around. He couldn't afford to leave it with Hamish. Changing leaders, mid-negotiations, might unbalance the whole thing. Rushing back to Los Angeles — to Jade — might make him feel better personally. Professionally, it would be a disaster. He knew Jade was safe. For now, that would have to do.

"Nate has a set of keys. You can get them from him."

At least he would know where to find Jade when he got back. Since she wasn't answering his calls, he would have to be patient. *Not* one of his best qualities.

"Lovely," Callie said. "When was the last time the place was cleaned?"

"Are you accusing me of being a slob? Wrong son. That would be Colt."

His brother never had to worry about dirty clothes or piles of dishes in his sink. He always had some woman or other happy to clean his house. They were thrilled to wash Colton Landis' dirty underwear. The man was one of the highest paid actors in the world, yet he had never spent one dime on professional maid service.

"I didn't think you had stacks of molding takeout containers lying around," Callie laughed. There was a pause. "Do I need to move out any porn?"

"Jesus, Mom." It was horrifying enough to hear his mother use the word. The idea of her searching his loft was almost too much to contemplate.

"Is that a *Jesus, Mom*, why would I have porn stashed under my bed? Or *Jesus, Mom*, you better get over there and clean it out before Jade moves in."

"Let's call it a *never mention the subject again*. And no," Garrett added, "Jade won't find anything embarrassing."

"Good," Callie said, obviously satisfied. "Still, some pornography can be beautiful. And quite stimulating."

"Mom..."

"Don't be a prude, Garrett."

"It isn't prudish. It's normal. Children, especially sons, don't want to hear their mother's opinion on pornography."

"I'll desist," Callie laughed. "Thank you, baby. Thank goodness Jade called me before she rented one of the holes we looked at yesterday."

"It's good she has you." Garrett silently said a prayer of thanks. "Are you certain she'll agree to the loft? She's bound to question the low price."

"I'm certain she'll balk. Leave it to me. Before I'm done, Jade will think she's doing me a favor. I can be very persuasive."

"Tell me about it," Garrett chuckled. "Mom?"

"Yes."

"I love you."

"Oh, sweetheart." He heard his mother draw in a breath. "Now you've made me cry."

"I don't say it enough," Garrett said, frowning. He planned on changing that. Three words. Easily said when you meant them. He planned on saying them a lot in the future.

"You tell me all the time," Callie corrected. "Usually when you're saying goodbye. Out of the blue like that was a lovely surprise. I love you too, baby. With all my heart."

"Am I your favorite?"

Callie's musical laugh carried through the speaker, warming Garrett's heart. It was one of his all-time favorite sounds.

"When was the last time you asked me that? When you were four? Maybe five?"

"I outgrew that stage," Garrett admitted.

"All you boys asked at one time or another."

"What was your standard answer?" Garrett asked. He knew the answer, but he wanted to hear her say it.

"I love you," Callie said.

"Then you would scoop us up and give a hundred and one kisses. We were laughing so hard when you were finished, we forgot to worry about favorites."

"You were too young to understand the pitfalls every parent tackles when faced with that question," Callie sighed. "I would give my life for you and your brothers. No hesitation. No question about it. There is no degree to my love. I hope you know that."

"I always have."

"Stay safe, sweetheart." Callie sent a kiss his way. "I'll see you soon."

Putting his phone away, Garrett thought about how lucky he was. Two parents who loved unconditionally. Not uncommon. However, when your mother deserted you and your father wasn't capable of a shred of affection, growing up had to be difficult. Could he blame Jade for pulling back? Her experience with men ranged from condescendingly indifferent to brutal. There didn't seem to be any middle ground. Believing in him would not be easy for her.

It was frustrating. For the first time in his life, he had found a woman he wanted to spend more than a few weeks with. Garrett wanted to see if they could build something lasting. He knew what forever looked like. His parents were a shining example of how it could be. That's what he wanted. Was Jade the one? He would never find out unless he could convince her to give him a chance.

Garrett stepped outside of his trailer into the mid-summer air. It wasn't the blazing heat they got in Los Angeles. This was Vancouver. One of the reasons he loved shooting here was the milder weather. Rain wasn't that much of problem this time of year. If he could settle everything on this trip, he would be back in a month to shoot the final exterior scenes. *Exile* would wrap in early October. Fingers crossed it would be ready for distribution late next year.

"Garrett. The car is waiting."

"Be right there, Hamish."

Garrett climbed into the back of the Cadillac Escalade with a calmer mind. Jade in his loft. He smiled at the thought. He doubted his mother would tell her who owned the place. When she found out, he wondered if she would be angry. God, he hoped so. He was in the mood for a fight. Whatever her reasons for turning away from him, it still pissed him off. They needed to clear the air. Then they needed to make love. On his bed. With all the lights on.

"I don't know what you're thinking about, but keep it up," Hamish said as they pulled into traffic. "That's the happiest I've seen you in days."

"I see the light at the end of the tunnel, my friend." Garrett patted Hamish on the back. "A few more bumps and then clear sailing all the way."

"I DON'T KNOW, Callie. How can this place be in my budget?"

"Trust me," Callie said. She tugged Jade through the door. "Think of it like house sitting more than renting. My friend needs somebody trustworthy to look after the place while he's out of town. I recommended you."

Jade tried not to gape. She was hardly a hick from the sticks, in the city for the first time. Up until now, her life had been a first class ride. The best hotels, the finest restaurants. She had seen bigger lofts. Though none in downtown Los Angeles. And none with a panoramic view of the city. It was tempting.

"I wanted something less..." Jade searched for the right word. "Something *less*. How can people live like this when they haven't earned it?"

"You think you should suffer first?" Callie hid her smile. "That rat-infested crack house? Really? No one deserves to live like that."

"It wasn't a crack house," Jade scoffed. "Was it?"

"I have no idea." Callie guided Jade to a stop in front of the floor to ceiling windows. "Look at this. Why would you pick urine-soaked hallways when you could wake up to this every morning?"

When Callie put it like that, Jade had no comeback.

When she walked out of her father's house, Jade had a plan. She would find a place to live that suited her budget. Then she would find a job. Without any set agenda, she went to a place she was familiar with. The motel where she and Garrett used to meet.

Garrett. The tightening in her chest became a familiar feeling. Loss. Sorrow. Guilt. He called her at least a dozen times in the past few days. So much for reducing temptation. She read each text. Listened to every voice mail. He was worried. Why wasn't she returning his calls?

After debating with herself, Jade finally gave in. One text. Brief. To the point. It wasn't fair to keep him completely in the dark. He needed to know that she was fine — safe and sound. Otherwise, he might contact the police. Or worse, he might continue calling until she did what her heart drove her to do. Tell him everything then beg him to stay.

Jade looked out over the city. It amazed her that out there and beyond were people who cared what she did — who she did it with. All because she had a recognizable name and a knife-wielding husband. The second she arrived at the hospital with life-threatening wounds, she became news. Worse. She became fodder for gossip. Tabloid papers, online bloggers. Whispers from friends and acquaintances.

Time and other scandals quieted the worst of it. However, it wouldn't take much to fan the still smoldering coals. One hint that Jade Marlow was involved with Garrett Landis and once more she would be the center of attention. She didn't care about that. Let them say what they wanted about her. She cared about Garrett. She refused to drag him down into muck and mire. With a stench attached to her name that she would never completely lose, he needed a woman whose past didn't have such a huge, ugly stain on it.

Late last night Jade sent her last text to Garrett. Short. To the point.

I'm fine. I'm sorry. I need to move on. A fresh start is the only way. Goodbye, Garrett. Thank you for a wonderful six months. Please, don't contact me again.

It wasn't the smoothest break-up. Texting was cowardly. What else could she do? If she tried to do it in person, Jade was afraid she wouldn't have the strength to go through with it. For her, this was the only way.

Ever since she hit send, Jade waited for Garrett to respond. All last night, then this morning, her phone remained silent. Apparently, he was honoring her wishes. Was it perverse of her that a little part of her was disappointed? She didn't expect him to suddenly appear, pounding the door down, begging for her to reconsider — but part of her secretly wished for just that. It was the part of her that still believed in white knights and happily ever afters. Impractical. Unrealistic. Little girl dreams that *this* woman couldn't afford to indulge in.

If Jade had learned one thing, it was this. She was stronger than she thought. A survivor. Now it was time to move forward — one step at a time. She was prepared to do it alone. Luckily, she didn't have to. She had Callie. The irony wasn't lost on her. She wouldn't allow herself to lean on Garrett. However, his mother stood not five feet away, her greatest advocate.

Avoiding Garrett would be impossible if Jade maintained her friendship with Callie. Was she strong enough to ask for his friendship and nothing more? Would he accept such an offer?

Fists clenched, Jade wanted to scream. *Enough!* If she let her thoughts keep running in circles, her head would explode. She needed a friend. Callie was that person. The rest she would deal with when she had to. Right now, she had more pressing matters.

"How long is your friend going to be out of town?"

"Indefinitely."

"Callie?"

"Yes?"

Jade looked at the other woman. *Garrett's eyes. Maybe she was a glutton for punishment.*

"Do you own this place?"

Callie's expressive eyes widened; the silvery gray deepened to the color of brushed steel.

"Why would you think that?"

"You are a wonderful actress," Jade said. "But a lousy liar."

With a chuckle, Callie slid an arm around Jade's waist.

"You have me there," the other woman admitted. "It was a talent I never mastered. However." She squeezed Jade affectionately. "I promise you I am not lying. I don't own this place."

"And the owner?"

"A very close friend." *Which was true*, Callie thought. She was fortunate to call all her sons friend. "He *is* out of town. I admit to fudging a bit on the rest."

"In what way?" Jade asked warily.

"The loft was on the market. All of the interested buyers have given lowball offers. Since my friend isn't in a hurry to sell, he agreed to let you stay here at a rent you could afford."

"You gave him a sob story on my behalf." God, Jade hated being pitied.

"No," Callie corrected. "I gave him a bare outline of your situation. Straightforward. No sobs involved. Being a generous man, he agreed to help."

"Callie—"

"Listen, Jade," Callie interrupted. "There is nothing wrong with taking a hand up. Notice I said *up*, not *out*. You have a friend who has a friend. So what if this place is a little nicer than your average apartment?"

"*A little?*" Jade looked around the room again. "You are the master of understatement."

"Do you plan on digging in? Are you going to stay here forever?"

"Of course not. Still…"

"A few months, Jade." Callie's eyes turned serious. "The building is completely secure. Camera. Alarms. A burly doorman. I know we haven't spoken very much about your husband."

"Soon to be ex."

"The sooner, the better," Callie said. "He's still out there, Jade. I don't say that to upset you. I want you to be safe. Realistically, all you can afford is a smelly walk-up and a few dead bolts. When your ex is in custody, we'll talk about you moving out."

"Wishing won't make that happen, Callie."

Jade knew that. She prayed every day for Stephen's capture. Six months on the run without as much as a sighting. It could be years before he was apprehended. Hell, it might never happen.

"I will stay here," Jade finally declared. "It would be foolish and ungracious for me not to."

"Wonderful," Callie exclaimed. "The first thing we need to do is give the place the once-over. Obviously the owner has someone come in to clean every so often."

Jade watched as Callie ran a finger over the kitchen counter.

"No dust," Callie said with satisfaction. She opened the refrigerator. "Sparkling clean. Groceries first. Then if there isn't any, linen. Sheets, towels. Soap. Essentials."

Since Callie was right, Jade didn't argue. She had never purchased these things for herself. Having someone with her who knew the ins and outs would be nice. Jade wanted to be independent. That didn't mean turning down help when she needed it. Besides, she loved being around Callie. She made shopping for groceries sound fun instead of mundane.

"I know the cutest little shops." Callie was already making a mental list of the places she would take Jade. "Are you free tomorrow?"

"I have to start looking for a job. I'm going to see what's listed in the morning paper."

"That's a good place to start." Callie gave Jade her sweetest smile. "Or, you could let me help. What kind of job did you have in mind?"

"I'm not qualified to do anything. I have a degree in graphic design. Not that it did me any good," Jade sighed. "As my father pointed out, it is a useless thing to major in."

"What did he want you to study?"

"Languages. He thought it would help to have someone around who could speak Chinese." Jade shook her head. "I tried. One class and I knew I didn't have the aptitude. Or the interest."

"Honestly," Callie scoffed. "The man has more money than he knows what to do with. If he wanted an interpreter, he should have hired one."

"As he loved to remind me, my father didn't get rich by throwing away money."

"In other words, he wanted unpaid labor."

"He paid for my education." Jade had no desire to defend her father. What she said was the truth.

"How did you end up with a degree in graphic design?"

"Sometimes having a father who wasn't interested in you could be a good thing," Jade explained. "When I changed majors, I never told him."

"Easy as that?" Callie thought it sounded *too* easy.

"He paid the tuition. During my four years of college, it worked fine. I went to class, came home, as expected. It wasn't until I graduated that the shit hit the fan."

"No Chinese."

"Not a lick."

They had moved to the large, chocolate-colored sofa. Callie patted Jade's hand. "What did your father say?"

"What he always said," she shrugged. "Or some variation on the theme. It was typical, he said in that controlled tone of his. He should have expected a worthless daughter to get a worthless degree."

Jade closed her eyes. She had to keep reminding herself that her father wasn't downstairs behind his office doors, ready to summon her for another round of *why Jade is a disappointment*.

"No!" Callie cried out. "How could he say such a thing? You poor, sweet girl."

"I didn't tell you this because I wanted more of your sympathy."

Jade wished she had kept her mouth shut. With every story she shared with Callie, she became more and more pathetic.

"No one should speak to another person that way, Jade. Especially a parent." Callie practically vibrated with anger. "I've never been sure what I believed when it came to eternal damnation. Now I hope Anson Marlow ends up in the deepest bowels of hell."

Surprised, Jade blinked once, then twice. Finally, she did the only thing she could do except cry. She burst out laughing.

"I've heard people tell my father to go to hell," she finally said, wiping the moisture from her eyes. "*That* is a new one. Thank you, Callie. I needed that. I hate to think about the years I put up with him. I was frozen. It took me forever to get past wanting his love and approval, realizing I would never have either."

"You got there, Jade. That's what matters."

It took almost dying. This was her second chance. Jade looked around. In much more luxurious surroundings than she could have imagined when she was planning her new life. *Planned* was an overstatement. When it came right down to it, Jade grabbed a bag and walked away. She had no work experience, no place to live. Her bank balance was decent. Enough to last if she was careful with her money *and* found work — fast. Los Angeles was not the best city to live on a budget. At least not the part that she was used to.

Now, because of Fairy Godmother Callie, Jade was sitting in a downtown penthouse loft. She could stop worrying about money. For now. She would find a job without having to settle for the first thing that came along.

"You do have skills, you know."

"I do?" Jade asked. That was news to her.

"Do you know how many parties, charity events, and benefits I attend every year?" Callie waved Jade off. "Don't try to answer that. We both know it's a lot. Too many. Then there are the ones I'm invited to but either can't or don't want to attend. In Hollywood, someone is always hosting an event."

"True."

"Some of them are first class all the way. Most are middle of the road. Too many stink. Bad decorations, terrible food, inept servers. Not to mention the indifferent hosts. I can say without qualification, you never fail to make organizing an event seem elegant yet somehow effortless."

"Callie. I… It's nothing. Really."

Jade wondered if she was blushing. She raised a hand to her cheek. Definitely hot. Praise was not something she was used to. She didn't know how she was supposed to react.

"Nothing?" Callie exclaimed. "Take it from someone who has gone through a dozen party planners over the years. What you do takes talent. Coupled with your experience, you'll be turning clients away."

"Do you really think so?"

"You won't have to advertise," Callie assured her. "Once you're ready, word of mouth will be all it takes. I doubt there's a person in this city who hasn't been to something you've organized and hosted."

"Then there's the freak factor."

"I won't lie to you, Jade," Callie sighed. "There will be people who will hire you because of your notoriety. Completely weeding them out will be impossible. Trust me; that will die down. By this time next year, the only reason they will come to you will be for your professional services."

"I have always enjoyed organizing those functions," Jade admitted thoughtfully. "I was in charge. People looked to me to make decisions. My opinion not only counted, it was law. Don't laugh. I felt like a field general, mustering my troops for battle."

"Why would I laugh?" Callie wanted to know. "I've seen the way the throngs descend upon a table of food. It's nothing short of a battle. Especially if you want to get a jumbo shrimp before they are all gone. One time I was close to spearing a man in the hand with my seafood fork."

Jade and Callie plotted for another hour. Now she had the beginnings of a business plan, Jade felt herself truly begin to settle. Her nerves were smoothing out. Her stomach was twisted in two or three fewer knots. At this rate, she might adjust to her new life faster than she ever imagined. All thanks to Callie.

Now, after all the things her new friend had done to help her, there was one more favor Jade needed to ask.

"I need to learn to protect myself. Can you recommend someone to teach me?"

THREE DAYS SINCE receiving Jade's text and Garrett was still fuming.

I need to move on? Thank you? He couldn't believe it. *Thank you?!* What the fuck? You don't end a relationship with a text. Or a fucking *thank you*.

"Excuse me? Did you say something?" a husky voice asked.

Garrett looked at the woman sitting next to him. Beautiful. Long, dark hair. A hint of cleavage. Nice shape. A smile that said she wouldn't object to him making a move. Just his type. Garrett sighed. Or she *was* his type. Before a certain long-legged redhead started monopolizing his thoughts.

"I'm sorry. I have a lot on my mind. Sometimes I mumble out loud."

"I understand," the brunette's smile widened. She leaned closer, the hint of cleavage turning into an invitation. "If you need to get something off your chest, I'm a great listener."

Not terribly subtle, Garrett thought, his eyes taking in the woman's obviously enhanced breasts and veneered smile. Fake. He didn't mind fake. He had lost track of how many of his past bed partners sported some kind of cosmetic surgery. Boobs, ass, nose, chin, cheeks. Hell, he made his living in Hollywood. Ninety percent of the town was plastic in one way or another. It never bothered him before. Now he was judging this stranger for her choices? Why now? Garrett didn't need to search long for the answer.

Jade. One hundred percent natural Jade. He couldn't get enough of her. Dumping him with a text. Think again. If she wanted him out of her life, she had to say it to his face. Which was why he was on a commercial flight to Los Angeles.

The negotiations with the union lasted into the wee hours of the morning. They could have called a halt at a decent hour. However, they were so close; it didn't take much persuasion on Garrett's part to keep everyone at the table. He wanted this done. He had a movie to make and a woman to strangle.

The moment after the papers were signed and hands were shaken, Garrett headed to the airport. His assistant had a ticket waiting at the counter. Forty-five minutes later, he was headed home.

Garrett needed a shower, some food, and eight hours of uninterrupted sleep — not necessarily in that order. Three days of living on bitter coffee and stale sandwiches didn't help his disposition. Right in the middle, he gets Jade's text. It wasn't the best timing — not that there was a good time for something like that. The problem was he couldn't do anything about it. Jade still wasn't answering his calls. He was stuck in a room with ten stubborn men who seemed to want ten different things. In the end, they all gave a little, walking out satisfied with the deal. He couldn't deal with Jade until they were in the same area code.

God, he must look a sight. He hadn't changed his clothes. Same t-shirt and jeans he put on two days ago. Did he stink? Probably, though his smiling aisle companion didn't seem to mind. Of course, she didn't mind, not if she recognized him. By looking at her, his guess would be aspiring actress. If that were the case, it wouldn't matter what he smelled like. She would smile and claim she loved his unique aroma. No harm in finding out.

"I didn't introduce myself. I'm—"

"Oh, everyone knows who you are, Mr. Landis. I'm Stella."

And there it was, Garrett thought. The batting of the eyes, the way she lowered her voice when she said, *Mr. Landis*. And that name. Stella. Very now. A serious actress name. At least it wasn't Jennifer. Hollywood had a surplus of those now.

"Nice to meet you, Stella," Garrett said, holding out his hand. He could play along. What better way to get his mind off one woman than with another. They would be landing in Los Angeles in less than an hour. A little harmless flirtation was exactly what he needed.

"Were you in Vancouver for business or pleasure?" Stella asked.

She wasn't a bad actress, Garrett decided. The trade papers, like the one sticking out of her bag, were full of his recent problems in Canada. Apparently, Stella wanted to keep the reason for her interest to herself — for now. That was fine. Garrett didn't mind playing along.

"All business, I'm afraid."

"Oh, that's too bad. Vancouver has some lovely places to take in the sun. Have you ever been to Wreck Beach?"

Wreck Beach was a legendary clothing optional hangout. Counter-culture hippy holdovers mixing with nudists of all ages. The come one, come all attitude was appealing to those who liked to let it all hang out. It wasn't Garrett's scene. Still, he admired anyone who could put aside both her modesty and the fear of skin cancer. Unless you liked strangers touching you, bringing along a sunscreen buddy would be essential.

"I've never been," Garrett told Stella. He waited for her next move.

"I hate tan lines," she whispered in a conspiratorial tone. "What do you think?"

"About tan lines?" Garrett shrugged. "I can't say I've given them much thought."

"I'd be happy to show you mine," Stella offered. "Or rather my *lack* of them."

The captain's clearance to land announcement made Garrett decide to put an end to this little diversion. In the nicest way he could think of.

"I'm sure you have very nice non-tan lines, Stella." Garrett pulled a card out of his wallet, writing a few lines on the back "At the moment, I'm not free to enjoy the experience. Call this number. My assistant will line up an audition. There's a small part in *Exile* I think would be perfect for you."

Garrett left the airport, Stella's squeal of excitement still ringing in his ears. He gave the woman points for fairness. She made it clear that her offer was still open. She offered her body, use of her shower, and threw in the temptation of a home cooked meal. Except he wasn't tempted. Not the least bit. Grabbing his carry-on, he left the slightly bemused actress to wrestle with her own bag.

The airport was crowded. Nothing unusual there. Garrett was used to weaving his way around masses of bodies. He had done it a thousand times. Today, his patience was at a premium. By the time he finally reached the sliding doors, he was ready to tear the head off the next person who got in his way. Luckily for everyone involved, his wait for a taxi was minimal — no innocent bloodshed.

He settled back in the cab. He gave the driver the address of the loft. The smartest thing he could do would be to go home and get some rest. Jade wasn't going anywhere. He was in no condition to have a reasonable conversation. Since he didn't want to be reasonable, this was the perfect time to have it out with her.

Garrett was going over in his head what words he would use, most them of the four-letter variety, when his phone rang. Wyatt. What now?

"If somebody scraped their knee in Vancouver, *you* can fly out. I'm not setting foot on another plane until shooting starts next month."

"Hello to you too," Wyatt snarked back. "Whose wrong side of the bed did you get up on this morning?"

"Funny," Garrett said. "You know damn well I haven't been to bed, mine or anyone else's. I hope to remedy that. Soon."

"I assume you're talking about sleep."

"Eventually."

"Jesus," Wyatt chuckled. "I don't know where you get the energy. Well, you are going to have to keep your dick zipped up for a while longer. Mom has called for a mandatory dinner. No excuses. If you can contemplate bedroom games, you aren't too exhausted for dinner with the family."

Garrett cursed his smartass mouth.

"What's up?"

"Nothing special. With our crazy schedules, Mom likes to act quickly when we're all in town at the same time."

"Shit." Garrett decided to get the salty language out of the way before seeing his mother. "Colt leaves for someplace or other in pretty soon, doesn't he?"

"Australia," Wyatt said. "He'll be gone for six weeks. So don't think you can whine your way out of it."

"I never whine." Okay, maybe that sounded a bit whiny. "As long as Mom doesn't mind me falling asleep halfway through the meal, I'll be there."

"If I see you nodding off, I'll pelt you with a dinner roll."

"You're a pal, Wyatt."

"What are big brothers for?" Wyatt laughed again. "Six sharp."

"Great," Garrett grumbled, putting his phone away. "I'm dead on my feet and no one gives a damn." Garrett looked up at the cab driver. "Did I just sound like I was whining?"

"A little bit," the older man nodded.

"That's what I thought."

Fucking Wyatt. There... one more cuss word out of the way.

Garrett slid down in his seat, his eyes closed. Jade would have to wait. With a sigh, he told the driver there was a change in plans.

"Forget downtown. Take me to Laurel Canyon."

"LASAGNA IS COLTON'S favorite. I want him to have a good meal before he leaves town."

"He's twenty-six years old, Callie. A big boy by any standards. He's going to shoot a movie, not fight a war."

Callie stuck her tongue out at her husband. Seeing the twinkle in Caleb's eyes turn from teasing to interest, she held a pair of salad tongs up in a defensive measure.

"Back, mister," warned. "I love that the sight of my tongue can still rev you up after all these years. Unfortunately, that will have to wait. We have a full house."

"Family." Caleb circled around the large, granite island to where Callie washed vegetables. "They won't mind if we disappear for a few minutes."

"Now you're insulting us both. When did we ever settle for a few minutes?"

"That Christmas we were visiting your parents. Remember the coat closet?"

"One time," Callie laughed. "I can still see the look on Aunt Wanda's face when we stumbled out, her faux-fur stole wrapped around your neck."

"Best four minutes ever."

Callie turned into her husband's arms. This was home. When the rest of the world seemed cold, unforgiving, and judgmental, Caleb grounded her with his love. She sometimes marveled at how a small town girl from Iowa found a rich, happy life so far away from rural wheat fields where she grew up. Glittery movie premieres, star-studded award shows were wonderful. The gold statues that lined her office shelves were gratifying strokes to her ego. Those things meant nothing compared to her husband, their sons, and the life they built together.

"Hey," Caleb lifted her chin. Her eyes were purple, full of love. The tears upset him. "What is this about?"

"I'm so lucky, Caleb." Callie burrowed closer, fitting her head under his chin. When she felt his strong arms tighten, she sighed with contentment. "My life is full of love. The last few days that I've spent with Jade have made realize how few people have what we do."

"My love." Caleb kissed the top of her head, breathing in her unique scent. *His Callie.* "There isn't a day that goes by that I don't thank heaven for you. What would have happened to me if you hadn't loved me back?"

"Am I a smart woman?" Callie asked, bringing his hand up to her lips for a kiss.

"Brilliant."

"Then why would I have been stupid enough not to love you?"

That was how Garrett found them. He stood in the doorway not wanting to interrupt an obviously intimate moment.

The love practically radiated off them. Caleb Landis, his big, rock-solid father. Callie Flynn, his beautiful mother who looked like an angel, but blessed with a devilish sense of humor. They raised their children with love, warmth, compassion, and the occasional boot to the britches.

Garrett felt his churlishness fall away. For hours after he got off the phone with Wyatt, he grumbled to himself thinking how annoyed he was over this mandatory dinner. Didn't he visit all the time? When he was out of town, he called one of his parents at least every other day. It was unreasonable to expect him to drop whatever plans he had because his mother insisted.

Now that he was here, seeing them in each other's arms, his resentment seemed childish. If his mother wanted her sons together, then that was what she would get. Garrett would gladly sit down with his family. Without the put-upon attitude he carried when he entered the house.

"I'd say get a room, except when did the two of you ever need one of those?"

"Garrett."

Callie rushed to him, her smile bright and welcoming. Garrett pulled her close. *Never take this for granted*, he told himself, thinking of Jade. Not everyone had a loving mother. Or a supportive father.

"Good to see you, Dad."

Garrett kissed Callie's cheek before exchanging hugs with his father.

"You look tired," Callie said, looking him up and down. "And skinny."

"Good eye." Garrett winked. "At least about the tired part. You can't get skinny eating fried food for every meal. I think those union guys were attempting murder by grease."

"Where was it written that you had to eat it?" Callie demanded. She raised her children with healthy, nutritious food. She expected them to follow that example whenever possible.

"I was trying to win them over, Mom." Garrett winked at his father. "It would have been rude to turn down that last helping of onion rings."

"I'm putting extra vegetables in the salad," Callie declared. "And no garlic bread for you."

"Hey." Garrett protested.

Callie didn't listen, pulling a head of broccoli out of the refrigerator.

"It's your own fault," Caleb laughed. He patted his son on the shoulder. "Tease your mother, pay the price. You do look beat. Sit. Do you want a beer?"

"I better not. Alcohol is likely to knock me on my ass. Sorry, Mom."

"Ass is acceptable under the circumstances," Callie assured him. "Caleb, the kettle is hot. Make him a cup of lemon balm and lavender tea. It helps you sleep."

"I don't need help sleeping," Garrett said. "I need to stay awake."

"Nonsense." Callie bustled around, checking the oven, grating cheese. "Some tea, a good, healthy meal, and the company of your family are what you need. You'll stay here tonight. I don't want you driving home in your condition. Especially at night on those winding roads."

"Don't argue," Caleb warned. "Your mother is right. You'll be much better off driving in the morning."

"You won't hear any objections from me," Garrett assured them. "My old bed plus one of Lorena's famous breakfasts. Sounds like heaven to me."

Garrett took the steaming mug from his father, breathing in the scent of lemon and lavender. In his experience, all herbal tea tasted the same. Like steeped grass clippings. Taking a sip, he decided this one was no exception. Seeing his mother's satisfied smile, he kept his opinion to himself.

"Where is everyone else? I saw their rigs in the driveway."

"Wyatt is in my office closing a deal. Colt is getting his dog settled out back. As usual we are sitting while he's out of town."

"You love Amos," Callie reminded Caleb. "I swear you can't wait for Colt to have a location shoot out of the country so you can play with him whenever you want."

"Did I say I minded?" Caleb rolled his eyes, making sure Callie didn't see.

Chuckling, Garrett selected an olive from the antipasto tray his mother set in front of him, popping it into his mouth.

"That takes care of two brothers. Where is Nate?"

"With our guest down in the workout room. Caleb, sweetheart, will you get a bottle of Chianti from the wine vault."

"We have a guest?"

"Mmm. I—"

"There isn't any Chianti," Caleb called out.

"Oh, honestly," Callie sighed. "The man can oversee multi-million dollar productions, but he can't find a simple bottle of wine."

Garrett smiled, watching his mother leave the room. Curious what Nate was up to, he walked down the hall to the left, taking the flight of stairs that led to the basement.

The workout room was added when Caleb and Callie bought the house. Over the years, they renovated the area, modernizing the equipment, adding a meditation room, then a Pilates studio. The weight room was always in a state of flux. Since it got the most use, they made sure the equipment was always state of the art.

When they were boys, Garrett and his twin brother had an ongoing friendly competition. They set goals to see who could lift the most weight. Or who could climb the rope the fastest. Nate always won. After a while, they gave up competing. Garrett graciously declared his brother the brawnier physical specimen. The only activities Garrett could beat Nate at were anything involving endurance. Nate might get there faster in a sprint. However, given enough time and distance, Garrett always overtook him.

From the sound of it, Nate and his guest were in the room at the far end of the hall. Most of the time it was lined with well-cushioned mats. Caleb Landis was a black belt in several martial arts disciplines. When he wanted to hone his skills, he flew in masters from all over the world. This is where they would meet.

He heard Nate's voice, instructing someone to lead with his or her shoulder.

"You need to put your body into a punch. If you only move your arm, you can't get enough force."

Good advice, Garrett thought. Normally, Nate had the patience of Job. He didn't mind going over and over something until his student caught on. It took a lot to frustrate his brother. However, when you crossed that line, watch out. Nate did not suffer assholes quietly. From the sound of things, Nate was in classic teacher mode.

Garrett looked through the open studio door. He planned on getting a peek without disturbing the occupants. What he saw froze him in his tracks. Standing in the middle of the room, Nate's hands on her waist, was Jade.

For the first time in over two years, Garrett saw Jade out of the darkened motel room. His eyes drank in every detail. She was dressed in skintight black yoga pants that showed off a nicely rounded butt and shapely legs. The weight she had put on in the last six months looked good on her. Her black t-shirt was loose, only giving a hint of the full breasts he knew were underneath. She wore her blazing red hair pulled back in a long ponytail and her feet were bare, her toes painted a deep magenta.

None of this was supposed to be for his eyes. Only a few days ago, she told him to hit the road. It seemed the fork in that road led her directly to Nate.

What the fuck?

"What do you think?"

Garrett almost jumped out of his skin. He was so engrossed in the unfathomable scene he hadn't heard his mother's approach.

"Well?" Callie asked; her voice lowered to a whisper. She stood with him in the doorway, her arm slipping around him.

"Well, what?"

Garrett was only half listening. Jade? With Nate? What the hell was going on?

"Garrett," Callie said impatiently. "I asked what you thought."

"I think Nate has his hands all over Jade Marlow," Garrett grumbled.

"Jade asked if I knew a good self-defense teacher. Naturally, I thought of your brother. He was happy to show her the basics."

Garrett's eyes narrowed when Nate's hand got a little too close to Jade's ass.

"He seems to be enjoying himself."

"I thought so, too," Callie beamed. "I think Nate would be good for Jade."

"Mmm," Garrett mumbled. "Wait. What? Nate and Jade? As in...?"

"Don't you think they make a good-looking couple?" Callie smiled. "I know Jade is skittish about men. Who could blame her? Nate is such a gentle soul. She needs to be treated with kid gloves. Your brother is perfect."

Garrett couldn't believe his ears. *His mother wanted to play matchmaker to Jade and Nate? Unbelievable.*

"My first thought was Wyatt."

"Wyatt." *Christ, this just got stranger and stranger.*

"It makes sense," Callie reasoned. "Two wounded hearts. They could heal each other."

"I don't think so," Garrett protested. Wyatt could get his own woman. Jade was not available.

"I agree," Callie beamed, unaware of Garrett's turbulent thoughts. "Wyatt isn't ready. I think Jade is. *If* it's with the right man."

"A man like Nate."

"Maybe. I'm still feeling out the situation. Hey, you two," Callie called out. "Dinner will be ready in twenty minutes."

"Sounds good," Nate grinned. He winked at Jade. "We've worked up quite an appetite."

Laughing, Jade turned towards Callie. It looked like she was about to say something. Then she saw Garrett. When she started to sway as if she would faint, Garrett instinctively took a step toward her. Nate, being closer, beat him to it.

"Hey, are you all right?" Nate gave her a concerned look, his hand on her arm holding her steady. "Did I push you too hard?"

"No," Jade assured him. "I'll be fine."

"You need a hot meal in your stomach," Callie said firmly. "Before I came down, I filled the tub in my bathroom. By the time you have a nice soak, dinner will be on the table."

Jade took the towel Nate held out. She walked across the room, wiping her face. Garrett kept his eyes locked on her, willing her to look at him. Daring her.

Jade passed him without a glance.

"Thank you, Callie. I won't be long."

"Such a sweetie," Callie said.

A few days ago, Garrett would have agreed. Now, he wasn't sure what Jade was. Cold-hearted bitch? No, that didn't fit. Tease? Nope. There was nothing sexual in the way she interacted with Nate. Something was going on that went beyond a simple break-up. Whatever it was, Garrett planned to find out.

"She started out timid." Nate joined them on the walk back upstairs. "That isn't unusual. If you've never hit anyone, it isn't an easy thing to do."

"I liked that part."

Nate grinned. "You're a natural, Mom. You also grew up on a farm with three older brothers. By the time you got to Hollywood, you knew how to give as well as you took."

"After eighteen years putting my brothers in their place, the male sharks in this town were a breeze."

"Jade needs to build some upper body strength" Nate explained. "She's started working out again, something she stopped doing after she got out of the hospital. I gave her a program of weight training and conditioning. I'll have her kicking ass in no time."

"Watch out for flying rice."

Nate's turned from grabbing a bottle of juice from the refrigerator. He was used to intense workouts. Unlike Jade, he hadn't broken a sweat.

"Rice?" Nate frowned. "What are you talking about?"

"Didn't Mom tell you?" Garrett tried to make his words sound teasing. Keeping the edge off was difficult. "She thinks you and Jade will make the perfect couple. Mind you, her original choice was Wyatt."

Nate barely saved himself from spitting the juice across the room. "Wyatt and Jade? No offense, Mom, but they would be a mess. Too much baggage on both sides."

"I realized that," Callie said. She gave Garrett a warning look. "I know you boys hate the idea of my matchmaking. I wasn't going to push, Nate. I simply thought if you hit it off, it would be good for both of you."

"Sorry, Mom. Jade and I edged into the brother/sister dynamic right away." Nate scratched his chin thoughtfully. "Not that she isn't gorgeous. And sexy. I can't say why there wasn't any spark. Maybe it's the sadness I see in her eyes when she doesn't think anyone is looking."

"My big protector." Callie cupped Nate's face with her hands. "I should have realized. You need a woman as tough on the outside as you are."

"With a marshmallow center," Garrett added. Good old Nate. The relief he felt at hearing his brother explain his feelings for Jade was short-lived.

"There's always Colt."

"What?" Garrett couldn't believe his ears. Different woman every night, Colt? Had Nate lost his mind?

"I thought of that. They are close to the same age." Callie smiled at Garrett. "Take the lasagna out of the oven, sweetheart. It needs to sit before we cut it."

"Colt is a bit wild," Nate mused.

"Exactly," Callie agreed. "He is having too much fun sowing his wild oats. Jade needs a man who can focus on her. Colt's eye wanders too easily."

Setting the casserole on the stove, Garrett added a silent, *damn right*.

"Sometimes, no matter how much you wish it, there isn't a good fit," Callie sighed. "We know plenty of eligible men. When Jade is ready, I'll set her up with one of them."

"Excuse me."

Callie smiled. "Did you need something, Garrett?"

"What about me?"

Callie and Nate exchanged puzzled looks.

"What about you?" Nate asked.

"Jade? And me?" Garrett threw up his hands. "Come on. You considered your other sons."

"Did I bruise your ego?" Callie reached over to squeeze his hand. "You were actually my first thought. *Fleeting* thought."

"Really? Why?" Garrett looked at Nate. "What am *I* lacking?"

"Don't ask me," Nate said. He kissed Callie on the forehead. "I need a quick shower. I'll leave you to soothe Garrett's ego."

As Nate passed by, Garrett punched him in the arm. It was like hitting galvanized steel.

"Need some ice for that?" Callie asked.

"No, my hand is fine."

"I meant for your ego." She smiled at Garrett's disgruntled look. "What is it with brothers? If one of you has something, the others suddenly need one too."

"None of them has *had* Jade." That distinction belonged to Garrett. And he planned on keeping it that way.

"Do you want to know why I dismissed you so quickly?"

"Please."

"When you are directing a movie, you can't think of anything else. It's one of the things that makes you so good," Callie explained. "That single-minded devotion has taken you to the top in a short period of time."

"You don't think I can split my focus," Garrett said.

"Jade needs to feel like the center of someone's world. She's never had that before. Trust me; it's a heady feeling for any woman." Callie sighed.

"With the right man," Garrett pointed out. "You like it because it's Dad. There's a fine line between devoted and stalker."

"Which is why I thought of Nate," Callie told him. "He knows how to hold something close while allowing it room to breathe. Your father is like that. Wyatt tried to be," Callie's eyes grew sad. "Unfortunately, his wife *wanted* to be smothered. That isn't a healthy trait on either side of a relationship."

"You don't think Colt and I are capable of giving a woman the kind of love Dad gives you?" Garrett hated to think that was true.

"Of course you are," Callie assured him. "Colt isn't ready for that kind of commitment. And you, Garrett, right now your love is your work. When you find the right woman, you'll make room for both." She pulled him down, kissing both cheeks. "Now, enough heavy stuff. Go remind Wyatt the work day is over."

When you find the right woman. The words rang through Garrett's head. For the past six months, he had found his thoughts divided between making movies and Jade. Until his mother verbalized it, Garrett hadn't given it a thought. Before now, he easily put his focus solely on the project at hand. Women were fun diversions he used to blow off steam during the few off hours he allowed himself.

Now, there was Jade.

She didn't pull his focus. Finding time for her and his work wasn't a hardship; it just... was. He could do both because both were important. No, not important. *Vital.*

Garrett needed a small list of things to survive. Food. Air. His family. His work. And now Jade.

The realization both frightened the hell out of him and made his spirit soar. His happiness was suddenly linked to another person. Without conscious thought on his part, Jade Marlow now had the ability to crush his heart with the force of a sledgehammer. No one should have that kind of power over another human being. Unfortunately, when you let yourself love someone, you didn't have any choice.

Garrett felt his knees grow a little weak. Love. He loved Jade. It seemed the old adage was true. Love came when you least expected it — at its own convenience. Ready or not, here it was.

Was Jade ready? If she was, could she love him? Garrett knew one thing. It was too soon. She was still regaining her strength, both physically and mentally. She was trying her wings for the first time. Flying solo for a while would be good for her. Garrett was fine with that. However, he wasn't stepping out of her life. If she wanted nothing more than a friend he could do that. Temporarily. The day would come, he hoped, when that wasn't enough.

In the meantime, despite being in love with her, he was royally pissed off. That break-up text she sent him still rubbed him raw. Garrett smiled in anticipation. Suddenly, the thought of sitting across from Jade at his family's dinner table held a lot of appeal. That touch of discomfort she was bound to feel would serve her right.

JADE WALKED DOWN the stairs. With every step, a feeling of dread settled over her like a heavy wool blanket on a hot August afternoon. Coming here tonight when she knew Garrett would be here was ten kinds of stupid. The moment she saw him she knew her plans were foolish. Why did she think they could be friends? The mere act of walking past him without touching him had taken more willpower than she knew she possessed. How was she going to endure an entire meal?

Jade wore the same jeans and cotton blouse she put on before arriving here. She left her hair loose, adding a touch of lip-gloss. Her skin had a healthy glow, the combination of exercise and a warm, fragrant bath. She no longer looked ill. Every day, the fragility that clung to her for months after the stabbing faded a little more.

As she approached the kitchen, the sound of masculine laughter rang out. She could do this. How different could it be than the thousands of times she would plaster a smile on her face to entertain her father's business associates? If she could sit through hours of mind-numbing conversations about the fluctuating foreign market, she could make it through this.

"I'm telling you, Judy Dench pinched my butt."

"She's lovely, Colt," Garrett said. "A great actress. But when you start fantasizing about women in their seventies, it's time to get professional help."

Wyatt high-fived Garrett. Nate doubled over with laughter.

"Stop teasing your brother." Callie gave her sons a warning look. She smiled at Colt, her silver eyes brimming with laughter. "Don't let them make you feel bad, Colton. It's the granny thing. Some men find it irresistible."

There was another burst of laughter. Caleb joined in the good-natured ribbing when he asked if Colt pinched Dame Judy back.

"Jade," Colt called out when he saw her. "Finally. Come join me. You can be my ally against this *loving* family of mine." Rushing forward, Colt took Jade's hand, leading her to his side of the kitchen island.

"You can't ask Jade to take sides, Colt." Nate swung Jade into his arms, depositing her on a bar stool between him and his father. "Until she gets used to us, consider her Switzerland."

"As in sweet and creamy, like fine chocolate?"

Jade knew Colt was kidding. Still, she couldn't control her blush. It wasn't every day the *sexiest man alive* flirted with you. No matter what his intent.

"Enough." Callie set a glass of Chianti in front of Jade. "Jade, I blame myself for getting caught up in the teasing. Once it starts, you never know where it will go."

"I don't mind," Jade assured her. She didn't want them to treat her like an outsider. "I've never been around a big family. This is nice."

"Show of hands," Callie declared. "All in favor of making Jade an official member of the family?"

Unable to stop herself, Jade's eyes slid to Garrett. His vote mattered. If he didn't want her there, she would accede to his wishes. Jade caught her breath. Not only was his hand up, he looked directly at her. Unwavering. The distance between them made it impossible to tell the color of his eyes. Maybe a clear gray? Silver? Either way, he didn't object to her being here.

"Unanimous." Callie opened her arms, drawing Jade in for a warm hug. "There's no getting rid of the Landis clan now, young lady."

"Sounds good to me," Jade said, her eyes once again meeting Garrett's.

Damn. She had to stop that. How could she insist on nothing but friendship if she couldn't stop looking at him? Or wanting to touch him. The answer to her problem was simple. She couldn't come to the house when she knew Garrett would be here. Plain and simple — he was too much of a temptation.

"Okay." Callie clapped her hands. "Now that we've settled that, let's eat."

Jade picked up her glass before she was swept away by the crowd of hungry men. She felt a hand on her waist, guiding her to her chair. Without looking, Jade knew who it was.

"I know what you were thinking back there," Garrett whispered as he held the chair out for her.

Jade sat, afraid to answer. Her throat felt tight. She couldn't force any words past the lump in her throat.

"You want to be friends."

How did he know?

As he pushed in her chair, Garrett leaned closer. "Friends? No fucking way."

It wasn't said as a threat. Jade didn't feel threatened or frightened in any way. There was a low, deep promise in Garrett's voice that made a shiver run through her body. Damn him. With only a few words, she felt that pre-sex languor pulse over her skin, through her veins, pooling between her legs.

"Are you wet?" Garrett asked her with a voice so low before she knew what she was doing, Jade leaned closer to his lips. Before he stood back, he added three more words that were bound to have her squirming all through dinner. "Think of me."

Evil. Diabolical. Jade had no idea Garrett was capable of such underhanded manipulation. *Think of him?* How could she do anything else? Especially when he sat directly opposite her. She couldn't avoid looking at him and the half-grin he sported whenever he caught her staring. Jade swore as soon as Nate taught her how, she was going to kick Garrett's ass.

The two were so busy they didn't notice Callie watching them. *Well, what do you know?* Garrett and Jade. After that long speech about why they wouldn't suit, she should have felt foolish. Instead, she was delighted. And curious. It was obvious this wasn't their first meeting. How long had this been going on? How far had it gone? Damn, damn, damn. The unanswered questions would drive her crazy. Still, she was a mother first. She wouldn't poke at Garrett for information. The friend in her wanted Jade to confide. Until she did so voluntarily, Callie would keep her suspicions to herself. Oh, it was hard keeping her nose out of their business when she loved them both. Then a thought occurred to her. If she let things develop naturally, who knew? By spring, she might be helping to plan a wedding.

Grinning, Callie looked around the table at her big, happy family. Life was good. Picking up the serrated knife sitting by the lasagna, she asked, "Who's hungry?"

Chapter Twelve

JADE SPENT A restless night. What little sleep she did get was filled with hot vignettes starring Garrett in various stages of undress. She would be much better off if she didn't know what it was like to be held next to his naked body. She didn't need an imagination. She knew what the real thing felt like.

Jade was determined to never be with Garrett again. Her resolve might slip when she was sleeping — in the light of day, she couldn't let herself weaken. No matter how many times he whispered sexily into her ear or gave her looks that melted her insides, she couldn't waver. Could she?

No! No! No!

Screaming the words in her head, didn't make Jade believe them. She wanted Garrett. More than that, she missed him. While the sex was phenomenal, it was afterward, when he held her. When they talked about everything and anything. An intimacy to those moments was new to her. Now that she knew what it was like to connect with another person on such a deep level, knowing she would never have it again made her want to weep.

What she needed to do was pull herself together. Stop thinking about what couldn't be. The best way Jade knew to do that was to immerse herself in work.

Party planner? Event specialist? Whatever she called herself, Jade knew one thing. No one was going to hire her if they didn't know she was open for business. Word of mouth was terrific. To get people to talk, someone had to start the conversation.

Jade's advantage over someone just starting out, were the hundreds of names, numbers, and emails that were already at her fingertips. Finally, all the years she was Anson Marlow's *hostess* paid off.

Energized, Jade decided her first course of action would be to build a website. True, most of her Beverly Hills contacts were not big cybersurfers. But their assistants were. Besides, she wanted to expand beyond the closed off group she had mingled in all of her life. A new world was out there, or at least new to her, that needed her services. She planned on tapping into it.

Jade spent the rest of the day getting the bare bones of her site put together. Deciding on a name was easy. She wanted something simple, yet elegant. Jade was a distinctive enough name — easily remembered. Why not use it? She wasn't going to capitalize on her Marlow connection or her own notoriety. Once word got out about who the Jade was in *Jade Events*, it would be impossible to keep away the rubberneckers and reporters. However, that would die down. If she dealt with the negative straight out, she hoped it wouldn't be long before the business was all she had to deal with.

For the first time, Jade found a practical use for her background in graphic design. She delighted in fooling around with different logo ideas. She discarded anything that was too complicated or too simple. Again, she wanted elegant and distinctive. The gold intertwined J and E that she finally settled on was perfect.

Jade rolled her shoulders, loosening the tightened muscles. Two-thirty? Could that be right? No wonder her muscles felt stiff. It was eight o'clock when she sat down in front of her newly purchased laptop. She had worked all morning, missing lunch.

Standing, Jade decided her body needed a workout before she filled her stomach. Sweet, patient Nate made it clear. If she was serious about protecting herself, she needed to work on her strength and conditioning.

The yoga she did every other day was a good foundation. After she was released from the hospital and her wounds were almost healed, she started an online course. She didn't have to go out or deal with anyone. In the privacy of her own bedroom, she learned how to center her thoughts through breathing. The moves were basic, yet still they worked wonders whenever Jade's thoughts would wander into dark territory. Long, deep breaths. Center her careening emotions. Yoga, along with her therapist, turned out to be a lifesaver.

And Garrett. Jade sighed as she changed into her running gear. Why did she always come back to him? Because. If the yoga centered her, and her therapist helped put things into perspective, Garrett brought her back to life. Without him, she wouldn't be out of her father's house, starting a new business. She owed him so much. Which was why she wouldn't give into her selfish impulses. Garrett didn't need the headaches she would inevitably bring him. She might need him — he didn't need her.

Jade left the building, turning right. She already knew the route she would take. It was exactly one mile to the shoe repair shop and back. She could handle that distance. Slow and easy. If she needed to walk every now and then, that was fine. Eventually, she would build up to running the entire way. A little faster, then a little farther. Endurance. That was her goal.

She didn't break any speed records, but she managed to jog the entire distance at a steady pace. Maybe all that yoga was good for more than steadying her nerves. Tomorrow she would hit the weights. Callie insisted Jade come to the Landis house to use their gym instead of joining a fitness club. They could be workout buddies. It was easier to stay motivated, Callie told her, when you had someone to push you.

Jade waved at the doorman as he held open the front door to her building. Feeling ambitious, she decided to take the stairs. She only made it six floors before dragging her butt to the elevator. Hey, that was six floors more than she did yesterday. Little steps that would lead to bigger ones.

She needed a shower, then something to eat. Jade loved having an appetite. Looking forward to planning her meals. Making shopping lists. Even before she was stabbed, food didn't hold much appeal. She would skip meals, never making them. So when she came home from the hospital, having lost her appetite altogether, it didn't take long for her to be reduced to a rack of skin and bones.

Once again, thank you, Garrett. He made eating fun. Before Jade knew it, she was twenty pounds heavier. Her doctor encouraged her to add another ten. With the muscle she hoped to pack on in the next few months, she might meet that goal.

Jade did a mental inventory of what she had in the kitchen. Milk, bread, and the leftovers from last night's dinner that Callie insisted she take home. A few pieces of fruit. All good, but she was in the mood for something else. A big, fat, greasy hamburger. With French fries. She wasn't familiar enough with the neighborhood yet to know where to get a good one or who delivered, so Jade called the front desk. Bruno was on duty. He claimed to have a study of every restaurant worth knowing. After she had hung up, she was convinced he at least could share a wide variety of places. She would judge for herself if *Manny's Burger Palace* truly boasted the best in the city. Jade called in her order. They assured her she had at least half an hour, so she headed for the shower.

The large stall with its multiple spraying jets washed away the sweat from Jade's body. She closed her eyes, running her soap-slicked hands across the zigzag of scars. Since moving into the loft, Jade no longer obsessed with how they looked. She didn't turn away if she caught her reflection in the mirror.

Last night, after returning home, she stood before the full-length mirror in the closet. She removed her clothes, refusing to turn away from her image. She wasn't horrified by what she saw. It wasn't as if she had never looked before. However, this was the first time she looked with a different perspective.

Before she was a victim, she saw the marks on the body as something to be ashamed of — to cower from. This time, she saw them for what they were. A crazy quilt badge of honor. Jade Marlow was a survivor. A cold, unfeeling monster for a father. An abusive marriage. Almost starving herself to death because she didn't care enough to eat the bare minimum required to sustain her body. After all that, she was still standing. Standing hell. She was thriving.

Jade took a pair of jeans from the built-in mahogany dresser, slipping them over a scrap of lace that could almost pass for underwear. Not bothering with a bra, she pulled on a bright yellow camisole. Her hair was still damp but since she wasn't planning on going out, she decided to let it dry naturally. She was just finishing rubbing in a lightly scented cream over her arms when the doorbell sounded.

Grabbing the wallet from her bag so she could reimburse Bruno, Jade hurried to the door.

"Perfect timing. I'm so hungry I could eat the bag."

"Let's hope it doesn't come to that."

"Garrett."

"Let me in, honey. There's little sadder than cold fries."

"Then hand me the bag and leave."

"Where's your curiosity? Don't you want to know why I'm here? Or how I got past the doorman?"

"I know why you're here. And I assume you tipped the doorman an outrageous amount."

Realizing Jade wasn't going to invite him, Garrett squeezed by her. At least she didn't yell, *You shall not pass*. Then again, he didn't know very many women who quoted Gandalf. That was more of a geeky guy thing.

"Give the guy some credit, Jade. The doorman can't be bribed. He would lose his job in a heartbeat."

With a sigh, Jade closed the door. She followed Garrett to the kitchen, watching as he took out a sheet tray before turning on the oven. He unwrapped the burger and fries, depositing them on the tray, before sliding it into the oven. He didn't hesitate or ask her where anything was. Almost as though…

"You've been here before. And take that back out. I'm hungry."

"I don't want it to get cold while we talk." Garrett took a bottle of white wine from the refrigerator. The glasses were to his right. Again, something he already knew."

"This is your loft, isn't it?"

"Mmm." Garrett handed her the half-full goblet. "I bought it six years ago. When I decided to build a house in Laurel Canyon, I put this place on the market."

"Callie didn't tell me."

"Because she was afraid you'd say no if you knew a family member owned it. Was she wrong?"

"I... Maybe. I don't know."

Jade felt like her brain was bouncing around like a half-inflated rubber ball. Her thoughts were jumbled — sluggish, instead of sharp. Garrett, the man she spent all day telling herself she had to avoid, stood five feet away. Handsome, sexy. Irresistible. Why did life have to be so unfair?

"I want you to leave, Garrett." Good. Firm voice, full of conviction. "I don't care if you own this place. I'll move out if you want. If I stay, you have to respect my wishes."

"Tell me about your wishes, Jade."

Garrett circled around her like a panther stalking its prey. Jade felt the hair on the back of her neck stand up. Not out of fear. He would never hurt her. However, he could easily break her willpower. One look into his clear, silver eyes and she could feel her resolve crumbling.

"You know what I want. I told you this; we are over. I thanked you." The moment she said the words Jade knew they sounded lame.

"Ah, yes. The text. Not cool, Jade." Garrett gaze sharpened. "What the hell were you thinking?"

"You're angry."

"Don't you think I have the right to be," Garrett asked. "Only a few hours after one of the best nights of my life, I get a message basically saying, thank you and fuck off."

Jade winced.

"You seem surprised," he continued. "What made you think this was over?"

"Last night," Jade said. "You were so… calm."

"I couldn't make a scene in front of my family. Trust me, when I saw Nate with his arms around you, I felt like someone had punched me in the gut."

"Nate?" Jade was confused. "He was showing me some basic self-defense."

"He's a man. He was touching you." Garrett leaned closer. "Brother or not, I don't want anyone else touching you."

"Garrett…"

"You don't know how to respond to that, do you?" Garrett stepped closer. "Part of you wants to protest. *How dare I presume to tell you who can and can't touch you?* Then there's the other part of you."

"What part?" Jade asked breathlessly.

"The part that likes it."

"Stay back," Jade warned, inching away. She had to stop when her back literally came up against a brick wall. "Nate showed me how to down a man with one kick."

"That rarely works when you warn your victim ahead of time." Garrett put a hand on each side of her head. "I could never hurt you, Jade."

"I know." Her eyes met his. Stormy gray. His emotions were as turbulent as hers.

"It does occur to me, though, that's it's time to stop treating you with kid gloves." He moved, brushing her chest with his. "You left fragile behind some time ago. I think I was too close to notice. You're stronger, aren't you, honey? You don't need to be petted like a wounded bird."

"No." Jade felt mesmerized. Between his voice. The words he spoke. His eyes. She was falling. No, not falling. This was completely consensual. She was going to jump. The hell with the consequences.

"I want to be treated like a woman, Garrett. I can take care of myself. No one will ever again take my choices away."

"Then tell me what you want."

Garrett's lips were so close she felt the breath of every word he spoke. Warm, sweet. Tempting.

Keeping her eyes locked on his, Jade took the hem of her shirt, pulling it over her head, daring him to look. She had no safety net this time. The bright afternoon light filled the room. There was no camera to switch off. Garrett wasn't hundreds of miles away. It was time to let him *really* see her. Every inch. Every flaw.

Less than a heartbeat later, Garrett dropped to his knees, level with her stomach. Silently, he wrapped his arms around her hips. He rested his cheek against her scarred flesh, simply holding on.

Jade closed her eyes, savoring the feel of him rubbing a day's growth of stubble across her skin. It was a familiar feeling. Garrett would do the same thing in that darkened motel room. She threaded her fingers through his hair, pulling him away. She slowly opened her eyes.

"Thank you." Garrett said the words against her stomach, the brush of his lips making her shiver.

Jade watched as Garrett traced each scar, first with his eyes, then his fingers. Finally with his mouth. Somehow, it was healing and erotic at the same time.

"I wish I could take away the pain — erase it from your memory."

Garrett bathed the longest, deepest scar with his tongue. Jade gasped. He seemed to have the power to give her so much pleasure, the pain no longer mattered. When he unbuttoned her jeans, finding the very edges of the indelible marks, she felt strength in her legs begin to falter. As though sensing what she was feeling, Garrett rose to his feet, his hands lifting her legs until they were wrapped firmly around his waist.

"I'll never let you fall, Jade," Garrett whispered near her ear. He bit the lobe, somehow finding the perfect balance between pain and pleasure. "Hold on. This is going to be fast and hard. Are you with me?"

Always. The word echoed in her head. All that came out of her mouth was deep, gasping groan of pleasure.

Garrett reached between them, pulling her jeans lower, and then fumbling to release himself. Jade felt the length of him, rubbing where seconds earlier his mouth had been.

"Tell me you need this," Garrett growled against her lips. "Tell me you can't live without it."

"I need you." Jade practically whimpered the words, straining to bring her hips closer to his. "Now. Please."

With one arm anchoring her to him, Garrett entered her, his thrust hard. True. He muttered something about finding heaven before his mouth crushed hers with a kiss filled with pent up passion and frustration. His tongue swirled against hers, caressing the inside of her mouth. He didn't take the time to soothe or coax. This was raw. Primal. Up against the wall. No holds barred. Exactly as she wanted it.

As Garrett's thrusts became faster, his hand slid into Jade's hair. He slanted his mouth over hers. Neither needed a gasp of air. They shared. Moan matched moan. Jade tightened her legs, grinding against Garrett, her breasts flattened against his chest, her hard nipples practically branding him. If she could make her mark on him, she would. Something permanent to remind him he belonged to her.

"You're mine, Jade. Say it."

As much as she wanted to shout it to the world, Jade couldn't say the words. So she pulled his mouth back to hers.

"Damn it," Garrett shouted as they both reached their peak. "You! Are! Mine!"

As she crashed over into a pleasure like none she had ever known, she cried out the words they both needed to hear.

"Yes! Yours. Only yours."

Garrett's harsh breath formed a light, damp, mist on her neck. They spent several moments, locked together, their heartbeats synched in pounding rhythm. Instead of letting Jade's legs slide to the ground, he held her tighter. Garrett made his way down the hall to the bedroom, turning at the last second so that, as they fell onto the bed, he landed on the bottom.

Jade kissed Garrett's shoulder before resting her head against it.

They were tangled together, clothing twisted, sweaty, sticky. It felt amazing. She tried to tell herself this was wrong. Summoning up all the reasons why this shouldn't have happened was too difficult when she had Garrett's arms around her. She promised herself she would move away. Soon. Tomorrow at the latest.

"Are you still angry?"

"Yes." Garrett smoothed back her hair. "Less angry. I'm still in recovery mode. After you tell me what all that crap was about, I'll probably scale back to mildly annoyed."

Jade hesitated. Telling Garrett was the smart thing to do. If he understood, he would stay away. The problem was she didn't want him to. After talking herself into believing she was doing the right thing when she cut him out of her life, what did she do? She went to his parents' house knowing he would be there. Then, she didn't simply welcome his lovemaking; she ripped off her shirt. If that didn't cry, *I'm ready and willing*, Jade didn't know what did.

Saying goodbye to Garrett was much easier when he was in another country.

"Speak to me, Jade."

Garrett pulled back until he could look her in the eye. What he saw made him laugh. The two of them looked as though they had been through a cyclone. Barely living to tell the tale.

"Hold that thought," Garrett said, untangling their legs. "Or maybe I should say, get your thoughts together. Once we have cleaned up, I expect answers."

Jade knew what needed to be said. Saying it to his face would be the hard part.

"First things first." Garrett kissed Jade. Thoroughly. "Damn." He kissed her again. "No more of that. Thinking straight around you is hard enough without fogging my brain with kisses."

"You kissed me," Jade reminded him.

"Details, details."

Garrett scooted off the bed. He stood looking down at her with admiration in his gaze.

"Looking at you seems to affect me the same as your kisses." He gave his head a quick shake. "I was going to undress you myself. Bad idea."

"Oh, I don't know." Jade tugged a little on the waistband of the jeans that were already down below her butt. "A girl can always use a helping hand."

"No more sex until we've eaten," Garrett declared. "I don't imagine that burger and fries are in the best of shape. I'll order us a couple of new ones while you start the shower."

"I showered before you got here," Jade told him. She sniffed her arm. "I don't want to wash you off my skin."

"Oh, honey," Garrett groaned. "If you keep saying things like that, we'll never get out of this bedroom."

"Promise?"

Chuckling, Garrett lifted Jade into his arms.

"Incorrigible." He took five steps, depositing her at the walk-in door. "I like the idea of having your scent on me while we eat. Find a shirt, though? Your breasts are too distracting."

She watched as Garrett walked away, adjusting his clothes as he went. Nice ass. Perfect for grabbing during sex. Jade grinned. She couldn't believe they had sex up against the wall. He still had on his shirt. His shoes were still on his feet. Jade felt a shiver of excitement rush through her body. Knowing she could make him want her that much was a heady thought. After a brief consideration, she decided she liked having that power. It was only fair. Garrett wielded the same over her.

Wearing a loose purple t-shirt, Jade joined Garrett in the kitchen. She had changed out of her jeans into cotton shorts. They showed off her long legs. She always considered them her best feature. Lately, they were becoming nicely toned as well as shapely. Showing them off seemed only natural.

"Hey," Jade cried when she saw him eating her French fries. "I thought you called in another order." Half the fries were gone. "I guess they were still edible."

Garrett shrugged, not the least bit chastised. "They're still in pretty good shape." He dredged a fry in ketchup. "Want a bite."

"Gee, thanks."

Sarcasm aside, the strip of potato looked good. She was starving. Jade opened her mouth.

"Oops," Garrett said. "There's ketchup on your chin."

Chewing the warm fry, Jade reached for a napkin. As she lifted it, Garrett snatched it out of her hand.

"Allow me."

Eyes sparkling, he tossed the napkin onto the counter.

"Don't you dare start something you aren't going to finish," Jade warned when he pulled her close.

"I'll finish." He licked the red sauce from her chin. Garrett leaned closer causing Jade to lift her lips in anticipation. "Eventually."

He pushed her away. Jade's eyes narrowed.

"I cry foul. I want my kiss."

"You can have as many as you want. After we talk."

Garrett poured them each a glass of wine, handing one to Jade. Then he took her free hand and led her to the sofa. Once they were settled, he turned to her.

"Honey, as pissed off as that text made me, I knew something had to have happened to make you send it." He linked his fingers with his. "When we said good night, you were happy. Hell, you were glowing. I was under the impression we had a breakthrough. I was making plans for the future."

"You were?"

Hearing the surprise in her voice, Garrett laughed.

"Guys do that too." He kissed the back of her hand. "When it's the right woman."

"I let myself dream too," Jade admitted.

"So tell me what happened. What changed in those few hours?"

"My father."

Garrett sighed. He felt a wave of anger he did his best to tamp down. Why did every bad story Jade had to tell, begin with her bastard father?

"What did he do?"

"He had me followed."

Before she started, Jade thought her explanation would take hours. In her head, it was an epic tale. Homeric. In reality, it took her fifteen minutes — start to finish. She was so nervous by the end she wished she had more to say.

For several moments, Garrett didn't respond. His eyes, though, were a stormy gray. That couldn't be good.

"Why does he treat you like that?"

Looking around, Jade spied her purse on one of the barstools. Without a word, she removed her wallet, taking out the picture of her mother. She handed it to Garrett.

"The resemblance is amazing." He looked from the picture, to Jade, and then back. "This is no excuse, Jade. You aren't your mother."

"No," she agreed. "I'm not trying to make my father out to be a sympathetic person. I'm simply sharing with you the only clue I have. He doesn't care about me, Garrett. I'm an annoyance. A daily reminder of a woman who did the seemingly impossible. She walked away from Anson Marlow. And now her daughter has done the same."

"I might feel sympathy for your mother. Except she left you alone with a man *she* couldn't live with. Nothing justifies that."

Jade shrugged. "I can't speak for her. She made her choice. I *do* understand the need to get out from under my father's thumb."

"Your father is the biggest son of a bitch ever born."

"Probably."

"Probably?" Garrett exclaimed. "He wins the contest, Jade. Hands down."

"I don't know any other sons of bitches." Jade shrugged. "I'll defer to your vast knowledge."

"Is that a joke? Because I don't find any of this funny."

"No," Jade conceded. "But at this point, it's either laugh or shoot him. I don't want to go to jail."

"Justifiable homicide. I know just the lawyer to get me off."

"You?" Jade frowned. "Why would you shoot him?"

"Because you're my woman. A real man steps in and does what killing needs doing." Garrett used his best Old West accent to emphasize his point. "Now. Take a sip of your wine."

Jade did what he asked.

"Good." Garrett did the same. Taking hers, he set their glasses on the coffee table. "Come here. I need to hold you."

Gratefully, Jade wrapped her arms around Garrett's waist, her head resting on his shoulder.

"Am I?"

"Are you what?"

"Your woman."

"From the moment you walked into that motel room." Garrett pulled her closer.

"You understand why this isn't a good idea." Jade took a deep breath. She needed him to examine all the angles before he made his decision. "Why *we* aren't a good idea."

"There isn't anything that your father or the press can throw at me that I haven't seen before, Jade," Garrett assured her. "Let them rake their muck. It won't last. Before you can blink, someone else will capture the public's attention."

"My father can keep it alive as long as he wants." Jade burrowed closer, a chill passing over her. "I don't know how he took my leaving. I expected him to call. Or send one of his lackeys. Nothing."

"Maybe he won't do anything." Garrett didn't believe his words any more than Jade did.

"His pride has been wounded. Or is it his ego?" Jade sighed. "Whatever it is, he isn't capable of letting it go, Garrett. When he finds out you're the man I was meeting, he will be livid. He hates looking foolish. I shudder to think what kind of crap his people will start throwing around."

"I have excellent reflexes."

"Some of it is bound to hit you," Jade warned. "I don't want you or your family to suffer because of me."

"None of this is your fault," Garrett said with absolute conviction.

"As for my family. Our business is movies. That means gossip. Ridiculous speculation. From my parents' first date, they have been tabloid fodder. I've lost track of how many times some rag has had them either divorcing, separating, cheating. We've all developed rhinoceros skins when it comes to such stories."

"But…"

"I don't care, Jade." Garrett pulled her up until they were face to face. "Understand? We'll deal with it. If and when it happens. No more hiding. And I'm sure as hell not walking away. Got it?"

Jade threw herself into Garrett's arms.

"I know I should argue," she whispered. "I want this so much I can't bring myself to."

"This?" Garrett slid his hand under her shirt, growling with satisfaction when he found her bare breast. "No bra and those shorts? You wanted to drive me crazy."

"You." Jade gasped. One touch and her nipple was hard. "I want you."

"The food will be here soon."

"Mmm." Jade ran her fingers through his hair, tugging gently until his mouth was close to hers. "Kiss me."

"You need to eat."

"Feel this." Jade pulled Garrett's hand to just below her breast. "No more protruding ribs. You've fattened me up nicely during the past six months." She gave him a brief, teasing kiss. "My appetite is better than ever. Didn't you notice how much food I put away last night?"

"A big slice of lasagna *and* dessert. Very sexy."

Jade laughed. "I don't know about that."

"It's true," Garrett said. He moved his hand back to her breast, the pad of his thumb running over the peak. "You would put a bite in your mouth then lick your lips. I was hard all evening. Thank God for that tablecloth."

"Now you're teasing me." Jade nibbled along the side of his jaw. "You looked like you didn't have a care in the world. I, on the other hand, was in misery. That was dirty pool, whispering in my ear while you seated me."

"Were you wet?"

Jade blushed. After everything they had done together, dirty talk was still new to her. She liked it. *Boy did she like it.* Still, the words heated her skin as well as her insides.

"You know I was. Am," she added.

"Let me take care of you." Garrett slipped his hand into the waist of her shorts. "The look in your eyes tells me I can get you off before the food arrives."

"Nope." Jade stopped Garrett's hand with her own. "I've decided you're right. We need some nourishment for what I have in mind."

Loving this teasing, happy Jade, Garrett wrapped her in his arms before teasing her ear with his tongue.

"Tell me what you have in mind."

Jade leaned closer, telling him in breathy detail.

"Now that is cruel," Garrett complained. His eyes were a fierce, molten gray. "I've dreamed of your mouth on me. Eat when I have that image in my head."

"Call it an appetizer."

Just then, the doorbell rang.

"Good timing." Garrett walked to the door. "I'll give you fifteen minutes. Burger, fries, milkshake."

"You ordered milkshakes? What flavor?"

"What else?" Garrett winked. "Chocolate."

Chapter Thirteen

JADE'S EYES OPENED slowly. A small beam of early morning sunlight streamed through the crack in the closed curtains.

Strong, masculine arms circled her waist, holding her close. *Garrett*. To wake up with him after a night of lovemaking was a luxury Jade had never expected to experience.

No more sneaking in and out of seedy motel rooms. No more worries about getting caught or the consequences that would surely follow. Garrett wanted to be with her. Out in the open. For the whole world to see.

Jade felt some lingering doubt. She knew better than anyone what her father was capable of. Especially when he felt the slightest bit of perceived embarrassment or humiliation. She had walked out without a word or a backward glance. She took nothing. Asked for nothing. For a man who prided himself on complete control of those around him, her actions had to rankle.

Whatever Anson Marlow threw at them, they would take. Head on. Together.

"That was a happy sound."

Garrett kissed Jade's bare shoulder, his arms pulling her close.

"Happy woman, happy sounds."

She turned to face him. Garrett's tousled hair and sleepy eyes were the best things she had ever seen this early in the morning. Feeling the nudge of his erection against her stomach, she smiled.

"Speaking of happy."

"Hmm," Garrett nuzzled the sensitive spot at the base of her throat. "Apparently, you didn't wear me out last night. And early this morning. Despite your best efforts, there's still life in the old boy."

Jade raised her leg over his hip, sliding her slick center over him. "Show me."

Garrett's eyes sharpened

"With pleasure."

"YOU LOOK LIKE the cat that got the cream. What were you up to last night?"

Looking at his brother with wide-eyed innocence, Garrett merely shrugged.

"Cut the bullshit," Nate scoffed. "Who is she? Wait. Is it the same woman? The one Wyatt thought might be married?"

"Wyatt has a dirty mind."

"We all do," Nate grinned. "Dad blames Mom."

"And Mom blames Dad." Garrett laughed. "The point is I don't do married women. Only a dirty mind would accuse me of such a thing."

The brothers had met for a late lunch. After reluctantly leaving a very warm and satisfied Jade, Garrett headed to the studio for another production meeting. Since this one involved his recent activities in Vancouver, he couldn't blow it off. Staying in bed with Jade all day was a much more appealing idea. The problem was he couldn't use it as an excuse to get out of the meeting. Addicted to Jade wouldn't cut it with Wyatt.

"I'm beginning to worry about my brothers," Garrett said, taking a bite of his BLT on whole wheat. "You equate happiness with sex."

"And you don't?" Nate slathered his Reuben with mustard.

"I don't have to have sex to be happy."

Nate gave him one of those *are you shitting me* looks that always made Garrett laugh.

"Don't get me wrong," Garrett said. "Sex never hurts."

"Damn straight," Nate nodded. "If you do it right."

"Idiot." Garrett wadded his napkin, hitting Nate in the forehead. Dead center.

"What are you, twelve?" Nate complained. Then proceeded to wing the piece of paper back at Garrett. It couldn't have hurt. When it stuck to Garrett's mouth, the victory was a moral one. Satisfying, nonetheless.

"Tell me about her."

He and Jade talked about this. How to let people know they were seeing each other. When it came to the general public, they decided to let it come out in its own way. Word of mouth, tabloids, bloggers. If any of them picked up the story, so be it. Garrett told Jade the best way to handle it was to let them have their fun. After a few days, a week at most, it would be old news. Jade wasn't as confident about that as Garrett was. She was positive her father wouldn't let it die that easily. Either way, they had a plan. No comment.

Garrett's family was another matter. Neither he nor Jade wanted his parents and brothers to hear about it from another source. Telling Nate would be a good place to start.

"I've been seeing the same woman for a little over six months."

"And you haven't said anything? What gives?"

Garrett shrugged. "The situation is sticky."

"Not married."

"No," Garrett sighed. "Technically, maybe."

When Nate put down his sandwich, Garrett knew his brother was taking the conversation seriously.

"Hell, Garrett. That can never end well." Nate frowned. "Kids?"

"No." Garrett leaned closer. The last thing he wanted was for any of this to be overheard. "It's Jade."

"Marlow?"

"Shh," Garrett looked around. No one seemed to be paying them any undue attention.

"Yes. Do you know another Jade?"

"When you said sticky situation, you weren't kidding." Nate gave Garrett a friendly punch on the shoulder. "I have to hand it to you. Keeping that relationship under wraps had to take some doing."

"You have no idea."

"I didn't catch any vibes the other night at dinner."

"Things had hit a snag. We were..."

"On a break?"

"Stop quoting *Friends*."

Nate loved that show. A few years ago when he worked on a Jennifer Aniston movie, he talked about her for weeks. She was his first major pre-teen crush. According to Nate, she was even more beautiful in person.

"You can never go wrong quoting the classics." Nate popped a homemade potato chip in his mouth. "I take it. Whatever the problem was, it has been settled."

"Between Jade and me? Things are golden." Garrett's grin turned into a scowl. "Her father is an asshole who won't go away."

Garrett gave Nate a rundown. He felt comfortable telling his brother about Jade's relationship with Anson Marlow, from the time her mother abandoned her, the neglect, verbal abuse. How her father turned a blind eye to Stephen Marsh's physical abuse. He ended with his own belief that Marlow was behind his son-in-law's disappearance.

"There is no way that psycho drunk could get out of town on his own. Let alone stay hidden all this time."

"Garrett." Nate pushed the rest of his food away, his appetite gone. "Anson Marlow is one fucked up bastard. We all knew the bare bones of what Jade went through, but man, I don't know how she came out the other side."

"She's tougher than she looks," Garrett said. He felt a surge of pride. His woman wasn't simply surviving. She was thriving.

"Tough, hell. That woman has a rod of steel running through her."

Nate shook his head. "Until that weak-ass abuser husband is found, she'll never be completely safe, Garrett."

"I have H&W Security working on that."

"Smart," Nate nodded. "They are the best."

"I'm hoping—" Garrett's phone buzzed. "Speak of the devil. Hey, Jack. Nate and I were just talking about the job you're doing for me. Please tell me you have some good news."

"Well," Jack Winston sighed. "I have news. Not good, not bad."

"I don't like the sound of that."

"I can't explain it, Garrett. Every time we get a lead on Marsh, he falls off the radar. Someone is shuffling him from place to place."

"I knew he had help." Garrett looked at Nate. His brother was trying to follow the conversation. He wanted Nate's input, but an increasingly crowded restaurant wasn't the place to get it. "Can you hold for a few minutes, Jack? I need to find some privacy."

"No problem."

Paying the bill, Garrett and Nate left the restaurant, walking a block to where Nate parked his truck. After they had climbed into the hot, stuffy cab, Nate turned the air conditioner on full blast. Garrett switched his phone to speaker mode.

"Go ahead, Jack."

"I told you I turned this over to Alex Fleming."

"Right." Garrett nodded. "Ex-Army."

"Alex knows how to find people. It's one of his specialties. Under normal circumstances, Marsh would already be in custody." Garrett could hear the frustration in Jack's voice. "Two days after you called, Alex had him traced to a small town in Montana. Before we could contact the authorities, he was gone. Vanished like a puff of smoke."

"It takes money to do that," Nate said. He and Garrett looked at each other, anger in their eyes. What little doubt there was had been wiped away. Anson Marlow had to be involved.

"I agree," Jack said. "Look, Alex just walked in my office. He's been on top of this thing from day one. I'll let him fill you in."

After they had taken care of brief introductions, Garrett and Nate listened as Alex caught them up on the frustrating situation.

"I'm positive Marsh has a handler," Alex began.

"You think Marlow hired a guy to keep Marsh in the wind?" Garrett clenched his fists. This was worse than he imagined.

"Don't assume a man is in charge," Alex said. "Whoever is with Marsh could just as easily be a woman. In fact, I would have gone that way. A man and a woman traveling together tend to raise fewer red flags. This person is good," Alex almost growled the words. He wasn't a man who liked being outmaneuvered.

"So basically, we're fucked." Garrett felt like punching his hand through the window.

"Did I say that?" Alex asked. "I'll get them. I found them in Montana. From there they moved to Indiana. The last sighting was Chicago. Smart to move to a bigger city. That last time was close."

"This isn't goddamned horseshoes."

"Garrett, calm down." Anticipating his brother, Nate narrowly saved Garrett's fist and his window from damage.

Garrett wrenched his hand from Nate's. Didn't any of them understand? As long as Marsh was in the wind, Jade's life was in danger.

"This has to be driving you crazy," Alex said. "The woman I love means everything to me. Look, I know it doesn't seem like much, but as long as Marsh isn't in California, Jade is safe."

Alex was right. It wasn't much consolation. However, it was something.

"Any suggestions on how I handle things here?" Garrett needed to do something. Anything. "Is it time to hire a bodyguard?"

"You read my mind," Alex told Garrett. "Sable will be there first thing tomorrow."

"Sable?" Garrett gave Nate a questioning look.

"She's the best I have," Alex assured him. "Remember. Men tend to underestimate women. No one, I mean no one, will get past Sable."

Garrett hung up, his mind racing with information. The good, the bad, and the confusing.

"What did you get from that?"

"Trust Jack and Alex to know what they're doing," Nate shrugged. "Sable. Interesting name. Like something from a James Bond flick. What do you think she'll look like?"

"I don't know. One of those East German swimmers when they were bulked up on steroids?" Garrett answered absently. He wasn't worried about Jade's bodyguard. He was worried about Jade. Then there was the problem of telling her about Jack, Alex, and now Sable. He wondered how she would react when she found out he did all this without consulting her first?

Nate shuddered. "A mustache and bacne? No thanks." When he noticed Garrett's distracted frown, Nate patted his brother on the arm. "Hey, we'll all be looking out for Jade."

"I don't know what I would do if anything else happened to her, Nate." Garrett stared sightlessly out the window. "When I think about how close that animal came to killing her… I have to keep her safe."

"Look at me."

"What?"

"Turn your head and look at me," Nate told him.

"What the hell are you jabbering on about?" Garrett asked, doing as Nate demanded.

"Holy shit!" Nate shook his head. "It's true. You're in love with Jade."

Garrett didn't deny it. What would be the point? Still, Nate seemed awfully sure of something he could only be guessing about.

"What makes you so sure?"

"What is it they always say about Mom? Her eyes ever lie? Look in the mirror, Garrett. Purple."

Pulling down the sun visor, Garrett looked into the mirror. Deep purple. It was a shade he had seen many times. In his mother's eyes. When his father walked into the room, or when someone mentioned his name. It was the color of love.

"All those years we teased you about the girls you dated," Nate grinned. "Checking your eyes to see if it was serious. Wondering if, even though your eyes were like hers in every other way, maybe the love thing skipped you. Take it from me; you are one hundred percent, full-bore, head-over-heels."

"Shit."

It was the only thing Garrett could think of to say. He barely had Jade out of the dark. She wasn't ready for *till death do us part*. Hell, he wasn't sure *he* was ready. They were just starting a normal relationship. Dating. Going away for a weekend. He was busy with *Exile*. Finding out how Jade dealt with the demands of his career would go a long way in finding out how compatible they were outside of the bedroom.

"I know that look."

Garrett mentally shook himself before turning his questioning gaze onto Nate.

"What look?"

"You're starting to overthink it," Nate said. "Your careening thoughts are so loud I swear I hear a slight echo."

"Are you suggesting my head is hollow?"

Nate grinned. "Only when that inner voice of yours makes a fool of itself." Nate started the truck, pulling into the busy Los Angeles traffic with the ease of a seasoned stunt car driver. "Let yourself enjoy what you're feeling. I like Jade. The whole family likes her."

"That is important," Garrett conceded. "Not only to me. Jade has never had a family, Nate. Not one like ours. The closer she gets to everyone, the more it will hurt us if we can't make it work."

Keeping one eye on the thick traffic, Nate leaned over, knocking Garrett on the head with his fist.

"Hey," Garrett protested. He rubbed the offended spot. "That's like being hit by a sledgehammer."

"Stop worrying about what might happen, idiot. For the first time in your life, you are in love. Do you know what I would give to feel that? It doesn't happen every day, you know."

Nate was right — an annoying habit of his. It was time to enjoy life with Jade. The danger surrounding her be damned. To hell with his crazy doubts. Loving someone was a new and heady experience. It was time to embrace every new, exciting feeling.

"One more piece of advice," Nate said, turning onto the highway.

"What's that?"

"Tell Jade how you feel. Soon. Otherwise, you'll be spending most of your time with your eyes closed."

AFTER CHANGING HER clothes five times, Jade left for her first official meeting as a full-time party planner. She could probably come up with a fancier title. It wouldn't change the facts. She knew how to organize and get things done. Without any conscious thought, she had compiled names, numbers, and email addresses of Los Angeles rich, famous and infamous. On the open market, she estimated A through L alone was worth a small fortune.

Unlike most of her competitors, Jade was starting out with a huge advantage. The people listed on her laptop already knew the kind of party she could put together. If they hadn't attended a function she personally organized, they knew someone who had. Jade might be unsure about her talents in many areas. Throwing a kickass party wasn't one of them.

You want elegant? No problem. A sit-down dinner for 200? Easy as pie. Buffet? Pool party. Beach barbecue? She had done them all. Multiple times. And if she unexpectedly ran into a theme she wasn't familiar with? She was bound to know someone who could help. Jade knew the best caterers. Decorators. Florists. Pastry Chefs.

Jade had dealt with bad weather, uninvited guests, food poisoning and — the horror of horrors — running out of champagne just before a big toast. When it came to rooms full of hungry, thirsty people, nothing could faze her. Meeting with her first potential client was another matter.

Selling herself was a new experience. Jade swallowed a giggle. Maybe she should put that in a different way. She was selling her knowledge. Her experience. She knew what Callie had said was true. Throwing a party was easy. Throwing one where everyone had a good time was something else. The key was for the guests never to be aware of why the party was running smoothly. You didn't notice clean silverware or a pressed tablecloth. However, you noticed smudges and wrinkles. It was Jade's job to keep the party moving with as little drama as possible. The thing about parties, no matter how *high class* the guests, there was always drama.

"You look very professional today, Miss Marlow."

Jade smiled. Leave it to her favorite cab driver to give her the boost to her ego she so desperately needed.

"My first official business meeting, Troy."

Jade smoothed down the skirt of her cream-colored sheath. Jade's closet sported five brand new outfits designed to impress. After they came up with Jade's new profession, Callie insisted she needed clothing to fit the image of a competent, fashionable woman. The labels weren't couture like the ones Jade left behind when she walked out of her father's house; they were better. Paid for with her own money. Approved by her new friend.

The sleeveless dress skimmed her knees showing just the right amount of leg. Sling-back pumps, the color of ripe raspberries, and a simple pair of hoop earrings were all the accessories Jade wore. Her hair was pinned into a neat bun at the base of her neck. Her stomach might be full of warring butterflies — on the outside, she looked cool as a cucumber.

"Back to Beverly Hills?"

When Jade walked out of the Marlow mansion, Troy had been her first call. He seemed to understand without words that she was finally cutting free. Strange, a man she knew only as a paid driver understood her better than most of the people she had known for a lifetime. There was something sad and yet terribly sweet in the thought.

"Let's call it going where the money is," Jade said, her smile widening when Troy chuckled.

As the cab wound through the familiar streets, Jade felt her nerves settling. She might not live here anymore, but she knew what these people expected. If she projected confidence, her clients would believe it. How hard could that be? She had a lifetime of experience hiding her true feelings.

Going to her clients, instead of them coming to her made perfect sense — at least for now. Once she was better established, Jade would worry about hiring someone to answer phones. A small, tasteful office. Perhaps an assistant. That was all down the road. Right now, she needed to get through this first meeting.

They went through the usual routine outside the security gates. Troy pulled the cab to a stop at the front door.

"Tag me when you're ready to leave," he told Jade. He gave her a friendly wink. "Knock 'em dead, kid."

Jade let herself out of the cab, walked up the marble steps, and then rang the bell. She looked at her hand. Steady as a rock. Her palm was dry. Her breathing steady. *Remember*, she could hear Callie telling her, *you are looking them over, too. If you don't like what you see, get up and leave. As soon as the word gets out, people will be clamoring for you.*

Jade didn't know if that was true. However, Callie was right about one thing. She didn't have to take the job. Armed with that knowledge, Jade felt her confidence rise.

"Hello, Marsden." Jade greeted the butler when he opened the door.

"Miss Marlow," the middle-aged man moved to the side, letting Jade enter. "Mrs. Stern is expecting you."

Agnes Stern. Once again, she had Callie to thank for setting up this meeting. Even though Jade knew the family, Callie knew about Porter Stern's upcoming seventy-fifth birthday. After one phone call, Jade had a meeting.

The Sterns were old money. Porter Stern didn't depend on her father's good will to bolster his fortune, so she didn't need to worry about Anson Marlow exerting his influence. Jade would get or lose the job on her own merit.

"Miss Marlow is here, madam."

Marsden left with a slight bow, closing the door behind him. It was a lovely, feminine room. Arrangements of roses sat on delicate, antique tables whose surfaces were protected by hand crocheted lace doilies. All the furniture looked like it belonged in a Victorian drawing room. A silver tea service adorned a gold cart. It was parked to the right of a tall, wing-backed chair, covered in a floral chintz. Flowers seemed to be the theme of the room. Even the lady who held out her hand was dressed in a pink suit with a large, bejeweled peony pinned to the lapel.

"Jade, darling girl. Come in."

Jade liked Agnes Stern. That wasn't something she could say about most of the people with whom her father socialized. Instead of false smiles and nasty words behind your back, Agnes let you know how she felt. That kind of honesty was rare in Beverly Hills. Jade imagined it was rare everywhere.

"It's good to see you, Mrs. Stern." Jade held out her hand.

The older woman simply shook her head, bringing Jade in for a hug. Surprised, Jade automatically hugged her back. Agnes Stern was a petite woman, coming up to just below Jade's shoulder. Whatever she did in her spare time, it gave her the grip of a lumberjack. Muscles wrapped in perfectly styled hair and the scent of lilacs. Who would have guessed?

"Sit. I have tea. Would you like something stronger? And please, call me Agnes."

Jade took the chair opposite Agnes.

"Tea would be lovely, thank you."

"I was prepared to push a plate of fattening food at you, but I see you've filled out nicely since the last time I saw you."

Jade wasn't offended. How could she be when Agnes was so bright and friendly? There was nothing malicious in her words. Nothing hurtful. If Jade had a grandmother, this was how she would want her to be.

"I've been getting a lot of that lately," Jade smiled. "Good food, provided by genuinely caring people is never a bad thing."

"Emphasis on the genuine." Agnes handed Jade a delicate bone china plate with, of course, a floral pattern. She held out a tiered server full of little sandwiches. "The round ones are salmon, the rectangles cucumber."

Jade took one of each. Genuine in this town was sometimes hard to come by. She weaved her way through the disingenuous so much of the time it was easy to become cynical. Or so hardened she assumed even the smallest gesture of kindness was attached to an ulterior motive. Jade had lived her entire life that way. Until Garrett. He showed her what real kindness was.

"I hope it's a man who put that look on your face," Agnes laughed. "Or a woman. I believe in loving who you love. Are those shining eyes for someone special?"

"I…"

Jade's first instinct was denial. Keeping Garrett to herself was a habit she realized she could break without worrying about the repercussions. They were going on their first public date tonight. Soon everyone would know. Sharing a little with Agnes couldn't do any harm.

"That blush tells me I'm right on target," Agnes said, a bit smugly.

"There is a man. He… He's very special."

"Mmm." Agnes sighed. "There is something about that first bloom of love."

"Oh, I don't know about love." The butterflies in Jade's stomach took flight again. At the same time, she felt a little tingling in the vicinity of her heart. "It's too soon for that."

"I knew five minutes after I met Porter." Agnes laughed. "I made fun of his name. It is silly. Who names a child after a kind of beer? When he laughed back, that was it. We've been married fifty years this November."

"That's incredible."

"No. It's sheer determination." Agnes set her cup on the table. Her dark brown eyes met Jade's. "There were days when I wanted to walk away. Sometimes I wanted to run."

"What made you stay?" Jade found herself unconsciously leaning closer, hanging on Agnes' every word.

"Something my mother told me on my wedding day. Before you do anything rash, ask yourself one question. *Have the good days outweighed the bad?* No matter what the problem was that we were currently facing, the answer has always been yes."

"That's lovely, Agnes." Jade wiped at something on her cheek, surprised when she found a tear. "I'm sorry. Crying isn't very professional."

Agnes handed Jade a tissue. "I hoped we've moved past that. I've always wondered what was under that cool exterior you presented to the world. I like what I see. Has that young man of yours helped you melt the ice?"

"With a blowtorch." Jade groaned silently. *Too much information.*

"Don't be embarrassed," Agnes laughed with delight. "I remember that feeling. You think of him when he's not there. When he is, you can't keep your hands off each other."

"Agnes…" Jade felt her cheeks heating up.

"Ah, so I'm right." She nodded with satisfaction. "Good. There is nothing wrong with starting with sexual chemistry. Sometimes you build on that, sometimes you don't. Either way, I hope you enjoy the ride."

Before Jade could decide how to answer that, Agnes patted her hand reassuringly.

"Never mind that. You came here for a reason. I want to throw my darling Porter a seventy-fifth birthday bash the likes this old neighborhood has never known. Since I've decided you're the perfect person to help, let's get started. Toss out some ideas. Let's see what sticks."

Chapter Fourteen

GARRETT CALLED JADE just as she left her meeting with Agnes. He was running behind, which meant he would be later than expected. The re-writes of the re-writes were still not what he wanted. Smoothing out the script and the screenwriter's ruffled feathers meant they would just make their reservation. There wouldn't be time for a drink before they left.

Jade had no problem with that. Her meeting with Agnes ran much longer that she had anticipated. Instead of an hour, by the time they were finished laughing, planning, and enjoying each other's company, three hours had flown by.

As long as she was in the neighborhood, Jade stopped to fill Callie in on her first paying gig. Naturally, Caleb joined them. Before Jade knew it, she was hurrying home to shower and change. She had hoped to spend a couple of hours primping for the big night. As she let herself into the loft, her watch read seven o'clock. An eight o'clock reservation meant no time to tarry.

Jade tossed her purse on the sofa. She would transfer her ID, comb, and lipstick to her little clutch before she left. Bouncing on one foot, then the other, she removed her shoes on the way to the bedroom.

Mentally running through her wardrobe, Jade lamented not buying that sexy little number Callie tried to talk her into when they went shopping.

It was completely impractical, Jade argued.

You're bound to find an occasion to wear it to, Callie countered.

Too sexy Jade pointed out.

Just the right kind of sexy, Callie said emphatically.

It didn't matter now. Jade left the store with her practical five outfits — nothing more. Now she would have to repurpose one of them for a night out with her boyfriend.

Jade almost giggled. At her advanced age, she had her first boyfriend. Her teenage years were filled with sons of her father's business associates and one fumbling make-out session with the bad boy who delivered groceries to the house. He was nice. Nicer than his reputation made out. Jade was a day away from her eighteenth birthday. She liked the way he kissed. In one of her few moments of teenage rebellion, she lost her virginity in the backseat of his borrowed Ford Escort. It was brief, cramped, and nothing to brag about in her diary. Thank God, he wore a condom.

Jade could barely remember what Tim Leggett looked like. Tall. Lanky. Brown eyes? Still, she would always be grateful. Her first time had been with someone of *her* choosing. A boy with ripped jeans, who smelled faintly of motor oil. Not a five hundred dollar a bottle, cologne dipped pretty boy who only wanted to get into her pants so he could brag to his friends that he bagged the ice queen.

The bad boy was a onetime deal. She would never call the other boys anything but what they were — smoothing the way for her father's latest business transaction.

It had taken twenty-seven years for Jade Marlow to find a boyfriend. She sighed happily. Boy, oh, boy, was it worth the wait.

A five-minute shower, then she would decide what to wear. As she reached to unzip her dress, Jade frowned. What was that on the bed?

A box tied with a large purple ribbon sat on the pale blue quilt. With a surge of anticipation, Jade reached for the gift. She almost hated to open it. Presents were not the norm in the Marlow household. Not personal ones. There were always expertly wrapped packages under the professionally decorated Christmas tree. It was hard to get excited when she knew a stranger picked them out and the only person who watched her open them was the maid who had to take the discarded paper out to the trash.

This gift was special. Her first from Garrett. One out of desire, not obligation.

One pull had the ribbon falling away. Sentimentally, Jade neatly folded the satin. Later she would tuck it away for safekeeping. Right now, she had to find out what was in the box. Lifting the lid, Jade pushed aside the tissue paper.

Oh, my.

It was a dress. With great care, Jade lifted the garment from the box. She moved to the full-length mirror, holding it up in front of herself. It wasn't the dress Callie urged her to buy. That one had been a low cut, shimmery silver lamé. This dress was red. *Really?* Jade worried. With her hair? But oh, it was beautiful. Hand-beaded. From her estimation, it would hit her mid-thigh. The material wouldn't cling. Instead, the weight of the beads would make it swirl around her body, teasing at what was underneath.

Sighing with appreciation, Jade laid the dress on the bed. That was when she noticed there was something else in the box. Two things. Jade picked up the first object, opening the felt bag to peer inside. A shoe. No, not a shoe. An Italian work of art. Gold, strappy, with a sky-high heel. Taking out its mate, Jade held one shoe in each hand. They weighed almost nothing. A few pieces of leather and some sparkle. Completely impractical. Jade loved them.

Setting them on the bed next to the dress, Jade hurried into the bathroom. The quicker she showered, the sooner she could try on her new things.

Ten minutes later, Jade was clean, dry, and thoroughly lotioned. Her skin was soft. The scent of a gentle spring breeze filled the room. She loved her new body wash. She was ready for the dress — and Garrett.

Looking at the clock, Jade decided she had enough time to give her toenails a coat of bright red lacquer. If they were going to peek out of the end of her gorgeous shoes, they should be suitably prepared. By the time she fixed her hair and makeup, the shiny polish should be dry.

Jade decided her eyes should have a smoky, dramatic feel. She didn't go all out very often. However, when she did, Jade had the touch of a professional. Some eyeliner, then mascara. She gave her cheeks a touch of color before she painted her lips a red as bold as her dress.

Jade took the pins from her hair letting it fall down around her shoulders. She ran her fingers through it giving her a tousled, sexy look. Perfect. She wanted anyone who looked at her tonight to see a strong woman who was proud to be on the arm of her man.

From her dress to her hair, tonight everything about Jade was bold and sassy. A new woman was emerging. No more hiding her emotions behind a wall. She felt as sparkly as the heels of her shoes. Inside and out.

Dropping the towel she had wrapped around herself after her shower, Jade picked up the beaded dress. The thin straps meant she either had to wear a strapless bra or none at all. Moving to the mirror, she looked her breasts over with a critical eye. Nice shape. Well placed. No visible sagging. The old Jade wouldn't have gone out in public without a complete set of underwear. That decided her. No bra tonight. Panties, yes. Jade slipped on a lacy red pair. She might feel bold, but there was a limit. No way was she providing a bare crotch shot to any lurking paparazzi.

The dress fit like a dream. As she guessed, the hem hit her mid-thigh, showing off her long, shapely legs to perfection. When she slipped on the shoes and picked up her small satin clutch, her ensemble was complete. Somehow, Garrett got her size perfect on every item.

Taking a deep breath, Jade looked at the finished product. What she saw took her breath away. No one would call her an ice queen tonight.

"I can feel the heat from over here, Jade. You are absolutely the sexiest woman I have ever known."

"Perfect timing," Jade turned to Garrett. She opened her mouth to say something sassy, but one look at him stole every thought from her brain. Except one. Holy cow!

"Surprised?" Grinning, Garrett did a slow turn. "You aren't the only one who cleans up nice."

"Nice?" Jade said. She slowly walked across the room. "You're wearing a suit and tie." She leaned closer. "You shaved. That isn't fair, Garrett."

"What do you mean?"

"In jeans and t-shirt you drip sex appeal. Tonight?" Jade ran a finger along one of his lapels. "Dressed like that? Every woman who sees you is going to hate my guts."

"And every man who sees you is going to wish he was the one taking you home." Garrett pulled her into the circle of his arms. His lips brushed her ear as he whispered, "Let them eat their hearts out. All I see is you."

Jade put her mouth against Garrett's. She didn't move to deepen the kiss. Being in his arms. Feeling his warm breath mingle with her own. If this wasn't heaven, she didn't know what was.

"You always smell so good." Garrett lightly kissed one side of her mouth, then the other.

"It's called Spring Meadow." Her lips parted, anticipating Garrett deepening their contact.

"It's called pure Jade."

Garrett took her mouth with his — Jade melted. His tongue didn't tease against hers. It tasted. Dipped. Swirled. Jade felt her body begin to burn. Much more of this and she would explode into a raging inferno.

"Let's forget about dinner," Jade gasped when Garrett finally raised his head. "I want you."

"Tempting," Garrett set her away from him. Giving her another look, he took a deep breath. "You have no idea."

"Then…?" Jade eased the hem of her dress several inches higher. She was almost to her panties when Garrett stopped her. He grasped her hands, kissed each one.

"We have plans. Fix your lipstick. If we leave now, we should just make our reservation."

"I'll fix mine if you fix yours." Jade held out a tissue. "That shade of red isn't your color."

Chuckling, Garrett wiped his mouth. "Well, it's certainly yours. I'm glad to see you embraced the color. I was afraid you might balk. The whole redhead shouldn't wear red. I've never understood that one. You look spectacular."

Jade emerged from the bathroom, her mouth wearing a fresh coat of *Passionate Crimson*.

"There is always the fear of looking like a circus clown."

Garrett held out his hand. Taking hers, he tucked it into the crook of his arm.

"Believe me. No one will be calling you Ronald."

They took the elevator, nodding to the concierge. The doorman anticipated them, sweeping the heavy door open mere seconds before they got to it. Frowning slightly, Jade approached Garrett's Lamborghini.

"Is something wrong?"

"No." She hesitated, feeling silly. "I miss the other car."

Realizing what she meant, Garrett smiled. "You mean Hamish's clunker?"

Jade took Garrett's hand, letting him help her into the passenger side of the low-slung sports car. In a blink of the eye, he was in the driver's seat, pulling into traffic.

"When I would get to the motel, I was always relieved to see that car parked in the lot," Jade explained. "Part of me was afraid you wouldn't come. I guess that old, brown car will always have a place in my heart."

"Be glad I gave it back to Hamish permanently. The springs stick up through the cushions. Not to mention the slight smell of cheese."

"You're making that last part up." Jade sat back, enjoying Garrett's easy driving style. Nothing flashy. He wasn't trying to impress her by zipping around other cars. He was relaxed while staying alert.

"I swear. My guess is gorgonzola. Hamish swears it was there when he bought the car."

"How much does he make?"

"Plenty," Garrett assured her. "Hamish calls it being true to his roots. I call it being cheap."

"As long as he's happy," Jade said.

"I'm not sure how long it will last." Garrett sighed. "Hamish is involved with an actress who is known for liking nice things. *Very* nice things. I don't know how she'll react to driving around in what amounts to a brown turd."

"She might really care about him, Garrett."

"Fingers crossed," Garrett pulled to a stop. They were fourth in line for the valet parking. "It's lasted longer than I imagined. If the relationship blows up before we finish shooting *Exile*, I'm afraid there will be a shit storm of massive proportions."

"How are you at shoveling?"

"This is Hollywood, honey. We are issued shovels along with our Director's Guild cards."

Laughing, Jade glanced around, noticing for the first time where they were.

"Garrett…"

"If we are going to do this, we might as well do it right."

Plush was the hottest restaurant in town. Securing reservations was impossible — unless your name carried weight. Garrett would have no problem — even on the shortest notice. As he pulled the car up to the entrance, any hope Jade had of slipping under the radar vanished. The flashes from cameras started before the car door opened. The photographers didn't know who they were yet. The pictures they took were in hope of catching a big name.

Congratulations, Jade sighed to herself. *Tonight, you've hit the jackpot.*

"Stay in your seat," Garrett told her. He brushed his fingers over her cheek in a brief, comforting caress. "I'll help you out."

Jade waited for Garrett to make his way around the car. It wasn't as quick a journey as it might have been. The paparazzi recognized him immediately. They made the usual push forward, blocking Garrett's path. Jade schooled her features. Some of the pictures were bound to catch her inside the car. She didn't want any of them to show her sporting a deer in the headlights expression.

However, instead of the old Jade. The one with the frozen half-smile. She reminded herself. Tonight is a new beginning. The face you show to the world has to reflect this life — not the old one. With that in mind, Jade remembered who was about to help her out of the car. Garrett. When she thought of him, her face lit up.

Garrett gestured the doorman away. He opened Jade's door, extending his hand. In one fluid movement, she stood. She blocked out the popping cameras and the shouted questions. She had eyes only for Garrett. In her heels, she was only a few inches shorter than he was. Their eyes met. The absurdity of the situation hit them at the same moment. Without a word, they laughed. That shot flooded the internet. It trended all evening. Twitter went crazy.

Jade Marlow and Garrett Landis. Hollywood's newest couple?

For the next few hours, Jade was blissfully unconcerned about the global stir she and Garrett's appearance together had created. He was her focus, not the world around them.

They were seated without delay. A secluded table meant to promote intimacy. The room was lit with a low-key, flattering light that made everyone look as though they were bathed in candlelight. A few people greeted Garrett as they passed by. He nodded politely, keeping his hand in the small of her back. They didn't pause. The curious onlookers would have to keep their questions to themselves. However, Jade noticed plenty of furious keyboard action. Being the first to spread a juicy piece of gossip was worth letting your dinner grow cold.

"I know you aren't a big fan of champagne."

Jade smiled, pleased that Garrett remembered something she mentioned months ago. He cared enough to listen then make a mental note. She felt her heart swell. If she wasn't falling in love with him, she was an idiot.

"I discovered this when shooting a film in Washington State."

Garrett nodded for the waiter to fill their glasses. "There is this little winery outside of Spokane. I bought every bottle I could get my hands on."

He waited until Jade picked up her glass.

"To the first night of many."

Jade silently applauded the toast, sipping the perfectly chilled Chardonnay. For a moment, when their eyes met, she thought the color of his eyes seemed different than she had seen before. Intrigued, she leaned closer. Before she could decide, Garrett shifted his gaze, taking several moments to drape his napkin over his lap. When he looked at her again, the color was the usual. A beautiful silvery gray. Whatever she thought she saw must have been a trick of the light.

They ordered from the limited menu. The specials changed daily depending on what the chef found fresh at the market that morning. Jade chose the oven-roasted salmon with lemon pasta.

"I'll have the pumpkin ravioli. For dessert," Garrett looked at Jade. "The chocolate soufflé?"

"Yes, please."

When they were alone, Garrett took Jade's hand. It was a simple gesture, holding hands across a table. Couples did it all the time. Jade was so wrapped up in the moment she didn't notice the attention it drew from neighboring diners. One more step, Garrett would say if she thought to ask. Soon, their actions would stop being news. No one except the two of them would notice their little gestures of affection.

"Tell me how your day went." Garrett kissed the back of her hand. He wasn't doing it for any reason other than he wanted to. Like Jade, he had ceased to notice anyone but her.

"I got the job."

Delighted she hadn't buried the lead, Garrett listened to Jade's animated recounting of her meeting with Agnes Stern. He insisted she leave nothing out. By the time Jade ended her day with her visit with his parents, the waiter was taking away their empty plates.

The memory of Jade's too slender body was still fresh enough in Garrett's mind that he loved seeing her consume her meal with obvious enjoyment. Gone were the days when he coaxed bites of food into her. The shadows were gone from her eyes. The hollows in her cheeks filled out. His beautiful Jade glowed with happiness. She was healthy in both her body and soul — he planned on keeping her that way.

Tomorrow her bodyguard would arrive. Garrett was looking forward to bringing Jade up to date on his efforts to track down Stephen Marsh. The chance that she would be angry with him for not consulting with her first was high. Hell, he wouldn't appreciate such high-handed actions — no matter the motivation. He hoped, once she had all the facts, she would understand.

Explanations could wait until after dinner. He didn't want to spoil these magical moments by letting reality seep in.

"Your soufflé will be out in ten minutes, Mr. Landis."

"Thank you. That will be perfect." Garrett held up the half-empty bottle of wine. Since he was driving, he settled for one glass. Jade could have as much as she wanted. "May I fill your glass?"

"No." Jade felt slightly giddy, the zing in her veins having nothing to do with the alcohol. She didn't want anything to override her natural high. "I would love a cup of tea with dessert."

"Very good." The waiter motioned for a busboy to clear away the wine bucket. "We have several choices. White. Darjeeling. A lovely green tea from India that is new to the menu."

"Darjeeling will be lovely."

Jade waited until the waiter was out of earshot before whispering to Garrett, "The man seemed so proud of the green tea, I didn't want to tell him it all tastes like steeped grass clippings. Weak ones to boot."

"A lot of people wouldn't care about hurting a waiter's feelings."

"A lot of people are self-centered nitwits."

Not you, Garrett thought. Jade had more reason than a lot of people to concentrate on her own problems. She could have shut herself away. Wallowed in her own self-pity. Instead, she found a way out. He saw a bright, intelligent, capable woman who won his heart without trying.

Garrett looked down at the table. There he went again. He wanted to *tell* Jade he loved her. With words. He didn't want the damn color of his eyes giving it away first. He had almost been caught once tonight. He needed to stop thinking lovey-dovey thoughts. Which was difficult. Especially when Jade's smiles were so open and warm.

"Is everything okay?" Jade asked, her voice concerned. "You're giving that tablecloth quite the dirty look."

"Sorry." Garrett mentally kicked himself. "I let work creep into my thoughts."

"Tell me about it." Jade smiled. "You spent all of dinner listening to me go on about my day. How is the movie going? Is everything in Canada back to normal?"

A safe topic. Garrett explained to Jade about the delays that seemed to be plaguing *Exile*. The latest ones concerned the script. Garrett saw the middle arc of the story as more character driven. A break for the audience after a fast, action-packed start. The ending was set to be emotional with a rousing climax that he hoped would have people cheering. Unfortunately, the screenwriter was convinced his original story was perfect as is. It stated in the writer's contract that Garrett had the right to make changes, within reason. The problem was the two men had different ideas about what constituted *reason*.

"What are you going to do?" Jade took a spoonful of the recently delivered soufflé. She sighed, smiling as the rich, airy dessert danced over her taste buds. Without a second thought, she dipped her spoon for another bite, holding out for Garrett to sample.

Garrett let Jade feed him. That was it. Any speculation about the intimacy of their relationship was no longer in question. Holding her hand across the table. Kissing the back of that hand. Now sampling food from the same spoon? They might as well have put out an official press release. Jade Marlow. Garrett Landis. Super couple.

"Should I not have done that?"

"Share your dessert?" Garrett asked innocently. "It would be selfish not to."

"Hmm." Jade shook her head. "I keep forgetting we are interesting to other people. From now on, I only feed you in private."

"It was a natural gesture, Jade." Garrett shrugged. "We can't be so self-conscious that we stop enjoying something as simple as a night out."

"Simple?" Jade looked around their luxurious surroundings.

Garrett chuckled. "You know what I mean. Not every night will be like this. Are we supposed to refrain from sharing a French fry the next time we stop for a burger?"

"Point taken." Jade licked the last of the chocolate off her spoon.

"Do that again."

"What?" She teased. Jade knew exactly what Garrett meant. His eyes followed the path of the spoon as she dipped into the soufflé, and then brought it back to her mouth. Slowly, Jade slid the dessert past her lips, her eyes locked with his. The smoky silver of his eyes told her everything she needed to know. Garrett wanted her. Since the feeling was mutual, Jade put the spoon down. At this point, licking it clean would be gilding the sexual lily. She would save the rest of the foreplay until they were home. Alone.

"Is there anything else I can get you this evening, Mr. Landis?"

"The check?" Jade suggested, her eyes sparkling with desire.

"Absolutely."

It turned out there wasn't a bill. Garrett took care of it when he made the reservation. They waited while Garrett's Lamborghini was brought around. Jade felt Garrett's mounting impatience. It fed her own. Finally, after what seemed like an eternity, the waiter informed them that their car was waiting. Garrett helped Jade from her seat.

After a wonderful meal, excellent company, and the anticipation of sex with Garrett, Jade forgot what was ahead of them. Fortunately, Garrett was on top of things. They didn't leave the way they arrived. To Jade's surprise, Garrett led her to the kitchen.

"Since we got here, the number of paparazzi has tripled."

"We're going out the back?"

"It won't be press free," Garrett said. They paused at the exit near a row of sinks and automatic dishwashers. "Keep your head up. When you look down, you look like you have something to hide. Smile if you want. Or don't. I won't let go."

A burst of light blinded Jade. Garrett hurried her along the short distance to the waiting car. Questions were shouted. Most were the usual. Generic. *How long have you been dating? Where did you meet?* Jade did as Garrett had instructed. She kept her chin up. It wasn't bad. She could do this. It was the question someone shouted just as they reached the car that made Jade stumble.

Jade! Jade! Was your affair with Garrett Landis the reason your husband attacked you?

If Garrett hadn't been there, Jade would have landed flat on her face. He held her upright, almost carrying her the final few steps. When she was in the car, door firmly shut, he ran around to the driver's side. Before she knew what was happening, they were away from the restaurant, on the way home.

"Goddamn vultures." Garrett reached for Jade's hand. It was like ice. "Are you okay?"

"My father."

"What about him?"

"That question about Stephen." Jade shuddered. "My father was behind it."

"Probably." No point in sugarcoating it. "The only weapon he has left is the press. I'm sorry, Jade. That wasn't how I wanted the evening to end."

Garrett took the side streets back to the loft even though it added time to the trip. He didn't think they were being followed. Still, there was no point in taking any chances.

"Is the evening over?"

Garrett glanced at Jade. Still a little pale, her expression was determined.

"I'm not going anywhere, honey."

"Good," Jade said firmly. "Tonight was perfect, Garrett. I'm not letting anything spoil it. Especially not my father."

A few minutes later, Garrett pulled into the underground parking lot. Unbuckling his seat belt, he started to exit the car.

"Wait."

"Is something wrong?"

Putting a hand on his chest, Jade pushed Garrett back into his seat. The interior of a Lamborghini wasn't designed for easy maneuverability or extraneous activity. Luckily, Jade's plans didn't call for either of them to move around very much.

"I've never given a man a blowjob in the front seat of a hundred-thousand-dollar sports car."

Garrett's reaction ranged from surprise to humor to desire. He decided to ride all three.

"It's closer to three hundred."

"Three hundred thousand dollars?" In the process of unbuttoning Garrett's pants, Jade hesitated. When she looked up at him, her eyes brimmed with laughter. "I'm not *that* good."

Garrett moved his seat back a few inches, then hit the recline button. When he was in the perfect position, he pulled Jade down for a long, passionate kiss.

"Honey," he breathed against her lips. "You are perfect."

"Keep that in mind." Jade slowly lowered his zipper. "This is my first time."

"But I thought…"

Jade licked her lips in anticipation. "It doesn't count when someone forces you."

Garrett lifted Jade's chin. "You really want this?" He had to be sure.

"I'll bet you taste like a big, salty lollypop."

"I couldn't say," Garrett laughed.

Measuring his length, Jade slowly ran her hand up and down his erection.

After teasing the damp tip, she licked the moisture from her thumb. Her eyes widened in surprise.

"Salty and …" Wanting to be sure, Jade took another taste. This time going straight to the source. Her tongue ran over him. She hummed with pleasure. Garrett moaned.

"Sweet." She beamed at him. "My favorite combination."

Not wanting to push, Garrett laced his fingers into Jade's long, silky hair. The red looked like fire dancing over his skin. His other hand gripped the edge of his seat with increasing pressure. If Jade was in the mood to tease, it was going to take all his will not to come too soon. Her hand, her mouth. Her hair streaming over him. He was close to sensory overload — and loving every second.

"When was the last time you did this?"

Before Garrett could answer, Jade took him into her mouth. After that, words were impossible.

"Well?" Jade had pulled back, her red, wet lips inches from his straining cock.

"Did you ask a question? Oh, right." He smoothed the hair back from her face. "Never. This is a first for me. I've made out in a car. That's it. We always moved the action someplace else before things got out of hand. So to speak."

That pleased Jade beyond measure.

"I get to take your front seat virginity?"

"I'd say be gentle—" Garrett gasped her name when Jade scraped her teeth along his length. "Ah, honey. The hell with that. Keep going exactly the way you are."

Jade discovered something new about herself. When it was right, pleasuring a man with her mouth was a beautifully intimate experience. Power surged through her with Garrett's every moan. She was in charge. How fast. How hard. When to pull back so he didn't come too soon. He didn't ram himself down her throat. He coaxed. Encouraged. The thrust of his hips. The way he massaged her scalp with his fingers. All of it told her how much he enjoyed what she did. When he reached his peak, it was because of Jade. He didn't take his orgasm. He let Jade give it to him. Of her own free will.

Jade slowly eased away. She licked her lips, savoring his taste. Instead of sitting up, she lay her head on his thigh, kissing the warm, firm skin. If Garrett continued to stroke her hair, she felt like she could stay like this forever.

"Thank you."

"Hmm." Jade finally raised her head, a contented smile on her mouth. "I would say my pleasure except that doesn't begin to cover how I'm feeling."

"Happy?"

"Yes," she sighed.

"Jade…"

The headlights of another car hit Garrett in the eyes making him blink. Startled, he realized he had almost told Jade he loved her in a parking garage with his pants down around his hips. Christ. What was wrong with him?

"Let's get out of here before someone catches on to what we've been doing." Garrett rearranged his clothing. Jade didn't wait for him to help her out, meeting him on his side of the car. Garrett wrapped her in his arms, giving her a sweet, lingering kiss.

"I don't know where that came from," Jade said as they waited for the elevator. "The idea suddenly came to me. Normally, I would never act on it. You bring out something in me I didn't know I possessed."

"Is that good or bad?"

Jade stepped into the elevator, watching as the doors closed behind them. Garrett pushed the number for their floor. At that moment, he looked like a man who was completely content. His hair was a little messy. There was a slight smudge of her lipstick on the corner of his smiling mouth. He hadn't bothered to tuck his dress shirt back into his pants and his tie was loose. Garrett Landis was the most beautiful man she had ever known. Inside and out.

"It's good that being with you brings out a bit of my bad girl."

Garrett took Jade's hand. If he didn't say it now, she was bound to see it in his eyes. He took a deep breath.

"I love you, Jade."

He waited for her reaction. The tears in her eyes he could deal with. If they were tears of happiness. Her words. They pissed him off.

"I wish you didn't."

"Fuck that."

The doors slid open. Jade quickly exited. She searched her purse, cursing when she couldn't find the key to the door.

"You can't run away, Jade. I'm right behind you." Garrett took her purse. With little effort, he removed the key, fitting it in the lock. "After you."

Without a word, Garrett watched as Jade hopped on one foot then the other, removing her shoes as she went. She kept on going, disappearing into the bedroom. He decided to give her five minutes. Then they were having this out. In less than one, Jade came storming back.

"I lied."

"About?" He could be calm when he saw her emotions were in turmoil. For some screwed up reason, he found it comforting.

"I have wished for months that you would love me." She stopped by the floor to ceiling windows, her arms wrapped around herself. "I have dreamed of looking into your eyes, hoping they would be that special shade of purple I've seen your mother's turn when she is thinking about the man she loves."

Garrett moved behind her. He moved her hair to one side so his lips could whisper in her ear. "Turn around, Jade. See the truth."

"I want you to love me, Garrett." Unable to help herself, she leaned back against him, sighing when his arms circled her waist. "You shouldn't. That's what I meant to say. Loving me would be a big mistake."

"Too late." Garrett picked her up, carrying her to the sofa. He sat, settling Jade on his lap. "Not only can't I change the way I feel. I don't want to. You can't make me stop." He kissed her cheek. "Any more than I can make you start loving me."

"I…" God, she wanted to say the words. It would change everything. Garrett was the kind of man who would want a wedding. Children. Forever. Jade was the kind of woman who longed for all of that without believing she could ever have it. If Garrett didn't understand that by now, she didn't know how she could explain it.

"I didn't tell you I loved you so you would feel obligated to say it back, Jade." Though he had to admit, not hearing the words returned hurt. "I can't hide how I feel. However, even if my eyes didn't give me away, I would want you to know. I don't want to hide anything from you. Especially my love."

"Full disclosure?" That would be new. Her father withheld everything. Garrett wanted it all out in the open. It would take some getting used to.

"Yes." He moved her off his lap, keeping her close. "Which leads me to something I need to tell you."

"There's more?" After their run-in with the paparazzi, then Garrett's declaration, she was already mentally exhausted. Jade didn't know if she could take anything else. "Can it wait until morning?"

"No," Garrett said. "Would you be able to sleep wondering what I had to say?"

"Probably not." Jade rolled her eyes. "You're right."

"Wait. Will you repeat that into my phone? I want to record it. Something tells me I won't hear it very often."

"You are hilarious." Jade hid her smile. "Tell me."

Garrett started with his initial call to Jack Winston. He explained to Jade about his suspicions concerning her father. Jade didn't comment while he told her everything. When he finished, he squeezed her hand.

"I'm sorry I didn't tell you from the beginning, Jade. I wanted to have some kind of confirmation before I accused your father."

"I've suspected him too."

"You never asked?"

"It wouldn't have done any good." Jade closed her eyes. The exhaustion was quickly seeping through her body. Would her father ever be completely out of her life? "This Sable. The bodyguard. She'll be here tomorrow?"

"Around mid-morning, if there aren't any travel delays." Garrett wasn't sure what to make of Jade's reaction. She hadn't said very much. Since her eyes were closed, he couldn't tell what was going on in her head. "I'm moving in here, Jade."

"Oh?"

Again. Very little reaction.

"My house in Laurel Canyon is too secluded. The loft has first-class security. Sable can have the spare room." Garrett swallowed. "I'll take the couch. If you want."

"Don't be an ass." Jade slowly opened her eyes. They looked weary — not angry. "That was your one."

"My one?"

"Not only did you keep a very big something from me," she said. "You and your friends made decisions that directly affect me without consulting me. I won't put up with that, Garrett. Never again. I lived with someone who made arbitrary decisions regarding my life. I can't remember one single time when he asked my opinion. You did it this time because you didn't want to hurt me." She looked him directly in the eye. "Never do it again."

"I understand." And he did. Taking away Jade's choice was the worst thing he could do to her.

"Good." She held out her arms. "Take me to bed. Where, by the way, you will sleep. Every night. The couch is for when I get really pissed at you."

That sounded fair to Garrett. The chances of them living an argument-free life were slim to none. As his father always said, the only people who never fight are the ones who don't care enough to bother.

Garrett carried Jade into the bedroom, her head resting on his shoulder. He closed the door behind them, shutting out the rest of the world. For tonight, he was with the woman he loved. He didn't want to think about tomorrow or the problems that went with it. They had these next few hours to themselves. He planned on making every second count.

Chapter Fifteen

"BREAKFAST IS NOT the most important meal of the day."

Jade watched in amazement as Garrett filled his plate with eggs, bacon, toast, and fried potatoes. Add a side of mixed berries plus a huge glass of orange juice? Jade couldn't believe anyone looked like him while eating like that.

"I agree." Garrett popped a blueberry into his mouth. "The most important meal is the next one." Seeing Jade's lips twitch, Garrett picked up another berry. "Open up."

"You think you can hit my mouth from there?"

Garrett gauged the distance. Jade was about five feet away, making herself a cup of tea. Easy. If she cooperated.

"I can get it there. The question is can you catch it?"

Jade set her cup on the counter, then squared her body up to his.

"Show me what you've got."

Five seconds later, Jade was enjoying the sweet, tart juice against her tongue while doing a victory dance around the kitchen.

"Impressive." Garrett laughed at her antics. "You have a lot of energy for a woman who kept me up all night."

"Ha." Deciding his bacon looked good, she swiped a piece off Garrett's plate. "I was being polite. You are the one who couldn't keep your hands off me."

"Funny. I don't remember it that way. Let me think." In a flash, Garrett had Jade wrapped in his arms. "Oh, that's right." He nuzzled her neck. "It was me. Aided and abetted by your hands." He kissed each finger. "And your mouth." The kiss took Jade's breath way.

"I'll concede I helped. If you'll admit that this," Jade cupped him between the legs. "This will not stay down. If I didn't know better, I would swear you have a stash of those little blue pills."

"Pure Landis testosterone, honey."

"I'd ask Callie about that except it would be too embarrassing." Jade frowned. "It's bad enough that I'm sleeping with her son. And was doing so when she befriended me. God, what is she going to say?"

"She will be thrilled."

"I hope you're right. Not that I'm going to bring up the sex part."

"For which I am eternally grateful." Garrett winked.

"What are—"

Jade was interrupted when the line to the lobby buzzed.

"That must be Sable." Garrett answered, confirming his guess, and clearing the woman to come up. "She's early. That's always a good sign."

For some reason, Jade felt nervous. A bodyguard was bad enough. Having a stranger follow her around all day? She couldn't get used to the idea.

"It will be fine," Garrett assured her on his way by to answer the door.

Jade followed, not knowing what to expect. Ex-Army. Tough as nails. A weapons expert with three black belts. She was ready to be thoroughly intimidated. When Garrett opened the door, Jade was certain there had to be a mistake. This was a supermodel, not a warrior.

"Hello," the woman smiled, holding out her hand. "Mr. Landis? I'm Sable Ford."

"Come in." Garrett stepped aside. He met Jade's surprised look with one of his own.

"And you must be Jade."

"I'm sorry," Jade said. "Where are my manners? It's nice to meet you."

Jade held out her hand. The other woman's grip was strong, though not aggressive. The calluses on her palms were encouraging. Still...

"I'm going to come right out and say it. You don't look like a bodyguard."

Unoffended, Sable waved off Jade's concern.

"Why don't you point me to where I can stow my gear. After I get settled, we can form a game plan."

"Let me show you."

Garrett led the woman down the hall. Jade cleaned up the kitchen while she tried to make sense of Sable Ford.

The problem, Jade realized, was that she had been expecting one thing and got something else altogether. Bodyguards were supposed to be big, strapping men with guns bulging at their sides. Sable was tall. A little taller than Jade. Dressed in loose, cotton pants and a silk blouse, she looked like she stepped off the cover of Vogue, not a military base.

"What do you think?" Garrett asked in a low voice. He took his empty plate, putting it in the dishwasher.

"I have no idea. I hate judging anyone by her appearance. Still..."

"Her nails are expertly painted some pale shade of pink. Her luggage is Louie Vuitton and she smells subtly like some high-end perfume."

"It's French," Sable informed them with a smile. She sat on the high-back stool that Garrett had earlier occupied. "It was a gift. I can never remember the name. I like that it has a light fragrance. Not too heavy."

"Sable. I apologize," Jade said.

"There's no reason to," Sable assured her. "I'm here to keep you safe. If you aren't comfortable with me, I won't be able to do that. You need to trust I'll have your back. I need to trust you will follow my lead if the situation turns hairy."

"She's right," Garrett told Jade.

"We need to get to that place fast."

"What do you suggest?" Jade asked.

"Get me the biggest, toughest guy you know." Sable rubbed her hands in anticipation. "And if he outweighs me by a hundred pounds or more? All the better."

"WHY ARE YOU making such a big deal about this?"

Garrett held up his phone, making certain he had a good shot.

"Because," he told Jade. "Chances are my brother is going to get his ass handed to him. By a woman half his size. Why wouldn't we want to see that?"

When Sable asked for a tough guy, there was only one person who came to mind. They needed someone who had hand-to-hand training. Martial arts skills. Someone who could hold their own without getting carried away if things got out of hand. Garrett was almost certain that Sable would live up to the hype. Jack and Alex wouldn't have sent her if she couldn't protect Jade. However, there was a slight chance her sparring partner could get the upper hand. If that happened, they didn't want some steroid-crazed idiot beating her to a pulp.

Then there was the need to keep Sable's identity under wraps. The idea was to introduce her as an old friend of Jade's in town for a visit. The fewer people who knew they had hired a bodyguard, the better.

Finding someone to take on Sable for a few rounds wasn't a problem. Gym rats were a dime a dozen in a town that was always in need of hulking extras for the latest action film. No, they needed a combination of brains, brawn, and discretion. With a big, fat dose of family loyalty thrown in for good measure. Only one man fit that bill.

"You want to see Nate get bruised and bloodied?" Jade asked incredulously.

"No." Garrett slung his arm around Jade. "Well. Maybe a little bruised."

"Garrett..."

"Don't worry. No one can take a punch like Nate. For all the rehearsing and blocking stuntmen do, it's inevitable that they take a few hits."

"That doesn't make me feel any better."

They decided the best place for Sable to show her stuff would be at the Landis estate. It was the only place big enough, outside of a public gym, that they had access to. All it took was one phone call to his parents explaining the situation. Not only did Callie and Caleb offer their workout room, Callie insisted everyone stay for lunch afterward.

Garrett had to chuckle. Only his mother would want to cater her own son's ass kicking.

"Nate is okay with this?"

"Look at him." Garrett nodded where Nate and Sable were huddled together. "He's like a kid in a candy store."

"What if she takes him down?"

"You mean will his big male ego be wounded beyond repair?"

"Something like that."

"Nate appreciates the kind of skills on Sable's resume," Garrett explained. "He'll do his best to win. If he doesn't, he'll shake her hand. Then he'll try to recruit her for his stunt team."

"I find it strange that they can be so relaxed when the whole purpose of this is to beat on each other."

Jade watched as Nate and Sable taped their hands. Did some warm-up stretches. Even exchanged easy banter. Every now and then laughter would float over to where she and Garrett stood. Jade couldn't understand the mindset.

"This is what they do for a living, honey. Nate's a physical guy," Garrett explained. "He loves pitting his skills against an equally matched opponent. If that opponent can best him, that's fine. You only get better if you allow yourself to be challenged."

"Do you really think Sable will provide that challenge?"

Seeing her would-be bodyguard next to Garrett's brother, Jade couldn't imagine the slight woman taking out the man who loomed over her. Nate was a good six inches taller. Sable wanted someone who outweighed her by a hundred pounds? Jade estimated the difference was at least that. Where Sable was sleek, Nate was thick muscles. Jade started to worry. She knew Nate would never purposely hurt the smaller woman. Still, accidents happened.

"Look closer," Garrett told her. "You're still seeing the stylish woman we met this morning. I see a trained fighter. Something tells me, when the time comes, she'll be just fine."

"Did I miss it?"

Jade looked around as Callie and Caleb entered the room followed by Wyatt.

"You called him?" Garrett asked his father.

"I did," Callie said. She linked arms with Jade in an unspoken show of female solidarity. "It never hurts for a man to see what a woman is capable of when she puts her mind, and body, to it."

"I thought I was here to see Nate taken down," Wyatt grinned at his father. "Now I find out it's an object lesson."

"Callie loves a twofer. Fun and learning rolled up into one colorful ball. She's in mom heaven."

"They do know I can hear every word, right?" Callie asked Jade in a conversational tone. "When you mock the mom, you pay the price."

"What kind of punishment do you dole out for this kind of an offense?" Jade glanced teasingly at Garrett, letting him know she was taking notes.

"Um, Mom," Garrett interrupted. "Maybe you should keep those secrets to yourself. You don't want to water down their effectiveness."

"It varies," Callie continued, ignoring Garrett. "There is a beautiful strawberry cheesecake in the refrigerator. It would be a shame if it mysteriously disappeared before lunch."

"I cave," Wyatt declared. He kissed his mother's cheek. "No more mocking. I apologize for myself and every man who came before me."

"Impressive," Jade said.

"Wyatt really loves cheesecake," Callie laughed with delight. She pulled her oldest into her arms, giving him a big, loving hug.

"Looks like the show is about to begin," Caleb observed, lacing his fingers with Callie's. "I wonder how long this will—" There was a loud thud as Nate landed flat on his back. "Take."

"Maybe she caught him off guard," Wyatt said. A few seconds later, Nate hit the mat again. "Or not."

Nate got in a few hits of his own, though none that did more than sting. Garrett called it. Some switch flipped when Sable went into fight mode. She morphed from an easygoing beauty to a warrior woman in the blink of an eye. Five minutes after they started, Nate held up his hands in defeat. Just like that, Sable was laughingly patting her opponent on the back — the intensity gone from her expression.

"Holy shit," Wyatt breathed. "Sorry, Mom."

"I'll give you one," Callie said, shaking her head in wonder. She turned to Jade. "I think that answers the question of Sable's qualifications. I'd feel safe with her if the Cossacks were invading."

"High praise indeed," Caleb nodded with a straight face. "Callie should know. She did a movie about the Russian revolution."

"Are you implying that all my knowledge of history has been gleaned from the movies?"

"Not *all*, my love."

Callie snorted. "This from a man who only knows who Wagner is because of Bugs Bunny cartoons."

"Are they arguing?" Jade asked as she watched the couple head upstairs, continuing their banter all the way.

"Around here it's called foreplay." Garrett shook his head with a smile. "Soon they won't be able to keep their hands off each other."

"How soon?" Jade asked. She found the Callie/Caleb dynamic fascinating.

"They'll make it through lunch. Probably."

"Only because they have guests," Wyatt said. "They've been known to disappear during the salad course."

Jade sighed a little wistfully. How wonderful to grow up with parents who showed affection so openly.

"Say the word and they can be your parents too," Garrett whispered for her ears only.

"Garrett..."

"Too soon?"

"A bit. Yes."

"Okay," Garrett said, completely unconcerned about pushing Jade out of her comfort zone. He could wait until she was ready. However, now that he knew what he wanted — *who* he wanted — he planned on making sure Jade understood. He wasn't going to change his mind. He was in. All the way.

Before Jade could comment, Sable and Nate joined them.

"That was impressive."

"Impressive?" Nate said to Garrett. "This lady is deadly. I'm lucky she wasn't really trying to take me out. I wouldn't be walking away under my own steam."

"I had excellent teachers," Sable told them. "Plus a certain amount of aptitude."

"That's one way of putting it," Nate laughed good-naturedly. He rubbed his backside with an exaggerated wince. "My ass is going to be black and blue."

"I have an excellent ointment for that. A couple of applications." Sable snapped her fingers. "It's magic."

"Maybe you could bring it by my place later. I might need help… reaching."

Garrett and Wyatt exchanged smiles. Nate wasn't just the easiest going of the brothers. He was also the fastest mover when it came to women. Colton was close. In a runoff, Nate would win by a nose.

"Tempting," Sable told him. "Unfortunately, I'm here to do a job. If Jade is okay with it, I'm her full-time bodyguard. I don't have time for any… ointment applications."

"I'm more than okay," Jade chimed in. "I hope I can talk you into showing me some of those moves."

"Hey," Nate protested. "I thought I was your self-defense instructor."

"What can I say," Jade grinned. "I'd be a fool not to learn from the best."

"Great," Nate grumbled, his eyes twinkling with humor. "Shot down by two beautiful women in a matter of minutes."

"Not to mention one of them knocking you on your ass. Repeatedly." Garrett hit playback on his phone. "I wonder how many hits this would get on YouTube."

Wyatt looked over Garrett's shoulder, the brothers laughing at the film.

"Add Instagram." Wyatt offered.

"And Twitter."

"Since when do you tweet?" Nate asked Garrett. He attempted to snatch the phone away.

"My assistant is an expert." Garrett tucked his phone safely into his pocket.

"I'm hitting the shower." Nate turned to Sable. "Want to join me?"

"Do you never give up?" Garrett asked in amazement.

"Come on, Sable." Jade ushered the other woman out of the room. "Callie's bathroom is gorgeous. And private," she said without turning. "One of you men, bring Sable's bag up when you come."

"Hey," Nate called out. "That came out wrong. Separate showers. I swear I was suggesting *separate showers*."

"Let it go, Nate." Garrett patted his brother on the shoulder before grabbing Sable's tote. "You can spend lunch trying to pull your size fourteen foot out of your mouth."

As he jogged up the stairs, Garrett could hear Wyatt giving Nate a hard time. Ribbing each other was a time-honored tradition. God, he loved this family. The only thing that would make it better was the addition of Jade. Soon, he promised himself. Once the threat from Stephen Marsh was behind her, Jade would be able to relax. Once she was relaxed, he would slip under her remaining defenses. He would have a ring on her finger before spring.

"You look like the proverbial cat. What's up?" Colt walked through the front door just as Garrett emerged from the basement. "Holy—. Forget about you. Who is that?"

Garrett followed Colt's gaze to where Sable, still in her black tank top and leggings, was laughing about something with Jade and Callie.

"Before you get carried away, Colt, you better see something." Garrett tossed his phone to his brother. "Hit play."

"Why?" Colt opened the phone. "What is it?"

"One kickass woman."

That video would either put Colt off or intrigue him even more. Either way, Sable had made it clear she wasn't looking for a fling. She took her job seriously. It was good to know they had the same priority. Keeping Jade safe.

AFTER LUNCH, JADE looked for Callie. With everything that was going on, there hadn't been time to speak with her unless they were surrounded by other people. What Jade had to say needed some privacy.

She found Callie in the breakfast nook going over the week's grocery list with her cook.

"I think double the milk and eggs. We've been getting more drop-ins lately." She held a hand out to Jade when she saw her. "I hope this sweet girl will make sure that trend continues."

"Do you have a few minutes?"

"What kind of question is that?" Callie patted the window seat cushion. "Sit. Talk to me."

This was harder than Jade imagined. How could she explain to Callie about Garrett? If the rule was, you didn't screw around with your friend's brother behind her back, what was the rule about your friend's son?

"Relax," Callie smiled, her eyes shining a clear gray.

"I want to apologize."

"Well, I know you didn't break the vase in my sitting room. Caleb copped to that one." Callie thought for a moment. "I'm at a loss. What did you do?"

"The internet must be full of the story. About Garrett? And me?"

"Oh, that. I've known about the two you since dinner the other night."

"How?"

"The way he whispered to you when he helped you into your chair. It was very... intimate."

"Intimate." Jade felt her cheeks heat up. "Now I'm sorry *and* embarrassed."

"You shouldn't be either." Callie squeezed Jade's hand. "I'm thrilled. Which is exactly what I would have told that nosy reporter who followed me to the hair salon this morning. If it was any of his business, which it isn't."

"Garrett and I went out to dinner last night. It was our first public date."

"I saw the pictures," Callie nodded. "The woman who has been doing my hair for years had some of them on her iPad. The two of you looked gorgeous together."

"You think so?"

"It was the consensus of the entire salon. Even Rhonda Baines, who has been trying for years to land Garrett for her daughter, had to admit how well you suit."

"I should have told you about Garrett before we became friends." Jade nervously smoothed an imaginary wrinkle from the skirt of her dress. "I didn't think there was anything to tell. I tried to break things off."

"Garrett wouldn't let you." Callie smiled happily. "Good for him. I didn't raise any fools. Obviously, whatever the problem, you've worked things out."

"I think so." She looked at Callie, trying to gage her reaction. "You honestly don't mind? I'm not exactly baggage-free. Illustrated by my new bodyguard."

"The perfect Hollywood accessory," Callie teased. Almost instantly, she turned serious. "I hate that you need protection. It isn't your fault, Jade."

"I know."

"I love my sons. I wouldn't trade them for anything." Callie draped her arm around Jade's waist. "My greatest hope has always been that one day, each one of them would give me a daughter to love. Ah, I can see the slight panic in your eyes. I know it's early days. Just remember this. You will always be the daughter of my heart. No matter what."

With tears filling her eyes, Jade said the words to Callie that she hadn't been able to say to her son. "I love you."

Callie gathered Jade close, telling her to have a good cry. Then proceeded to join her.

"What is it about the two of you?" Caleb asked as he entered the room. His voice was gentle, not accusatory. "Tears, my love?"

Callie took the tissues Caleb offered, handing one to Jade.

"I'm a weepy person. You knew it when you married me."

Caleb lifted Callie's chin. At the same time, he ever so briefly skimmed a hand over Jade's hair. The gesture was so gentle. So sweet, Jade almost started crying again. Was it possible she had not only gained a mother, but also a father? It was too much to take in all at once.

"I'm going to find Garrett."

Caleb took Jade's seat, pulling the love of his life into his arms. "Well?"

Callie happily rested her head on his shoulder. She sighed with contentment. "I've always loved a spring wedding."

Chapter Sixteen

"YOUR BEST WEAPON is the element of surprise. Most attackers expect *some* resistance. Give them everything you've got. Cause as much pain and damage as quickly as possible." Sable demonstrated. "Stomp on the arch of the foot. An elbow to the bread basket."

"Hey," Colt objected when Sable's *demonstration* caused him to double over. "When I agreed to help teach Jade some self-defense moves, I didn't mean for you to use me as a punching bag."

"Oh, did I hurt the big action star?" Sable crooned the words. "In *Trance,* you took out fifty Russians, dismantled a nuclear bomb while bedding half-a-dozen scantily clad women. Where's the tough guy now?"

"You go to see my movies?" Colt grinned.

"They showed them at the base I was stationed at in Afghanistan. It was either that or check my toes for trench foot. Your movie won — barely."

"Can you get foot rot in the desert?"

Jade shook her head. The obvious sexual tension between Sable and Colt was interesting. Amusing. After an hour, it bordered on annoying. Not that Sable wasn't doing her job. In the few days since her arrival, she had taught Jade some invaluable tricks for protecting herself. This morning's distraction was Colt's fault. The plan had been for Garrett to help. When he was called to the studio at the last minute, they decided to go ahead without a man to practice on. They arrived at the Landis home to find Colt just finishing breakfast. He insisted on stepping in for Garrett.

It hadn't occurred to either woman that the main reason for his generosity was his desire to flirt with Sable. Jade's bodyguard tried her best to keep the session professional. It worked — at first. However, the point of this workout was to show Jade different methods of getting away from an attacker. That meant getting up close and personal with Colt. After almost an hour of touching, prodding, and poking, his comments grew increasingly pointed. For the most part, Sable treated him like a slightly amusing gnat. She skillfully swatted away his attempts to engage her. Until now. They were so focused on each other Jade wondered if they remembered she was in the room.

"Why don't we call it a day?" Jade called out.

"Now see what you've done?" Sable said to Colt, her voice dripping with sarcasm and a tinge of humor. "I'm trying to help Jade. Mr. Movie Star had to make it about himself."

"Bitch," Colt whispered with a grin.

"And proud of it."

Colt gave Sable a dirty look, and then turned to Jade.

"I'm sorry." He grabbed a bottle of water from the built-in cooler. Taking off the lid, he handed it to Jade. "I honestly meant to help. Things got…"

"Out of hand?" Jade smiled. Colt's apology was so earnest her frustration fell away. "It's fine, Colt. Callie has some new orange blossom bath salts I'm dying to try." She gave him a sisterly peck on the cheek. "I'll leave you with Sable to finish whatever it is you're doing. One warning?"

"What?"

"Watch your balls."

"Relax," Sable said after Jade was gone. "I have no interest in your balls or any other part of you."

Colt watched as Sable put a few things into her bag. Lord, she was a stunning woman. Not that he didn't see beautiful women every day. Sable's beauty was different. Any man would be attracted. Tall, lean, but with curves in all the right places. He would bet the twenty-five million he was making on his next film that her breasts were spectacular. He would give the back-end profits he was going to make to find out.

The problem was, Sable seemed more amused by him than attracted. On top of that, she was dedicated to her job. It came first. Cole understood. Professionalism mattered. When he was working, nothing got in the way. That meant no late night drinking, no on-set affairs. He was paid a shit-load of money to carry a film. He owed it to everyone involved to give one hundred and twenty percent of himself. He had plenty of time between movies to take advantage of the perks his status provided.

Jade was safely upstairs, taking a bath. To his thinking, that meant Sable was on a break. Time to have some fun.

"I am sorry."

Sable gave him an uninterested look over her shoulder before turning back to her bag.

"Come on." Colt put out his hand. "Truce?"

"Fine."

Sable reached back to shake Colt's hand. In a split second, she was flat on her back, a grinning Colt lying on top of her.

"Surprise."

Smiling back, Sable slowly ran her hand down his side.

"This is nice," Colt said. "Why don't we—"

Before he could finish his proposition, Sable shifted her hand, grabbing him by the balls. Hard. There was nothing fun or sexual involved.

"Surprise."

"Hey," Colt yelped when her grip tightened.

"Jade warned you."

"You said you weren't interested in my balls."

"And you believed me," Sable laughed. "That's so sweet. Naive. But sweet."

Letting him go, Sable pushed Colt off her. She jumped to her feet then held out a hand. Good-naturedly, Colt let her help him up. Not ready to throw in the towel, he leaned close, a teasing quip on his lips. Before he could blink, the quip was replaced by Sable.

As first kisses went, this one hit it out of the park. Home run. Touch all the bases. Sable's lips were a heady combination of soft and sweet. Her tongue swept through his mouth, sparking his desire — feeding the instant need that coursed through his body.

Then as quickly as it started, Sable ended the kiss.

"What was that?" Colt asked. He hadn't held her more than a few seconds, yet his arms felt empty.

"I call it a kiss."

"I meant, why start something you have no intention of finishing?"

"I wanted to know what it was like to kiss the sexiest man alive."

"And?" Colt hated asking, but the question slipped out before he could stop it.

"Nice." Picking up her bag, Sable headed for the shower.

Nice? Colt stood in the middle of the room staring sightlessly at the closed bathroom door. Damn. He wasn't certain how he felt. Annoyed? Confused? Turned on? That woman could kiss — a whole lot better than nice.

Cole knew one thing. Sable Ford was an intriguing woman full of contradictions. Too bad he didn't have the time to uncover what made that woman tick.

With a wistful sigh, Colt headed up to the kitchen to say goodbye to his parents. Sable had a job to do. So did Colt. He was heading to Australia to make a good old-fashioned swashbuckler. By the time he got back, Sable would be gone. Just as well. A woman like that could get under a man's skin fast.

No thanks. He was too young, too busy, and having too much fun to get serious about any woman. He would leave that to Garrett.

IT WAS STRANGE. Technically, he and Jade had been seeing each other for over six months. The circumstances were a trifle skewed. Unusual was a better word. Still, it was strange that during the time they had known each other, Jade had never been to his home in Laurel Canyon. An oversight he planned to fix. Today.

"I feel like a little kid being given a treat."

Jade slipped her feet into a pair of bright yellow canvas Keds. If they were going to be exploring Garrett's house, she wanted comfortable shoes. Some women might be able to walk around, up and down stairs, in four-inch heels. Jade wasn't one of them. A loose pair of cream-colored cotton cargo shorts and a sleeveless blouse rounded out her ensemble. She wore her hair in a long, French braid. Neat. Elegant. Stylish.

"What flavor are you today?"

"Raspberry cream."

Jade had discovered a line of flavored lip-glosses. Now that she was kissing a very desirable man on a very regular basis, she stepped up the product she put on her mouth. Garrett didn't like the heavy, sticky glosses. Jade didn't blame him. They left behind an unpleasant film, inside and out.

This particular gloss was lighter weight than most. It conditioned her lips, making them soft and supple. She liked the colors. Garrett loved the fruity flavors.

"That's one I haven't tried. Let me see."

He teased her lips with his tongue, swiping the bottom one once, then twice.

"Mmm." He tasted again, deepening the kiss. When he finally pulled back, Jade was breathless and in complete agreement. The raspberry was a keeper.

"I need to put on another coat."

"Let me.

Garrett reached for the little pot of color.

"No, you don't." Jade moved it across the table. "If you start fooling around, we will never get out of here." She quickly dabbed the gloss onto her lips. "Sable is waiting."

"How do you think that stuff would look on your nipples?"

"The same way it looks on my mouth."

"I will bet there's a difference," Garrett said, his voice deepening with interest.

Jade would not let him pull her into one of *those* conversations. The kind where she ends up with reddened cheeks. She put an end to this before it got that far.

"If we leave right now, I promise to let you find out. Later. After we go to bed."

Garrett took hold of her finger — the one she used to apply the lip-gloss. Keeping his eyes on hers, he lifted it to his mouth, sucking it inside. His tongue rubbed the tip, removing all traces of flavor.

"Garrett…"

Jade couldn't shift her gaze. He knew exactly how to make her heart beat faster. When her legs started to weaken, Garrett removed her finger. With a knowing wink, the stinker took her hand, leading her out of the room.

"IT'S BEAUTIFUL, GARRETT," Jade declared, leaning back against Nate's truck.

Rather than make Sable and her long legs suffer the long trip crammed into the Lamborghini's backseat, Garrett had borrowed his brother's rig. He had to admit, he liked the way the big vehicle handled. With another person to think about, it might be time to consider a second car.

"Thank goodness you decided to stay in town. This place has way too many security dead-zones." Sable walked to the side of the house, shaking her head. "Call Alex. You need a complete overhaul of the system." She tested the cable leading to a camera mounted on the porch. "Did you get this at a going out of business sale? In the seventies?"

It seemed Sable didn't require an answer. Mumbling to herself, she wandered out of sight.

"She just security shamed you," Jade laughed.

"Annoying. However, she has a point. Since the place was finished, I haven't spent much time up here. I haven't thought much about security. The builders picked out the cameras. I should have paid more attention. Come on. Let me show you the inside." Garrett held the door for her.

"Don't leave the house without telling me," Sable called out. She had already done a room-to-room check declaring it safe for Jade to enter.

"She's scary." Garrett closed the door. "Eyes in the back of her head scary."

"Impressive." Jade corrected. "In another life, I want to be Sable Ford."

"I like you exactly the way you are." Garrett slipped behind her, his arms circling her waist. "Perfect for me."

Jade turned in his arms, giving him a sweet, lingering kiss.

"Give me the grand tour."

Jade couldn't remember having a dream house. Oh, she dreamed of living anywhere but with her father. Or her husband. When she fantasized about that, there was never a specific place. Her only thought had been *anyplace but here*. As she looked around Garrett's house, she realized what this was. A house to build a dream on. As long as the man came with it.

One entire wall was nothing but glass. Sunlight filled every corner of the room. Hardwood floors gleamed. The smell of citrus filled the air. Not that fake, cleaner smell. Actual citrus.

"I smell lemons."

"There's a big bowl in the kitchen. I have three trees in the backyard."

"Callie once told me that you love fresh lemonade." Jade picked up one of the yellow pieces of fruit, bringing it to her nose. "It's one of my favorites too."

"Serendipity."

"Do you believe in such things?"

"Call it what you want," Garrett said with a shrug. "I believe we fit."

"Maybe."

"What do I have to do to convince you?"

Jade cupped his face with her hands. There it was. That little catch she felt in the rhythm of her pulse when she looked into his eyes. The love she saw in the purple depths.

"You're doing it," she sighed against his lips.

"I love you, Jade."

"I know."

Jade deepened the kiss. Without a trace of hesitation, Garrett kissed her back. Loving him would be so easy. If only she could let go of the doubts. Not about him. About herself. As far as she had come, there was still a part of her trapped in that house — a woman who couldn't find the strength to walk away from the pain and humiliation. Did she deserve a man like Garrett? Until she could answer with an unequivocal yes, she could never give him what he wanted. Her absolute love and commitment.

"Want to see the bedroom?" Garrett gave her an exaggerated leer.

Jade laughed. "Yes, please."

"It isn't exactly a den of iniquity, but with your cooperation, I have hope."

Garrett grabbed Jade's hand. They were halfway to the stairs when his phone rang.

"Take it," she said when Garrett hesitated.

"Wyatt knows where we are," Garrett told her. "He wouldn't call if it wasn't important."

"Go," she urged. "I'll check my messages. You have to love the cellular age."

"Not when it interrupts some naked time with my woman."

"Who said we were going to get naked?"

Garrett gave her a knowing look. "Naked. Pantyless. Potato. Potahto. I'm good either way." With a wink, he answered the phone. "What's up?"

Smiling, Jade scrolled through her missed calls and texts. Nothing that couldn't wait. A caterer she was lining up for Agnes Stern's party. A few interviews for the assistant job she decided she needed to fill. It was the last text that gave her pause, turning her happy expression pensive.

"Something wrong?" Garrett asked. Whatever it was Wyatt needed, it must not have taken very long.

"Not wrong," Jade said slowly. She handed the phone to Garrett.

"This Stacy is reminding you about a party tomorrow night? You don't want to go?"

"I do." Jade took back the phone. "It's a fundraiser for the Wounded Warrior Foundation. I helped with the preliminary organization."

"I think Mom and Dad are going to that. It's something we all contribute to. We can meet at their place, and then all go together." When Jade hesitated, Garrett tugged on her hand. She gladly went into his arms. "What's the problem, Jade?"

"The venue."

"What—? Oh." The light finally dawned. "Your father's house?"

"Yes."

"Then we'll send a big, fat check. We'll plug in a movie. Pop some corn. Make out."

"With Sable watching?"

"She's cool," Garrett pointed out, pulling Jade closer. "She won't mind going to bed early."

It was tempting. Garrett gave her the perfect out. A quiet night at home. No prying eyes. No drama. When Jade walked out of her father's house, she swore she would never set foot in it again. At the time, she meant it. Now, thinking back, it seemed a bit melodramatic. It was just a house. Unless she faced it, and her father, the progress she had made was wasted. It was as her therapist said; problems get bigger and bigger the longer you put off dealing with them. Sometimes the only way to move forward is to retrace your steps.

One more time, Jade decided. It was just a house. Her father was just a man.

"I need to go, Garrett."

"Then we'll go."

Just like that. No questions asked. Garrett had her back. He also had her heart. Whatever doubts Jade had clung to dissolved in that instant. What was she waiting for? The heavens to open up? Neon lights to flash the news in huge multicolored letters? Nothing was going to change. Tomorrow wouldn't be better than right now. She was through being a fool. At least where Garrett was concerned.

"I love you."

"Say that again?"

Getting close to his ear, Jade said in a clear, steady voice, "I. Love. You. Like it or not, you're stuck with me, Garrett Landis. I have you and I'm never letting go."

Garrett picked Jade up, swinging her around. His laughter filled the room. "Honey, I wouldn't have it any other way."

Chapter Seventeen

"POPCORN IS SOUNDING awfully good about now." Garrett squeezed Jade's hand. "Say the word, honey. We can be back at the loft before you know it."

Having that in the back of her mind was what would get her through tonight. That and Garrett. Plus most of the Landis clan. Callie, Caleb, Wyatt, and Nate were there to support a worthy cause. At the same time, they were there for Jade.

"I didn't expect your brothers to come."

"Nothing could have kept them away." Garrett handed Jade a glass of wine. "If Colt weren't in Australia, he'd be here too."

Jade shrugged. "I feel like they barely know me and I'm already turning out to be more trouble than I'm worth."

Garrett's eyes sharpened to a steely gray. "First? We're a family. Rallying around is what families do. Second? Never question your worth." He lightly kissed her lips. "Priceless."

Jade felt a warmth spread through her body, chasing away the chill that had tried to settle in her bones from the moment they entered her father's house. *Remember*, she told herself, *you get to leave at the end of the evening. With Garrett.* If nothing else would get her through, that thought alone would.

Looking around, Jade was surprised nothing had changed. As soon as the idea popped into her head, Jade realized how silly it was. She had only been gone a short time. Just because she wasn't the same woman who walked out didn't mean her old, velvet-lined prison would transform as well.

"I'll be watching from a distance," Sable informed Jade. "I have your back so enjoy the party. As much as the situation allows."

Watching her bodyguard casually navigate through the crowd, Jade was struck once more by how looks could be deceiving. In her long, crimson gown, Sable blended in with ease. Her grace and beauty drew plenty of attention. To the casual observer, she was another guest. Only a select few knew that her beaded handbag contained a deadly weapon. Almost as deadly as the woman herself. Those men considering hitting on Sable might reconsider if they knew she was capable of snapping them in two with her bare hands.

"I like that smile," Garrett whispered, his breath gently caressing her ear. "Want to share what put it there?"

"What do you think would happen to all those admiring looks if they found out what a hard-ass Sable is under her designer gown?"

"Some would be scared off," Garrett admitted. "Some would call her Mistress and beg her to walk across their back with her four-inch stilettos."

"As long as you don't go there with me, I could care less about other people's kinks."

"No stilettos," Garrett assured her. "I prefer…" He leaned close to Jade's ear, whispering his sexy request.

Jade's eyes widened. "Really?" She asked.

"Doable?" Garrett took her hand, his thumb tracing a small circle on the back.

"Remind me when we get home." Jade's smile let Garrett know she was very much on board with his sexy suggestion.

"How much longer do we have to stay?" Garrett looked at his watch. "From the moment I saw you in that dress, I've been fantasizing about removing it. Those thin, crisscrossing straps are driving me crazy."

It wasn't an elaborate gown. It consisted of a whisper of purple silk and cords of braided satin that weaved an intricate pattern down her back. It skimmed the ground as she walked, the high side slit showing off a hint of long, shapely leg. She chose the design because it was comfortable while flattering to her figure. She chose the color because it reminded her of Garrett's eyes. The color of love.

"One more hour should do the trick," Jade said, running her hand down his arm. Lord, he looked handsome in a tuxedo. A look that worked for most men. On Garrett's tall, lean frame, the tailored suit showed her man off to mouthwatering perfection.

Jade was aware of how much attention she and Garrett were drawing. *Let them look*, she thought. Seeing a particularly interested woman giving Garrett the eye, Jade deliberately moved a little, not so subtly brushing against him.

"I won't last another ten minutes if you keep that up," Garrett growled under his breath.

"I'm staking my claim. There are too many beautiful, young women here who want to get their lacquered claws into you."

"My skin is claw-proof," Garrett assured her. "Always has been. I was waiting for a woman with brains and a core of steel to match her beauty. Add killer legs? Is it any wonder I'm putty in your hands."

"Putty, huh?"

"A goner," Garrett's eyes met hers, letting her see what he was feeling. "Is it too corny to say you had me at hello?"

"Definitely," Jade nodded. "Is it weird that I like corn? When it's coming from you."

"I'd say that makes us a practically perfect pair."

"Practically." Jade smiled. "I like that. Absolute perfection would be boring. Not to mention, a little creepy."

"Hey, you two." Nate joined them, casually draping his arm over Jade's shoulders. "I hate to break up the lovefest."

"Then go away," Garrett told him.

"Charming. It isn't too late, Jade." Nate pulled her close. "Mom and Dad are crazy about you. They won't object if you switch brothers midstream."

"Jade has taste, Nate. Go find a woman without any. You know, the kind you usually date."

"Sorry to interrupt this sidesplitting comedy routine," Jade chuckled. "There is a very animated man across the room trying to get your attention."

"Which one of us?" Garrett asked, scanning the crowd.

"My guess is both," Nate said. Plastering on a fake smile, he waved back. "Landon Weeks."

"Well, shit." Garrett sighed. "He's an old friend of our father's. We have to say hello to the gassy windbag."

"Gassy?" Jade asked.

"As in he lets out gas. Periodical, smelly, silent farts," Nate grimaced. "Dad thinks it's hilarious. Mom puts up with it for Dad."

"And you guys?"

"Three hours trapped in a car with Uncle Landon. No air conditioning."

"Enough said." Jade laughed.

"Save yourself," Garrett said, kissing Jade's cheek. "You can meet him at the wedding."

Garrett and Nate were halfway to Uncle Landon before his words sank in. Wedding? What wedding? *Whose* wedding?

"I'm surprised you had the nerve to show your face tonight."

Mandy. Her father's assistant had poured herself into a strapless black satin gown. Her breasts spilled out of the top in such a precarious manner, Jade worried that if the other woman inhaled too vigorously, they might plummet out. Since it was impossible to estimate how much damage the surgically enhanced balls of saline might do, Jade shifted to the side, removing herself from the direct line of fire.

"I'm surprised you care," Jade countered.

"*I* don't," Mandy sniffed disdainfully. "All of my concern is for your father. Haven't you caused him enough pain?"

Jade wondered if they were talking about the same man? *Pain? Anson Marlow?* Either Mandy had no concept of the man she worked for, or she was shooting smoke up her ass for the hell of it. Jade guessed it was a little of both. Happy to leave Mandy with her twisted illusions, Jade shrugged.

"I won't be here much longer. Call this my last farewell. Lose the sour look, Mandy. You can relax. I'm never coming back."

Flagging a passing waiter, Jade set her half-empty glass on his tray. Without another word, she headed to the open balcony doors. After her little run-in with Toxic Mandy, she needed some fresh air.

All evening, Jade had been waiting for some feeling of nostalgia. Even the slightest tinge of a happy memory. How fitting that when it finally happened, it was because of Garrett. She ran her hand over the smooth oak railing. This was the spot, almost three years ago, where she first flirted with him.

Running away, even for a few hours, had been so unlike her. Exciting. Forbidden. The possibilities seemed endless. Until she let reality sink back in. If she had gone with Garrett. Given into temptation. Would they have fallen in love? Would they still be together? There was no point in such speculation. Jade was a different person now. A better match for him. Stronger. In mind and body.

The hell with staying another hour, Jade thought. She had told herself that she could come back here without falling apart. Who cared what anyone else thought? Garrett and his family— No. *Their* family. What their family thought was all that mattered to Jade. Callie, Caleb. Wyatt, Nate, and Colt. They opened their arms, welcoming her in with a warm acceptance that took her breath away.

Jade smiled. Time to go home. As she turned toward the ballroom, the sound of raised voices froze her in her tracks. Not just any voices. Her father. Jade shivered. And the man she hoped to never see again. Her ex-husband. Stephen Marsh.

"WHAT THE HELL do you think you're doing?" Anson Marlow seldom showed an outward demonstration of anger. He prided himself on always having a tight grip on his emotions. It made him sloppy. Sloppy led to mistakes. Mistakes cost money. Money was his religion. Power his God. He refused to let temper or sentimentality loosen his grip on either.

However, there were exceptions to every rule. When his ex-son-in-law appeared out of nowhere, Anson Marlow came as close to losing control as he could ever remember. It was all he could do not to strangle the idiot. They were in the garden. The freshly turned soil in the rose bed would make a perfect place to bury the body.

"I knew I would find you out here." Stephen tried not to slur his words. Half a bottle of vodka was nothing. He wasn't drunk. He was… relaxed. "Such a creature of habit, Anson. Why do you insist on hosting these ridiculous parties when you hate to socialize? Like clockwork, you disappear into the garden to smoke one of your godawful cigars. I knew if I waited, it would only be a matter of time before you strolled by."

"Where is Teresa?"

"You mean my handler," Stephen sneered. "Shoving me from one shitty town to another?"

"She was keeping your ass out of jail. With my help and money, I might add."

"Stop making it sound like you were doing me a favor. Everything you do is for the good of Anson Marlow. No one else. All those lofty promises you made when I married your cold fish daughter. *Someday you'll take over, son.*" Stephen's voice took on a singsong quality. "*In another ten years, all this will be yours.* Bullshit. You never planned on giving me anything."

"I thought you might be groomed for the top spot. It didn't take you long to show how worthless you are. I could overlook your marital problems," Anson shrugged. "As long as you kept it behind closed doors. It was your drinking I found untenable. Did you honestly believe I would hand over my empire to a lush? You had vodka with your Corn Flakes. Whatever hope I had in the beginning, dissolved with every drink you took. Along with your few remaining brain cells."

"I know things, Marlow. Things you don't want the Feds to get wind of."

"Which is why you have money in the bank."

"Not enough." Stephen swayed slightly, blinking to refocus his eyes. "My new girlfriend and I want to leave the country. That should make you happy, Daddy-in-law."

"Girlfriend?" Anson spat the word out with disgust. "What the hell is wrong with women?"

"The heart wants what the heart wants, Anson." A tall, sturdily built blonde stepped out of the shadows. She was dressed head to toe in black. In her right hand, she carried a gun — pointed directly at Anson Marlow.

"If your heart wants a worthless fall-down drunk, Teresa, be my guest. Coming back here is the best way for us all to end up behind bars."

"Your problem has always been overconfidence, Anson." Unlike Stephen, Teresa was steady as a rock. "Face it; you aren't always the smartest person in the room. We want twenty million dollars and a private plane to take us to South America."

Anson barked out a laugh. "The hell with the plane. Why don't I get Tinker Bell to sprinkle you with fairy dust so you can fly there under your own power?"

"Sarcasm? Really?" Teresa moved closer. "You aren't in any position to mock us, Anson. How long do you think all this would survive if Stephen and I made a deal with Uncle Sam? Orange isn't your color, old man."

"All you had to do was stay away," Anson reminded Stephen. Knowing the weak link in this duo, he chose to ignore Teresa. "You're wanted for attempted murder. Have you forgotten that little fact?"

Stephen laughed. "What was it you said to me after your man hustled me away? *If you were going to stab her, why didn't you finish the job?*"

JADE'S FEET FELT like they were frozen to the ground. The rest of her was pure, horrified, angry heat. She thought there wasn't anything her father could say or do that would shock her. She was wrong.

Why didn't you finish the job? How cold could another person be?

Jade's death held no meaning for Anson Marlow. Except it would have made his life easier. No wonder he fired the maid who discovered her bleeding body. It wasn't because the woman had been traumatized. It was a punishment for finding Jade too soon. Another half hour, maybe less, and problem solved. A dead daughter was something he could have worked with. The fake grief. A huge, elaborate funeral. The press would have eaten it up. Instead, he found himself stuck with a live, damaged daughter and the persistent rumors that he knew about the abuse that led up to the stabbing. If Jade had done the right thing — if she had died — all of that could easily have been swept under the carpet.

The more she heard, the angrier she became. The old Jade would be in tears by now. A puddle of inconsolable dysfunction. If she needed proof that she was no longer that woman, this was it. Her cheeks were dry. Instead, they flamed with rage. All she wanted to do was leap over the railing like an avenging warrior. Self-preservation kept her rooted to where she stood. Two men twice her size and a woman wielding a gun. In her head, Jade pictured herself as Wonder Woman. The reality was much different.

Time to stop listening. She needed to call the police before Stephen got away again. When a hand slipped over her mouth, Jade barely swallowed her scream.

"It's me," Garrett whispered. "Back up. Slowly."

Breathing deeply, Jade followed Garrett's lead. Before she knew it, they were in a secluded alcove between the balcony and the ballroom.

"Damn it, Jade," Garrett hissed, wrapping her in his arms. "Why didn't you come get me the second you saw your ex-husband."

"I couldn't move," Jade explained. She burrowed closer. "Don't jump down my throat, Garrett. I wasn't in any danger. I needed to hear what they were saying."

"That's no—"

"There isn't time for this." Jade started at the sound of Sable's voice. "I had an eye on her the entire time, Garrett. Though I wasn't aware of the floor show until I noticed how fixated you were on the lawn. Grass isn't that fascinating."

"I know I should have come to you right away."

"We'll talk about protocol another time." Sable pulled the gun from her purse. She calmly did a quick check of the bullets before flipping off the safety.

"Shouldn't we call the police?"

"Already taken care of. My boss called me just before you went outside. Alex was giving me a heads up that Marsh and his companion were heading west. The plan was to get you out of here, just to be safe. Once we realized what was going on, Alex put in the calls to the proper authorities."

"Good," Jade nodded. "Great. Wait." She put out a hand when Sable started to leave. "Wait for help."

"I won't move unless I have to," Sable assured her. "That's an unstable group, Jade. If it looks like Marsh is going to bolt or his friend is about to blow your bastard father's head off, I'll step in." Sable gave Jade a cool, emotionless look. "Unless you'd prefer I let nature take its course?"

Let Teresa kill her father? They all knew that was what Sable meant. After everything, Jade didn't hesitate. "Unlike my father, I refuse to play God. I'm happy with the thought of him rotting in a cell for the next few years."

"Fair enough." Sable turned to Garrett. "Take Jade out of here. You can't go home. The FBI will want to talk to both of you."

"Need some backup?" Nate stepped into the alcove.

Sable lifted her skirt revealing another gun strapped to her thigh. Acting as though she did it every day, she pulled it from its case, and then handed it to Nate.

"How much did you hear?"

"I caught the gist." Nate checked the gun.

"Good. One thing. Don't play the hero," Sable said, her eyes serious. "I can handle the bad guys. What scares me is having to tell your mother I stood by while one of her babies took a bullet."

"I hope they'll be okay."

"Nate can take of himself." Garrett took Jade's hand. "You heard

Sable. The plan is to keep an eye on things until the authorities get here."

"The FBI."

With impressive ease, Garrett ushered Jade through the crowd. Somehow, he avoided anyone who wanted a moment of his time. Every time it looked like they were approaching a talker, Garrett made a detour until they were across the room and out the door.

"Where can we go so we won't be disturbed?"

"This way."

Jade knew the perfect place. Keeping a hold of Garrett's hand, she went down the hall to her left. The art gallery where she used to hide from prying eyes when she texted Garrett. It was bound to be locked. With so many strangers wandering around, her father wouldn't take any chances. However, unless things had suddenly changed, the key wasn't far away.

"You have got to be kidding." Garrett watched in amazement as Jade lifted the Ming vase on the nearby table. "What's the point of locking it in the first place?"

"My father has no idea the housekeeper leaves the key here." Jade unlocked the door, and then put the key back in its hiding place. "One time she lost the original. Naturally, my father had an important guest that he wanted to impress. You can imagine his reaction when a locksmith had to be called. After that, an extra key was never far away."

She shut the door behind them. Before Jade could turn on the lights, Garrett kissed her. Melting into his embrace, she gave herself up to the sensations. Desire. Warmth. Love. The feeling that she was home.

"When I realized that monster was outside, only a few feet away from you, it was all I could do not to grab you. It's a good thing Sable has a stable head on her shoulders. If she hadn't held me back, he might have gotten away."

"Sable is trained to keep her cool." Jade nuzzled his neck. "Besides, she isn't in love with me."

"That does make a difference."

"All the difference in the world."

Jade. Garrett. A darkened room. She felt the tug of the memory of another time not so long ago. So much had happened since the first night they met in that seedy motel room. A different part of Los Angles. A different woman.

Reaching over, Jade flipped on the lights. She no longer needed the dark. She had a life. Outside this room. A life with Garrett.

"Behold the Marlow treasure trove."

"I love Chagall."

Jade smiled. "Me too." She slowly turned in a circle, silently greeting her old friends. "I've always hated that he squirrels these masterpieces away. They need to be seen — enjoyed."

"A museum?" Garrett picked up a Rodin, examining it closely.

"I once suggested a traveling exhibit. It would be a chance for people who never get to New York or Paris to see each piece in person."

"How did that go over?"

"Not well."

"Jade." Garrett set the statue down. "I didn't hear everything that went on out there. Do you want to talk about it?"

Jade ran her hand over the Picasso. The Renoir. The Matisse.

"He wishes I had died."

Garrett didn't argue. He didn't tell her she must have misunderstood. Or her father didn't mean it. How could he? What would be the point of lying when Jade was all too aware of the truth? So he did the only thing that was in his power to do. Someone to listen.

He led her to the leather sofa, gently pushing her onto the cushion. Then sat down next to her, their knees brushing.

"Tell me everything."

In truth, there wasn't very much to tell. Once she moved past her initial shock of seeing Stephen again, Jade shared the rest with Garrett without hesitation.

"Is it too late to change your mind? Who would mourn if that son of a bitch got a bullet through his cold, dead heart?"

"I can't think of a single person." Jade sighed. "Why put him out of his misery? I would rather he pay with the loss of his freedom than the loss of his life. When all this hits the fan, he won't be able to buy his way out."

"Honey…"

"What?"

"I wouldn't bank on seeing your father go to prison."

Jade knew what Garrett was going to say. In all likelihood, his money would buy Anson Marlow his freedom. She could testify to what she heard. There was no reason for Stephen not to roll over on him. Jade hadn't a clue what Teresa knew. She could sing to the rafters. One thing remained true. Money bought you a lot of leeway in the world.

The sound of yelling drew Jade and Garrett into the hall. She didn't know if this was the definition of all hell breaking loose, but she would bet it was damn close.

A crowd of people hated nothing more than to be told they couldn't leave. When those people had money and power behind their names, it made the situation in the Marlow mansion a chaotic mess. Uniformed police officers sealed off the exits then did their best with crowd control. Some of the older party guests yelled their displeasure. Everyone else frantically called or texted their lawyers. It didn't matter that they hadn't done anything wrong. Securing representation was a knee-jerk reaction of the rich and famous.

"I saw the valets moving cars," Nate said as he joined them. "The police and the Feds are letting everyone leave."

"Nate." Garrett sighed with relief. "You seem to be in one piece. Where's Sable?"

"Conferring with a couple of guys in black suits. FBI, I assume." Nate shook his head. "It's nothing like the movies. Thank God."

"What happened? Is Stephen in custody?" Jade asked, her hand reaching for Garrett's.

"He isn't getting away this time," Nate assured her. "Sable made sure of that."

"We didn't hear any shots." Now that it was over, Jade felt her first bout of nerves. Aftershock. Garrett gently rubbed the back of Jade's hand with his thumb. A small, yet comforting gesture.

"We stayed out of sight, waiting for the police," Nate explained. "For some reason, your father kept antagonizing the woman with the gun."

"Teresa."

"Right." Nate smiled at Jade. "Instead of respecting the fact that she held a deadly weapon, he wouldn't stop. He called her stupid. A whore. I think it was that last one that pushed her over the top. She was going to shoot your father, Jade."

"He has that effect on people." Jade leaned closer to Garrett. "Most of them aren't carrying guns."

"I didn't see Sable move," Nate said in amazement. "I swear, one moment she was by my side, the next Teresa was on her ass."

"And Stephen?"

"He started babbling incoherently." Nate grinned.

"What?" Garrett demanded.

"Sable clocked him. One punch. The bastard was out like a light. That was when the police swarmed in. Teresa and Stephen were cuffed and led away. End of drama."

"I see what you mean," Garrett nodded. "In the movies, that final scene would have taken at least thirty minutes."

"Explosions, fire." Nate made exaggerated motions with his arms. "Half the house would be smoking rubble."

"This is a better ending," Garrett said, slipping his arm around Jade. "I prefer my mayhem up on the screen."

"No argument here."

Jade felt the tension draining from her body. After all this time, it was over. Stephen was no longer a threat.

"Is it really over?"

"Almost." Garrett nodded to where her father was being led in.

It didn't appear to Jade that he was in custody. His hands were free of any restraints. However, he was flanked on both sides by uniformed police.

Sable entered the room with the two men Nate had told them about. She appeared completely unruffled. Not even her lipstick was smudged. To look at her, no one would guess what she had been up to a few minutes earlier. Seeing Jade, she said a few quick words to her companions before making her way across the room.

"Are you okay?" Just because she looked fine on the outside didn't mean Sable hadn't been hurt. No one knew better than Jade how clothing could cover a multitude of injuries.

"Not a scratch. Well." Sable grimaced. She looked down at her hand. "My manicure has been shot to hell."

With a relieved laugh, Jade hugged Sable. "I'll take you for a new one tomorrow. My treat."

"About your father."

Jade glanced his way again. Anson Marlow had the look of a man without a care in the world. A sick feeling crept into her stomach.

"He's going to get away with it."

"Jade…" Garrett exchanged worried looks with Nate.

"I don't know, Jade." Sable shook her head. "If Marsh and the woman roll on him, he won't be able to wiggle away."

"Why do I think there's a but coming?"

"Before everything went down," Nate told her, "your father offered Marsh and Teresa a shit-load of money to keep their mouths shut. That and a guarantee of top-notch legal representation."

"What do you think?" Jade asked Sable. "Will they take the money?"

"They are both going down," Sable said. "The charges against Marsh are more serious. He's bound to do a larger amount of time. Still…"

"Still?"

"With the right lawyer, they could plead diminished capacity because of alcohol abuse."

"Fuck that," Garrett growled.

"I agree." Sable gave Jade a reassuring smile. "Marsh isn't walking away from this. He might be seduced into thinking he could. If that happens, your father will walk. What you overheard won't hold enough water, Jade. Any lawyer worth his salt will claim hearsay."

"That son of a bitch thinks he's home free. I want to knock that smug look off his face." Garrett took a step forward.

Nate put a restraining hand on his arm. "At this point, all it would accomplish is you getting arrested for assault. That won't help Jade any."

"No," Jade agreed. "It's time I helped myself."

"What do you have in mind?"

"Come with me." She took Garrett's hand before turning to Sable and Nate. "I need five minutes."

"Go," Sable urged without any question. "We have your back."

"Are we about to do something illegal?" Garrett followed Jade, looking over his shoulder. No one seemed to be paying any attention to them. "Because I'm okay with that."

"This might be one of those gray areas." Jade paused outside a large door. On a long table, an arrangement of roses sat looking completely innocuous.

"Another hiding place?"

Jade tilted the vase, revealing a key. "The little things always slide by my father. I'm hoping it will be his undoing."

She unlocked the door. Garrett slipped in behind her, shutting them into darkness. Jade didn't bother with the light. Nothing ever changed in her father's office. The furniture was never rearranged. It was a straight path from where she stood to where she wanted to be. In a heartbeat, she was across the room.

"Is your phone handy?"

"Who do you need to call?" Garrett's finger was poised to dial.

"I'm afraid we're in this one alone, my love. I need the light."

"Sounds cozy." Garrett moved to her side.

Jade took down the abstract painting to the side of her father's desk revealing a large wall safe.

"Hold the light up so I can see the keypad."

"Jewels? Bearer bonds?"

"Nothing that sexy." Jade pulled the handle, swinging open the heavy door.

Jade ignored the piles of money and the stack of velvet-covered boxes. She knew what she wanted and it had nothing to do with shiny baubles.

"The Feds tried everything to take down Al Capone." She removed a small, green book and several files. "Do you know how they finally got him?"

Garrett grinned. Well, hot damn. "Tax evasion."

"Give the man a cigar." Jade closed the safe, letting Garrett replace the painting. "With his usual arrogance, my father has been defrauding the U.S. government while keeping the paper trail ten feet from his desk. On top of the misdeeds they'll find in these files, he won't buy his way out of this."

"He'll know that you're responsible." Garrett gave her a fast, hard kiss. "I can't wait to see the look on that old bastard's face. It should be plastered on every news cycle for quite some time."

"Hide these under your jacket." Jade handed Garrett the book and files. He pushed the papers into the waistband of his pants, tucking his shirt in. When he buttoned his jacket, there was only a barely discernible bulge. "Good. I don't want my father to realize we have them."

As it turned out, they finished just in time. No sooner had they locked the office door and returned the key, the FBI led her father to the room. They stopped when they saw Jade.

"Miss Marlow." The taller of the two agents spoke. He held out his identification. "I understand you witnessed what took place in the garden between your father, Stephen Marsh, and Teresa Benson?"

Jade briefly looked at her father. There was a warning in his eyes.

"Witnessed?" Jade moved her gaze to the agent. "I don't know if you could call it that. I overheard part of the conversation."

"We'll need you to make a statement."

"Agent…?" Garrett gave the man a friendly smile.

"Simms."

"Agent Simms. Miss Marlow is exhausted. You can imagine how traumatic it has been for her seeing her ex-husband again, even from a distance." Garrett took out a card, handing it to the agent. "Here is the number where you can reach her. Tomorrow should be soon enough."

Before anyone could object, Garrett hustled Jade past the agents and out of the house.

"Slick." Jade gave him an admiring smile.

"Let's keep moving. I won't feel safe until we're home."

Jade wouldn't feel safe until they put those papers into the proper hands. Agent Simms and his partner seemed a bit too chummy with her father. She wasn't going to trust just anyone. The first thing to do was make copies. Multiple copies. She wasn't taking any chances that the papers would *mysteriously* disappear before they could be processed. Then they needed to figure out to whom they should go.

"With this line, we'll be lucky if we get home by dawn. The mass exodus of guests is running the valets ragged." Jade suddenly smiled. Of course. She had the perfect solution. "Let me have your phone again." Taking it, she tapped the keys. She didn't have to look it up; she knew this number by heart.

Intrigued, Garrett listened to the one sided conversation.

"Hi. Are you busy? Beverly Hills. No, the old place. Right. Bye." Jade handed the phone back. "Gather the troops. Troy is on the way."

IT WAS AN interesting group that piled into the yellow cab. A legendary screen siren, her equally famous producer husband, and their stuntman son took the backseat. The front was occupied by Hollywood's hottest director and his notorious girlfriend. Certain his wife would never believe him, Troy worked up the nerve to ask them to pose with him for a picture. To his surprise and delight, they not only agreed, but Callie Flynn also kissed his cheek. He had proof. On his phone. In color. Troy would be dining out on this story for the rest of his life.

"Come by for dinner tomorrow." It wasn't a question. Callie blew kisses at Jade and Garrett before she took the hand Caleb offered her. They entered their house arm in arm.

"I can't wait to hear what you two were up to," Nate got out of the cab. He leaned back in through the open door. "Are you good?" he asked Jade.

"I've never been better." She patted Nate's hand.

There was little said on the ride home. Jade and Garrett were content to hold each other. Silently, they weighed the implications of the night's events. What it meant to them and their future.

"Thank you, Troy," Jade shook the cabbie's hand after Garrett paid him. "You've been more than a driver to me. You've been a friend."

"I'll miss you." He nodded toward Garrett. "Something tells me you won't be making any more late night rides."

"No." Jade smiled when Garrett gave her a long, speculative look. "At least not alone."

"I wish Sable had left with us." Jade removed her shoes as soon as she was in the door. Deciding a cup of tea sounded like a good idea, she headed for the kitchen.

"She'll want to get as much taken care of as possible," Garrett said. Seeing what she was doing, he took two mugs from the cupboard "My guess is she'll head home tomorrow. She can always fly back if they need her."

"Tomorrow? So soon?"

"You don't need a bodyguard anymore, thank God."

"I know." Jade hadn't thought this far ahead. She would miss her new friend. "Harper Falls sounds like a nice place."

"It is," Garrett nodded. "Only seventy or so miles away from the Canadian border. Where, coincidentally, I will be filming *Exile* starting next week."

"I forgot about that." Jade scooped some loose tea into a strainer." You'll be gone for over a month."

"You could come with me. Hear me out," Garrett continued before Jade could answer. "I know you have a business to get up on its feet. I can't expect you to drop everything to spend time with me."

"Why not?"

Puzzled, Garrett took the cup Jade handed him. "Why not what?"

"Why can't you expect me to spend time with you? I only have one job booked. I can plan that from anywhere." Jade sipped her tea. "I've never been to Canada."

"I'll be busy most of the time."

"I can entertain myself, Garrett." Jade hid her smile behind her drink. "Even in the bedroom."

"Put the cup down, Jade."

"Why?" Jade gave Garrett a wide-eyed innocent look. "I just fixed it."

"In two seconds, I'm going to kiss you." Garrett set his mug on the counter. "I might stop. *Might*. Around dawn."

"*Just* kissing?" Jade carefully placed her mug next to his.

Garrett put a hand on each side of Jade's face. His eyes were such a deep purple it took her breath away. Sometimes she would fantasize about a man loving her. It seemed like a wild, far away kind of thing that happened to other people. Even then, she never dreamed of being loved so deeply. It made her want to laugh and cry all at once.

"Happy tears?" Garrett wiped them away with the pads of his thumbs.

"You have no idea."

Garrett kissed her with all the love she had seen shining in his eyes.

"I tell you what," he lifted Jade into his arms. "Between kisses, you can tell me all about it."

"PROMISE YOU'LL COME back for a visit."

"And you promise to stop by Harper Falls on your way back from Canada."

"Deal."

Jade sat on the edge of the bed as Sable packed her bag. Garrett had called it. When Sable finally took her leave of the FBI, she made sure they had all the information they needed from her. She assured them she would return to Los Angeles if necessary. The way things looked, she didn't think that would happen.

"Those FBI guys were damn pissy considering we did most of their work for them. By the time they left, their case was wrapped up in a pretty bow. I hate to call sexism," Sable sighed. "Unfortunately, sometimes it is what it is."

"You work in a testosterone-driven business." Jade watched with admiration as Sable fit everything neatly into one suitcase.

"I knew what I was getting into." Sable closed the bag. "First the Army, followed by personal security. They are worlds still dominated by men."

"For now," Jade added.

Sable laughed. "That's what I said to my last C.O. He believed men ran the Army, so I should get on my knees and do what comes naturally."

"What did you do?"

"I blew." Sable winked. "Right out of the Army. Women are making strides in the military. Slowly. To do so, you need a sympathetic Commanding Officer. Even if I had given him what he wanted, I never would have risen very far in the ranks."

"I'm sorry." Jade understood on some level. There came a point when you had to walk away.

"It's time." Sable held out her arms. "Give me a hug."

Jade squeezed hard.

"I wish you would let me drive you to the airport."

"Airport goodbyes are the worst." She picked up her bag. "Better to do it here."

"All set?" Garrett gave Sable a warm hug. "Your taxi is waiting."

"Troy?" Jade asked.

"Who else?"

Garrett handed Sable a manila envelope. After a brief discussion, they decided that Alex Fleming and the others at H&W Security would know how to handle the papers Jade took from her father's safe. Sable was happy to play messenger.

"It won't take long," she told them. "Alex knows the highest of the high. You're hitting your father where it hurts the most, Jade. In the bank account."

Later, Jade sat curled up next to Garrett. They were watching one of his mother's movies. Jade's favorite. It was a love story with plenty of laughs mixed with a few tears. Best of all, it had a happy ending.

"She was a legend in the making," Garrett said, pride in his voice.

True, Jade thought, snuggling closer. However, no matter how many movies his mother made, as far as Jade was concerned, Garrett was her best production.

Epilogue

THERE IS AN amazing thing that happens when you open your life and your heart to another person. So many old hurts drop away. Not because they no longer exist. It's because they cease to matter. You now have another person to focus on instead of yourself. A partner to help ease your worries. Garrett didn't suddenly become everything. He became a large, important, central piece of the puzzle. Right next to her. Over the coming years, the other parts would shift. Change. Morph into other things. Jade knew that Garrett wasn't going anywhere.

The sun was setting in the Vancouver sky. The days filming on *Exile* were done. They had been in Canada for almost two weeks. The time that she and Garrett spent together was limited. He was busy juggling shooting schedules and temperamental actors. Not to mention broken hearts.

As predicted, Hamish's affair with Lynne Cornish had ended. Badly. To help his friend, and keep his sanity, Garrett juggled the shooting schedule to make sure the ex-lovers were never on set at the same time. Not an easy task considering she was the leading lady and he was the assistant director. Somehow, Garrett made it work.

Jade spent her time selling herself online. So to speak. Word of mouth was all it had taken for her calendar to fill up. She neither needed nor wanted to accept every job that came along. She picked the ones that interested her. All the preliminary work could be done on her computer. It filled up her hours. When Garrett found some free time, she put work away. It worked out perfectly.

Tonight they were relaxing on deck of their rented cabin after a romantic dinner for two.

Sable had called that afternoon to inform Jade that the government had frozen all of Anson Marlow's assets. The ball was rolling. It would be interesting to see where it stopped. Interesting, but not vital. Her father was the past. As was Stephen Marsh. She wanted them to pay. However, she wasn't going to obsess about it. She would rely on the judicial system to do its job. Jade had more important things to occupy her time.

"I've been thinking."

"I'm all for that." Garrett smiled before his sipping his beer.

"Garrett Landis. Will you marry me?"

Garrett looked at the box Jade held out to him. A square box. One that looked like the kind a man would give a woman.

"Open it."

"Honey," Garrett took the box. He didn't have any choice. Jade practically shoved it into his hand. "I know our relationship has been anything but traditional."

"Exactly." Unable to wait, Jade took back the box. She lifted the lid. "Ta da."

"That's…"

"An earring." She removed the single stud. "Your mother told me you got your ear pierced when you were a teenager."

"I did," Garrett nodded. "Did she also tell you that she made such a fuss that I took the earring out that night and never wore it again?"

"She mentioned it. She helped me pick this out. Purple jade."

Garrett took the stud. The color was deep and intense. Almost one of a kind.

"Looks like I'll be getting my ear pierced. Again."

With a delighted laugh, Jade threw her arms around him.

"Is that a yes?"

Holding her close, Garrett whispered, "You'll never get rid of me now."

Jade melted into Garrett's kiss.

Forever with the man she loved. This was better than any dream.

How to Get in Touch

Please visit me at these sites, sign up for my newsletter or leave a message.

http://www.maryjwilliams.net/home.html

https://www.facebook.com/pages/Mary-J-Williams/1561851657385417

https://twitter.com/maryjwilliams05

https://www.pinterest.com/maryj0675/

https://www.goodreads.com/author/show/5648619.Mary_J_Williams

COMING IN MARCH 2016

Dreaming with My Eyes Wide Open

**BOOK TWO OF THE
HOLLYWOOD LEGENDS SERIES**

Made in the USA
Charleston, SC
04 November 2016